THE
RAGING STORM

Ann Cleeves is the author of more than thirty-five critically acclaimed novels, and in 2017 was awarded the highest accolade in crime writing, the CWA Diamond Dagger. She is the creator of popular detectives Vera Stanhope, Jimmy Perez and Matthew Venn, who can be found on television in ITV's *Vera*, BBC One's *Shetland* and ITV's *The Long Call* respectively. The TV series and the books they are based on have become international sensations, capturing the minds of millions worldwide.

Ann worked as a probation officer, bird observatory cook and auxiliary coastguard before she started writing. She is a member of 'Murder Squad', working with other British northern writers to promote crime fiction. Ann also spends her time advocating for reading to improve health and well-being and supporting access to books. In 2021 her Reading for Wellbeing project launched with local authorities across the North East. She lives in Northumberland where the Vera books are set.

You can find Ann on Twitter and Facebook @AnnCleeves

Ann Cleeves

THE RAGING STORM

PAN BOOKS

First published 2023 by Macmillan

This paperback edition first published 2024 by Pan Books
an imprint of Pan Macmillan
The Smithson, 6 Briset Street, London EC1M 5NR
EU representative: Macmillan Publishers Ireland Ltd, 1st Floor,
The Liffey Trust Centre, 117–126 Sheriff Street Upper,
Dublin 1, D01 YC43
Associated companies throughout the world
www.panmacmillan.com

ISBN 978-1-5290-7773-5

1 3 5 7 9 8 6 4 2

A CIP catalogue record for this book is available from the British Library.

Map artwork by ML Design Ltd

Typeset in Plantin Light by Palimpsest Book Production Ltd,
Falkirk, Stirlingshire
Printed and bound by CPI Group (UK) Ltd, Croydon, CR0 4YY

Visit **www.panmacmillan.com** to read more about all our books
and to buy them. You will also find features, author interviews and
news of any author events, and you can sign up for e-newsletters
so that you're always first to hear about our new releases.

This book is dedicated to the staff and volunteers of the RNLI, especially to the crews in Cullercoats and Ilfracombe.

Acknowledgements

I couldn't write these books without an amazing team to support me. I'd like to thank all my agents: Sara and her co-agents and scouts throughout the world, Rebecca, who looks after my television and broadcast interests, and Moses, who represents me in the US. Emma has shared PR tours and laughs, and I couldn't have a better publicist. I've been published by Pan Macmillan for thirty years. That's longer than most marriages and now they feel like family! A special mention to Vicki, my editor, Charlotte, who's in charge of copy-editing and proofs, Jamie in marketing, and the whole team of reps. Also, to another Charlotte, for being a willing partner in my passion to spread the word about the benefits of reading for pleasure. The Minotaur team – Catherine, Nettie, Martin and Sarah – have supported me wonderfully in the US, as have Pan Mac Aus in Australia. Candice and Praveen, that tour was a blast! Jill and Jane have kept me on track administratively, and Geoff and Steve of Benchmark have got me to where I need to be. Thanks to Prof Lorna Dawson, Prof James Grieve, Dr Nicola Grieve and Helen Pepper for their advice and for great times spent together. Love to good friends in the places where my books are set: to Sue in North Devon, Ingrid in Shetland, and Martin and Paul in Tyneside. And of course, as ever, to my wonderful daughters and their families.

Author's Note

This is a work of fiction, and the villages of Greystone and Morrisham are fictitious and aren't based on real places. I'm hugely grateful to Cullercoats and Ilfracombe lifeboats, not just for their magnificent work but for taking the time to talk about the boats and the procedures. As usual, any mistakes are mine.

NORTH DEVON

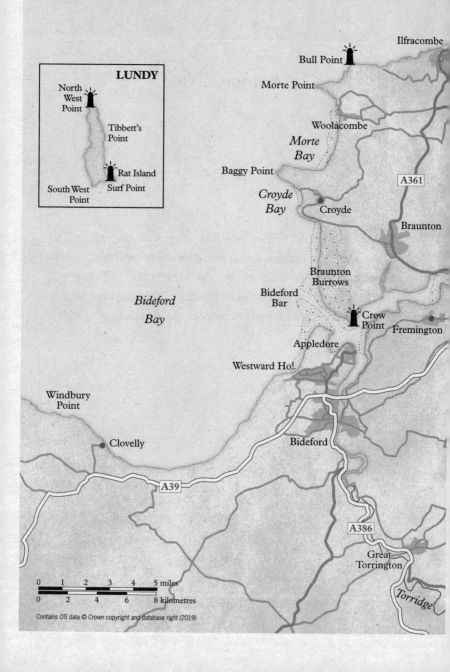

LUNDY

North West Point

Tibbett's Point

Rat Island

South West Point

Surf Point

Ilfracombe

Bull Point

Morte Point

Woolacombe

Morte Bay

A361

Baggy Point

Croyde Bay

Croyde

Braunton

Braunton Burrows

Bideford Bar

Crow Point

Fremington

Bideford Bay

Appledore

Westward Ho!

Windbury Point

Clovelly

Bideford

A39

A386

Great Torrington

Torridge

0   1   2   3   4   5 miles

0   2   4   6   8 kilometres

Contains OS data © Crown copyright and database right (2019)

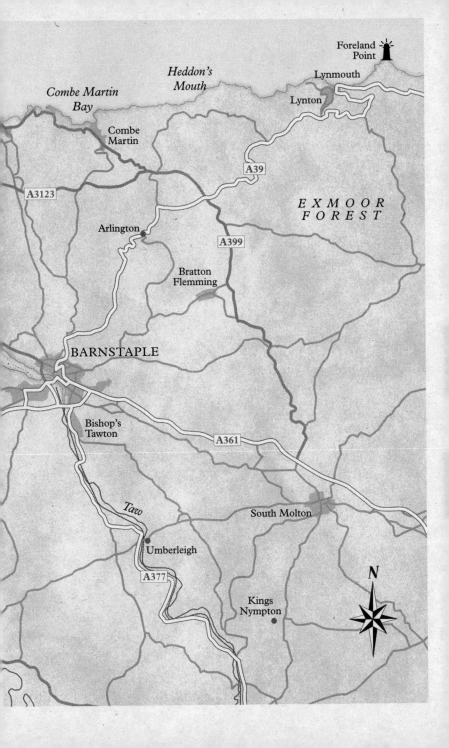

Chapter One

THE MAN BLEW INTO GREYSTONE AT the height of a
September gale. That was how the story went, at least. Suddenly
he was there, leaning against the bar of the Maiden's Prayer,
face as brown as a nut, white hair so short that it must have
been cut that day, laughing at one of the landlord's jokes. The
rain dripped off his waterproofs, and all his worldly belongings
were in an oilskin bag at his feet. There was no indication as
to *how* he'd arrived. He hadn't driven himself. There was no
car. But somehow Jem Rosco, adventurer, sailor and legend,
had arrived in their midst.

He told them that he'd rented one of the cottages that
climbed up the bank behind the pub.

'But I was desperate for a pint, boys, so I called in here on
my way.' A wink.

Harry Carter, the landlord, couldn't tell if the wink was meant
to indicate that this was a lie, a joke, or to include the other
customers standing at the bar in his desire for a drink. They too,
the wink seemed to imply, must know how it felt to be so
desperate for a pint that they wouldn't drop a heavy bag off first.

1

Rosco had two pints of local, cloudy cider, then he slung the bag, which was big enough to hold a child, onto his back and was on his way.

He was in the Maiden's every night after that. There was never a specific time. He'd appear suddenly, all smiles. Sometimes he'd stay at the bar, chinwagging with Harry. Other nights he'd drift around the room, landing at a table – the playgroup mums on their regular night out, or an elderly couple playing dominoes by the fire – like a piece of flotsam washed up by the tide. He was always friendly, always chatty, but he never really gave anything away. When anyone asked if the move to Greystone was permanent, or if he was there on a holiday, planning another journey perhaps, he'd only touch the side of his nose and grin.

'I'm here to meet someone. Someone special. I'm expecting them any day.'

He never stayed for more than two pints and then he was off again, sometimes with a little wave to the other customers, sometimes just disappearing, so that suddenly they realized he was no longer there.

They all knew which cottage he'd rented. It was at the end of the terrace, right on the top of the hill, owned by Gwen Gregory, who'd grown up at Ravenscroft Farm, and who cleaned in the Maiden's. It had the view across the village to the sea. Nobody had any need to walk past it. Beyond the single row of houses, there were only the remains of the quarry, which was the original reason for the village's existence.

But now people walked past the house anyway, out of curiosity. They were interested to know if Jem Rosco's mysterious visitor had arrived yet. They'd see the man sometimes looking out of the upstairs window, focused on the horizon, as if he was watching for a boat. Even in this stormy weather, a skilled sailor might float in and tie up at the jetty. There were two curved piers to shelter the narrow bay, built when stone from the quarry was carried out on big, flat barges. People said that one of his madcap adventuring friends would appear. Or the woman he was waiting for. Because most of the villagers had convinced themselves that it would be a woman.

Then one night, a few weeks after his arrival, Jem Rosco didn't come to the Maiden's for his usual two pints of rough cider. The regulars immediately noticed his absence. They chatted amongst themselves and speculated that perhaps the expected visitor had finally arrived. Perhaps old Jem would bring the stranger into the bar the following night, and finally they'd know what all the secrecy was about.

But Jem Rosco didn't appear again. They felt cheated. He might be an outsider but for a while he'd become part of the community. He was a celebrity, who'd been on television, sharing his travels – making his way up the Amazon, sailing single-handedly around the southern oceans – with the world. Part of his glory had rubbed off on them, but now the excitement was over.

Until the following morning, when the coastguard received an emergency call from a fishing boat in difficulty, sheltering from the storm in the lee of Scully Head.

Then, it seemed, the excitement had only just started.

Chapter Two

MARY FORD WAS WOKEN BY HER pager. She looked at the bedside clock. Five in the morning. She'd marked herself as available on the lifeboat rota because her father was staying, and there'd be someone to look after the kids if she were called out. Time was slipping away for adventures like these. Soon, Arthur would need a full-time carer, and she couldn't expect her dad always to be there. So, she'd thought, she'd best make the most of it while she could. She was out of bed and dressed almost without thinking. She loved this. The excitement of a shout, the camaraderie and laughter with the guys. And she was helm now. Almost three years of training and she was in charge. In a place like Greystone, a woman in charge didn't happen very often. Sammy Barton was lifeboat operations manager this morning, and he'd like it even less than the others. But Sammy could stuff it.

She knocked at her father's door. He'd most likely be awake already. Since Mary's mother had died, the man slept poorly. Mary often saw his light on in the early hours, and knew that he was scrolling down his phone. Sometimes she heard the buzz of the radio and the measured tones of the BBC World Service throughout the night. Her father stayed over quite regularly now, ostensibly to help with babysitting – Mary had sent her bloke packing soon after Arthur was born – but really because he found it hard being alone in the cottage in the woods just outside Morrisham. It had been easier when her mother had been alive, even after they'd moved her into the hospice. Then her dad had a purpose: planning the visits, and the treats to brighten his wife's day. Now, he was bereft.

Dad *was* a real help, though. Since Arthur had become ill with the dreadful Jasper Lineham Disease, her father had become an important part of the household. She'd never heard of JLD until Arthur's diagnosis and now she could think of little else. The cruel disease ate away at her son, like the tide eroding a sandstone cliff. There was the occasional good day when she had a flicker of hope, but it never lasted. She wouldn't have trusted anyone other than her father to stay with her boy. She'd never have gone out with the lifeboat, for example, if he hadn't been there, and that gave her the freedom and the excitement she craved.

Today, Alan Ford was lying on his side and looking at his phone. Checking Facebook or Twitter. Finding the company that her mother would once have provided, in social media friends and old work colleagues.

'I've got to go.'

'The lifeboat?'

Mary nodded.

'In this storm?' Her father was trying to keep the anxiety from his voice, but Mary knew what he was thinking. Bad enough to lose Claire. He couldn't bear to lose a daughter too.

'The wind's dropped. Can't you hear? It's not supposed to

blow up again for several hours. We wouldn't be allowed to launch if the forecast was too poor.' A pause. 'I have to go. There's everything Isla needs for school in her bedroom, but I'll probably be back by then. Artie can go too if he's feeling up to it.'

'Sure. Of course. On your way.' Despite his anxiety, Alan wouldn't want to deny Mary the adventures that *he'd* experienced throughout his life.

Outside, it was strangely quiet after the storms of the previous days. A lull between westerly fronts. There'd be a big sea still, but wind shouldn't be a problem. It would soon be light; there was already a grey sheen to the sky behind the houses to the east. It would be quicker on foot than to drive and Mary hurried down the street to the quay, but she didn't quite run. The pavement was still slick from rain and the last thing she needed was to break a bone, which would keep her out of the boat for weeks. She loved this – being out when everyone else was in bed; the adrenaline already starting to pump, knowing that she was being useful, that she might save someone's life.

Sammy Barton was already there when she got to the lifeboat station, and she arrived at almost the same time as a fellow crew member: Ollie Shebbeer, a mechanic in Greystone's only garage. Paul, the tractor driver was already working on the beast of a machine, which would push the lifeboat onto the shingle beach and drag it into the water. The sea was too shallow here for a conventional slipway, and this tractor had cost more than the boat itself. It could be almost wholly submerged and still work. In the kit room she started getting into the suits which were hanging under her name. An inner all-in-one to keep her warm, and an outer waterproof, which was supposed to keep her dry, but never quite managed it in very bad weather. The other two crew members arrived just as she was ready.

Sammy, the lifeboat operations manager, joined them and started passing on information.

'Coastguard received a mayday on channel sixteen. A fishing boat out of Ilfracombe called the *Anna Louise*, sheltering just the other side of Scully Head. Then they lost contact.'

'Any other vessel nearby?'

Barton shook his head. 'Nobody else had responded to the call.'

Mary grabbed the first-aid bag with the O_2 kit and the pump, and then they were in the boat. Mary was in charge, but she let Ollie sit in the front seat and take the wheel. He was less experienced, but she preferred to sit just behind, where she could see the radar, and be in charge of the navigation.

The Atlantic 85 was a rigid inflatable boat, a RIB, but solid and beautifully proportioned. And bright orange. She was named the *Lesley Alexander*, after the woman who'd left a legacy to pay for her. The station door was opened, and the tractor nudged the boat and the trailer down onto the shore and over the shingle until they were floating. Then the trailer was pulled away and they were on their way. The waves breaking on the beach were as big as Mary had expected, and the boat pitched and bucked like a fairground ride. She'd never been seasick but she knew some people had thrown up just watching from the shore.

The water close to Scully Point was shallow, and Mary had suspected that the *Anna Louise* might have gone aground on rocks. The spring tides of the equinox were very high and very low, and it had been dead low water at four in the morning.

When they hit thirty-five knots, out on the open water, the swell was rolling and the *Lesley A* was bouncing. The boat was open to the elements, and spray covered the bow, blowing into her face and making Mary laugh. This was the real buzz. The rest was important, but this was what Mary had joined up for.

It only took fifteen minutes to arrive at the recorded position. They slowed as they rounded the headland. Behind her, Mary heard a muttered incantation. The older crew didn't like coming into Scully – an old superstition – and mouthed words to ward off bad luck. Not really believing they'd help, but not willing to chance it. Saying the words, just in case. They were a religious lot, the people of Greystone, but that didn't stop them buying into the old stories of wrecks and drownings.

They had on the headlights, but Mary saw no sign of a trawler, not even one of the smaller boats that went out after crab and lobster. It occurred to her that this might be a hoax – it happened occasionally – but surely not in the early hours of a day like this. Pissed fishermen would be in bed by five. Then Ollie gave a shout and pointed to port. It was just light enough to see a small, dark shadow, moving with the swell. Not a fishing boat, but a small dinghy or tender, closer into the shore. It wasn't stranded on rocks. Mary knew this part of the coast and could have drawn her own chart. She'd studied it. For months the maps had been her bedtime reading. The dinghy disappeared, the view of it hidden by a rolling wave, and then it was there again. But the wave didn't carry it towards the headland.

'Anchored.' Mary was running scenarios through her head. 'Why would anyone want to do that?'

The lifeboat slowed again to walking pace and they drifted towards the dinghy. It wasn't until they were almost onto it that the man in front of her, who had a better view, yelled, suddenly tense.

'Casualty. Casualty.'

The spotlight from the boat lit up the dinghy and she turned so that the GoPro video camera on her helmet captured the scene. There was a body in the dinghy, curled into the curve of it. She was suddenly reminded of Arthur as a baby, lying in his Moses basket. He always managed to turn onto his side, even as an infant. But Arthur had been wearing a sleep suit, had been covered by a blanket, and this person was naked, the skin white in the bright lights.

Almost immediately, the training kicked in. This was a dash and grab moment. This was what she'd trained for. She was sitting where the side of the inflatable was at its lowest. As Ollie allowed the lifeboat to touch the dinghy, she slid into it, steadying herself as it rocked with the movement, then she lifted the casualty into her arms. He was less heavy than she'd been expecting. She held him low and rolled him over to the remaining crew members, who were waiting in the *Lesley A.* They laid him across the second seat, just as they'd been taught in exercise, Ollie holding his head. They wrapped him in a foil space blanket and Mary started CPR.

But as she was counting the compressions and the breaths, she knew this was useless. They'd been told this was what should happen. *Unless the body's rotting or it has no head, you try CPR.* That was what the trainer had said, a grin on his face, and they'd all chortled along as if it were a joke. *It's not your job to declare life extinct.*

This man was cold as ice and lifeless, though, and the limbs were rigid.

Seth was on the radio, organizing another lifeboat to launch in case the *Anna Louise* was still around somewhere, and in trouble. Calling for the helicopter to be on standby now it would soon be light. 'I'll call the ambulance, shall I?'

'Nah,' she said. 'We'll be back in Greystone well before the ambulance will get there. We need a doctor to declare him dead, and the police.'

Ollie turned the boat for home and the wind was already stronger. Force seven at least now. They'd be lucky to get back before the tide made it tricky on the beach. For the first time, she looked closely at the casualty's face, and realized that she recognized him. Jem Rosco, national treasure and her one-time hero.

Chapter Three

GREYSTONE BROUGHT BACK MEMORIES FOR MATTHEW Venn. There was a meeting hall in the village and he'd been brought here by his parents. A visit to the village had always been a treat, and he remembered this odd, isolated place with affection. There'd been a big community of Brethren, with more children than he'd ever encountered in Barnstaple. Outings had been organized: trips to the beach at Morrisham, picnics, social evenings. His parents had been more relaxed and Matthew had been given the chance to shine, to show off his bible knowledge and his faith. He'd basked in the admiration of the older members.

'What a clever little chap he is!' they'd say. And Dorothy would glow.

Since losing his faith, and marrying Jonathan, he hadn't been back. As they approached, he felt a little embarrassed by the boy he'd been, but interested to visit again a place where he'd been so happy.

Greystone wasn't somewhere that attracted tourists; especially now at the end of September, there was nothing appealing

11

about the place. The beach was rocky, and the gaps between rocks filled with shingle. The rocks were pocked with cockle shells and barnacles, and black with bladderwort. The cove faced north. The cliffs were hard and forbidding, and for much of the day there was no sunlight. The pub served the local cider, but there were no fancy meals. When houses came up for sale, potential second-homers came to look, but never bothered buying. This wasn't the North Devon of their dreams. The village was still scarred by the enormous quarry on the hill beyond it. It felt industrial, not idyllic. Real. As a precocious adolescent, he'd appreciated that.

Because there was nothing pretty, or appealing, about the place, locals could afford to live in Greystone. Young couples stayed out of necessity, because housing was cheap to rent and to buy. There was broadband, so remote working was possible. A few cottage industries had grown up – cider-making, a pottery – and they employed a handful of people. Just inland there were farmers who needed occasional contract labour. Commuting to Bideford was just about possible. The village had its own primary school, and there was a high school in Morrisham, five miles along the coast, for the older kids. This was a community where many people were related and everyone knew their neighbours; no effort at friendliness was needed, and grudges grew unheeded.

Inspector Matthew Venn had a clear sense of the place. He'd heard his parents talk about Greystone often enough. His mother had wanted to move there at one point, but, for once, his father had stood firm. It was *too* remote. *Too* self-contained.

Matthew had always been an inveterate eavesdropper, and as a youngster he'd store away details, running over them later, trying to make sense of them. He didn't think that much would have changed. Now he drove to the village through wind that made steering tricky, and rain so hard that the wipers on full speed wouldn't clear the windscreen. The storm had returned big style since they'd left Barnstaple. He passed on his thoughts to Jen Rafferty, his sergeant, who was sitting beside him.

'It feels different from anywhere else in the county. It's very remote.' He paused. 'A bit bleak, I suppose.'

Jen Rafferty didn't answer directly. She was a Scouser, passionate and impulsive. She'd left her home city to escape an abusive marriage, but Venn knew she still missed the Liverpool skyline, seen from the west side of the Mersey. She thought everywhere in North Devon was remote. Now, it seemed, she was more interested in the victim than the geography. 'Who *is* this Jeremy Rosco?'

'Haven't you heard of him? At one time, he was never off the television. He's a hero. Well, almost. He grew up just round the coast and went to school in Morrisham. The only son of a single mother. He didn't do well at school; he was only ever interested in being on the water.'

This was the story told in documentaries and interviews. Matthew wondered how true it was, but he continued:

'Rosco went on to become the youngest person to sail round the world single-handed, and he became a kind of legend. He moved on to other expeditions: he did both Poles with just a small team, and walked up the Amazon. For his subsequent adventures he had a television camera crew in tow, so he became a kind of media celebrity.' Venn paused. 'I've not heard so much of him in the last few years, though. He must have been in his late fifties. Perhaps he retired.'

'So, what was he doing in Greystone?'

Venn turned to her. 'That's what we're here to find out. Why he came back here, and why he died close by.'

The journey through the village was precipitous, made even more dangerous by the wet roads, the water forming a stream on each side. The houses were grey: stone from the quarry, the roofs slate. Where the land flattened, they passed the school, a shop and the pub, the Maiden's Prayer, named after a wrecked ship, but considered a little blasphemous by Matthew's mother. Behind the pub, a steep row of terraced cottages led to the abandoned quarry. The pub sign, painted with a ship in full sail, swung dangerously in the gale. Venn drove on to the quay.

The rain stopped when they arrived, but the wind seemed to increase. It blew from the north-west, straight into their faces. A uniformed officer, anonymous in navy waterproofs, was sheltering behind the wall formed by the quay and the lifeboat station, looking out for them. Presumably his colleague was inside. The officers had driven their car as near as they could, down the slipway which led to the beach. Venn parked behind it. He struggled to hold on to the car door when he opened it. The wind caught it and seemed about to tug it from his grasp, to rip it from the chassis.

It had taken Venn and Jen an hour to drive from Barnstaple. The officer was young and obviously relieved to see someone senior in charge. He was wet and cold. Venn wondered why he hadn't waited inside. Perhaps this was his first dead body, and he was of a squeamish disposition.

'Just show us where he is and then grab a coffee in the pub.' Venn wasn't sure that a pub like the Maiden's would serve coffee, but word about the incident would have spread and the village would be glad to have more news. They'd make an exception for someone in uniform.

The constable was local. 'There's a doctor in the village and the crew had him waiting for them. Usual procedure if there's a death.' He paused. 'They had to lift the body into the lifeboat to bring him back. That's standard apparently, unless it's so far gone that you know for certain there's nothing you can do. They left the dinghy where it was. Appledore lifeboat will tow it in. They know not to touch it more than they need to tie a line to it. Jimmy Rainston will have made sure of that. They'll take it back to their station. In this wind, it's too dangerous to try and get it in here. Their operations manager wasn't even sure he wanted them to go out to fetch it, but they decided to give it a go.'

Venn nodded his approval. 'Rainston's your colleague?'

'Yes, sir. We were here waiting when the lifeboat came in and one of us has stayed with the body all through.'

'Good. Doctor Pengelly is on her way.' Matthew was speaking almost to himself.

Jen was out of the car, red hair flying in the gusts of wind, a bright banner against all the grey. 'A bit odd, isn't it? Was Rosco killed in the dinghy?'

'The doctor says not. There was not enough blood apparently. The crew said the dinghy was clean. He reckons the man was stabbed elsewhere.'

'Then put in a dinghy and floated out to sea?' Matthew frowned.

'Towed most likely. Because of the anchor. Or rowed.'

'Of course,' Matthew said. 'It'd be impossible to do that remotely.'

'Like I said.' Jen pulled her coat tight around her. 'A bit odd.'

There were lights on inside the lifeboat station, very bright, casting hard shadows. The police officer had shown them in through a small side door and, for a moment, nobody noticed them because of the sound of the weather outside. Four men and a woman in RNLI jerseys stood in the kit room, clutching mugs of coffee. Matthew could smell it and was jealous.

A man of around Matthew's age, in jeans and a Barbour jacket, stood a little apart and was drinking coffee too. The doctor, Venn decided, but he could wait. There was a constable in uniform waterproofs, who must be Jimmy Rainston.

Venn introduced himself to the crew.

'You brought back the body.'

'He was dead when we arrived.' The woman spoke. She had long dark hair tied away from her face, thick dark eyebrows, and eyes which were almost black. 'I tried CPR, but really it was clear there was nothing we could do.'

'Where is he now?'

'Still in the lifeboat.' It was the oldest man in the room. Short and powerful, with a thick neck and a head like a fighting dog. He'd described himself as the lifeboat operations manager, Sammy Barton. 'We wanted to put him in a body bag. For a bit of dignity. But Jimmy here said to leave him be.'

'Quite right,' Matthew said, but he thought the dead man had been grabbed out of the dinghy and been exposed to the weather on the trip back. Any evidence might well have been washed away by now. 'The forensic pathologist is on her way. We'll move him as soon as we possibly can.'

'No rush.' Barton's voice was deep and rough. 'Even if we got a shout, I wouldn't allow a launch in this gale anyway. Must be near force nine out there now.'

'You all recognized him?'

'Oh yes,' Mary Ford said. 'It was definitely Jem Rosco.' A pause. 'He'd been staying in the village for a while. And, of course, we all knew him by sight.'

Venn turned to Rainston. 'Let's go and see him then.'

The constable led him through into the main body of the lifeboat station. The boat was on a trailer, attached to a huge tractor. It glowed orange. Rosco seemed very small. He was laid across the widest seat of the RIB, his head resting on a folded tarpaulin on the side of the boat. He was quite naked, his hair short and white but there was a strength to him in the shoulders and the arms. No spare flesh, and muscles a younger man would be proud of. Venn could see why Barton had wanted him covered. He'd been a proud man and this was a sad end for him.

He turned to Rainston. 'Thanks for this. You've done all the right things. I've told your mate to go up to the Maiden's to warm through. Why don't you join him? One of us will head up and chat to you when we've finished here.'

'Sir.' Rainston was a big man but he scuttled quickly away, giving just a brief last glance at the body before making his exit through the door into the kit room again.

Venn stood for a moment looking down at Rosco. The silence was broken by a squall, the rain battering against the big doors. The walls were covered by photos of other rescues, a roll call of lives saved. But not this one. There'd be nothing to do for a man who was already dead.

Back in the kit room, Venn approached the man in the Barbour jacket. He was dark-haired, slight.

'You must be the doctor. Thanks for turning out. You live in the village?'

'For my sins.'

'Pete grew up here,' one of the crew said. 'He ran off to do his training, but we couldn't keep him away.'

'My wife had a romantic notion about a practice by the sea.' The man smiled at Venn. 'Peter Smale. I'm a GP. I work mostly out of the health centre in Morrisham, but I hold a surgery here two mornings a week.' He looked at his watch. 'I should go back there. They'll be queuing into the road.'

'Of course. Perhaps we can catch up later.'

'I've taken over an empty shop in the main street. It used to be a greengrocer's but we've done it out. Not the slightest smell of cabbage left.'

The crew grinned politely. Perhaps it was an old joke.

'I know it,' Matthew said.

And I know you too. We sat together through the Brethren meetings as young adolescents, as pompous as each other. Our parents were friends of a kind. And so were we.

Smale looked at him as if he, too, had a moment of recognition, but said, 'I'll be there all day and I'm usually patient-free for a couple of hours in the afternoon.' He paused for a moment and then went out through the narrow door onto the quay, letting in a blast of cold air.

Matthew turned to the people who remained. 'I'm afraid you'll have to talk us through it right from the beginning, while we wait for the rest of my team to arrive.' He looked at Barton. 'So, tell me what happened.'

'We got the shout from the coastguard. They'd had a mayday by radio, channel sixteen, a vessel in trouble. No details apart from the position. The call was cut short.'

'But you went to investigate?' It was hardly a question. Matthew knew they would investigate. A mayday was the equivalent of a 999 call.

'Of course.'

'What time was that?'

'I got the call from the coastguard at four fifty-five. Our boat was in the water by five twenty.'

Matthew was taking that in. He looked at the remaining three men and the woman. 'You're all local?'

'They are.' Sammy spoke for them. 'All Greystone born and bred, apart from Mary here. She's the helm.' His voice was flat, but Venn could pick up the edge in it. He'd developed a nose for bias of any kind. Being gay in the police service gave you that. What did Sammy disapprove of in Mary? Matthew wondered. The fact that she was an outsider or that she was a woman?

'How long did it take you to get to the headland?'

This time Mary answered. 'Less than twenty minutes. The wind and the tide were behind us.'

'And you were expecting a bigger boat?'

Sammy Barton jumped in. 'The coastguard had said a fishing vessel called the *Anna Louise*.'

'At first, I thought the dinghy was a tender,' Mary said, 'and that the bigger boat must be lost. Then we saw what was inside. And anyway, with the anchor—'

Barton interrupted her again. 'The coastguard has been back to us, and said there's no boat with that name registered anywhere along the North Devon coast.'

'So, it was a hoax call,' Venn said. 'But they wanted you to find him.' He thought that was the strangest part of an already bizarre murder. Why not just make a hole in the dinghy and let it sink? Rosco's body might not be washed up for weeks. Perhaps it would never appear.

He looked at Barton. 'What's happening to the dinghy?'

'Appledore coastguard has towed it in. They're holding it there.'

Venn nodded. Another complication to a case that was already the strangest he'd ever investigated.

Chapter Four

VENN LEFT JEN IN THE LIFEBOAT shed to talk to the crew and wait for the pathologist and crime scene manager. Sally Pengelly and Brian Branscombe were regulars, part of the team. He thought that perhaps Brian would have been better heading straight to the lifeboat station in Appledore to check out the dinghy. Sometimes, though, the CSI said, the body itself was a crime scene. Branscombe was already taking his video, photos from every possible angle. The wounds looked like stabbings to Venn, but the death would remain unexplained until Sally Pengelly had seen the man. In the meantime, he would treat it as murder. It could be nothing else.

Venn stood in the porch of the Maiden's Prayer. He'd never been inside, and he smiled, wondering what his mother would say. The thought came less often these days, but still her voice was at the back of his head at times of crisis. Jonathan always said he shouldn't blame his mother for his self-doubt.

She's a lonely old woman. You're an adult, and you should be content in your own skin. Own your own shit and give her a break!

For Matthew, it wasn't that easy. Dorothy was his mother, and, when he'd lost his faith, she'd chosen the Brethren over him.

He walked inside. It was too early for lunchtime opening and the two constables were alone with the landlord. The pub was less gloomy than he'd imagined. There were pale wood tables and the walls were white, recently painted. The old traditions had been kept, though. Above the bar were curling pictures of bearded men, former lifeboat helms, and newspaper clippings describing apparently heroic rescues. A photograph of the darts team holding a trophy. The funeral service sheet for an elderly regular. Venn introduced himself to the man behind the bar.

'Harry Carter. I own this place. For my sins.'

It was the second time the phrase had been used that morning. For someone with Venn's upbringing, the words resonated.

'Any chance of a coffee?' He saw the policemen had mugs on the table in front of them.

'Sure.' Carter disappeared into a room behind the bar.

Venn turned to the officers. 'Where are you based?'

Rainston spoke. 'Morrisham, but it's a bloody big patch.'

'Of course. Get much bother out this way?'

They shook their heads. 'Never been here before,' Rainston said. 'I get the impression that they sort out their own problems. You saw the lifeboat guys. Any bother here in the pub, they'd soon calm things down. You wouldn't want to take on that Sammy Barton.' There was a pause. 'I'm not saying there's no crime. Bound to be. Underage drinking. Drugs. Drugs everywhere, isn't there? But nothing anyone would feel the need to call us out for.'

Venn wasn't sure what he made of that. A community that policed itself sounded dangerous to him, with an undercurrent of control, bullying. The Brethren had never liked outsiders looking into their business, and perhaps he was wary because of his experience with them. He wondered how many of the younger villagers were still members.

'Anything else you think I should know? Did anything about the crew's story strike you as odd? You were first on the scene when the boat got back.'

'It's *all* bloody peculiar, isn't it, sir?'

'It is.' Venn thought that summed up the case in one sentence. 'Write it up as soon as you get back, and get the statements across to me. You can go now, if you've warmed through.'

They'd left by the time Carter came back with the coffee. The man set the mug on the bar, and Venn took a stool there and wrapped his hands around it.

'Poor Jem,' Carter said. 'We thought he'd just left. It seemed a bit weird that he hadn't said goodbye, but he'd turned up out of the blue and it was in character for him to leave in just the same way. We wondered if maybe his mysterious visitor had finally turned up.'

There was too much here to unpick all at once, so Venn started with the basics. The facts.

'When did he arrive?'

'The first storm of the autumn.' There was a calendar hanging behind the bar and Carter consulted it. 'September the second. It was a Thursday night because a couple of the oldies were in playing crib. Always cribbage on a Thursday.'

'That was the day he appeared in Greystone? Not the first time he came into the pub?'

23

'Both,' the landlord said. 'He'd been travelling all day, he said, and he was desperate for a pint.'

'You must have been surprised to see him.'

'I recognized him as soon as he walked through the door. There was something about him. Not just because he'd been on the telly, but because he had a presence. You knew there was something special about him, even if you didn't know who he was.' Carter shrugged apologetically. 'That must sound a bit daft.'

'There are some people like that.'

The man who'd run the Brethren in Barnstaple had been one such. He could light up a room. And persuade people to do just what he wanted.

'Charisma,' Carter went on. 'Isn't that what they call it?'

Venn didn't answer. One of his annual appraisals had said that he lacked charisma. He'd seen that as a compliment, almost a badge of honour. He was drawn to Jonathan's charisma like a moth to a flame, but it wasn't a trait he desired for himself. He thought that policing was about intellectual rigour and honesty, not personality.

'You didn't know Mr Rosco? He grew up locally, went to school in Morrisham.'

Carter shook his head. 'He was fifteen years older than me. He was already famous by the time I was there. He came once for prize-giving.' His voice tailed off. 'He said in his speech that he was an example of how anything was possible. You just had to know what you wanted and follow your dreams.' He gave a wry smile. 'It didn't work for me. I'm back running the pub where I grew up.'

Venn wanted to ask what dreams the man had when he was growing up, but he couldn't see how that could be relevant.

Curiosity was part of his make-up, and he'd learned to live with it.

'How did Mr Rosco get here? I presume he had a car.'

Carter shook his head again. 'He must have got a lift. Or a taxi from Tiverton Parkway or Barnstaple if he came by train.' A pause. 'He never said. I think he enjoyed being mysterious; he liked people wondering about him.'

'He grew up along the coast. He hadn't kept a base locally?'

'I wouldn't have thought so. Why would he come and stay here if he had his own place a few miles away?'

Because he needed to be in Greystone specifically? But Jonathan always said people created narratives of their own lives. Perhaps Rosco had wanted to feature in *his* story: a stranger landing up at a village on the coast, attracting speculation in a community where nothing much happened. Perhaps he needed the envy that Venn had sensed in Carter's response to the man's life. It would make him the centre of attention again, if his celebrity had been waning.

'Where did Mr Rosco stay when he was here?'

'Quarry Bank. He was renting the top cottage. Just out of the pub and up the hill.'

'Who owns it?' The CSIs would need to go in, of course. It could be their murder scene, but Venn hoped he could get an hour on his own there first, suitably suited and gloved. He needed a sense of the man, and if Rosco's belongings were still there, that would give him a start. He knew it was easy to be misled by a public persona. Charisma could be added as part of a performance.

'Colin Gregory. But he's just gone into a care home. I assume it was his daughter Gwen who leased it out.'

'And she'd have a key?'

'Bound to have.'

'Where will I find her?' Venn just about managed to control his impatience.

'In the back. She cleans for us five days a week.'

Gwen Gregory was small and round-bodied, of indeterminate age. She had tight grey curls and a sharp little face, which gave her the appearance of an amiable sheep. She was still wearing an apron over jeans and a sweatshirt, and she seemed in a state of excitement. Perhaps she hadn't known Rosco well enough to be sad about his death, and she was enjoying the drama.

'Harry says you think he might have been killed in Dad's cottage.'

'I don't think anything at this point.' Venn's voice was mild, but he shot Harry a glance. He wondered if the constables had been indiscreet while they were drinking their coffee. It was more likely, though, that the lifeboat crew had been spreading the word about the circumstances of Jem Rosco's death. There'd probably be a Greystone village WhatsApp group, full of gossip, as well as the usual offer of free, unwanted furniture and outgrown kiddies' clothes. 'I'd like to see inside, though. Harry said you'd have a key?'

'I do!' Her excitement now seemed to have reached fever pitch. 'It's in my bag. I'll just get my coat and then I can let you in.' She was already reaching behind her back to untie the pinafore.

'No need for that,' Venn said. 'Just let me have the key and I'll let myself in. We try to limit the number of people in potential crime scenes. You probably know that yourself.' He already had her down as an ardent viewer of true crime documentaries.

'Of course!' The sting of disappointment appeared tempered by his acknowledgement that she would understand how the system worked. 'You'll probably have to wear one of those white suits.'

'Indeed,' he said, his voice serious. 'And a mask.'

She nodded and disappeared into the kitchen, returning with two large keys. 'This is the one to the front door, leading straight into the house from the pavement, and this is for the kitchen door into the yard.'

'It would be good to talk to you later. You must have taken the booking from Mr Rosco, and, if you don't mind, we'll need a statement. How long will you be here?'

'Only until one o'clock,' she said. 'And I don't mind at all. I'll be glad to help. This is such a terrible thing to have happened in the village. He was a lovely man.' A pause. 'You can find me anytime, though. I only live next door to where he was staying.'

'You've been very helpful,' Venn said. 'We'll definitely need to talk to you then. You'll be a valuable witness. I'll be in touch.'

She flushed and scurried away behind the bar and out of sight.

Outside, the rain was keeping off but it was as windy as before. He walked back down the hill to see what was happening in the lifeboat station, and to collect the scene suits from the car. He recognized Sally Pengelly's vehicle, and when he went into the building, she was there, just arrived, standing by the lifeboat and peering inside. She heard Venn approaching and turned to face him.

'He was a hero,' she said. 'When I was a youngster, I wanted to be a female Jem Rosco. I thought he might end his life on one of his crazy expeditions. I thought he might even be lost at sea. Not like this, though.'

'We don't think he did die at sea, do we?'

'No,' she said. 'He was dead when he was placed in the boat.' A pause. 'Perhaps someone thought it was fitting to tow him out onto the water. It would be where he'd want to end his days.'

Venn shook his head. 'It doesn't feel like a gesture of respect to me. More an act of mockery.'

She smiled. 'Luckily that's not for me to decide. I'll do as much as I can here, and then I'll get him to the hospital for the post-mortem.' She looked up. 'Have you seen the forecast? I'm worried we won't get back if we don't leave soon. They're predicting hurricane force winds for later today. Brian's heading to Appledore to look at the dinghy.'

'I'll leave you to it. Let me know when you have a time for the post-mortem.' Venn was aware of the remorseless routines of an investigation rolling out, although this case felt anything but routine.

Jen came with him to the small house where Jeremy Rosco had been living for the previous month. They didn't need Gwen Gregory's key to get in through the front door; it was already unlocked.

'Standard practice in a village like this?' Venn wasn't asking this as a serious question to his sergeant. Jen didn't know anything about small villages and her opinion wouldn't help much. He was muttering to himself. His ideas seemed more concrete when he spoke them out loud. 'Or did he invite someone in? Then the killer didn't bother locking the door behind him. Hard to carry a grown man down to the quay without anyone seeing, though.

'He was expecting a visitor.' They were standing now in a neat front room. An old man's room. A two-seater sofa under the window and a high-backed chair, easy to get out of for someone with limited mobility, facing the electric fire. An old, bulky television on a stand. On the mantelpiece a pile of books. Rosco's books. No sign of a struggle. No immediate sign of blood.

'How do you know?' Jen asked.

'The whole village knew, apparently. Rosco told everyone who asked that he'd be here for as long as it took his mysterious visitor to arrive. No time scale and no explanation. No real opinion about whether he was waiting for a man or a woman, but the consensus was a woman. They liked the idea of a romance.'

Venn walked through into the kitchen, which was at the back of the house, looking out into a yard surrounded by a high wall. There was no gate in the wall. Venn had noticed, walking up the hill, that dustbins were left in the tiny front gardens. The search teams were on their way. Jen stood in the doorway, watching.

In the kitchen there was a stained enamel sink under the window. Cupboards and appliances which could well date back to the seventies. Everything immaculate. No used plates or mugs, the draining board wiped and shining. Venn thought he should have asked Gwen Gregory if she cleaned for Rosco. Or perhaps he'd been a naturally fastidious man.

Jen followed him in now and was opening the cupboards. Again, they were ordered. Tins in rows. Cannisters for tea and instant coffee. Some of the goods, Matthew thought, would be more to Rosco's taste than Colin Gregory's. There was a packet of real coffee, and a small AeroPress with filters. In the narrow fridge, a bottle of Veuve Clicquot. Was that chilling, waiting for the mysterious stranger? If so, that probably did imply that the anticipated guest was a woman. Immediately Venn thought he was jumping to conclusions. Jonathan would mock him for that. He had no knowledge of Rosco's sexuality. If the sailor did have a lover, it could be a man.

Narrow stairs led up to two bedrooms and a tiny bathroom, one bedroom looking out at the yard to the quarry beyond, one at the front. The back room had a single bed and a chest of drawers, empty and lined with newspaper that dated back twenty years. No space in the room for anything else. The bed had been stripped and blankets were folded at one end, two thin pillows on top of the pile. The place felt damp and chill. There was no double glazing.

The front bedroom was even more draughty; the sash window was streaked with salt spray and rattled in the wind, despite a folded piece of paper intended to keep it in place. Venn remembered a Golden Age detective novel – one of Dorothy Sayers', perhaps – where the plot hinged on a piece of paper wedged into a sash window to stop it rattling. He'd read through the canon of the Golden Age when he'd first left home and life had been chaotic, unanchored. The stories had been an escape and had seen him through. He pulled it out. Card, not paper, with orange edges. A train ticket. Liverpool to Tiverton Parkway. One way. Dated the month before. That might be useful.

This room was a little larger, with a double bed and a wardrobe, a bedside cabinet. The bed was made up with sheets, blankets and a candlewick quilt. No duvet here. Venn was reminded of his mother, who still rejected the duvet as a foreign invention, to be regarded with suspicion. He stood for a moment at the window, looking down at the village and on to the quay. From here everything was visible: the school, the hall where the Brethren had held their meetings, the pub and the lifeboat station. If Rosco had been as curious as Venn, there'd have been no secrets kept from him.

Jen opened the wardrobe door, then stood aside so Matthew could see in. On one side there was space for clothes to hang. A tweed jacket, a couple of shirts, a pair of trousers, a fleece and an expensive waterproof. On the other a row of narrow shelves, which held underwear, jeans, T-shirts and jerseys. This must have been all the clothes the dead man had brought with him. Matthew didn't touch anything. He'd leave that to Brian and his team, though there was nothing here to indicate that the room was a crime scene.

'Where's the suitcase?' Jen's words broke into his thoughts. He'd been speculating about what Rosco had been doing here. Making up a story of his own to explain the man's behaviour.

'Sorry?'

'Well, this stuff. And the books. The food downstairs. I doubt the local shop sells champagne and fancy coffee. Rosco must have carried it somehow.'

'I don't know.' Matthew tried to focus. He supposed this was important but he was still preoccupied with his own thoughts. 'Is there an attic? A cupboard under the stairs?'

'Or maybe some storage in the bathroom?' Jen pushed open the third door, and stopped. Matthew almost walked into her, was so close to her that he could smell her shampoo. Citrus. He looked over her shoulder.

There was blood. A lot of blood. In the bath and spattered onto the tile walls. So, he thought, aware of a trace of irony: this was certainly murder, and they could stop looking for their crime scene.

Chapter Five

JEN RAFFERTY THOUGHT THIS LOOKED LIKE something from
a cheap horror movie made years ago. The blood in the bath
and on the walls had dried and darkened, so it could almost
have been filmed in black and white. It seemed to her that the
whole of Greystone had a strange, unreal, almost other-worldly
quality: the village that time had forgotten. She'd never before
been anywhere that felt so cut off from the rest of the world,
and the sense of isolation sapped her confidence. She wasn't
sure how to work here, how to conduct interviews, or make
people talk. The constant noise of the wind outside, howling
like an animal in pain, added to her unease.

She longed suddenly for the comforts of home. When she
got back to her little house in Barnstaple, she'd switch the
heating full on, pour a large glass of pinot, and curl up in front
of something trashy on Netflix. Have the sound on loud enough
not to hear the gale outside. But that would have to wait.
Matthew Venn seemed lost in his thoughts for the moment;
soon he'd start to issue instructions again.

'There's no shower curtain,' he said. 'Look, there's a shower over the bath and a rail, but no curtain.'

'You think the body was wrapped in it?'

He turned and smiled at her, glad that she was following his reasoning. 'It's possible, isn't it?'

Then he was focused again on the immediate situation. 'Let's get Ross here. I'll tell him to bring enough stuff for a couple of days. You can't stay overnight because of your children, but he and I can book rooms at the pub. It will save the trek each day and we'll be on site.'

She nodded her agreement. She hated missing out on anything work-related, but Venn had got this one right. The kids were teenagers now and they'd had to learn to be independent. She'd come to North Devon as a single mother with no friends or family on hand, and a demanding job. But she didn't know how long this investigation would last. She didn't mind leaving Ella and Ben overnight at the weekend – she'd been doing that for a while, because she occasionally needed to let her hair down – but not when they had to be up for school the next day. Besides, she'd rather do the daily drive than stay overnight in this strange village.

Venn was still speaking. 'I'd like you to talk to Gwen Gregory. Her father owns this house and she looks after the letting. She lives next door and cleans at the pub.' He looked at his watch. 'She should just be home from work. Let her talk. She'll be keen to be involved. The killer might be Rosco's mysterious stranger, but it could be one of the locals and she'll know the background to everyone here. I'll get hold of Brian and let him know that we've found our crime scene. Then I'll talk to the doctor. He grew up here. He's someone else who'll understand the place and its secrets.'

Outside on the pavement, the wind almost took her legs from under her, and tore at her scene suit as she tried to take it off. The storm seemed to be getting fiercer, rather than abating. The neighbour's door opened before Jen could knock. Gwen Gregory must have been looking out for a detective to call. Jen could feel the heat before she stepped inside. The layout of this house was identical to the one next door but this felt very different, more personal, with photographs on the mantelpiece and a women's magazine on the arm of the sofa. The furniture wasn't to Jen's taste – chain store contemporary and too big for the room – but it was comfortable. A large flat-screen television in the corner showed a lunchtime show, where a chef was filleting a mackerel. Gwen left the television on but switched off the sound. The warmth came from a solid fuel boiler, which must run the central heating.

'You're here about poor Mr Rosco,' Gwen said. 'Inspector Venn said someone would call.' A pause. 'I thought he might come himself.' She sounded disappointed.

'He's very busy.'

'Of course, he will be.' Gwen seemed to think she'd been rude and hurried to make amends. 'You'll be freezing if you've been next door. My dad kept it like an ice bucket. We offered to put in central heating, but he couldn't stand the thought of the mess. I'll put the kettle on. I've not long got in. Just make yourself comfy and I'll be back soon.' She disappeared into the kitchen, leaving the door open so Jen could hear the sound of a tap and the clink of crockery. The heat was making Jen drowsy and she was almost asleep when Gwen returned with a tray. She set it on a glass-topped coffee table. 'I'm guessing milk and no sugar.'

'Yeah, that's right.'

It was strong as Jen liked it, and there was homemade flap-jack on a plate. Jen thought a rush of sugar was just what she needed. She supposed she should stay impartial, but she was starting to warm to the woman.

'How did Mr Rosco come to be living next door?'

'He wasn't living there, not permanent like. More paying guest. Our dad went into a home at the beginning of the summer. We kept him in his own place as long as we could, but, in the end, we couldn't manage even with carers coming in twice a day. It was my brother Davy who suggested we put the house on one of those websites, for people wanting some-where to stay.' Gwen looked up at Jen. 'Those nursing homes are so pricy, and Dad's savings were being eaten away, but he wouldn't think of selling up. He always believed he'd get back there one day. We thought it might bring in something towards the care costs.'

Jen nodded to show she understood.

'We had a few takers. People walking the coastal path. But most visitors are looking for something with a few more facil-ities, and families want a sandy beach, don't they?'

'But that's how Mr Rosco got hold of you? Through the website? Did you recognize the name?'

'Not when he booked. It's not such an unusual name down here in the south-west. Of course, we all recognized him from the telly when he showed up. I was worried he'd turn up his nose at the house when he saw the place, but he said it would suit him perfectly.' Gwen looked at Jen again. 'Those were his exact words.' There was a pause before she added, 'He was such a nice man.'

'How long did he book it for?'

'He told us he wasn't sure how long he'd need it. He asked if he could pay for a fortnight and renew weekly after that. We were delighted. Nobody had stayed more than a couple of nights before and we weren't really expecting any new bookings now the season's over.'

'And how long had he been there?'

'For nearly a month, then he came in two nights ago and paid for another week.' Gwen looked awkward. 'I suppose we'll have to pay some of it back, though I'm sure I wouldn't know who to send it to.'

Jen thought that was something that the police would have to follow up on too: tracing the victim's family. They still hadn't tracked down any next of kin, and Matthew hated news of a suspicious death getting into the press before the relatives had been informed. Jeremy Rosco had been a celebrity, though, and she'd bet that news of his murder was already all over social media. Greystone wasn't so isolated that its residents weren't on Facebook and Instagram.

'Mr Rosco didn't mention any family to you?'

Gwen shook her head sadly. 'We didn't speak about anything personal at all.'

'You didn't know him? You must have been at the same school if you grew up here.'

'We were at school at the same time,' she said, 'but he was a bit younger and he moved with a very different crowd. More adventurous. I was a timid little thing in those days.'

Jen remembered Matthew's instructions to prize information from Gwen about the locals. 'So, you've lived here all your life?'

'Oh, we've been in Greystone for generations. You just have to look in the churchyard to see that. It's full of Gregory graves. Always farmers too. Never fishermen, like most of the village.'

'Your dad was a farmer?'

'Until he had to sell up.' Her voice was suddenly hard, bitter.

'What happened?' Jen couldn't see how any of this was relevant, but it was better being in here, chatting in the warm, the relentless sound of the wind dulled by efficient double glazing, than being out in the storm. Besides, Venn would love these snippets of background.

Gwen shrugged. 'It never made much of a living. Poor soil and it was hard work keeping the place going. My dad was never one for new ideas and though Davy had plenty, Dad's as stubborn as a mule. He wouldn't change a thing. So, when the quarry wanted to expand and made an offer on the land, he sold up. He bought these two cottages as a sort of investment, and after a year or so he moved into number one, and Davy kept the old farmhouse. The quarry didn't need it, and at least Dad had kept hold of that.'

'When was that?'

'Years ago. My mum had just died. Cancer. I'm not sure Dad would have sold if she'd been alive. He was still grieving. He told himself and everyone else who would listen that he was doing the village a favour. A bigger quarry would bring new jobs. That never happened, and later the whole place closed down. The workers who did remain were made redundant.'

'What does Davy do now?'

'He runs a taxi business.' She sniffed as if she disapproved. 'He's got a couple of cars. His wife's younger and teaches in the school here. They never had kids. There's no mortgage on the house, and I think her family had money. They do all right.' A pause. 'More than all right.'

'How did Mr Rosco get to the village? We haven't found a car.'

'No,' Gwen said. 'He didn't have a car.'

'Perhaps Davy gave him a lift from the station?'

'Perhaps he did. That would have been a good fare. Tiverton's probably the nearest and that's a good hour away.'

Jen wondered why the woman didn't know for certain. Wouldn't Davy have bragged about bringing the great Jeremy Rosco into the village? Perhaps the siblings weren't very close.

'You must have met Jeremy that first night,' she said. 'To let him into the house. Did you see how he got here?'

Gwen shook her head.

'He told me when he booked that he wasn't certain when he'd arrive. I left keys for him under a flowerpot by the side of the front step. That was what we arranged.'

'You live next door. Did you hear him come in?'

Gwen nodded. 'I was getting ready for bed. I was just shutting the curtains upstairs when I saw him. There's only one street light at the bottom of the hill and I saw him walking up. He had a great bag on his back, and I thought how strong he was for such a short man. Striding up the bank, even with that weight on his shoulder. I would have gone down to greet him – I like to welcome the guests – but I was already in my night things and I knew by the time I'd changed again he'd be inside. So, I just watched him find the keys and let himself in. I waited until he'd switched on a light and then I went to bed. By next morning, it was all over the village that Jeremy Rosco was staying here. I heard all about it when I started my shift at the Maiden's. Everyone wanted to know about him, but I had nothing to tell them.'

'Last night,' Jen said, 'were you in?'

Gwen nodded.

'On your own?'

Another nod. Jen didn't say anything and Gwen felt the need to fill the gap. 'I've never married. Had a long-term partner, but he worked at the quarry and buggered off when it closed. He asked me to go with him, but he was from the North, and a city boy at heart. I knew I wouldn't settle. Besides, I had Dad to think about . . .' Her voice tailed off and Jen thought Gwen was dreaming of her man, and what might have been if she'd had the courage to go away with him.

'Did you hear anything?'

'You think that's where he was killed? Last night?' Gwen's voice held a mixture of horror and fascination.

'We don't know anything for certain yet, but we need to explore all possibilities.' Jen paused. 'Did you hear anything? We know Jeremy didn't go to the pub last night. Perhaps he had a visitor?'

Gwen shook her head. 'The walls are thick and I always have the telly on. I wouldn't hear a thing.'

'You didn't see anything? Perhaps as you were closing the curtains when you were on your way to bed, like you did the night he arrived?'

'I didn't.' The woman sounded disappointed that she couldn't be more helpful.

'What about early this morning?'

'I sleep like the dead,' Gwen said. 'I never wake until my alarm goes off.'

'What time is that?'

'Seven. I start my shift at the Maiden's at eight.'

Jen thought that wasn't helpful. Rosco's body would have been removed long before then.

She knew she'd have to move. The heat was making her lethargic, too settled. Venn would be needing her. She got to her feet and looked at the window, the rain so heavy against it that all she could see was a shroud of grey.

'When did you last see Mr Rosco?'

'The night before last. I'd met Davy and his wife in the Maiden's. It was darts night and Davy plays. They were up against one of the Morrisham teams. Jeremy was there.'

'He went to school in Morrisham, didn't he? Who did he cheer for?'

It was a throwaway line but Jen came from Liverpool. She understood partisan support. She was expecting an immediate response, something light, almost playful to end the interview, but it took Gwen a moment to reply.

'You know, my love, I think he found it a bit awkward. Usually, he'd always cheer on our boys, but that day, he just stood at the bar, chatting to Harry, and he left before the end of play.'

'Could he have seen someone he recognized in the Morrisham team?'

'Perhaps he did, but if so, it wasn't anyone he wanted to meet again. He kept his distance, and he ran away after one pint. And that wasn't like Jem Rosco at all.'

Leaving Gwen Gregory's house, Jen almost bumped into Matthew Venn on the pavement. He was talking to Brian Branscombe, the wind snatching at his words so he had to shout. The crime scene manager nodded and went into the house where Rosco had stayed.

'What now, boss?'

'Lunch. Ross is on his way and I've said we'll meet him there.'

They fought against the storm and by the time they reached the pub they were both drenched.

Chapter Six

It seemed that most of the lifeboat crew were in the public bar when they arrived. Their oilskins hung from hooks along the counter and they were gathered around a table in the window, pints in front of them along with plates covered with crumbs. There was no sign of Mary Ford, the helm. Perhaps she hadn't been invited. Or perhaps she had better things to do with her time.

The LOM, Sammy Barton, watched them come in. 'They've taken him away,' he called over to Venn. 'That pathologist of yours has gone too.'

Venn nodded. He had nothing to say at this point.

There was a small room at the back of the pub, labelled THE SNUG on a faded gold sign over the door, and Venn pushed his way into that. In contrast to the public bar, the room hadn't changed for decades. There was nothing snug about it. A fire had been laid in the grate but it hadn't been lit. The furniture was scratched, the tables covered in a sticky varnish. It *was* private, though. There was a hatch into the bar and Harry Carter stuck his head through, looking suddenly comic, like a puppet in a *Punch and Judy* show.

'What can I get you?'

Venn took a box of matches from the mantelpiece, struck one and threw it onto the fire, before turning back to the landlord.

'Coffee, please. What do you do in the way of food?'

'I *could* make a plate of sandwiches.' As if he'd be doing them a huge favour. 'Or there's pasties. We get them in from the butcher in Morrisham. Proper job.'

Venn looked at Jen, who nodded. 'Two pasties then. And I'd like to book a couple of rooms.' He didn't ask if there were any vacancies. This was hardly peak visitor season.

All the same, Carter made a show of coming into the snug with a big diary to check availability. 'How long would you be staying?'

'Until the weekend at least.' Because how could they know how long this would take?

'No worries.'

'We'd want bed, breakfast and dinner. You could manage a proper meal for us in the evenings?' Venn's mother had believed junk food to be a sin against God's creation, and despite himself, the notion still lingered.

'Of course!' Carter feigned offence. 'Gwen Gregory comes in to cook for us when needed. She's a proper home cook. Nothing fancy, like, but everything fresh.'

'Perfect.' Venn paused. 'Could I have a double room? Just in case my husband decides to join me at some point.' He knew it was ridiculous, but a statement like this still seemed brave. Or provocative.

There was a pause. Venn couldn't tell whether the hesitation was caused by surprise or distaste. Eventually Carter re-arranged his face into an accommodating smile.

'Of course. There's a lovely double at the front. With its own bathroom. You'll both be very happy there.' Another pause. 'So, it'll be a double for you and a single for the lady. I'll need your details, miss.'

'No,' Venn said. 'Sergeant Rafferty won't be staying over-night. She has commitments at home. The second room is for another officer. His name's May. Ross May.'

And at that point, as if the name had conjured him out of the storm, Ross May opened the door and stood looking in at them. His usually gelled hair was wind-swept, and it seemed he'd stepped in a puddle on his way from the car: there were splashes of mud on his trousers. Venn thought that Ross, too, was out of his comfort zone here. He might have been born and brought up in North Devon, but he wasn't a country boy at heart, and he and his wife Mel had aspirations. They might never move away from Barnstaple, but they'd like to climb the social ladder within the town, and Ross would never haunt a pub like the Maiden's Prayer through choice.

'And here he is,' Venn said easily. 'So, another coffee and pasty, please, Harry. And I wonder if you could put some more coal on the fire before you go?'

Harry gave another awkward smile and did as he was told.

'I nearly didn't make it. A tree had blown down across the road and I had to shift it to get past.' Ross was excited, full of his adventures. There was nothing he liked better than a drama, as long as he was the hero of the story. Venn and Jen looked at each other, suspecting exaggeration. After all, it couldn't have been a very *big* tree if Ross had moved it on his own. But they said nothing. Let him have his moment of glory.

Venn quickly brought him up to speed.

'It's all a bit elaborate, isn't it, boss? Why not just leave the body where it was? Or put a hole in the dinghy and he might never be found? Someone playing silly buggers, do we think?'

'Perhaps,' Venn said. He thought it was too early yet to come to any sort of decision. Ross was right, though, and if they could answer those particular questions, they might know why Rosco had died.

'So,' Venn continued. 'Actions for the rest of the afternoon . . . I'm going to visit the doctor – Peter Smale – in his surgery. If Jeremy Rosco had any connection with the place, he'll know about it. He grew up here. Jen, can you canvas Gwen Gregory's neighbours, and then the street which leads down to the quay? Or make a start at least. I've been promised a team to help, but you know what resourcing's like. They might arrive just before it gets dark, then disappear again, especially in this weather. Someone killed Rosco in that house, carried him through the village, put him in a dinghy and towed it out to the headland. That would have taken a boat too. Something with a motor. So, Ross, talk to Barton, and if you don't get any sense from him, speak to the coast-guard. Who would have had access to a boat like that? There can't be that many people living in Greystone and Barton would know them all.'

Harry Carter's head appeared once more at the hole in the wall. He passed through the coffees. 'Pasties won't be long!'

They waited for him to move away before continuing the conversation, though the wind had increased even further, and seemed to have blown down a fence that banged in the yard at the back. It would be hard to overhear anything. All the same, Venn shifted his chair so he could see through the hatch into the other bar. Carter was back chatting to the lifeboat crew, gathering as much gossip as he could from them. It was impossible to see through the windows at the front of the pub now. Waves of grey rain broke across them.

'It wouldn't have to be a Greystone man, would it?' Ross said. 'The killer could have come from outside, driven in. Then you'd just have to carry the body to the car or the van.'

'You're right. And the bigger boat could have come from further along the coast. It would take a good sailor to moor at the quay in last night's gale, though.'

'I've checked that out.' Ross was ridiculously proud of himself. 'The wind dropped in the early hours as a depression moved through. It was pretty calm between three and six.'

'Really? That makes a difference then, though I imagine the sea would still be pretty wild. Good work then, Ross.' Venn saw Carter emerge from the kitchen, steaming pasties in hand, and gestured for them to be quiet until the landlord had disappeared again. 'So, explain all that to the lifeboat operations manager, Sammy Barton, and definitely explore possibilities with the coastguard.'

Ross seemed to glow in response to the praise. Jen rolled her eyes. That, Venn thought, summed up the relationship between the two. Everything was a competition.

Venn wanted to phone Jonathan, but as he got to his feet to go to his room, all the lights went out. The snug grew even gloomier. There was a mutter of disapproval from the public bar. A little while later, Carter stuck his head through the hatch.

'I've just been on to the power grid. The whole village is off. Line's down at Sandyfoot Farm at the top of the bank. They don't know when it'll be fixed. The gale's caused damage all along the coast.'

'Perhaps we should go back to Barnstaple then.' Venn thought the investigation would be impossible without power to run laptops and phones.

'No chance of getting out now.' Harry grinned. He seemed to be enjoying the thought of their discomfort. Or he was someone else who liked a drama. 'The lines were brought down by an oak, which is blocking the road. Huge beast it is. No way out unless you want to walk most of the way to Morrisham. You'd get as far as Ravenscroft in the car, but the road's blocked again beyond that.' He looked across at Jen. 'I'd best make a bedroom up for the young lady too.'

Venn went to his room to check the situation for himself. He couldn't imagine that they were really trapped here. Not in this day and age. He had reasonable signal on his mobile and dialled the police station. It took a long time to get through and Vicki Robb sounded harassed, overwhelmed. 'There are power cuts all over the county. And roads blocked so the engineers can't get through. Most places will be off at least until tomorrow. It's already getting dark.'

Matthew had never been good in enclosed spaces and sensed the steep sides of the valley closing in. He dialled Jonathan's number. His husband ran a community arts centre in Barnstaple, which was his passion and his joy, and when he answered, Venn heard conversation in the background, and preschool children singing a nursery rhyme. Normal life, it seemed, was continuing in the town.

Jonathan must have moved somewhere quieter, because when he spoke his voice was clear and full of affection. He had a lovely voice.

'Hello, you.'

'I'm not going to make it home. I'm sorry.'

'But I was going to cook for you. Don't you remember? A night in. Neither of us working. And both with a day off tomorrow.'

'Of course, I was looking forward to it.'

'So, you *are* working?' The tone was teasing, not resentful. Matthew loved that about Jonathan. His inability to be hurt when Matthew had to put work first. At the beginning, he'd taken it as a sign that Jonathan didn't care. Now, he valued it as a gesture of support, an understanding that Matthew was as passionate about his work as he was.

'A murder. Miles from anywhere in Greystone.' A pause. 'I've got to stay over. The storm's blocked the road and the power lines are down.'

'In Greystone? I don't envy you that. I took a kids' theatre group there once to the community hall. I've never been any-where quite so bleak.'

The community hall was where the Brethren had met. Perhaps where they still did. 'Did you get much of an audience?'

'Nah, it was the worst gig of the tour.' There was a brief pause. 'Look, I've got to go. We're closing the Woodyard early too because of the weather.' Another pause. 'Stay safe.'

Venn had expected the doctor's surgery to be closed, but the door was unlocked, and there was even a light inside. He'd been blown along the only shopping street in the village, and found the doctor's surgery easily enough. It stood between the post office and a general store. The greengrocer's shop window had been replaced by frosted glass, and there was a sign above the door. *Greystone Health Centre*. When he pushed open the door, he saw a small waiting room and a desk with a woman sitting behind it. Health centre seemed rather a grand term for the premises. Two doors led off the waiting room. Nobody was waiting.

One wall was covered with shelves, but instead of books they contained hand-knitted toys; they seemed to be staring down at him from googly plastic eyes. There were teddy bears and animals: cats, dogs, penguins and an enormous giraffe. All brightly coloured and a little grotesque. On the lower shelves, there were hats and mittens and children's jerseys, and jackets hung from clothes hangers. One little mannequin with a blank white face was modelling a child's stripy dress. A printed, laminated sign said: *Knitting for Artie. All for Sale. All proceeds to the fund.* There was a photograph of a little boy with curly hair and big eyes.

The receptionist was knitting too, something complex with different coloured yarn. She set down the needles and looked up. 'Can I help you?' Then before he could reply, 'Oh, sorry. You must be the detective. The doctor's expecting you.'

'You still have power?'

The place seemed ridiculously normal after the chaos outside.

'Oh yeah. The last couple of years the lines have been going down quite regularly. Peter invested in a little generator.' She looked up. 'The whole village will be in soon to charge their phones and boil a kettle.'

She moved round from the desk and Venn saw that she must be in the last stages of pregnancy. Her body was enormous, but her legs, in thick black tights, were so skinny that it seemed they must buckle under the weight. She knocked at one of the internal doors and stuck her head in. 'Pete. The inspector's here.' She left the door open for Venn and walked back to her desk.

The office was more comfortable and professional than Venn had been expecting. No strange woollen creations in sight. Besides the desk, with a computer, and the examination couch, there was a coffee table with a couple of easy chairs. Smale moved away from the desk and the men stood for a moment, looking at each other, before taking the seats.

'I recognized you,' Smale said, 'from the meetings. You came with your parents.' A pause. 'You were Dennis's golden boy.'

'Until I lost my faith and got cast away.' Venn kept his voice light. He thought this was an odd way to start an interview about a murder. 'Are you still a member?' Venn thought it unlikely. How could a doctor, a scientist, believe in the Rapture and the end of days? When the chosen few would be saved and the rest would be cast out.

'I still go to meetings,' Smale said, and then, almost to explain the statement, 'I married into the Brethren. We moved away for me to train, but my wife missed the place, the sense of community, and we have children now. We want them to have the same supported childhood that we enjoyed.' He smiled. 'We did have *such* good times, and there are Barum Brethren nowhere else in the country, after all. It's a unique experience for our kids.'

So, nothing to do with faith? Everything to do with feeling special, entitled.

'They see us caring for their grandparents,' Smale went on, 'for all our elderly. The girls might make their own choices later, but they've grown up with the right values.'

Venn nodded. He too had enjoyed good times in Greystone and he wasn't here to discuss matters of theology. But he was curious. 'You live in the village?'

'Just outside. We've got the old rectory at Willington on

the way to Morrisham. The girls come to school here and Ruth can see her parents every day.'

'Greystone is still a stronghold then?' Venn tried to keep any trace of judgement out of his voice, but he wasn't sure that he'd succeeded. 'There are fewer and fewer young people where my mother worships in Barnstaple.'

'The group is flourishing, actually,' Smale said. 'Perhaps there are fewer distractions here than in town. We're a very close community, very supportive.'

'It must be hard for outsiders to fit in.'

'Oh, I don't think so.'

But Venn thought he heard some doubt in the man's voice. Perhaps it wasn't just the village's isolation that prevented strangers from choosing to live here, but the locals' hostility.

There was a moment of silence within the room, which made the noise outside seem even more threatening.

A thought occurred to Venn. 'Jeremy Rosco, was he a brother?' It might be one explanation for the man's choice of Greystone as a place to wait for his visitor.

Smale shook his head. 'I don't think so. He never attended meetings while he was here.'

'Any other connection to the place?'

'I never had a conversation with him. I'm not a regular in the pub and that was the place where most people got to speak to him.'

'But you might hear the gossip going around. A doctor's waiting room, people chat.'

Smale smiled. 'Not to me, Inspector. When they get in here, they're only interested in their ailments and what I can do to make them better. You'd be better talking to Rebecca. She's the person on the front line.'

'Rebecca's your receptionist?'

He nodded. 'That's right.'

'And a knitter . . .'

He smiled. 'There's a child in the village with a serious illness. Some of the community believe he has a better chance of a cure if they can get him to the States. The village is fundraising.'

'You're not convinced?'

He shrugged. 'The boy has a rare genetic condition. Jasper Lineham's Disease. His mother understands that her son is most likely to die in his teens, but the family is still hoping for a miracle. I suppose we believe what we have to believe to survive.' A pause. Venn wondered if the last statement was as much about the man's own faith as the boy's family. 'There's a doctor in Illinois who's researching a form of gene therapy, and claims he might have a cure. There's been no peer review, and he's charging a fortune for the treatment. I think the mother knows in her heart that it's probably a con, but she's clinging to that glimmer of hope. The grandfather certainly is. He's the leading force behind the fundraising.' He looked at Venn. 'I don't feel I can disillusion them.'

Venn wanted to suggest that honesty might be more helpful, but he remained silent. He got to his feet. He'd expected more from the interview, perhaps because of their previous connection, and he was disappointed. 'I'll have a quick word with Rebecca then?'

'Sure,' Smale said. 'Then I'm going to shut up shop while I can still get home.'

There was an awkward moment before they parted, as if some gesture might be required, a brief hug perhaps, because they *had* been friends, but there was a divide between them.

They'd made different choices. Matthew straightened, and moved to the door. He didn't regret his choice at all.

In the empty waiting room, Rebecca was sitting back in her chair and stretching her legs out in front of her. She was still knitting.

'Shouldn't you be on maternity leave?'

'Nah,' she said. 'Not for another three weeks. I'm just enormous. I see pregnancy as a licence to eat cake.'

'I'm here about Jeremy Rosco.'

'Of course,' she said. 'It's all that anybody's talking about.'

'And what are they saying?'

'That his mysterious visitor finally turned up and killed him.' She had brown eyes and a smattering of freckles over her nose and cheeks. Straight brown hair cut in a long fringe.

'I don't suppose anyone *saw* the mysterious stranger?'

She gave a little giggle. 'Not that I've heard.'

'And surely you *would* have heard?'

'Probably. I hear all sorts in here. People don't really notice me. I'm a part of the place, like the public health posters and the no smoking signs.'

'What were they saying about Rosco before he died?'

She sat up and leaned forward across the desk, as far forward as the belly allowed. 'That he was a lovely chap. Friendly. He stood his round in the Maiden's and that went down well with the old boys. Lots of speculation about what he was doing here.'

'What conclusion did people come to?'

She giggled again. There was something of the schoolgirl about her. 'Everything from the possibility that he was planning to set up a business here – a hotel or a fish restaurant or a sailing school – to the fact that he was tracing long-lost family in the area. I don't think there was anything concrete behind any of the theories.'

'And the mysterious stranger?'

'Oh, even more ideas about that. Some said it would be a wealthy business partner, others a childhood sweetheart, previously lost to him. Dead romantic, that one.'

'And you?' Venn asked. 'What did you think was more likely?'

She shrugged. 'I didn't believe any of them. They were just stories. And the wind makes people a bit crazy this time of the year. You've only got to look in the school playground, the kids tearing around like mad things. They were just wild imaginings.'

Chapter Seven

JEN RAFFERTY WAS PANICKING. SHE'D HATED this place from the moment they'd driven down the steep road into the village and now she was stuck here. There was a sense of helplessness, a lack of control that pressed too many buttons and reminded her of her old life. And then there were the kids, on their own at home. She went to the tiny room at the back of the pub that Harry Carter had prepared for her. She could lie in the single bed and touch both walls. It felt like a coffin. Outside, the battered fence banged relentlessly. She'd have to pull it down completely and stack it before bedtime, or there'd be no sleep at all.

She phoned Ella but there was no response. The girl might still be on her way back from school. No point trying Ben. He never answered, so the next call was to Cynthia, her best friend and drinking companion.

'Hiya!' They'd had their bad times, but these days Cynth was always pleased to hear from her.

Jen explained where she was and what was happening.

'No worries. I'll pop in this evening and take in some food.

I promise they won't starve. And I'll make sure they're off to school in the morning. There was talk about the schools closing, but apparently the worst of the storm is supposed to pass through tonight.'

'I have no idea how long I'll be stranded here.'

'I'll keep an eye. Promise.'

So now, Jen Rafferty was out in the storm, knocking on doors. Usually, these interviews would be brief and conducted on the pavement, the questions routine, the canvassing a chore to finish as soon as was possible. Today, she accepted all the invitations to come inside, even those from people who had no specific information to share, but were curious, excited, anxious. She understood Venn's priorities. He wouldn't reject the gossip, the snippets of history. He'd embrace them. He always said that the police needed to know the community to understand individual offenders and victims. Besides, the freezing showers came suddenly, soaking her without warning, and the gale rattled around her head, making sensible thought impossible. There were no cups of tea because of the power cut, but the conversations in the warm tiny living rooms provided a welcome respite.

She started with Gwen Gregory's immediate neighbour, a young mother named Katie Brennon who was at home with her toddler. The guard around the fire took up much of the room, and a wooden clothes horse with steaming baby clothes most of the rest. The child seemed happy to sit on the floor and play with coloured blocks. Neither of Jen's kids had been that compliant. The woman seemed to appreciate the company.

'Usually, I'd be out with the mums' and babies' group, but I couldn't face it in this weather.'

'Is it only mums? No dads?' Jen couldn't help herself.

The woman looked up sharply, suddenly defensive. 'Oh yes, only mums. Fathers would be welcome, of course, but our men are all out working.'

And the women don't work? But Jen let that go. Maybe she should have spent more time with the children when they were younger. Maybe she should give them more of her time now.

'We're just asking everyone if they noticed anything odd happening in the village last night. You'll have heard about Jem Rosco's murder.' It wasn't a question. Brian Branscombe's team had already sealed off the top of the alley, and white-suited CSIs had made their way past the woman's house, carrying their kit.

'I didn't see anything. The baby sleeps like a dream. She's very content.'

Of course she is. Jen felt a moment of envy that was close to hatred. Her children hadn't slept through the night until they'd started school.

'And your husband?'

The woman stared into the fire and Jen had to wait for a response. Perhaps this wasn't such a happy family after all.

'He works from Bideford. But he does weird shifts, and he's often late getting back. I was asleep when he got in.'

'So, he might have been around in the early hours of today?' Jen marked the man down for a follow-up.

'I suppose.'

'What work does he do?'

'He's an HGV driver.' Katie looked up. 'It's important, keeps the country moving.'

'Bit tough on families, though.'

'Yeah,' Katie said. 'Sometimes it's tough. But I've got family in the village. Loads of support. And Billy loves it.'

'He's back at work today? Even after finishing late last night?'

'No, he's still asleep. He had a nightmare drive back to the village.' Katie looked up. 'I'm not going to wake him. Not for a couple of hours at least.'

'But you have no idea exactly what time he got in?'

She shook her head. 'He's very quiet. He doesn't want to disturb us.' A pause. 'Nights when he's that late, he sleeps in the spare room. I have Milly in with me.'

'Very thoughtful.'

'It's a hard job. He needs his rest.' Defensive again. Too defensive? Or was Jen being ultra-sensitive because her own husband had been a controlling bastard, too quick with his fists?

'We'll need to speak to him. When would be a good time to call round?'

'I'm not sure.' Now Katie looked directly at Jen. 'He's on a rest day tomorrow, even if the road's open again, and he might want a couple of pints this evening. He's had a heavy shift. He might not be at home.'

'That's okay then.' Jen kept her voice easy. After all, another couple's marriage was hardly her business unless it had a bearing on the investigation. Just because this woman had been on her own with the child and might fancy a bit of adult company, it wasn't her place to comment. 'We might catch up with him in the Maiden's?'

'Yeah. He'll probably be there.' Katie picked up her still silent daughter and stood up. An indication that it was time for Jen to leave.

Until she reached the bottom of the hill, where the terrace joined the main road into the village, Jen had no more useful information. Most of the residents were elderly, cheery couples who were happy to talk and would have liked to help, but who had gone to bed early and drawn their curtains and bolted their doors against the wild weather.

'This time of year, us don't get out much.' An old man with a walking frame seemed to speak for them all. 'And us don't see much either.'

The last house, the end terrace with a strip of grass to one side and a dormer showing a roof conversion, looked more promising. There was a child's swing in the garden; concreted into the ground, the rope connected to the wooden seat, which was wrapped around one of the supports to stop it banging in the wind. Jen knocked on the door and a woman answered almost immediately. She looked to be in her early thirties and was wearing jeans and a sweater. Jen recognized her immediately as Mary Ford, the helm of the lifeboat.

The interior of the house was as different from those belonging to the other terrace residents as it was possible to be. The ground floor had been knocked through to provide one space, the floorboards had been stripped and stained, and one wall had been covered with a flamboyant wallpaper depicting giant flamingos. The others were hung with paintings and prints.

'Wow,' Jen said.

'Do you like it? I'm rather proud, myself.' She nodded to the walls. 'The prints are mine. The paintings have been done by friends.'

'This is an arty community?'

The woman laughed so much that she almost choked. 'You must be joking! No! But there are civilized hubs not very far away.' She nodded for Jen to take a seat on a low grey sofa resting against the pink flamingo wall. 'And honestly, that's what I love about Greystone. The fact that it's a working community. No pretension or bullshit. And, of course, the houses are very cheap. I wouldn't have been able to afford *anything* anywhere else on the coast.'

It seemed that she had two kids in primary school – Isla and Arthur – and there was no partner on the scene. She earned a living from her woodcuts – she'd converted the loft into a studio – and from teaching a few hours a week in the high school in Morrisham.

'You must be investigating Jem Rosco's murder,' Mary said then.

'Did you know him? You said you recognized him when you pulled his body into the lifeboat.'

'I met him once in the Maiden's. Until recently, Lily, the old lady next door, has come in to babysit on Fridays to give me a night out. My dad stays over quite often now he's on his own. I've been allowed into the ladies' darts team.'

'Allowed?'

Mary laughed again. 'I'm not local, not born and bred here. Only inland from Morrisham, though to them it's the end of the known universe. They're not entirely sure I should be playing for Greystone. Or working in the lifeboat. But they know they wouldn't win without me.' She paused for a moment. 'I had a real fan girl crush on Jem Rosco when I was a kid.' Jen fancied that the woman was blushing. 'I had posters of him on my bedroom walls, sent him endless letters asking for signed photos, or a chance to crew for him.'

'Did he ever answer?' Jen's posters had been of boy bands and footie players. She couldn't remember ever sending fan mail.

'Nah. I guess every teenager who loved sailing sent him something similar, but he'd been to the same school as my dad, and he had a place in Morrisham, so I hoped for special treatment. I doubt any of them were read.'

'You didn't talk to him when you saw him in the pub?'

There was a moment's hesitation, then Mary shook her head. 'God, no! The embarrassment.'

'We think Mr Rosco was killed in his own house late last night, or in the early hours of this morning. Did you see anything? A strange car or a person you didn't recognize?'

'I didn't, but my father might have done. He's staying for a few days. My son's ill and Dad came across to give me support. It gives me some kind of life. To play the occasional game of darts.' She paused and Jen waited for some explanation of the child's illness, but the woman's face only clouded for a moment, and when she spoke her voice was as cheery as before. 'Dad's upstairs having a rest; he doesn't sleep too well at night and sometimes naps in the afternoon.'

'Maybe I shouldn't disturb him then.'

'Oh, I'm sure he won't mind. Since Mum died, he's been bored. They used to travel a lot together, and he's been at a loose end. He retired to lead wildlife trips around the world, but then Arthur got ill and he feels he should stick around to lend support.'

She left the room and returned almost immediately with a man in late middle age. He was tall, fit and wearing a sweater with a Devon Wildlife logo and jeans. Only his bare feet suggested that he'd been resting.

'You'd heard that Jeremy Rosco was found dead this morning?'

'Of course,' he said. 'Mary told me as soon as she got in. We had a late breakfast together once I took the kids to school.'

'We think he might have been killed in the early hours of

this morning. I don't suppose you saw or heard anything unusual.'

Alan Ford sat in a small armchair, which had been upholstered in deep green velvet. 'There was a car,' he said. 'It stopped at the bottom of the terrace and a woman got out, then the car drove off. I assumed it was a taxi, though I don't think there was any sign on it.'

'What time was that?' Jen asked.

'Late. The early hours of the morning. Past one o'clock because Radio 4 had finished and the World Service had started.'

Jen nodded, though she wasn't entirely sure what that meant. Ella was a geek and listened to Radio 4. Jen liked her music, streamed it, danced around the kitchen to it.

'Can you tell me anything about the woman?'

The man paused for a moment. 'I didn't see her face. There's a street light at the end of the terrace, but I was looking down on the top of her head. She wasn't dressed for the weather. Not for the rain at least. She was wearing a coat, very long – it almost reached the floor – and boots. Her hair was pale, nearly white in that light, and long enough to tuck into the collar of the coat. No hat.'

'Wow!' Jen was impressed by the detail.

'Dad's a naturalist.' Mary sounded proud. 'His specialism is damselflies and dragonflies. He's used to recording detail.'

Alan Ford smiled. 'I worked for the Devon Wildlife Trust for thirty years. I suppose noticing things has become a habit.'

'Any colour on the coat?'

'It's hard to judge colour with street lighting, but I think dark green.' He paused. 'She was wearing a scarf, loose around her shoulders, wide, more like a shawl. I'm pretty sure that was green too, but it had flecks of gold thread in it. I could see it shining in the light.'

'Did you see where she went?'

'Of course! She'd caught my interest. She seemed an exotic creature to turn up in Greystone in the middle of the night. I was fascinated. She walked up the hill, up towards the top of the terrace, but from here I couldn't tell how far she actually got, which house she went into.'

Jen thought she knew where the woman was headed, though. None of the other residents she'd spoken to had mentioned a visitor in the early hours. Most of them had been asleep for hours when this person climbed the hill. This must be Jem Rosco's mysterious visitor. And if she'd arrived in a taxi, perhaps Gwen Gregory's brother, Davy, might have more information about who she was, and where she'd come from. She felt the thrill of new information. This was why she loved this work; why she'd never have been able to give it up to spend more time with the kids.

'The car,' she said. 'Any idea of the make? A colour?'

Alan shook his head. 'I'm much better at identifying living creatures than machines. A lack of interest, I suppose, and my attention was drawn to the woman. It was a dark saloon. Grey or black. I can't tell you any more than that.'

'Which direction did it go when it drove off?'

He thought for a moment.

'Towards the village. But then that was the way it was facing. Even if it was heading back inland and up the main road out, it would be easier to drive down to the quay to turn round than do that here where the terrace is so narrow.'

'If it had done that, it would have driven past your window. Did you see it? Hear it?'

Alan shook his head. 'But then, I might not have done. Once the woman was out of view, I went back to bed, and I drifted very quickly off to sleep. A good night for me. I didn't wake again until just before Mary came in to tell me that she was going out on the boat.'

Jen thought it would be pleasant to sit here, in this glorious space, and talk to the father and daughter, but she had to speak to Venn. In this house, she might have found their first positive lead.

Chapter Eight

Ross May found Sammy Barton at home. He lived in a whitewashed cottage close to the quay, so near to the water that the spray must hit the windows at high tide. It wasn't Ross's idea of a perfect home; it was too wild, too insecure. *Too* close to nature. In summer, that smell of rotting seaweed must find its way in, and in this gale, it felt as if the whole building could be swept away at any time.

Inside, though, the place was tidy, civilized in contrast to the wildness outside. The man was sitting at a dining table at the front of the house, with a view of the sea, a laptop in front of him. His wife had opened the door to Ross, introduced herself as Jane, and had returned to a more comfortable chair by the fire. She'd picked up the knitting she must have been working on when he'd knocked. A paraffin lamp gave enough light for her to see what she was doing.

'I'm just writing up this morning's call-out,' Barton said. 'Though I'm not sure they'll believe it in Poole.' He looked up. 'That's where our HQ is based.'

'Is it a full-time job? Working for the RNLI?' Ross took a chair at the table opposite to Barton.

'No! We're all volunteers here. They have a couple of paid staff at HQ, but the rest of us do it for love. Because it could be one of our boys needing to be rescued.'

'Sammy was helm for thirty years.' The woman set down her knitting again and looked up, proud of her man. 'He only stopped after the heart attack and that wasn't his choice.' She got to her feet. 'Now I've finished this line, I'll make some tea, shall I? We're lucky we have a Raeburn in the kitchen and a load of logs that Sammy chopped from some pitch pine that washed up in the summer. Luckier than some in the village. I'll make a pan of soup in a while and get it out to some of the older folk who have no power. You've got time for a cup of tea, Constable?'

'I'd love one.' The woman reminded Ross of his grandmother. As a small kid, he'd always been happier in his grandparents' house than his own. His father had suffered from bouts of gloom, and had been a prickly bastard when the darkness hit. Depression, they might call it now. They'd probably have called it that then, if his dad had found the sense to ask anyone for help, or if Ross's mother had shown any sympathy.

The woman went out and Barton switched off the laptop. 'Best to save power though they seem to think we'll be back tomorrow.'

'What's your regular job then?' Ross suspected that Barton was retired. He'd hardly be sitting here in the middle of the afternoon if he was in full-time employment. But he knew too that people could be sensitive about stuff like that, and the

67

man certainly didn't quite look old enough to be getting a pension.

'I do a bit of fishing in the summer. Lobster. Crab. The fancy restaurants round the coast will pay a good price. Tourists like the fact that they're locally caught. The boat's pulled up in the yard behind the house for the winter.' He paused. 'When I was still working full-time, it was more of a hobby, like. Now, it's turned into a little business.'

'What were you doing before?'

'I was up at the quarry. Foreman. The last man standing when they decided to close it.'

'That must have been a blow for the village. All those proper jobs lost.' Ross's dad had been in a proper job once. He'd been a serving policeman. Then he'd lost his nerve and ended up selling menswear in the only department store in Barnstaple. *That* had never seemed much of a real job for a man to Ross.

'Ah,' Barton said. 'We could all see it was coming. The site nearly worked out and the transport costs so high. There was a bit of hope when they bought up Colin Gregory's land, but it never came to anything.'

'Did you know Jeremy Rosco?' Ross thought it was time to get to the point. 'Before he turned up in the pub a couple of weeks ago, I mean.'

Barton shook his head. 'Only by reputation.'

'You'll have gone to the same school, though, if you grew up here.'

'Only for a couple of years,' Barton said. 'Rosco was a bit younger than me, and you don't mix much with the young kids, do you?'

'I guess not.' Ross paused for a moment. 'What was he like

at school? Did everyone think he'd end up being special? Famous, like?' Oldham, the superintendent, would have thought a question like that was irrelevant, would even have mocked it, but Venn liked background, and Ross was starting to understand his way of working, and to appreciate it.

Barton took a while to answer. 'Jem Rosco was always a good sailor. There was talk of him being in the Olympic team while he was still at school, but he never quite made it.' There was another moment of silence. 'He had a bit of a reputation as a cocky bastard. The staff would have loved it if he'd made the squad for the kudos of the school, but, secretly, I think the other kids were pleased when he missed out. They didn't mind seeing him taken down a peg or two.'

'Maybe they were just jealous that he was getting all the attention.' Ross knew that *he'd* be jealous.

'Perhaps you're right. It's a terrible thing, envy. It can eat away at you.'

Barton's wife came in then with a tray. Tea in a pot. Chocolate biscuits on a plate printed with flowers, cups and saucers. Again, Ross was reminded of his gran.

'Were you there when he turned up suddenly in the Maiden's Prayer that first night?'

Silence.

'We're not really drinkers.'

Ross thought that wasn't any kind of answer.

'We go to the Maiden's, though,' Jane said. 'Just for the company. It's where the community gets together these days. It's like a second home for the lifeboat crew. Nothing wrong with that.'

It seemed an odd response. A bit defensive. It reminded Ross of Matthew Venn when occasionally he came to the pub with the team after work. He always seemed a bit awkward there, never quite relaxed.

'So, you were there that first night when Rosco came in?'

'We were just on our way out, weren't we, Sam?' It was Jane again.

'Yeah, we just crossed in the doorway,' the man said.

'Did you recognize him?'

'I did,' Jane said. 'Not at first, but when he went inside and the light caught his face. I like those natural history programmes on the TV. But I didn't say anything. Famous people must want to be private sometimes, don't you think? They wouldn't want to be bothered all the time by strangers.'

'Did you see how he arrived? We can't find a car.'

'He was in Davy Gregory's taxi.' Still, Jane was the person to answer. Sammy Barton remained silent. 'He'd already climbed out when we opened the pub door, but I saw it drive away.'

Ross thought this was a new piece of information, and his heart sang. He'd only just arrived on the scene and already he was making a difference. Ross saw this case as his opportunity to shine. His phone rang. He apologized and went outside to take the call. The wind blew his words away and he struggled to hear what was being said. He had to ask Venn to repeat his instructions.

'One of Brian's team is in Appledore to check out the dinghy where Rosco was found. It has a name on the side. *Moon Crest*. If you're still with Barton, can you ask if he recognizes it? It might belong to one of the fishing boats based in Greystone.'

'Sure.'

Ross opened the door to Barton's cottage without knocking,

and caught the couple in the middle of a conversation. They stopped talking immediately, as soon as he entered. He hadn't made out any of the words, but sensed there'd been some disagreement. They stared at him awkwardly.

'Is there anything else?' Barton was gruff, almost to the point of rudeness. 'I've spent all day on this.'

'Just one more question.' Ross kept his voice pleasant. 'We've been looking at the dinghy where your crew found Rosco's body. It's called *Moon Crest*. The boss thinks it was the tender for a bigger boat. Does that mean anything to you?'

There was another moment of awkward silence. Jane looked at her husband.

'That's the name of my boat,' Barton said at last. 'She's *Moon Crest*. But she's been in the yard at the back of the house since I brought her in at the end of the summer.'

'You have a tender?' Ross asked.

Barton nodded. 'In summer, I anchor *Moon Crest* out in the bay. Saves having to bring her ashore every time I go out. I use the tender to get to her.'

'You haven't missed it?'

Barton shook his head. 'But then I haven't looked. It's under tarpaulin.'

'We'd better go and look now then, hadn't we?'

Barton didn't speak. He pulled on the pair of wellingtons which were standing by the door and a yellow oilskin hung on a hook above them. He led Ross outside. The woman stayed where she was. There was an alley at the side of the house, wide enough for a car and trailer. Behind the house it widened into a yard, surrounded by a high wall. Ross could see the trailer out there, covered by flapping tarpaulin. Barton lifted a corner and Ross saw a white hull, a narrow deck leading down to a small cabin.

'The tender would usually be tucked under there too.' Barton's voice was loud and bleak. 'You can't think I had anything to do with Rosco's death? I wouldn't be daft enough to use something that could be traced back to me.'

May didn't answer that. 'When was the last time you saw the tender?'

'When I brought *Moon Crest* in at the beginning of September.'

Suddenly, the cloud thinned. The storm still raged but the scene was lit by an odd milky light. It caught Barton's face as he tilted his head towards Ross. The man wasn't playing the hard man any more. He was almost pleading.

'Look, man, you can see that anyone could have come in and stolen the thing. The yard isn't locked. You need to get this sorted. Not for me. But for our Jane. Word gets out, people start talking. You know how it is in a place like this.'

Ross nodded, but really, he had no idea what it must be like. He had friends on the shiny new estate where he lived with his wife Mel. But there was no real intimacy. He hadn't grown up with them, been to school with them. Most of them were incomers, looking for the good life in the West Country.

They walked back to the front of the house and paused on the pavement. The strange light had cast a sheen of copper on the boiling water.

'It couldn't have been done by one person,' Barton said suddenly. 'Think about it. You'd row the tender out to the point and drop the anchor. How would you get back ashore? Someone else would have to come and get you. Unless it was towed out by a bigger vessel. You saw my *Moon Crest*. It's bone dry, not been anywhere for weeks. Besides, it'd be hard to get a boat that size into the water quietly. Someone would have noticed.'

'Even at that time of the morning? We know the wind had dropped in the early hours. It would have been possible to get out then.'

'I don't reckon you'd want to take the risk. And the wind might have dropped but the sea was crazy.'

'What are you suggesting?'

'I don't know,' Barton said. 'I just know it had nothing to do with me.'

They stood for a moment on the pavement at the front of the house.

'Thank Mrs Barton for the tea.'

The man nodded and went inside. All the way back to the pub, Ross was wondering why Barton's tender had been chosen as a last resting place for Jem Rosco's body. If the man wasn't the killer, who had disliked him enough to implicate him?

Chapter Nine

IT SEEMED THAT MUCH OF THE village had gathered in the Maiden's Prayer that night. They'd fought their way through the gale to get there and weren't going to leave until they were thrown out. The fire roared as the wind blew down the chimney, and Carter had lit paraffin lamps and candles that flickered in the draught. Gwen Gregory provided food for the detectives in the snug, a feast of local produce.

'We use propane gas for cooking here, my dears. We don't depend on the electricity.' She cleared their plates and returned with blackberry and apple pie. 'The brambles were early this year. And I was out and up the cliff path before the others. Bags of them in the freezer, so let's hope the power's back on before they're all ruined. And the apples came from Davy's orchard.'

Davy the taxi driver who, according to Ross, drove Jem Rosco here in the first place and who, according to Mary Ford's father, could also have brought in the mysterious woman who walked up the hill towards Rosco's cottage and then disappeared.

'I'll go to see Gregory in the morning,' Matthew said, once

they were alone again. 'According to Carter, the road's clear that far.' He listened as his colleagues continued to sum up the case. He was trying to make sense of the complicated, twisted threads and tangled relationships. It was always like this at the beginning of a case. There was too much information, and it was impossible to tell what was important. He wondered if Peter Smale might make a good ally. He was part of the community, but he'd lived away for a while during his medical training, so could have a clearer perspective. Matthew had sensed an ambiguity in his relationship with the Brethren. He might give an honest opinion.

'And we need more information on the woman who was seen late last night. Ross, go and talk to the witness tomorrow. Alan Ford, the helm's dad. Take a statement. Let's pin him down.'

'There's one other potential witness,' Jen said. 'A truck driver. A guy called Billy Brennan. His wife said he might be in the pub tonight.'

Venn thought *everyone* was in the pub tonight. They'd gathered not just for warmth and food, but as a kind of wake for the dead man who'd livened life up in the weeks before his death, and who still provided excitement; an object for gossip and speculation. No one *really* knew him after all.

In the end, they moved into the public bar too. Harry said they were serving coffee in there, and Venn took the hint: his detectives couldn't justify a light and a fire all to themselves. As they moved to join the others, the details of the case were still swimming around his brain. He thought the whole murder was meticulously planned. A show. Almost a performance. And the people from the village, laughing and joking now in the bar, were the audience. Perhaps by listening in on their conversations, the team would learn more than they would here, in lonely isolation, poring over the details.

The room was hot and packed. The noise of voices almost drowned out the sound of the weather. Venn found himself sitting next to a frail old man with a wispy grey beard, squashed into a corner, in shadow. Harry brought Matthew a mug of tepid coffee, in thanks perhaps for their abandoning the snug. Jen and Ross were at a table close to the bar, and they already had pints in front of them.

The old man gripped Harry's arm. 'What's all this about? The village gone dark.'

'It's the weather, Norm. It's brought down the lines and blocked the roads.' The landlord's voice was kind.

'Nothing to do with the body they found at Scully, then?'

'Nah, nothing to do with that.' He turned to Venn. 'Take no notice of Norman here. He gets a bit confused and superstitious at times. Lives in a world of his own.'

The pub door flew open, banging violently. The lantern hanging on a beam in the middle of the room swung and the candles blew out. A big man walked in and shut the door behind him, pulling it against the force of the wind. The room had been shocked by the noise, and stared towards the newcomer. Even when the conversation started up again, Venn sensed a wariness. The man took off his Barbour jacket and hung it up before making his way to the bar. He was wearing pressed jeans and a shirt and looked too smart for an evening like this.

Venn turned to Norman. 'Who's that?'

'Billy Brennan.' The mouth clamped shut. No further information was forthcoming.

Brennan bought a pint and stood at the bar. Venn

approached him. This wasn't the best place for an interview but he needed to speak to the man.

'Mr Brennan?'

'Who wants to know?'

Venn introduced himself. 'We're investigating the death of Jeremy Rosco. Your wife said you were late home from work last night. We wondered if you saw anything unusual in your street.'

'I was tired. It's mad busy at the moment at work, and the weather was a nightmare all day. No chance to relax when you're driving a truck through it. Then nobody to help me unload when I got to the end of it. I was dead on my feet.' He seemed not to realize what he'd said.

'You'd have noticed, though, if anyone was about that late? In that weather.'

'Maybe. I don't remember seeing anyone, though.' He looked straight at Venn, challenging him to dispute it.

'What time, exactly, did you get home?'

'Half past midnight. Almost exactly. I was in my own car and had the radio on.'

So perhaps a little too early, Matthew thought, to have seen the woman climbing out of the dark car, and making her way up to the top of Quarry Bank.

'Did you go straight to bed when you got in?'

The man looked at him as if the question was daft. 'I made myself a cup of tea and watched a bit of telly. It takes me a while to wind down after a day like that.'

'It would have been about one in the morning before you went upstairs then?'

'Yeah,' he said, 'something like that.' He paused. 'I went outside for a fag before I went up. Katie doesn't like me smoking in the house. Not since the kiddie was born. Even when the weather's as bad as it was last night.' There was a niggle of resentment.

'You didn't see anyone walking up Quarry Bank while you were there?'

There was a brief moment of hesitation. 'Why? What have people been saying?'

'Nothing.' Venn's voice was bland. 'I'm just asking the question.'

'I didn't see anything. The wind had dropped a bit, but nobody would have been bonkers enough to be wandering around at that time of night.'

'Thanks, Mr Brennan, that's helpful.'

'That's it?' He seemed surprised. What else was he expecting? Venn wondered briefly if the woman in the long coat had been visiting him, not Rosco. But the man surely wouldn't have entertained a woman in the house when his wife and child were asleep upstairs?

'Yes, that's it.' Matthew left a pause. 'For now.'

The man turned away and found a seat as far from Venn as he could. Matthew joined Jen and Ross. They were onto their second pint and were talking to one of the lifeboat crew, laughing at a joke he'd made. They seemed to find it so easy, fitting in. Suddenly, he felt as if he were drowning here in the heat and the noise, that he couldn't breathe.

He nodded across to the truck driver, and bent close to Jen so he wouldn't be overheard. 'That's Brennan. He claimed not to see anything last night. See if you can dig up any info about him from the locals. I'm heading to bed.' Even those words took an effort.

She nodded, and stuck up her thumb to show she'd understood.

*

He used the torch on his phone to find his way upstairs. The room felt damp and cold. He stood at the window. No street lights or light spilling through curtains in neighbouring houses. He thought Greystone would have been just like this a hundred years ago. He considered phoning Jonathan, but at the last minute decided against it. There was no hot water so he threw some cold over his face before climbing into bed. He was still awake when the drinkers spilled out of the pub, laughing and shouting, at midnight. The wind seemed less noisy then. Perhaps the storm was moving through.

Chapter Ten

VENN WOKE EARLY TO STILLNESS AND quiet. It was a very different day. He opened the curtains to a grey and pink dawn. The sea was still ferocious, breaking in huge, relentless waves over the jetty, but there was no wind and no rain. He tried the light switch. No power.

Downstairs, Carter was clearing up the mess of the night before, whistling. Venn supposed takings would have been remarkable and would easily have made up for the cost of free coffee.

'Road should be clear in an hour or so,' Carter said. 'A couple of the boys are heading up now with a chainsaw. They reckon the power should be back in time for the school to open too.' He put a tray on the bar. 'Coffee? Breakfast? Gwen won't be in yet, but I can do some toast on the grill.'

'Perfect.'

He took the coffee and toast to his room and phoned Jonathan. The sense of dread that had overwhelmed him the night before had dissipated altogether.

'You survived the night then?' His husband's voice was cheery. 'It looked pretty horrendous there on the news.'

'I don't suppose you could bring some overnight things for me?' Venn hated asking for favours, but he couldn't see that this investigation would be over quickly. 'The road should be clear later this morning. We could have dinner?'

'Why don't I stay the night? I've got a couple of days owing. There's Wi-Fi. I can get some emails cleared.' There was a pause while he waited for a response from Matthew. 'That *is* okay? I won't be in the way? I promise I won't interfere in your investigation.' Because he knew that had been a problem in the Nigel Yeo case. Work and friendships had tangled, and caused tension between them.

'It's not a very exciting place to be!'

'I don't need exciting. I might walk the coastal path tomorrow and there's a mate in Morrisham I could look up.'

'Sure,' Matthew said. 'Why not?' But although he'd booked the room, thinking that Jonathan might join him, he was thrown by his husband's decision to stay, by the reality of it. He was happier with boundaries. Work and the personal completely separate. Still, Jonathan wanted to spend time with him and nobody else had, once he'd left his parents and gone out into the world. And the thought of the man here, waiting for him at the end of the working day, made him feel lighter. There was something to look forward to.

Matthew had looked at the Ordnance Survey map before setting out for the Gregory farmhouse. He'd never travelled much, but he'd always loved maps. They'd been a vicarious escape when he was growing up. They gave a glimpse of another, more exciting, world.

This was a back lane to Morrisham. Not a shortcut by any means, but a diversion of a road, single-tracked, surely, linking hamlets and settlements, curving round hills, following valley bottoms, approaching the coast in places, then heading back inland. Venn saw that he would pass through Willington, where the doctor, Peter Smale, lived.

He had the map on the passenger seat beside him, but he didn't need to look at it. He had an internal compass, an instinctive sense of the landscape. Besides, a signpost showed the way from the main Morrisham road to 'Willington' and 'Ravenscroft'. The hedges were high and splashed with colour, red like blood spatter: hips and haws. He had occasional views of hills in one direction, and the sea in others, through gaps and five-bar gates. In places there were signs of the previous night's storm: the debris of snapped branches, berries scattered on the road, crushed by traffic, pools of standing water in the fields.

Willington was tiny. No pub, no shop, no post office. A farm right in the middle of the village, with a sign saying there was a field for camping. A lovely squat church, very old, was surrounded by a graveyard, the stones covered in a golden lichen, and next to it the rectory, almost as big as the church itself. Venn slowed as he drove past. A woman, presumably Smale's wife Ruth, was in the garden, pegging washing on a line, fighting with the sheets.

Ravenscroft was an even smaller hamlet. A terrace of three cottages and the farmhouse where Davy Gregory and his wife lived. Venn came to it almost as soon as he left Willington. He wondered if the two families – the Smales and the Gregorys – were friends. There was a difference in their ages, but there were few other neighbours, and out here you'd need to find company where you could.

He wasn't sure what he'd been expecting at the Gregory farm, but it wasn't this. It wasn't this solid house built of mellow stone, nestled in a gentle curve in the hill, and a garden, the grass mowed short and already prepared for autumn. A fuchsia hedge, the blooms a deep red still, leading to the front door. A neat orchard at the back, the trees in rows, loaded with apples. He'd expected someone who had to supplement his income by driving a taxi to live in a place a little less attractive, and possibly in need of some care. The terraced house where Davy's father had lived was modest and spartan. But, Matthew thought, he of all people should know not to make assumptions.

The wind had dropped completely and it was a clear day. Up on Exmoor, there might even be a touch of ground frost. Perhaps it was the sunlight that made the place so appealing, and the view down the valley towards the sea.

Davy Gregory appeared while Matthew was still on the path leading to the house, having stopped to look back down the combe.

'Lovely spot, isn't it?' The man had been walking on the grass and Matthew hadn't heard him approach.

'Glorious.'

He was tall, grey-haired, younger than his sister, or at least better preserved. Good-looking if you went for older men. A bit of extra weight around the stomach, but concealed by the knitted navy sweater. Leather shoes despite the damp grass. 'The house has been in the family for generations. We lost the land, but we kept the view.' His voice was neutral. It was impossible to tell whether the loss of land rankled, or if the view made up for it. 'You're the detective, aren't you? Gwen said you might be stopping by; she pointed you out in the snug at the Maiden's last night.'

'I wondered if I might talk to you.'

'Of course. Come in.'

They walked round the side of the house, past a walled vegetable garden where autumn vegetables – leeks, sprouts, cabbages – grew in neat rows.

'Are you the gardener?' Venn asked.

'Yeah.' The word came out as a deep growl. 'As close to farming as I can get these days.'

So, Matthew thought, the loss of land did still rankle.

'Who owns the land now?' he asked. 'If the quarry decided not to expand, what did they do with it?'

'They hung on to it as an investment. Grazing is rented out to a local chap.'

'You weren't interested?'

Gregory stopped and turned back to face Venn. 'In paying rent for what should have been my inheritance? Where I'd been working ever since I was a boy? No, I couldn't stomach it.' A pause. 'I offered to buy it back, but I couldn't raise what they wanted. I think they're hanging on to it in the hope of development.'

The inside of the house was another revelation. Venn couldn't believe that it had been like this when Colin Gregory lived here. Davy and his wife must have knocked down walls to let in the light. They went into a kitchen the width of the house, with wide glass doors leading into the garden, one wall painted deep red. Jonathan would have loved it.

'Coffee? We've still got power here.'

'Please!'

'I hope you don't mind instant. Tilly, my wife, likes the fancy stuff, but I can never see the point of all the faff.'

'Of course,' Matthew said. 'Instant's fine.' Though he too would have preferred the fancy stuff, given the choice.

He waited until a mug was in front of him, a packet of digestives still in the wrapper on the table.

'You work as a taxi driver?' He tried to keep the surprise from his voice. Again, he thought he was making assumptions. Why shouldn't someone who drove taxis live in this beautiful house?

There was a pause. 'I always thought I'd be a farmer. It was what I wanted, what I grew up believing I'd be.' He gave a wry smile. 'I thought it was my destiny, if that doesn't sound too grand. Then I found I had no choice but to look for something else. I was never much good at anything academic at school, but I like driving. I bought myself a smart car, a Merc, for the business people and the rich tourists who like the idea of something fancy. I dress up for them. Not quite a chauffeur's hat, but a shirt and tie. The Honda is for the locals, and for the short hops to the supermarket or the dentist in town.' Another pause. 'Most of my smart work is contract. Some of the posh hotels up the coast provide station or airport pickups for a price. I quite often go up to Bristol or down to Exeter for the airports.'

'Why did your father sell the land?'

Silence.

'He'd got into debt,' Gregory said at last. He looked sharply at Venn. 'Gwen doesn't know. You mustn't tell her. We fed her a line about poor land and sheep prices, but there's nothing wrong with this land. And I had *such* plans to make a go of it.' Just in that sentence, Venn could hear the dreams, and the disappointment.

'Gwen said that you had ideas for the place,' Matthew agreed. 'How did your father get into debt?'

For the first time during their conversation Gregory seemed

uncomfortable. 'Is all this relevant to poor Jem Rosco's murder?'

Venn smiled. 'Probably not. But I'm curious. About everything. It's what makes me a good detective.'

There was another silence and Venn thought that the man would refuse to answer, but, in the end, he shrugged.

'It was after my mother died. He was conned into making a foolish investment. If he'd asked one of us, we'd have advised against it, but he thought he was being so clever.'

'What was the investment?'

'Someone had the bright idea of opening a restaurant down by the quay. It'd be a destination venue, they said. Tourists would come if the food was good and they served local fish, straight from the harbour.'

'But it didn't work out?'

'It was never going to work out. It was never going to happen at all. It was just a scam to con a load of money from a grieving elderly man.' His voice was hard, bitter.

'Were they ever charged, the fraudsters?'

'Nah, Dad would never even go to the police. It was just a mistake, he said. Just bad luck. He made me promise not to tell anyone. He was scared of looking foolish. Worried what people would say, think. He had a position in the village.'

'Is he a member of the Brethren?'

Gregory was surprised by the question, but he nodded. 'An elder. Until dementia took away his dignity.' He was looking out of the window. 'The sisters still looked after him, though. Someone came in twice a day to keep him company when he was living at home, to do the things that the official carers didn't have time for. And they still visit him in that place in Morrisham, though he won't recognize who they are. They're good people.'

Some of them are.

'And you?' Venn asked. 'Are you a member?'

Gregory shook his head. 'Not in my heart. I still go to meetings for Tilly's sake, but I can't believe it all. The Rapture for us and damnation for the rest. What sort of God is that?'

'Your wife believes?' This was, Venn realized, an odd conversation, but that was why he loved his work. The curiosity satisfied. He could ask the questions that nobody else had the right to ask.

'That was what brought her to Greystone. The fact that there's a thriving community of the Barum Brethren here. She grew up in Bideford, in the community there, and then her folks moved to Barnstaple.' He looked at Venn. 'You a member, then?'

Matthew shook his head and there was another moment of silence.

'Who conned your dad out of the money?' Venn thought if the fraudster were Jem Rosco, they'd have a motive for the killing, and a prime suspect.

'Harry Carter, who owns the pub.' Gregory spat out the words. 'I can't believe Gwen works for him. Cleans for him.' A pause. 'But then I still go there, buy myself a pint and laugh at his jokes. That's Tilly's doing. She says I shouldn't harbour a grudge and that we're luckier than most. I suppose she's right. She usually is.'

Perhaps the windfall from Colin Gregory provided the new en-suite bathrooms and light wood furniture. Perhaps the rest kept the pub ticking over.

'You drove Jeremy Rosco into the village on the night that he arrived?'

'Of course! Only natural that I should get him.'

'You were friends?'

'We were at school together,' Gregory said, which didn't quite answer the question. 'Both into sailing. Both wild boys. He was a year younger, but always part of the gang.'

'Where did you pick him up from?'

'Tiverton Parkway station. He was on the Manchester train. The seven o'clock.'

That made sense, Venn thought. There was no direct train from Liverpool. The man must have changed at Manchester.

'Did he have a suitcase with him?'

'Not a suitcase, but a big canvas duffle bag. Old-fashioned. Like sailors used to have in the old days.'

'How big?'

'Huge! I dunno what he had in it. Most of his worldly goods.'

Venn wondered if it had been big enough to carry a small man, wrapped in a shower curtain. And where was it now? Not in the house where he'd died, and not in the *Moon Crest* tender.

'Gwen thought he'd booked the cottage through an accommodation website, by chance.'

'He did! That was how it started. But I recognized the name and got in touch with him, offered him a lift in. He said I shouldn't tell anyone he was coming. He wanted it to be a surprise.'

'Did he tell you why he'd come? You must have had a conversation in the car. It's a good long way.'

'Nah, I asked, of course, but he wouldn't tell me. He just tapped the side of his nose. "You'll find out soon enough, Davy boy." Mostly we talked about the old days. We had a lot to catch up on.' Gregory paused. 'The last time I saw him, I hadn't even met Tilly. Never even thought I'd marry!' He looked across the table at Venn. 'I sowed my wild oats well into middle age. Then along came Matilda Mead, twenty years younger than me, looking like something out of a fairy story – long golden hair and skin like cream – to be teacher in the primary school here, and she changed my life.'

Just as Jonathan changed mine. Although I wouldn't have used such poetic language.

'Was Mr Rosco married?' He hadn't got as far as being able to find that out the day before, but Davy might have knowledge of a partner. 'Apparently he had an agent, who'll be able to help with that sort of information, but we're still trying to track them down.'

'Yeah, Jem did marry once,' Davy said. 'It didn't last long. He had plenty of women, though. Never short of a beauty on his arm, not even when he was still living round here, and hardly more than a boy.'

'Had you kept in touch with him over the years?'

'On and off.' Gregory's voice was breezy, making Venn think it was more off than on. The man might like to claim intimacy with a famous man, but there seemed to have been no real friendship there.

'Did he mention a partner when you were driving him back?'

Davy thought for a moment. 'No, but like I said, we were mostly talking about the old days. I suppose school was what we really had in common. We were always the boys at the back of the class causing mischief.'

'When was the last time you saw him before he arrived back here?'

'That was a reunion at the school ten years ago. He was guest of honour, but he remembered me and we hung out together all evening. Since then, we've been keeping in touch. Mostly emails, but that's how it is these days, isn't it?' He sounded a little sad.

'You had another fare,' Venn said, 'the night before they found Mr Rosco's body. Or rather in the early hours of the same morning. Yesterday morning. Can you tell me about that?'

Gregory shook his head. 'I didn't have any calls that night. I was here all evening.'

'Are you sure? A car was seen dropping a woman off at the bottom of the terrace where your sister lives, at about one o'clock.'

'I don't get call-outs at that time. Certainly not midweek. Weekends sometimes, some of the lads go into Bideford or Morrisham for a few beers and a meal, and I get a shout to bring them home. Occasionally I'll do an airport run at odd hours, but very rarely for Greystone residents.'

Venn wondered if this explanation was too detailed. Too complicated. He couldn't understand, though, why Gregory would lie about giving a customer a lift.

'Might they have used a different taxi service?'

'Depends where they came from. Not if it was a short distance and local. I'm all there is within five miles of here. Next nearest is based in Morrisham.'

So, how did the mysterious woman seen by Mary Ford's father get to Greystone? If she was implicated in the murder, did her accomplice bring her? Or was Ross right? Had Mary Ford's father imagined the whole thing?

Venn could think of nothing specific to ask Davy Gregory now, but still he sat in the beautiful kitchen. He wanted to know more about the equally beautiful wife, who seemed to have blown in, just like Jem Rosco. In the end, Davy answered the unasked question.

'The inside of the house is all my Tilly's work. She's the one with style.'

'How long have you been married?'

'Eight years. She arrived at the school just before Dad sold off the land. I was a wreck. Bitter, angry, depressed. She brought me back.' He looked up at Venn. 'She saved me.' He got to his feet and brought a framed photograph to the table. Matilda Gregory was indeed beautiful. She looked like a figure in a Pre-Raphaelite painting. Long hair and deep blue eyes. She was sitting in a white wrought-iron chair in the garden, smiling.

'We were never blessed with children,' Gregory said. Another unasked question answered. 'Tilly would have liked them but she accepted it. She says she's got a family of her own at the school.'

Of course! As my mother accepted my father's lingering illness and death as the Lord's work.

'Where was your wife last night?'

'She was at our neighbour's house. She was babysitting for them and then she stayed over. You'd think she'd have enough of kids during the day, but she's kind.'

'Would that be the Smales?'

'That's right. She and Ruth Smale have become good friends.'

Venn nodded. *Of course. Sisters in the Lord together.*

He got to his feet. 'Thanks,' he said. 'You've been very helpful.'

Gregory walked with him out to the car. He was still standing, looking down at the valley, as Matthew drove away.

Chapter Eleven

MARY WAS WOKEN EARLY, BEFORE IT was light, and very suddenly, as if by a noise or flash of light. But the room was quiet, and there was no sound in the street outside. The storm had blown out. Until Arthur's diagnosis, she'd slept deeply and nothing would wake her until the alarm rang very loudly from the small clock on the bedside table. Now, there were these sudden starts of wakefulness, moments of panic as she remembered anew that her son was dying. Occasionally, the boy called out in the night. There was a monitor in his room. Last night in the storm it hadn't been working and because of that, she'd stayed awake, anxiously listening out for him, until the early hours when she'd fallen into a fitful sleep.

Today, she'd escaped from a different sort of nightmare. In her head, she saw the shrivelled man, who'd once been her hero, curled into the small boat, and realized that she'd been dreaming about him, that she'd floated to consciousness to avoid having to take him into her arms again.

She thought perhaps she should get up and work, before the domestic routine of breakfast and walking the kids to school. A couple of hours in the studio in the attic might settle her. But, in the end, she walked downstairs, to the kitchen, and she sat in the cold, still house, thinking about the future, until the power and the heating came on, the children started to stir, and she could put the kettle on for tea.

Her father was still in bed when she took the kids to school. She pushed the boy in his wheelchair, bitter again at the disease that was limiting her son's life, knowing she'd give anything – her own life, of course – to make him well. They sang and joked all the way there – Mary had always been good at putting on a show – with Isla walking beside the chair, chatting to him about the autumn fayre that would be happening in the school later that day. Arthur was already starting to lose his vision. They'd been told that there'd be seizures, a loss of cognitive facility, before he died in his teens. Her father, scouring the internet in the hope of more information, and some hope, had come across the hospital in Illinois where there was a clinical trial into Jasper Lineham's, some form of gene therapy. He'd emailed the doctor and started the fundraising that morning, tears running down his face.

Look, my love! We can get him well again!

She'd wanted that to be true. Of course she had. But in her heart, she'd known it would take a miracle to cure her son and she was too rational to believe in miracles. She couldn't understand how her father, who'd been trained as a scientist and had brought her up to believe in facts, could be taken in by an obvious con. She thought the community fundraising, the knitting, the sponsored walks and cake sales, were about making Greystone feel good about itself, not helping her boy. Greystone kids had been quick enough to mock Artie's clumsiness when he was first ill, before the diagnosis. Perhaps there was some guilt in there too.

Arriving back at the house after the school run, she took her father a mug of tea. Seeing him propped up against the pillows, she thought for the first time how old he was looking. His face seemed to have shrunk a little, so his teeth seemed too big, and his neck was becoming wrinkled and leathery like a tortoise's. She'd always seen him as a strong man. Her rock, when her rat of a husband walked out on her, then caring for her mother through her illness and comforting Mary when the woman had slipped away in a morphine haze. Now, because Mary had been so close to another death the previous day, she saw her father as vulnerable and felt suddenly anxious on his behalf. She couldn't bear it if he disappeared too.

'Why don't you have a bit of a lie-in?' she said.

'Don't be daft! I'll get up when I've had this! I'll get some coffee on the go.'

And there he was fifteen minutes later, in the kitchen, his hair damp from the shower. Fully dressed, he didn't look frail at all, and his smile hadn't changed since she was a toddler.

The chat in the playground had all been about Jeremy Rosco's murder, and the investigation, the tone gossipy and excited, even when the children were still around to hear. Mary had wanted to shout at them: *Show some respect! Someone died and it was horrible! And do we really need our kids to listen to this?*

She'd talked to Isla and Arthur about Rosco's death when they'd come in the day before, keeping her tone calm and impersonal. 'A man died. That shout this morning – I had to bring back his body. The police are in the village trying to find out exactly what happened.' Then they'd moved on to other topics. Isla's weekend sleepover with a friend who lived at the edge of the village. Artie's project on tadpoles and frogs. He'd inherited his grandfather's love of the natural world.

After the kids had chased in to class, and on her way out through the school gates, Mary had heard two older women, grandmothers, talking about one of the detectives.

'I recognized the name. His mother was Sister Dorothy. Do you remember her? Dennis brought them over sometimes for meetings.' A pause. 'The boy broke her heart.'

Mary had thought immediately that they must be talking about the inspector, the person who'd first come to the lifeboat station. There was something reserved, contained about him. He had the air of a man who had struggled. But surely he couldn't belong to the Brethren? A detective would need to be ruled by logic, not superstition. There was enough of that already in Greystone.

Now, back in her house, with its smell of coffee and paint, she thought how good it was to be here. This house defined her: Mary Ford, daughter, mother, artist and lifeboat helm. The unease that had hit her since Rosco's death would pass. His killer would be caught and she would no longer be troubled by nightmares of a shrivelled body in a small boat, curled tight like a walnut in its shell. The old life would return, and, perhaps, with it, a glimpse of hope. If they could get Artie to the clinic in Illinois, maybe her father was right and she was wrong, and the boy would reclaim his health and his strength.

There was a knock on the front door, just as she was settling in her studio to work. Her father answered it and she could hear voices in the hall at the bottom of the stairs. She made her way down and found her father pouring coffee for a young, fit man, with gelled hair and a local accent.

'I told the detective that you were working and that we shouldn't disturb you.' Her father sounded irritated, a little put out.

'No worries, I hadn't quite started.' She turned to the young man. 'How can I help you? I've already spoken to Inspector Venn at the lifeboat station, and Sergeant Rafferty was here yesterday.' She disliked the fact that the killing had intruded once more into her home, her life, but of course it wasn't this young man's fault. There was something engaging about him, an innocent enthusiasm. He had the pent-up energy of an overactive child.

'I really wanted to speak to Mr Ford.' His voice was confident. He liked the authority of being a police officer and all that went with it. He wouldn't be easily intimidated. 'But it would be great if you could spare a bit of time for me too.' As if her father wasn't quite competent to speak for himself, as if she were some kind of minder. Although it was Alan who was really holding the whole family together, who'd found a new energy in his search for a cure for her boy.

'Of course,' she said, because now, after all, she was rather reluctant to leave her father to the mercy of this man.

They sat at the kitchen table. Ross May took the chair at the head, where her father usually sat, and she felt a stab of resentment. She was left to sit on the kids' bench.

'How can we help you?'

May turned to the older man. 'This woman you thought you saw on the morning of Mr Rosco's disappearance . . . We need a statement, if that's okay. You're an important witness.'

'I didn't *think* I saw her. I did see her.'

'However, nobody else did,' the detective said, 'so we need as good a description as you can give. Another witness was out on Quarry Bank, but he didn't see anyone.'

'I've already given the description. I spoke to Sergeant Rafferty.'

Mary was pleased that her father was keeping his cool. If anything, this arrogant young detective was amusing rather than irritating him.

'If you wouldn't mind going through it again, and I'll record the conversation. If that's okay with you, of course. Then we'll have a record.'

'I don't mind at all.' Alan turned to her and slightly rolled his eyes. Mary suppressed a smile. 'I suffer from insomnia and I was still awake at one o'clock. The wind had dropped, and I heard a car driving down the hill from the main road. My bed is close to the window and I pulled back the curtain to see who was out at that hour. An old man's nosiness. The car stopped at the bottom of the terrace, just outside the house, and a woman got out. Because of the angle I couldn't really see her face, but she was wearing a long coat, and boots. There's a street light there, but it's hard to make out colour. I think she had fair hair. Long fair hair. She moved out of my line of sight and, really, the only way she could have been going was up the hill towards Rosco's place. She could have stopped at any of the houses between here and there, though.'

Mary could tell that the officer was impressed by the clarity of her father's statement.

So, stop being such a patronizing young git.

'Can you tell me anything about the car?' the detective asked. 'You thought it might have been a taxi?'

'That was an assumption,' Alan said. 'Because it just stopped and dropped her off. I didn't see any sign on it. Nothing to identify it as a taxi, and of course I didn't think to make a note of the registration. I was just being a curious old man looking out of the window.'

Again, Mary suppressed a smile. Her father never usually described himself as old. And he wasn't, of course! That was for the detective and the recording. A kind of mockery of young people's attitudes to older people.

'That's very helpful. What colour was the car?'

'I've been thinking about that. Dark certainly. Black probably, but it could have been dark green or grey. The street light seems to drain away the colour.'

'Yet you saw the woman's hair?'

'Yes,' Alan said. 'I did, just as she started walking away, and the light wasn't quite so harsh.'

There was a silence, broken again by her father.

'I'm sorry, I don't think I can help you with anything else.'

Mary waited until Ross had stopped recording on his phone. She didn't want to make this official, but she couldn't let it go either, although it would be awkward if word got out that she'd made any sort of accusation. Not against a woman who was such a stalwart of the community.

'Dad, could the woman you saw have been Tilly Gregory? She has long blonde hair.'

'Tilly Gregory?' Ross May turned to her, eager again. Immediately, Mary regretted that she'd spoken in front of him. She should have waited until he'd gone before asking her father. Then they could have gone back and spoken to the police. Perhaps to Jen Rafferty. Mary liked the teacher. This man would be like a terrier with a bone.

'Her real name's Matilda. She's one of the teachers in the

primary school,' Mary said. 'Her husband, Davy, is a taxi driver.'

'Well?' Ross May turned to her father. 'Could she have been the woman you saw?'

Alan shook his head. 'I'm sorry, it could possibly have been her – I've seen her, of course, when I've taken the children to school for Mary – but I didn't see the woman well enough to say more than that.'

Mary saw that the detective would push the point, would worry away at it, so that finally her father would become irritated. 'I don't think we can help you any further. Not now at least. Do contact us again if anything else comes up.' She stood up to make it clear that she wanted him to go. He looked at her, surprised – perhaps he wasn't used to assertive women – and for a moment she thought he'd refuse to leave the house, but finally he got to his feet.

She walked with the constable to the door. She was worried that he would continue pestering her father on the pavement if Alan saw him out. But in the end, he directed more questions to her, pleased, it seemed, to have got her alone.

'This Tilly Gregory, what sort of woman is she?'

Mary wasn't quite sure what he meant, but answered anyway, sounding, she realized, as if she were providing a reference for a job. 'She's a great teacher, devoted to the kids, very well liked.' A pause, needing to add more, to make the comment more personal. 'She's a good woman.' Because Tilly Gregory had always treated Arthur with such tenderness that when Mary saw them together, she wanted to cry.

'Happily married?'

'Oh yes!' Mary paused then, because how could she comment on another couple's marriage? Outsiders had probably seen her and Tom as an ideal partnership until he'd run off with another woman. 'She's a lot younger than Davy, of course, but they seem very close, very loving.'

She expected the man to walk away then, towards the village, but still he hovered on the pavement. She was aware that her whole morning's work had been disturbed – she would struggle now to concentrate – and, hoping to end the conversation once and for all, she said:

'She's very religious, you know. Quite a number of people here belong to the Barum Brethren and she's a part of that community. Really, she's the last person you could suspect of wrong-doing.'

She thought that might convince the detective and send him on his way, but if anything, he was more excited.

'Who should I talk to then? About this cult?'

'They don't see themselves as members of a cult.' Mary was quite irritated by now, and she let it show. She wanted to be back in her studio with more of her father's good coffee. Even if she couldn't focus on her work, there were emails to answer, a tax return to complete. 'And I'm not a member, so really I'm not the right person to ask.'

He nodded as if he accepted the justice of the remark, as if he might even have his own source of information, and, at last, he turned away and made his way back towards the centre of the village. Mary watched him go, worried that at the last moment he might turn back.

Chapter Twelve

JEN'S WAS ONE OF THE FIRST cars out of Greystone through the newly cleared road. The men from the village hadn't waited for the council to clear it. They'd cut the huge tree into manageable chunks with a chainsaw and towed them onto the verge using a tractor. She recognized some of the men from the night before. Ollie, the young guy from the lifeboat who'd been flirting with her. Definitely flirting, despite the difference in their age. And Brennan, the truck driver, strong enough to lift huge pieces of wood himself. There was a gap in the hedge where the tree had stood, a hole like a pit and the enormous roots lying on their side. She wondered how long the oak had stood there since it had first started growing.

Jen had a hangover. Not the sort of hangover that made you throw up, with the need to lie in a darkened room for most of a day, but that faint heady queasiness that made it hard to think clearly.

The Barnstaple schools weren't opening until midday, so she could be there to see the kids before setting off for the post-mortem, which had been scheduled for later in the day. She felt the usual recurring guilt that she couldn't be there for them every morning. She knew that her children didn't get enough of her time or her attention; that they'd become independent through neglect, not through her care. Ella had eaten and stacked her plate in the dishwasher before Jen had arrived home.

'I'd thought we could all have breakfast together.' Jen knew she sounded needy. 'I got pastries in Lidl on the way through. A treat.'

'Sorry, coding club before lessons start.' Ella was already out of the door. She'd meet her equally geeky boyfriend on the way and they'd talk about their twin obsessions of science and fantasy gaming. Jen supposed she should be delighted that she'd never caught Ella drunk or smelling of weed, that she was in a stable relationship with a young man who was an academic high achiever, but it didn't seem as if El had much *fun*. Jen had married too young, had children too young, had waited too long in an abusive marriage before cutting her losses, and now, fun seemed important.

She let Ben sleep in. He was a growing boy and needed his rest. But eventually she stood at the bottom of the steep stairs, in her narrow, terraced cottage, and shouted to him that he'd be late.

He clattered down half an hour later. She hadn't heard the water running and suspected he hadn't showered. How often *did* he shower when she wasn't here to check? Or change his clothes? But it was too late to send him back now. He grabbed a pain au chocolat from the plate on the kitchen table and opened the door to leave. At the last moment, he came back into the room. She thought he'd forgotten a piece of coursework, or his games kit, but he kissed her on the cheek. 'Bye. Thanks.' Then he really was gone, leaving the house quiet, and Jen with a strange sense that was close to bereavement.

Sally Pengelly was already in the hospital mortuary, gowned and masked, when Jen arrived, and waved at her. The body on the table looked very small, very old.

'I don't think I need to keep you for long,' Pengelly said. 'The cause of death is obvious. There are multiple stab wounds. He'd have bled out very quickly.'

'Would he still have been bleeding when he was carried from the scene?'

'It depends how soon the killer moved him.'

'He must have been moved before rigor, mustn't he? To have been curled into the dinghy?'

'The blood spatter is in a bathroom. He could have been placed in the bath, don't you think? In the same foetal position? Then there'd have been no rush to move him.'

Jen thought about that. The rage implied in the repeated stabbing seemed at odds with the meticulously planned removal of the body, the staging of the boat anchored just offshore. Why bother with that? Why not just leave Rosco where he'd been killed? Had he been put in the boat as a mark of respect – he'd spent his life on the water after all – or, as Venn had suggested, was this a kind of mockery? It certainly wasn't an attempt to mislead the investigators. The killer would know there was no way this could be put down as an accident.

She was still going over the details in her mind on her way to Appledore, to hook up with Brian Branscombe's team. She waited outside the lifeboat station for one of the CSIs to come out to speak to her.

The young woman removed her mask and they sat together on the sea wall. The autumn sun bounced off the water and they were surrounded by gulls. Jen was tempted by the thought of a Hockings ice cream or a bag of chips. It almost felt like being on holiday.

'We're nearly finished. There's not much there to help you, I'm afraid. One set of fingerprints, but we've checked against the owner, and they belong to him.'

Sammy Barton. Which didn't mean he wasn't the killer.

'I'd guess whoever placed the body in the boat was wearing gloves,' the investigator went on. 'There's some soil at the bottom of the dinghy. Still damp, so maybe it's relatively recent. The body would have shielded it from the worst of the weather that night. It could have come off the boots of the person who placed him there. They probably had to step inside the dinghy to position him properly. We'll get an analysis, but again, it's most likely to have come from the owner. It was raining hard and the water *could* have seeped in under the victim.' A pause. 'Brian is heading up the scene at the house in Greystone. It would be interesting if he found similar soil traces in the bath-room there. That really would be significant.'

Jen nodded. That, at least, would be a crumb to hand over to Venn; something concrete. So far, all they had were stories and speculation.

She used the satnav on her phone to get from Appledore to Greystone. Venn always used a paper map, studied before setting off. Ross seemed to find this amusing, but Venn said it was important to understand the region's geography, phys-ical and human. 'We're all a product of the place where we were born, where we grew up, and where we live.' That made sense to Jen. She'd always be a Scouser at heart.

The route took her inland across farmland separated by tangled hedges, bent by the westerly winds. Then there was a glimpse of the sea between the curve of two hills, and she was starting the descent into the village. It seemed slightly less grim now the rain had stopped, but still the road was in shadow, enclosed by the narrow valley. After the open landscape, she felt hemmed in by the terraced houses, and the grey cliffs of the worked-out quarry behind.

She parked on the main street and, looking up the hill towards the house where Rosco had been killed, she saw a team of officers, searching the tiny front gardens, emptying bins. It seemed that the knife that had stabbed the man still hadn't been found. She walked towards them to see what was going on, felt the pull on her calves as she climbed the hill, and found Venn and Ross watching the action too.

'Nothing yet,' Venn said. He turned away and they all started back down the slope towards the village.

The salt air seemed to be doing wonders for Jen's headache. She turned to Ross. 'What did you make of Alan Ford then? A reliable witness?'

'Yeah,' he said. 'You were right. Very sharp and not the sort of person to make anything up. He thought the woman he saw in the early hours had long blonde hair.'

'Davy Gregory's wife has long fair hair,' Venn said. 'I saw a photo of her.'

'Mary Ford said the same,' Ross said. 'She suggested the woman might be Matilda Gregory, school teacher and leading light within the Brethren here.'

'It's hard to think why a religious woman would be

wandering the streets in the early hours of a stormy morning.' Jen pictured the scene. There was something romantic about the image of a woman walking on her own through the gloomy village. It was the stuff of films, a period melodrama. 'It sounds as if she was desperate.'

'Davy Gregory claims that he didn't work that night,' Venn said. 'He can't give his wife an alibi because she wasn't at home. Apparently, she was babysitting for a friend. Ruth Smale, wife of the doctor who was in the lifeboat station when we first got there.'

Jen nodded. She could picture the man, who'd formally pronounced Rosco dead, standing a little to one side. 'She wouldn't still be there at one in the morning, would she?'

'According to Gregory, she stayed over.'

'A bit odd, isn't it, for a school night? You wouldn't be up drinking with a mate after their night out if you had to face a class of kids the next day.'

'From what I hear,' Venn said, 'Matilda Gregory isn't the partying sort. Like Ruth Smale, she's a member of the Brethren.'

'That's two more witnesses we need to talk to then.' Jen couldn't imagine a woman stabbing Rosco in his bath and carrying his body through the village to the quay, but she was curious to meet them. Sisters of the Brethren. Women who lived such different lives from her own.

They'd almost reached the Maiden's Prayer when there was a noise behind them. Heavy footsteps. A shout. It was Jimmy Rainston, one of the first officers to arrive at the life-boat when Rosco's body had been brought ashore. He'd obviously been running: he was beetroot red and heaving for breath.

'Sorry, sir, we'd have called but there was no mobile signal.'

'So,' Venn said. 'What have you got for us?'

'A knife.' A pause. Rainston was enjoying the moment of glory. 'We reckon we've found the murder weapon.'

Chapter Thirteen

Matthew and Jen followed the officer up the hill. Ross had wanted to come too. When Rainston had joined them, he'd been like an overexcited kid offered the prospect of a mound of sweets, ready to race ahead.

'No need for us all to go,' Venn had said. 'We still have to consider Sammy Barton as a suspect. He's got no motive that I can see, but all the opportunity in the world. And the best knowledge of the coast. You need to go back to his house at some point, Ross. Get a sample of soil from the yard where the dinghy had been kept, and from the garden. Also, a scraping from Barton's boots.' He'd sensed Ross was about to argue and went on before the man had a chance to speak. 'Then give Brian a shout. He's still at the murder scene. I need to know if they found any soil samples there. I didn't see anything when I was in there, but I wasn't looking and it wouldn't take much for a comparison. They'll be taking scrapings from the drainpipes.' A pause. 'Once that's done, we're still waiting on details of Rosco's next of kin. I can't believe he was completely alone in this world. Get on to it, will you?

He must have had some cash squirrelled away. Let's see who inherits.'

Now, walking beside the local cop, who was beefy in build, but not as fit as he should be, still wheezing as they climbed the steep bank, Venn wondered why he hadn't let Ross come along. Was it a kind of spite? He *had* taken a moment of pleasure in Ross's disappointment. But, after all, a young detective needed to know that a murder investigation wasn't all about dramatic revelations and murder weapons. It was about detail. And there was nothing a jury liked more than concrete forensic evidence. Jonathan always said Matthew overthought things, and perhaps that was true now as he analysed his response to the DC's disappointment. Guilt lurked always, ready to pounce. Part of his own inheritance.

The three of them walked up Quarry Bank, past Gwen's cottage, and past the cottage where Rosco had spent his last few weeks. That had been cordoned off from public gaze. The houses only ran on one side of the path; on the other was a strip of wasteland with a few scrubby bushes, a scattering of brambles. Venn saw that this had been the main area of search. Men and women were crouching, prodding the undergrowth. But Jimmy Rainston was still walking on up the footpath towards the quarry.

The boundary was marked by a rusting metal fence. There were holes in the wire, caused, Venn suspected, by local kids. He'd only learned as an adult that, to most teens, there was nothing as attractive as forbidden ground. He'd been a very different kind of teenager, a rule keeper, a little priggish. He'd probably have shopped anyone breaking through the fence to his parents or teachers. Jonathan would have been leading the fray with his bolt cutters.

Matthew wondered what that would be like: to be part of a gang of kids, released occasionally from parental authority, running wild, forming alliances with children different from himself, kids with different faiths or none. He struggled even to imagine it.

He was so lost in thought that when the policeman stopped at the fence, Matthew almost bumped into him. Beyond the boundary Venn could see a grey granite bowl of rock. A moonscape, pitted and uneven. The cheap set for a sci-fi movie. Large boulders littered the base and there were already saplings growing out of cracks in the cliff. Nature had started taking over what had once been a large industrial site. To one side, a piece of machinery had been left and had rusted so badly, corroded by salt and weather, that it was hard to guess what its function had once been. A group of white-suited officers stood in a group looking down at an object that was out of Venn's line of sight. Venn heard footsteps behind him and turned to see Brian Branscombe.

'They found our weapon then?'

'Looks like it.' Brian was local, and had a slow, careful voice and a very sharp wit. 'I won't go in. I'm still working on the scene in the house and the last thing you need is any sort of contamination for a defence lawyer to pick up on. There's no rust, according to the boys, so it can't have been there long and it's the shape and size Sal Pengelly described when she first looked at the wound.'

'Sal said it could be a kitchen knife,' Jen said. 'Wide bladed at the hilt but sharp. The sort a chef might use, but really anyone who liked cooking could have one.'

Venn turned to Branscombe. 'Was it hidden?'

'Nah, not really. It was lying on the ground behind a pile

of rock. Not visible from this side of the boundary, but easy enough for the team to find once they'd started searching properly. Like I said, no rust or corrosion, so not left over from the time that the quarry was active.'

'Could it have been thrown over the fence?'

Venn was trying to picture the scene. The killer would be left with a body in the early hours of the morning. They'd want to get it down to the tender. That at least had been planned. The quarry was in the opposite direction from the sea. He couldn't see why someone would make even a short detour to dispose of the weapon.

But Branscombe shook his head. 'You'd have to be a bloody good shot to get it that far. I think someone went in and left it inside.'

Why would you do that? The killer would have known it would be searched for and found. Easier, surely, just to leave it in Rosco's bathroom? No effort had been made to hide the fact that it was the scene of the crime. Or if the knife was in any way distinctive, why not throw it into the sea while you were rowing out with the tender? It would be unlikely ever to be discovered then.

Again, Matthew thought this was staged in a childish sort of way. The killer was playing ridiculous games.

'Did you find any soil in the house?'

'DC May has just been in touch about that. There was nothing obvious in the bathroom, but we'll be draining the plughole and taking samples from the stair carpet. Don't hold your breath, though. Even if we find anything, we won't get the analysis back immediately.'

'You can get started on the stuff in the dinghy tender?'

Branscombe nodded. 'Yeah, that's already on its way to the lab.'

They watched him walk back towards the cottage crime scene, head bent, preoccupied.

Matthew stood for a moment, weighing priorities. The only person who'd been seen anywhere near Jem Rosco's house at the time of the murder was Alan Ford's mysterious woman. He turned to Jen, who was fidgeting, waiting for him to move.

'The school day finished at three fifteen. It's not much after that. Let's go and talk to Matilda Gregory. I don't suppose she'll leave immediately, so we should catch her.'

When they arrived, however, it was clear that this wasn't the end of a normal day. People of all ages were going towards the school, not walking away from it. It was a small building, dated, Matthew guessed, from the thirties, when the quarry would have been at its most productive. Four classrooms faced onto the playground. Bunting had been strung over the door and a poster, painted by a child in orange and yellow, announced the school's autumn fayre.

'What do you think?' Matthew asked. 'Shall we come back another day?'

'Nah.' Jen was already making her way to the queue by the door. 'Bet there's a cake stall, and it'll be a good way to get the village on side.'

They paid the pound entrance fee and followed the flow of parents and grandparents into the school hall. Stalls had been set up round the walls. It was a cross between a jumble sale, a craft sale and a fairground, with a coconut shy, raffles and sales of bric-a-brac, jars of homemade jam and home bakes. More of the grotesque knitted animals. Matthew recognized some of the lifeboat crew. Peter Smale and Harry Carter were manning stalls. Gwen Gregory was serving teas in one corner.

The conversation dropped a little when the detectives walked in and there were stares, not of hostility exactly, but wary curiosity. They could have been poisonous snakes in a zoo.

A woman moved towards a low stage at one end of the hall and called the room to order. Matthew recognized her from the photo he'd seen in the Ravenscroft farmhouse as Matilda Gregory.

She had a singer's voice, deep and smooth, with a hint of a local accent. 'Thank you so much to you all for coming. And to our children for all their hard work. I'm sure you'll agree that the hall looks magnificent. This year, we're raising money for Artie's Fund. So, dig deep, so we can send a very special pupil to America to make him better.'

There was a loud cheer. Matthew looked around but he couldn't see Mary Ford or her son. Maybe the child wasn't well enough to attend, or perhaps the woman would find the idea of the charity deeply embarrassing. He knew that he would.

Jen nudged him and pointed to a grey-haired man who'd just come through the door, pushing the small boy in his wheelchair. There was still no sign of his mother.

'That's Alan Ford.'

As they watched, a young girl, whom Matthew supposed to be Mary's daughter, ran from behind a stall towards the man. Ford swung her into the air and made her giggle. Matthew had a jolting memory of his father doing exactly the same thing, of the world tilting, of feeling safe in his dad's arms, of finding himself laughing. His father had never done anything like that when Matthew's mother was around. She disapproved of what she called 'silliness', and Matthew's dad had always acceded to her will, in her presence at least. These rare moments between father and son had been secretly shared and now that he was dead, they were treasured.

Matthew waited until the small crowd of parents around Matilda Gregory had dispersed, and then he approached her. She frowned, but led them out of the hall and into a classroom.

'This really isn't a good time. As you saw, I'm rather busy. We weren't even sure we'd go ahead with the fayre until this morning.'

'Because of Mr Rosco's death?' Jen asked.

The teacher looked up sharply. 'No! Because of the power outage. They promised it would come back on today, but these things are never certain.'

She was wearing a long cord skirt and a rust-coloured cardigan, autumn colours, matched by the children's art on the walls, a collection of collages made up of dried leaves and berries. Through the long windows there was a view of the grey sea.

Matthew introduced himself and Jen. 'You'll have heard that we're investigating Jeremy Rosco's killing.'

'Of course. Davy phoned at lunchtime and said you'd been to the house to speak to him. I never met Mr Rosco in Greystone, though. I'm not sure how I can help.' There was that frown again. An indication of things not being quite as they should be, or not as she would like them to be. Venn knew the feeling. He'd grown up with the Brethren too and understood their need for certainty, for unspoken rules to be kept.

'We're talking to most people in the village,' Venn said easily. 'It's routine. The way we always work.'

She nodded as if she could accept the need for the routine.

'Just a few questions.'

They sat on the children's tables, rather than the chairs, but still Venn felt uncomfortable, undignified, too close to the ground. Matilda Gregory had a proper grown-up chair at the front of the class. She was wearing brown leather ankle boots with a small heel and she crossed her feet. Everything about her was modest, but she managed to look stylish.

As they'd decided, Jen took the lead. 'Could you tell us where you were in the early hours of yesterday morning, Mrs Gregory?'

'Is that when Mr Rosco was killed?'

Venn expected an evasive response, but Jen answered. 'We're pretty sure that it was.'

'I was fast asleep,' Matilda said. 'I'm not one for late nights, even at the weekend. Certainly not when there's school the next day.'

'You were at home in Ravenscroft?'

She shook her head. 'Some friends had an emergency. Ruth and Peter Smale. Peter's the doctor here. Ruth's mother's very ill and they were called to the hospital in Barnstaple. They asked me if I could babysit their daughters in the old rectory in Willington. It's only just down the road from us, but I wasn't sure what time they'd get back, so I took an overnight bag.'

Venn thought that was something they could easily check. He made a mental note.

'What time *did* they get back?' Jen kept her voice easy, conversational.

'Just after eleven. The crisis with Ruth's mother had passed, so they felt able to leave her and come home. I was already on my way to bed, so I decided to stay.'

'And you didn't go out again?'

'No! Of course not. What is this all about?'

'A woman matching your description was seen getting out of a car at the bottom of the terrace where Mr Rosco was staying. Of course, your sister-in-law lives there too. Perhaps you were going to visit her?'

The teacher looked bewildered. 'At that time in the morning? Why would I?'

Jen's voice was gentle. 'If Gwen was having a crisis of some sort? Surely you'd be one of the people she'd call? She has nobody else, does she?'

'You think Gwen killed Rosco and called me to help her get rid of the body? That's crazy, the stuff of horror films.' She gave a little laugh. 'Or comedies. You've talked to Gwen! She wouldn't hurt a fly.'

'Had you ever met Mr Rosco? Before he turned up here in Greystone?'

She was quiet for a moment. 'Not that I remember,' she said at last.

'I'm sorry?' Jen made it clear that she didn't understand.

'He knew my parents. Apparently, they were close when they were younger, all members of the Morrisham Yacht Club, but as far as I know, I never met him.'

'He was at school with your husband. Yet you didn't invite him to your house when he was in Greystone? Have him round to dinner to chat over old times?'

Watching, just out of Matilda's sight line, Venn thought that was a great question. He wasn't sure he'd have asked it in the same way. Jen was making a splendid job of the interview.

There was another silence. 'We did invite him,' the teacher said at last, 'but he made excuses. He said he was expecting a visitor and he wasn't sure when they'd turn up. He didn't want to be too far from home when they arrived.'

Jen didn't respond immediately and when she did her voice was a little firmer. 'Just to be clear. You didn't visit Mr Rosco in the early hours of yesterday morning? It seems such a coincidence, you see. You have a very striking appearance. It's hard to believe that two women who look like you could be seen in the same place.'

Matilda looked up sharply. 'I don't lie, Sergeant. I think it's a sin. Your witness is mistaken, or another woman who looked like me was there. Either explanation is more likely than that I'd be out on my own, visiting a man who's not my husband, and that I'd lie about it.' There was a moment of silence. Jen was hoping Matilda would say more, but in the end, *she* was the person to speak.

'I'm sorry, Mrs Gregory. I don't mean to upset you. I hope you understand why we have to check these things. A man has died.'

'Of course.' Matilda seemed a little more relaxed, even gave a smile. 'And once the Smales got back from the hospital, they were in the house with me all evening. There were no mysterious disappearances. I can assure you of that.'

She got to her feet. 'If that's all, Detectives, I should get back to the fayre. The fundraising is important to us all in Greystone.' When they didn't immediately move, she stared down at them, the iciness returning. 'I don't know why you're asking us all these questions. Mr Rosco only spent a few weeks here with us. Surely you should be asking the people he spent most time with: his family and close friends? They'll be able to tell you more about him than we can.'

Jen glanced at Venn. He nodded his agreement that the interview was over, and they left together. Glancing back at the school as they passed through the gate, Matthew saw Matilda Gregory watching them through the classroom window, her phone to her ear.

Chapter Fourteen

AFTER THE BOSS AND JEN RAFFERTY left to talk to the teacher, instead of going straight to the Bartons' cottage, Ross May headed back to the pub. A minor gesture of rebellion, to prove to himself that he couldn't be pushed around. He'd try Barton later. He made an effort not to care, but he felt like the youngest in a family, always left behind, always treated like shit, never listened to. He worked harder than Jen – not surprising because he didn't have the distraction of children – but Venn never seemed to notice. He and Mel intended to have kids sometime. Of course they did. But not until they'd established themselves in their careers and maybe not until they'd moved up the housing ladder a step. And then, Ross wouldn't let kiddies get in the way of his work. It wasn't *his* fault that Jen Rafferty had moved down here, leaving her husband behind. She'd chosen to be a single mother. Let her deal with it.

On the way, he phoned Brian Branscombe and received the information that the soil in the dinghy had already been sent to the lab and that nothing of interest had yet been found in Rosco's bathroom. It would take time to collect all the samples,

Branscombe said, implying that Ross should know that and was hassling him.

'Sorry,' Ross said. 'The boss told me to ask.' Let Venn take the crap.

There was a note on the door of the Maiden's saying it would be closed all afternoon because of a community fund-raising event. Ross had a key and let himself in. At least he'd be able to sit in the bar, instead of the poky room at the back. He set about struggling to get a handle on Rosco, to track down any recent contacts for him. There was a Facebook page, but that seemed to be professional rather than personal, and nothing had been added in the last six months. There were lots of photos of fancy yachts, gleaming in the sunlight against a backdrop of impossibly blue seas. Sailing porn. But few facts.

There was a phone contact for an agent, but when Ross phoned it, he was told that Jeremy Rosco was no longer a client.

'Had he found a new agent? Could you give me the details?'

The voice at the other end of the line was frosty. 'Mr Rosco decided that he could manage his own affairs. He resented paying our very reasonable commission.' A pause. 'He could be a little demanding. We weren't sorry that he'd made the decision to go it alone.'

Ross was still working out the implication of that, and forming another question, when he saw that another call was coming through: his colleague Vicki. He apologized and told the agent that he might need to speak to her again.

Vicki had been helping with data collection in the station in Barnstaple and had found an address for the man: a flat in Morrisham. Once she had that, she'd traced his GP.

'Not that it did much use,' she told Ross. 'Apparently Rosco hasn't visited the doctor for at least five years.'

'They'll have a next of kin for him, though.'

'Only an out of date one. An ex-wife. They divorced twenty-two years ago. She's living in Barnstaple now.' Vicki read out the address. 'I asked someone to go round to inform her of Rosco's death, but she'd already seen it on the news. Apparently, she wasn't heartbroken.'

Left on his own in the Maiden's Prayer, Ross tried to google Rosco again and came across an old episode of *Desert Island Discs* from Radio 4. Ross's mother always listened to it while she was preparing Sunday dinner, so he knew the format. The adventurer was picking the eight records he'd want with him if he was stranded, and talking about his life. Ross thought much of the music was a bit boring. Though there was a bit of punk and some classic rock, it was mostly country. It was interesting, though, to hear the man talking about himself and his childhood, growing up on the North Devon coast.

'I was an only child and my dad left when I was a baby. Probably just as well. He'd drunk himself to death by the time I was ten; they found his body in a hostel for the homeless in Plymouth. Yeah, it was tough growing up. My mother worked in a cafe – long hours in the summer and bugger all work in the winter. What you'd call a zero-hours contract these days. As a young teenager, I got into bother. Nothing serious. Mucking around. Always hyper, always wanting to be in on the action. Couldn't see the point of school. It was the sea that saved me. There was a poster on the noticeboard in the class-room. *Learn to Sail This Summer*: hand-drawn pictures of dinghies in full sail. Turned out one of our teachers was into sailing. Suddenly, more than anything I wanted to be there, out in the bay with the wind in my face. I'd always been a water rat. I spent my days on the beach while my mother was working in the caff, looking for treasure on the tideline, poking around in the rockpools. I guess the club wanted some younger members, though I doubt they were expecting someone like me. I turned up to the yacht club with a couple of posh girls, and that was it. Love at first sight. With the sailing and with one of the girls.' He gave a strange snort, which could have been regret. 'I never looked back.'

The rest of the interview was about his success, the round-the-world record, his expeditions. But there was no explanation as to how he'd made the adventures happen. Ross couldn't see how he'd turned from a schoolboy, crewing on other people's boats, to a round-the-world yachtsman. A boat like that would cost a fortune, wouldn't it? It would take sponsorship and Rosco wouldn't have had those sorts of connections. They'd been told that the man had ambitions to sail in the Olympics, but he'd never made the team, and Ross couldn't see how sponsors would be interested in 'might have beens'. It could be worth a trip to the yacht club. Someone there might remember the real man, rather than the legend.

Then there was the posh girl who Rosco had fallen in love with. There'd been something in his voice as he'd spoken about her on the radio broadcast . . . It was a leap, Ross knew that, but could she have been the mysterious woman the sailor had been waiting for? A romance from the past? His very first love?

He was still pondering this when Venn and Jen Rafferty came in, bringing a blast of cold air with them.

'How did you get on with the teacher?' Ross was about to ask if she was as glamorous as they'd been led to believe, then thought better of it. Neither Venn nor Rafferty had a sense of humour about stuff like that.

'I'm not sure.' Venn sat at the table. 'She was very hard to read, and she was distracted. There was an event going on at the school. She claims that she was staying with friends on the night Rosco died.'

'You didn't believe her?'

Venn shrugged. 'Not sure. The friends were in bed soon after eleven. We'll have to check with them, of course, but she *could* have gone out again. Davy *could* have picked her up in his taxi. I can't see why he would bring her into Greystone, if she and Rosco were having an affair? If she was his mysterious visitor. She might not be telling us everything she knows, but in an investigation, everyone's got something to hide. It doesn't mean she's guilty of murder.'

'Matilda Gregory said we should look into Rosco's past for a motive,' Jen said. 'That makes sense, I suppose. As she pointed out, he was only here for a few weeks. But it did sound as if she was directing our attention away from the village. I wonder if it's the community she's trying to protect, not just herself.'

'I *have* been doing a bit of digging into Rosco's past,' Ross said. 'Vicki tracked down an address for his ex-wife.' He'd been tempted to claim the discovery as his own, but Venn had a way of sniffing out that sort of deception. 'They've been divorced for donkeys' years, but she's still living just outside Barnstaple.'

'I could go and chat to her on my way home,' Jen said. 'At the very least she can give us some background, but she might have more recent information.' A pause and a wry smile. 'I suppose some divorced couples stay friends.'

'I've had another idea too.' Ross explained about the radio

broadcast and Rosco's early days of sailing. 'I thought I'd visit the yacht club and see if anyone there remembers him and can explain how he funded his first trips. And he mentioned falling in love with a posh schoolgirl who learned to sail when he did. He comes across as a romantic sort of chap, doesn't he? He might still have been holding a candle for her. I wondered if she could be the mysterious woman he was expecting to turn up at the cottage.'

'Will anyone be at the sailing club?' Venn sounded doubtful. 'This sort of weather, nobody will be out in a boat.'

'This time of year, it won't be about the sailing.' Ross was a member of the rugby club and, he thought, out of season, it wouldn't be very different. 'It's more like a social club. Old guys sitting at the bar and chinwagging about past glories.'

Venn nodded.

'I thought I might head out there this evening.' Ross could see the prospect of an evening's escape from this drab, depressing village. 'It's only a few miles away and I might turn up something.'

'Sure,' Venn said. 'Good idea. Let's catch up when you get back.'

It was almost dark when Ross arrived in Morrisham, a stately town with wide, tree-lined streets leading to the waterfront, with its marina. This felt nothing like the North Devon Ross knew. It was genteel, with a faded grandeur, the main street flanked by a couple of large churches. Surrounded by gently rolling farmland, it had a vibe more reminiscent of the south of the county. Coaches full of elderly tourists regularly stopped here on their way to Torquay. There was one very grand hotel, with manicured lawns, and terraces where afternoon tea was served. The shops sold the sort of clothes his gran might have worn. He thought it must be a nightmare to be a teenager here. No wonder Rosco had been a bit wild.

The sailing club must have been built in the sixties or seventies. It was made of concrete and glass and looked down over the marina. Beyond it, a beach, backed by a wide promenade, led away into the distance. This, presumably, was where Rosco had gone beachcombing as a boy.

Ross May turned his vehicle into the club car park, and walked to the front of the building to get a sense of the place before going inside. Perhaps because the marina was so sheltered, some boats had been left there. The metal rigging sang in the breeze, a strange, slightly eery sound. The bar was at the top of the building and had a view of the water. The lights were on and Ross looked up to see couples sitting at the tables by the glass. The only young people in the place were the workers.

The door was at the back next to the car park, and was locked. It would take a code to get in. Ross pressed a buzzer, and waited.

'Yes?' The voice impatient and a little haughty. This wasn't one of the young waiting staff.

Ross introduced himself. 'It's about the murder of Jeremy Rosco. I'd like to speak to anyone who knew him.'

A pause, a little laugh. 'Oh, we all knew Jem Rosco. All the established members. He was quite a fixture when he was in town.'

The door clicked and Ross pushed it open. Inside, the lights must be operated by a sensor, because they suddenly switched on. There was a lift, a Perspex box, to carry the elderly or disabled to the first floor, and a set of varnished stairs, which

Ross took. An overweight, florid man was waiting for him at the top. He held out a sun-spotted hand.

'Barty Lawson. I'm commodore here. Come along in.'

He must have warned everyone in the bar of Ross's arrival, because the whole room turned and stared, before pretending to be engrossed once again in their conversations. Now, it was quite dark outside, and Ross was mesmerized for a moment by the flashing buoys in the bay, and the sweep of the lighthouse beam from the headland beyond the beach.

'Glorious, isn't it?' Lawson sounded as proud as if it were his personal property. 'Takes a fortune in upkeep, of course. The salt wind eats away at the concrete. Now, what would you like to drink?'

Ross was tempted. Despite his swagger, he felt out of place in this sort of company, and a drink might relax him. But Venn had an uncanny way of sniffing out misdemeanours, and the breaking of rules.

'Coffee,' he said. 'Thanks.'

Lawson ordered a coffee and a whisky from a middle-aged woman behind the bar, and led Ross to a table by the window. He must have been sitting there before Ross showed up, because a whisky glass, with a little left, remained on the table.

'It's really just background,' Ross said. 'We know very little about Mr Rosco's personal life and it would be useful to speak to his friends.'

'Ah.' Lawson was looking out into the darkness. His face was reflected as a shadow in the glass. 'Everyone here thought they were Jem's friend. Once he became famous, at least.'

'Not so much before that?'

Lawson turned back into the room. The hand holding the glass trembled a little. Ross thought the man was already drunk, in that contained, unobtrusive way of the seasoned alcoholic. It was the cloudy eyes and the effort to concentrate. Venn's superior, Joe Oldham, could get that way at times, more often recently, though Ross was reluctant to admit it.

'Well, he was quite an irritating oik as a boy. He never really fitted in.' There was a pause. 'This place was always a second home for me. My grandfather raised the cash to build it and my father was in charge until he died.'

'And then you took over.'

'Voted in!' The man bridled a little. 'We don't believe in nepotism here.' There was a pause, while he seemed to reconsider. 'Having said that, I probably got a sympathy vote. Poor Papa committed suicide.'

Ross was saved from answering by a young barmaid who brought his coffee on a little silver tray – milk on the side and a biscuit – and another large whisky for Lawson.

'So, what was Rosco like as a youngster?'

'Cocky,' Lawson said. 'And he took too many risks when he was out on the water. We didn't mind him drowning himself, but there were times when he put other people in danger.'

'I don't understand how he could afford it.' Ross sipped the coffee, which was weak and much too hot. 'Sailing's an expensive hobby.'

'He started off crewing for older members, working his passage as it were. Cleaning here and working behind the bar when he was older. But he was never really happy playing second fiddle. He always wanted a boat of his own.' A pause. 'He was good, but not as good as he thought he was. Not then.'

'There was talk of him sailing for Team GB in the Olympics.'

'Ah.' The fresh glass in front of Lawson was already almost empty. 'He was very good at talk.'

'How did he get the money to buy a boat good enough to sail single-handed round the world?' It was time, Ross thought, to be more direct. Otherwise, Lawson would lose it altogether. The man was at that stage of drunkenness when he was unguarded, but still relatively coherent. One more drink and he'd be over the edge.

'That was what we all wanted to know. Jem Rosco left here to seek his fortune. That was what he said when he resigned from the club. As if he was bloody Dick Whittington. It seemed fortune found him, and a bit closer to home.' Lawson stared at his reflection in the glass. He seemed lost in thought.

'I don't understand.'

'He had a sudden windfall.' The man's voice was ragged, bitter. 'A year later he was sailing out of the marina, with the country's press here to watch him set off.'

'Where did he get his money from? To buy the boat?'

'Oh, we all wondered that. There were stories, of course. Most of them made up by Rosco himself. But we all wanted to know who paid for the *Nelly Wren*.'

'Of course,' Ross said. 'That was the boat he broke the round-the-world record in. A strange name. Was it called that after anyone special?'

The girl he lost his heart to when he first learned to sail?

Lawson looked up at him, bleary-eyed. 'Oh yes! It was named for the woman who went on to be my wife. Who was already my girlfriend. Eleanor. Bloody cheek.' He turned round to catch the eye of the barmaid. 'Nell, he called her. Then Nelly Wren. He said the Wren was because she was so dainty.'

'Is she still your wife?'

'Yes, she bloody well is.' He'd raised his voice and there were disapproving looks from the other members. Nobody seemed very surprised, though. Perhaps Lawson regularly turned from affable to aggressive at this time of the evening.

'She's not here this evening?'

Lawson shook his head. 'She doesn't get out much these days. Not with me, at least. These days, she's a bit of a home bird. Not even her good works take her out any more.' It took him a moment to realize what he'd said. 'But not a wren. Not to me. To me, she's always been Eleanor. Eleanor Lawson.' The emphasis on the surname. His voice was loud again: 'My *wife*.' He could have been a child claiming possession of a fought-over toy.

'Does Rosco have any surviving relatives locally?'

'Not as far as I know. No siblings certainly. I seem to remember his mother died when he was out on one of his adventures.' Lawson waved his fingers in the air to suggest quotation marks around the last word. There was a moment of silence. 'Eleanor might know.'

'Perhaps you should go home to her,' Ross said. 'I have to leave now. You've been very helpful.' He felt sorry for the man, embarrassed on his behalf and wanted to get him away before the audience had anything further to roll their eyes at.

He was thinking he should check that Lawson didn't have his car with him when the older woman appeared from behind the bar.

'Your taxi's here, sir. Downstairs and waiting for you.' She winked at Ross and whispered as Lawson stumbled off to find his coat. 'I get his keys from him as soon as he comes in. We don't want him losing his licence, do we? Not when he's a magistrate and all.'

They walked together down the stairs. At one point Ross took the older man's arm to stop him falling.

'I might want to talk to your wife,' he said, just before they went outside. 'As you suggested. Is there a good time to call at your house?'

'Come anytime!' The man was suddenly jovial again, the melancholy gone. 'Always open house at the Lawsons'!'

Ross held the door open to let the man go ahead of him. A dark car was waiting. A man got out and opened the back door of the vehicle. 'Come on, Barty. Let's get you home to your missis.' His voice warm and friendly. Almost affectionate.

Ross recognized him from a photo Venn had shared to the team. Davy Gregory, taxi driver and former farmer. And minder, it seemed, to the rich and entitled.

Chapter Fifteen

Jen phoned Rosco's ex-wife before setting out from Greystone. The woman sounded distant, a little bored by the idea that she should give up part of her evening to discuss her dead former husband. 'I suppose I can stay in, but I don't know how I can possibly help.'

'We're just looking for background,' Jen said. 'I won't take up any more of your time than we need.'

It occurred to Jen that she too would hardly be heartbroken if she got a call saying that her ex had died. She'd be curious, of course, but there'd surely be a moment of relief, a sense of lightness, of a burden being shed, because she would no longer have to worry about what poison Robbie might be feeding her children when they went on their increasingly infrequent visits. Perhaps, too, there'd be no more of the nightmare memories. The man screaming at her that she was an unfit mother. Slapping her. Punching her in the gut. No, she thought. Her first response to learning of Robbie's passing wouldn't be one of relief. It would be of joy, of total delight.

Selina Vickery lived in a large, detached modern house on

a hill at the edge of Barnstaple. It was a part of a small new estate of executive homes, and stood on the largest plot, with a view of farmland at the back and over the town at the front. It was just getting dark when Jen arrived. She'd parked in the street and stood for a moment looking in. There were lights on in the large kitchen, but the blinds hadn't been lowered. Selina and a man in his sixties were sitting at a breakfast bar drinking tea.

This must be Terry, the new husband.

Jen rang the bell and the woman slid from a tall stool to answer the door.

'You must be Sergeant Rafferty.' She wore jeans and a silk blouse and looked good for her age. Well-cut hair and subtle make-up, which, Jen thought, hadn't been put on just for *her* benefit. This was a woman who cared about her appearance and wouldn't meet anyone without it. 'You don't mind sitting in the kitchen? I've just made tea.' She led Jen into the room and now she did pull down the blinds at the long windows. Everything was very clean, very shiny.

Jen took a stool, accepted the offer of tea.

'As I said on the phone, I don't know how I can help you. Jem and I divorced twenty years ago. Terry and I have been married for fifteen.'

'I'm just after background information,' Jen said. 'We haven't worked out what he was doing in Greystone. Did he have any contacts there? Relatives? Friends?'

'There might have been schoolfriends. Kids from the village went to Morrisham High, I think, but I didn't know Jeremy then.'

'How did you meet?'

'I was working for my father. He had his own business, a

shop, in Morrisham. The town had a different feel then, before the smart set moved to Croyde and Woolacombe. It was more fashionable. The tourist board called it North Devon's answer to Nice, and it did have a glamorous feel. There were fancy bars and clubs. We sold quality clothes, not just for the twinset and pearls brigade who visit now, but for the younger crowd. Men *and* women. We had regular customers but the tourists came too. And the grand sailing fraternity. Dad had an eye for fashion and design.'

'Which you've inherited.' Her husband spoke for the first time, his voice proud. He was stocky, grey-haired. 'Selina has her own textile company. She sells worldwide.'

The woman smiled at him, with real affection, before continuing her story. 'Jem came in looking for an outfit for some awards dinner and I served him. I recognized him at once, of course. He was a local hero in those days, not long back from sailing round the world. Still in his mid-twenties. Very cool, in a wind-blown, boho sort of way. He asked me out for a drink that night. We had several drinks and I was still there for breakfast. A month later I'd moved into his flat. I was younger than him. Dazzled, I suppose, by his celebrity.'

'Where was the flat?'

'It was in one of the newly built apartment blocks looking out over the promenade in Morrisham. All white and clean, and pretending to look like somewhere on the French Riviera, with palm trees in the communal garden at the front, a sleek wine bar on the ground floor. His place had a balcony and we'd sit there in the evenings to watch the sun set over the sea. I thought it was so cool. Dad's business was in Morrisham, but I'd grown up here in Barnstaple. This is quite different, ordinary, real.'

Jen thought that probably tied in with the address that Vicky had found. Rosco might still own the flat. 'How could he afford a place like that?'

Selina thought for a moment. 'I'm not sure he could afford it. Jem was a charmer, and very plausible, but everything was precarious. He might get what seemed like a ridiculous sum to endorse new sailing gear, or open a restaurant, or give a team-building speech, but then he'd splash out on a holiday in the Maldives and it would all disappear. I understood business. It's what I'd grown up with. At first I just enjoyed the ride – the big wedding and the honeymoon in St Lucia – but then I started to worry about whether or not he was paying his VAT or filling in his tax form.'

'Is that why you divorced?'

Selina didn't answer immediately. 'No, not entirely, though his reluctance to take *anything* seriously made me uneasy. As I said, he was a charmer. He told me he didn't need to worry about the financial detail, that he had an accountant to deal with the tedious stuff, and a lawyer to get him out of bother. But by then, I'd stopped quite believing him.' She looked up at Jen. 'I'm not saying he was a liar, but he made up all these stories in his head. Real life bored him and he was like a kid living in his own daydreams. He had to play the lead role in his made-up adventure stories. I'm sure he believed in the fantasy. As I said, he wasn't a liar. But for Jem, everything had to be romantic, exciting.'

'I don't suppose you remember the name of the accountant or lawyer?'

'Not the accountant. The lawyer had a weird name. I think that was why Jem had picked him. We used to laugh at it. Bottle! He was called Rodney Bottle.' She looked at Jen. 'He was already middle-aged then. I'm not sure he'll still be practising.'

Jen's phone buzzed in her pocket. She apologized, took it out and looked at it. A text from Ross.

Ask her about Eleanor. Known to him as Nell. The girl Rosco fell for when he was still at school. The girl he named his boat for.

She switched it off and stuck it in her bag. Selina and Terry were staring at her, obviously curious.

'Did you ever meet a woman called Eleanor? Nell. Apparently, he named his boat after her. The first boat that he sailed round the world in.'

'Ah,' Selina said. 'Nelly Wren. She was another of Jeremy's make-believes.'

'She didn't exist?'

'Oh, I think she existed, but nobody could have been as pretty, as innocent or as good as Jem made her out to be. She was his first girlfriend. The love of his life at least. I'm not even sure he actually went out with her.'

'But he married you!'

'Nell was unattainable. Engaged to someone else. I'm not sure why he married me. To distract himself perhaps. We did have a lot of fun together and I adored him, in the beginning at least. He would have loved the adoration. Then the gloss wore off. I'm sure the same would have happened if he'd been married to the perfect Eleanor. His passions were only fleeting. Soon, he'd move on to the next thing: the trip up the Amazon or walking to the North Pole.' A pause. 'Or a younger and more glamorous lover.'

'Is that why you divorced then? He'd found someone else?'

'No,' she said. 'I left him before it happened, but I could

tell he'd decided I wasn't really what he needed. I'd never be able to live up to Nell. When he was drunk, he'd tell me about her, about how lovely she was. There's only so much of that a girl can take.' There was a pause. 'You know what Diana said about Charles and Camilla – that there were always three people in her marriage. That was how it felt with Jem. In a way it was worse because I wasn't even sure that he'd ever made love to her. She was inside his head. The ideal woman. I was real and so I'd never match up.' She smiled at her husband. 'And then I met Terry, who's very real too. He's a builder. Practical like me. This is his development. We married as soon as my divorce came through. Two teenage sons, and we've never looked back.'

'Jeremy had already done his round-the-world trip when you first met him?'

'Yeah, he was still living off the glory of that.'

'Do you know how he raised the money for that first trip? He didn't have a wealthy family, and at that point he wasn't well known outside local sailing circles.'

Selina shrugged. 'I suppose he found some rich backer who'd been taken in by his charms.'

Jen thought about that. Wouldn't a backer want something in return? A company name splashed all over the boat? 'Did Jeremy ever mention anyone specific?'

Selina thought for a moment. 'No. He always said that first trip was down to luck.' A pause and then she grinned. 'Perhaps he'd won the premium bonds!'

The suggestion was meant as a joke, but Jen wondered if it was worth checking out. There was something of the fairy tale about Jem Rosco's background, and a lucky premium bond number didn't seem as outrageous as it might otherwise do.

The contemporary equivalent of five magic beans in *Jack and the Beanstalk*.

'When was the last time you saw your ex-husband?'

'Not very long ago – at the beginning of the summer – and it was quite by chance. I'd been out with some friends in Morrisham, and Terry offered to pick me up after the meal. For some reason the evening ended earlier than I'd expected, and I had forty minutes to wait before we'd arranged for him to collect me. I walked along the prom to kill time. It was one of those beautiful June evenings, when the sun is low over the horizon and seems to send a path of gold across the water.' Selina paused and pulled a face, mocking herself for the poetic thought, before she continued. 'It was midweek and there weren't many people about. That's when I saw Jem. He was sitting on a bench, hardly more than a silhouette in that odd light, but I recognized him. I sat beside him. We hadn't ended on bad terms and I was interested to find out how he was.'

She paused again, caught up, it seemed, in the memory. 'It took him a while to realize who I was, and then he became the old Jem, full of life and chatter, telling funny stories about his last expedition, asking for my news. We were very at ease with each other and I was nearly late meeting Terry. But when I first saw him, from a distance in that dying light, he'd seemed rather old and sad.' Selina looked across the breakfast bar at Jen. 'I'm sure he'd been crying.'

Chapter Sixteen

THE BAR HAD OPENED AGAIN WHEN Jonathan arrived and Matthew heard his husband before he saw him, calling across the room to Harry. 'Hello, mate, lovely to see you again!' His theatre group must have stayed in the Maiden's when they were on their tour.

'Your bloke's in the back.' Harry's reply was warm, welcoming. Of course. Jonathan made friends wherever he went.

Venn was alone in the snug, his makeshift office. He thought the team would be here in Greystone for a while, unless there was a sudden break in the case. More storms were forecast for later in the week. There were flood warnings, and the tides were high. If they left Greystone now, there was no guarantee that they'd get back.

There was still a little light left in the day and the couple went for a walk, through the village and along the jetty. They sat there for a while, their backs to the wall, watching the dying sun catch the waves as they broke on the shingle.

'Thanks for bringing my stuff.' Matthew could never quite

put into words what Jonathan meant to him. It always came out like this: boring and banal.

'I wanted to see you,' Jonathan said. 'I miss you when you're not there.' A pause. 'Besides, it's good to get away for a while. There's something I need to decide.'

'Would it help to talk?'

'Not yet. My shit. My decision.'

Matthew felt a sting of rejection, but said nothing, and Jonathan went on speaking. 'I'm meeting an old friend tomorrow. He's a teacher at the high school in Morrisham, so we're catching up for an early lunch.'

'How old is he, your teacher friend?'

'Mid-sixties, just about to retire. He arrived there in his early twenties as a newly qualified teacher, and has been there for the whole of his career. He teaches art and brings a group of sixth-formers to the Woodyard to most of our exhibitions. We run workshops for them.' Jonathan squeezed Matthew's arm. 'There's no competition, I promise! He's grey and wrinkled and very unfit.'

'He could have taught Rosco,' Venn said. 'And Davy Gregory and Harry Carter here.'

'You're surely not asking me to interfere in your work?' His voice was still teasing but it had an edge. Matthew had accused him of doing that once before and he still hadn't forgotten the hurt of it.

'No,' Matthew said. 'Of course not.' He stood up and held out a hand to pull Jonathan to his feet. The only light now came from street lamps in the village and a flashing buoy marking the entrance to the harbour.

Ross had returned to the Maiden's Prayer when they got back. Jonathan stayed in the bar, chatting to Harry, drinking the local cider, joining in a game of darts. Venn caught up with Ross in the snug.

'So, at least we know a bit more now about Jeremy Rosco.' Venn was drinking coffee, his elbows on the table. He needed a sharp mind for this. At the moment, everything seemed woolly and blurred at the edges. There was little that was concrete to get hold of. Even Ross, usually so fixated with facts, was speaking of impressions and feelings.

'Bartholomew Lawson,' Ross said. 'Commodore of the sailing club, husband of Nelly Wren and general pisshead. He really didn't like our victim. He called him a little oik.' A pause. 'I think he was jealous. Really, really jealous. There was this boy from a single-parent home who swanned into the yacht club and was a better sailor, and who then had the nerve to fall for Lawson's girl.'

'Jealous enough to kill him after all this time?' Venn was sceptical. But envy was corrosive. If he were still religious, he'd say that it ate away at the soul. He'd seen colleagues, brooding, desperate, because someone else had been given the promotion they'd thought should be theirs.

'To be honest, I don't think he'd be upright in the early hours of the morning, never mind competent enough to organize that sort of murder.' Ross paused. 'He has a taxi to take him home every night. The guy got out to help him into the car. I recognized him from the photo you circulated.'

'Davy Gregory?'

Ross nodded.

'Did they seem friendly?'

'Not what you'd call friendly. Even drunk, Lawson still thought he was boss, but they knew each other well enough. Gregory appeared to be acting like some sort of minder.'

'I've heard back from Jen,' Matthew said. 'It sounds as if Rosco was obsessed by Lawson's wife. She was a part of his life, in his imagination at least, even when he was married to someone else.'

'I suppose,' Ross said, 'that would be a kind of motive for Lawson, but I still can't see him as a killer. And why now, after all this time?'

'I'll go and see Eleanor Lawson tomorrow.' This woman seemed to have haunted the dead man's dreams since he was a boy.

'Want me to come along?' There was little enthusiasm behind the offer. Middle-aged women didn't quite catch Ross May's interest.

'No.' Matthew's voice sounded sharper than he'd intended. He realized that he'd caught something of Rosco's obsession with the woman. Now, he wanted to form his own impression of her, and it would be easier to do that alone.

'I still need to get those soil samples from Sammy Barton.' Venn thought that should already have been done, but said nothing. He was learning to pick his battles with Ross. 'Then, can you see if Rosco still owned an apartment on the Morrisham seafront? Selina, his ex, saw him there at the beginning of the summer.' He paused for a moment. 'And, through Selina, Jen has tracked down his lawyer, the guy who once was his lawyer at least. He went by the name of Rodney Bottle. I'm sure you'll be able to find out if he's still working in the town, or if someone has taken over from him.'

'If Rosco owned a place locally, why come to stay in Greystone?' Ross said. 'Especially if Eleanor was his mystery woman.'

Venn thought for a moment. 'I think when we know that, we'll know who killed him.'

He stood up. He wanted to speak to Jonathan. He felt home-sick for the long, low house by the estuary. He wished they were there, alone.

Chapter Seventeen

THEY WOKE EARLY AGAIN. JONATHAN WAS immediately out of bed, making tea, planning a swim; sea swimming was a recent passion, a daily ritual when they were at home. From the bedroom window, Matthew watched him walk across the street and into the shadowy water, and stayed watching until Jonathan strode back onto the shore, laughing and shaking the water from his hair like a dog. Matthew ran downstairs to his car then and drove off, before Jonathan came back and saw him. He felt like a voyeur, as if Jonathan was a stranger and he had no right to be staring.

Driving inland, there was mist on the low ground and a strange diffuse light filtering the rising sun. The Lawson house was some way inland of Morrisham, surrounded by woodland and a high stone wall. Matthew left his car on the road and walked up a twisting drive through trees. He hadn't expected the grounds to be so extensive. There was a small pool, almost a lake, with a jetty rising out of it. Everything was untamed, a little overgrown, as if the place had seen better days.

A wooden swing on long ropes hung from a huge tree on

the lawn. Ross hadn't mentioned the Lawsons ever having had children, but perhaps it had been left there by former owners. Matthew had a brief moment of temptation. What would it be like to swing in long arcs under the tree? The whole place had a dreamlike, ghostly quality. He imagined a grand Edwardian party, children playing, jumping from the jetty into the lake, adults dressed in white sitting on blankets on the grass, enjoying an elaborate picnic as they watched.

Only then did he remember that he had been in this garden before, and that he *had* briefly been on the swing. The memory returned with a force that stopped him in his tracks. He shut his eyes and he was on the swing, his head tilted back, the sun filtering through the leaves onto his face as he moved. It was the height of summer. It had been one of the Greystone Brethren outings and he'd been very young. Four? Five? His mother had been wearing a pretty yellow dress with a white belt. He had a picture of her laughing, obviously relaxed, eating an ice cream cone. The lawn had been crowded with people.

A cockerel had been crowing since he'd left the car, and now it brought Venn back to the present, to the chilly autumn morning. He turned a curve in the drive, and he saw a woman walking ahead of him, carrying a basket of eggs, most of them brown with muck. She could almost have stepped out of his daydream, but she must have heard his footsteps on the gravel, because she stopped and turned.

'Hello.' She sounded surprised, but friendly enough.

Venn could see how she'd got her nickname. She was small, a little round, and dressed all in brown apart from black wellington boots: long brown mackintosh over a skirt and jersey, the colour of the earth, the coat unbuttoned.

'My name's Matthew Venn,' he said. 'I'm a detective,

investigating the death of Jeremy Rosco.' A pause. 'You must be Eleanor Lawson. I wondered if I could talk to you?'

'Ah,' she said. 'Poor Jeremy. I always thought he'd meet a dramatic end, but I didn't imagine anything like this.'

They walked on side by side up the drive. There were bushes and shrubs on either side, everything covered in cobwebs, lacy and sparkling with dew. They turned another bend in the track and then the house became visible. It was large and grey, a Victorian Gothic pile with a turret in one corner and stone steps leading to a grand front door. Another jolt of memory, although Venn thought he'd never been inside. Through a first-floor window, he saw a face. A rocking horse, paint faded, which seemed to be staring out at him. Eleanor saw him looking up and laughed.

'That's Dobbin, mine when I was a girl here. I haven't had the heart to get rid of him, although we never had children of our own.' Sadness in her voice.

'I think I've been here before. Some sort of garden party. It would have been about thirty years ago.'

'Ah, my parents would have been running the place then. They threw the gardens open every midsummer's eve in aid of the lifeboat.' A pause. 'It's all become rather run-down since then. I don't think anyone would consider it worth paying for a visit now.'

'You grew up here?'

'I did! It's been in the family since it was built. My great-grandfather came over from Ireland and made his fortune. He founded the Greystone quarry on the coast and owned most of the village there at one time. Now this house is all that is left.'

Another connection, Venn thought. *Another complication.*

She led him round the side of the house and in through a small door to a stone-flagged room, smelling of dogs and mud, where she took off her boots and hung up her coat. He hesitated for a moment, wondering if he should take off his shoes, and she noticed his awkwardness.

'No, no, they're perfectly clean. Cleaner than anything else in this place. We don't have any help in the house these days.'

The kitchen was big and cluttered, but actually not dirty. The windows were clear and there was no grease on the work surfaces. Venn thought that little would have changed since the place had been built. A retriever lay on a mat in front of a giant range. Eleanor moved him gently with her foot, to slide a kettle onto the hot plate.

'This is Frankie. He's so very old, and he spends most of his time asleep. There's always been a Frankie in the house, but I suspect we won't replace him when he dies.'

For a moment she seemed so sad again that Venn had the urge to comfort her, but she turned to him, her voice bright. 'Tea or coffee? And will you have some breakfast? All these eggs need to be used, and Barty rarely emerges until lunchtime after an evening at the sailing club. Some days I seem to live on eggs, and what I can scavenge from the garden.' A pause and a grin. 'It's a wonder I can shit at all!'

That shocked and amused him at the same time, which is what, he suspected, she intended.

'No need for breakfast,' he said. 'I had some at the Maiden's Prayer before I set out. But I'd love some tea.'

'Is that where you're staying? Well, I hear it's a lot more comfortable than it used to be.' She looked across at him. 'But then, Greystone has never been a particularly comfortable place for us. They still blame my father for selling the quarry to a national company, and besides, we're a Catholic family. You know that most of the village is Barum Brethren?'

Venn nodded.

'We're considered worse than heathen.'

It was leaf tea, made in a cream china pot. She brought out mugs and a strainer, and poured milk from a carton in the fridge into a jug. 'I still have some standards.' Another grin.

They sat opposite each other at a table covered by an oilskin cloth, patterned with small red flowers.

'So,' she said. 'What do you want to know about Jeremy?'

'He named his first boat after you.'

'So he did.'

'You were very close?'

'Very close,' she agreed, 'when we were young.'

'According to his wife, you were always the love of his life.'

She bent to stroke the dog's head, so Matthew couldn't see her face. 'Ah,' she said. 'Perhaps he was always the love of mine.'

'So, what happened?' *What kept you apart?*

'I was young when we first met. Easily influenced. My family didn't take to him. They thought it was all this that he wanted. Not me.' She made a sweeping gesture to include the house and the land outside. 'I knew that wasn't the case. He was a romantic soul. But restless. I realized I'd never keep him at home.' She sat upright again. 'I suppose I went for the safer option.'

'Bartholomew Lawson?'

She nodded. 'Barty and I had been pals since we were toddlers. Our families were friends and we went to the same church, took our first communion on the same day. He got sent away to boarding school; I was a day pupil at the convent school in Bideford. We met up in the holidays.'

'You joined the sailing club?'

She nodded. 'Where his father was commodore.'

And *he*, Matthew thought, was the man for whom Matilda Gregory's father had worked. A coincidence? Probably. In these small communities, everyone was linked in one way or another.

Eleanor was still speaking: 'Jem became a junior member on the same day.'

'And fell for you.'

'Fell for the thought of me. The idea of me.'

'You were already going out with Barty at that point?'

'I suppose I was. We'd snogged certainly, and he'd taken me to the pictures. He felt a certain kind of ownership.' For the first time, her voice was hard.

'Do you know how Rosco got the money to buy his first boat?'

She laughed and Venn saw her as the girl she once had been. 'That was pure luck! Classic Jem. You couldn't make it up.'

Venn said nothing and waited for her to tell the story.

'He and a couple of friends were beachcombing,' she said. 'He found a piece of jewellery on the tideline, mixed with the sea glass, the shells and the weed. A locket. Gold. The catch was broken and it must have dropped from the owner's neck. There'd been a picture inside. The saltwater had rotted that away, but there was an inscription on the back. *My darling Grace*. He could have sold it for the value of the gold, but as I told you, he had a romantic nature. He wanted to trace the woman who'd owned it. He asked me to help him.'

'And you found her?' Venn thought Eleanor was a great storyteller. He was already caught up with the narrative.

'We did! He was like a terrier when he set his mind to something. She was an elderly woman called Grace Fanshaw, and she lived in one of those stately Georgian houses in Morrisham High Street.'

'How did he track her down?'

'There aren't that many women of the right vintage who regularly walked the beach. Jem and I asked around. It seemed that Grace's lover had given the locket to her when she was a girl. It was old, already an antique, when the man bought it, but he had the inscription done. He was a naval officer and there was an accident in the Atlantic just after the war. He drowned. She never married and seemed haunted by the sea.' Eleanor looked up at Venn. She seemed close to tears, but Matthew wasn't convinced by the tale. It seemed like something a man like Rosco might make up from fragments of other stories, scraps from films and popular television dramas. Rosco had been the hero of his own adventure story.

Eleanor must have sensed his scepticism. 'I met her,' she said. 'She and Jem became friends of a kind. He visited her regularly, did her shopping and kept her company. She was very frail by the end. She stopped her daily walks on the beach, but he pushed her along the prom in a wheelchair. He was kind to her. She had no family.'

Matthew was starting to guess what was coming. 'Grace remembered Jeremy in her will.'

Eleanor nodded. 'She left him everything. The house and all her savings. It was enough for him to get the *Nelly Wren* and to plan his trip.'

'There was definitely no family?'

She shrugged. 'Nobody local. I think there was a nephew. I remember Jem was contacted by some lawyer in London, who queried the will, but though Grace was frail in body, she was in sound mind. There was nothing they could do.'

'You and Jem must have been close at that time,' Venn said, 'if you went with him to visit Grace.'

'We were friends. Close friends.' She sounded a little defensive.

'You were still going out with Barty?' *Pleasing the family. Keeping your options open.* 'He told one of my detectives that he didn't know how Jeremy got the money for his round-the-world adventure.'

'I was young! I couldn't take anything too seriously. And Barty was away, first at school and then at university. I always stayed at home.'

'It was serious for Jeremy, though, wasn't it?'

Silence. 'He was heading out on his trip,' Eleanor said at last, 'and his head was full of his boat and the sea. Of becoming the youngest man to sail single-handed round the world. When we met up, the talk was all about that. It seemed as if I was his audience. Nothing more.'

'Did he ask you to wait for him?' Venn thought that was the kind of romantic gesture the man might have made.

She was as still as the stone her grandfather had cut from the quarry. Outside the kitchen window a robin was singing. 'He did. But he was drunk, that night before he set off, wild with excitement. I thought it would be forgotten by morning.'

'But he'd meant it. And when he came home, you were engaged to Bartholomew Lawson?'

Another silence.

'I was,' she said at last. 'I've regretted it every day since.' She looked at him. 'Jem turned up here, the day before the wedding, asking me to run away with him. He'd proved what sort of man he was, he said.' There was a long silence. 'I didn't have the courage to do it.'

'Had you heard from him recently? We know he was expecting a visitor at the place he was renting at Greystone.'

'No,' she said. 'I knew that he wouldn't ask again. Jem had too much pride. It would have been different if I'd gone to him, and I wish I'd contacted him years ago. But I wasn't brave enough, and, by then, I could tell that Barty needed me. I'd made my choice and I had a duty to live with it. If I'd left, there'd be nothing remaining of him. It would have been easier if we'd had children. He'd have been a different man then.' A pause. 'But that was down to me too. It was *my* body that let us down. I suppose I felt we had to rattle along together.'

There was another, longer silence. She was stroking the dog and Venn thought the conversation might be over. He was about to get to his feet to leave, when she started speaking again, her voice flat and sad.

'Jem was always in my head. In my dreams, he was a potential escape from a meaningless relationship. I thought that if I really couldn't stand it any more, I'd get in touch with him and he'd gallop to the rescue. No judgement. No recrimination. We'd sail away into the sunset. We'd have fun. The possibility kept me going through the dark times. Now the hope is gone and everything seems rather bleak.' She looked up and gave a wry smile. 'But of course, I'll survive. I love this house and I have a better life than most. Besides, I can't complain because, as I've explained, it was my choice. How do the young describe it? My bad.'

Now, Matthew Venn did get to his feet to go. Eleanor walked with him to the back door. The sun was up and the dew on the cobwebs had disappeared. The long swing hung still from the tree in the middle of the lawn. Before he reached the bend in the drive, Matthew stopped to look back at the house. There was a face at an upstairs window – human, not a wooden horse. Bartholomew Lawson, staring down at him.

Chapter Eighteen

Ross was still in the Maiden's Prayer when Venn arrived back there from the Lawsons' house. Gwen Gregory had cleared the table of the remnants of his late breakfast and he was working at his laptop. 'I went to see Barton first thing. I met Brian there and he got the soil samples you were after.'

The boss nodded. 'How was Barton? Any resistance?'

Ross thought about that. 'Not really. He was polite enough. He said the weather's due to break again tomorrow night.'

Venn seemed preoccupied. 'Have you seen Jonathan?'

'Yeah,' Ross said, 'we had breakfast together when he came back from his swim. He said he was going into Morrisham. Jen's on her way. She won't be long. She called into Appledore to see how the CSIs were getting on with the dinghy. Nothing useful so far.'

Venn nodded. Ross thought it was always impossible to tell what he was thinking. What was the word? Inscrutable. That was the boss to a tee.

'So, I've been to see Eleanor Lawson,' Venn said. 'I know now how Rosco got the cash to buy his first boat.'

Ross listened to the story of Grace Fanshaw and the finding of the gold locket. It all seemed very unlikely to him. It could have been a kids' fairy tale, or something out of the women's magazines Mel read when they were on holiday.

'Did you believe it?'

'There's something so weird about this investigation that I'd believe almost anything.'

That didn't sound like Venn, who was rational and always instilled in them that the facts mattered more than guesswork, or any notion of gut feeling.

Matthew was still talking. 'We can check, though. There'll be a record of the will. A distant relative contested it.' He paused. 'If Rosco was waiting for a mysterious woman, surely it must have been Eleanor Lawson. She was obviously the love of his life. But she looks nothing like the woman Alan Ford described as getting out of the car on the night of the murder, and she denies being there, or even having heard from Rosco recently. Why would she lie?'

May thought this was obvious. He wondered if the boss was losing his grip. 'Because she killed him?'

'Why would she do that? After all this time. And she came across to me as rather a gentle soul.'

Ross was tempted to remind Venn about the importance of sticking to the facts, not relying on superficial impressions of character or personality, but at the last minute he held his tongue. Probably best not to provoke him while he was in such a strange mood. 'Rosco's solicitor, Rodney Bottle, is still alive and willing to talk to us. His son runs his business now, but Rodney remembers Rosco. He sounds as if he has stories to tell. I've said we'd see him at his place in Morrisham.'

'Great. It seems we're finally getting some real information on our man.'

'And I've tracked down the freeholder of the flat Rosco still owned in Morrisham. The concierge has a key and will let us in. They can't remember the man using it for ages.'

'Why did he pay to stay here in Greystone when he could have stayed in his own flat in Morrisham?' The same question again, but this time Venn seemed not to expect an answer. He hadn't taken a seat when he came into the room, and now he was pacing, walking backwards and forwards in front of the unlit fire.

Ross May answered all the same. 'Perhaps the flat's a dump. There might not even be any furniture in there.'

Venn came to a rest. 'You might be right. Let's go and find out, shall we?'

From the outside, Rosco's Morrisham home was definitely more an apartment than a flat, and was far from being a dump. The individual blocks must recently have been painted, because they were startling white in the autumn sunshine. The apartments were arranged in wide steps, each looking out at the sea, giving the impression of a cliff sloping away from the shore. On the ground floor, there was a bar, sleek and stylish. Rosco's apartment was on the top floor of the five-storey building, and would surely have a spectacular view of the coast.

Inside, the communal areas were spacious. There was a discreetly positioned lift, but a grand staircase also led up to each floor. Glossy-leaved pot plants were as tall as small trees. It felt more like a hotel than an apartment block. The building might have been built relatively recently, but there was a sense of an older, more gracious age. The idea that a concierge was available on site to provide a service to residents seemed odd, anachronistic. Ross couldn't imagine what a place here would cost.

The man who met them in the lobby was small and dapper. Elderly but well-preserved. His bald head shone as if it had been polished. He'd worked there since the flats had been built, he said, and remembered Mr Rosco as an early resident.

'He'd just come back from the round-the-world race, and he was famous. The developer felt it was a coup that he'd chosen to take up residence here. There was a lot of local publicity about his homecoming. I suspect he got rather a good discount. Having Jem Rosco here certainly attracted other people to buy.'

'Had he stayed recently?'

The bald head shook. 'I haven't seen him for a number of years. I suspect he regarded the apartment as an investment these days.'

'He could have let it out,' Ross said. 'Airbnb or a holiday rental. A site like this, he'd make a fortune.'

The head shook again, and the voice sounded disapproving. 'That's not allowed within the original purchase contract, though we suspect that occasionally the rules *are* broken.' Despite his age, he'd not bothered with the lift and was walking ahead of them up the carpeted stairs. His movement was sprightly. He was almost dancing. 'Many of our residents are elderly now, and I've had complaints about rowdy gatherings. When I've checked, the people inside always claim to be relatives of the residents.' He paused, not, Ross thought, because he needed to draw breath but to emphasize his disapproval. 'The stories are so similar that I suspect some sort of agreed fabrication.'

'A cover story suggested by the owners?'

'Indeed.' He continued bounding ahead of them up the stairs.

They came out into a wide hallway, where, ahead of them, was a huge window looking out over the bay. In the evening, the sunshine would be flooding in, but even now, in late morning, the space was airy, filled with light. There were two doors, one to the left and one to the right. The man turned left. 'This is Mr Rosco's apartment.' He pulled out a bunch of keys.

'That's fine.' Venn had managed to position himself between the man and the door, but still sounded polite. 'If you can let us have the key, we can take it from here.'

Ross half expected an objection, but the man only nodded, slipped a key off the ring and handed it to Venn. He smiled. 'If you need me, I'll be waiting downstairs.' And he'd gone.

Venn unlocked the door. They moved straight into a large living room, with double glass doors leading onto a balcony formed by one of the steps of the building. While the lower floors were two apartments wide, and the back one would have no view, this one covered the whole width of the block. It was, Ross thought, like the top of a pyramid, self-contained and glorious. There were two white leather sofas and a glass coffee table, all a little dated, but substantial, expensive pieces. Through an open door, they saw a kitchen, with marble work-tops and upmarket appliances. Also in white. There were two bedrooms, each with its own bathroom.

Venn pulled a gloved finger across a pale chest of drawers in the largest bedroom. 'No dust. If Rosco really hasn't stayed here for years, there must be a cleaner.'

Ross was again reminded of being in a plush hotel. A rich

relative of Mel's had bought them a night in a flash place in London as a wedding present before they jetted off to the Canaries on honeymoon, and this had the same vibe. Great for one night, but not very homely. He wasn't sure that he'd want to live here.

'Why wouldn't he wait here for his mysterious visitor?' Ross couldn't understand it. It might not be very cosy, but this was a palace in comparison to the cold, damp cottage in Greystone. 'It's so much more comfortable than where he was staying when he died.'

Venn considered the question seriously. 'Because he didn't want people to know he was back in the area? I imagine word would soon get out if he was staying here. Especially if, as the concierge said, most of them were of the same vintage as him. He'd be recognized.'

'He was in hiding?'

'Well, that seems a little melodramatic, but perhaps. Not for any sinister reason, but because he didn't want the hassle. Maybe he had things to do that made it necessary for him to go under the radar, and not play the role of great adventurer for a week or two.' Venn had walked back into the living room and was staring out at the sea. 'Of course, there might be another reason.' The boss seemed to be talking to himself, and not to Ross at all. 'Perhaps the mysterious visitor was a fiction, made up by Rosco to explain his presence in the village. Perhaps, all along, he was there to meet a local.' He turned so he was looking back at Ross. 'I think that's where our focus should be.'

Ross thought this meant they were about to head back to Greystone, but the boss continued prowling around the room. He landed in front of three small photos, framed and propped on a shelf. He stood staring at them, searching, it seemed, for some link to their investigation.

'That must have been Eleanor with Rosco when they first met.'

May looked too. Two young people stood on a shingle beach next to a wooden dinghy. Both had their jeans rolled up to their knees and the water washed over their feet. The girl was small, with pixie-cut hair. The boy wasn't much taller, and was obviously Rosco. Both wore sweatshirts with MYC embroidered on the chest.

'Morrisham Yacht Club, don't you think?' Again, Venn didn't seem to expect a response. 'But that's not the beach here in Morrisham. It could be Greystone. Eleanor's grandfather owned the quarry there at one point, so there would have been a connection.' A pause. 'This would have been long before selfies became popular. I wonder who took the photo?'

The next picture was of three young people, aged fifteen or sixteen. This could have been taken on Greystone beach too. Certainly, there was a grey backdrop, shingle in the foreground and cliffs behind them. The light was poor. It was almost dusk and they were sitting around a makeshift firepit, dug out of the pebbles, driftwood was burning and they had cans in their hands. May thought it was some sort of beach party. He recognized Rosco, right at the centre, because of his small stature, but the photo was so blurred that his features meant nothing. He couldn't tell the others from each other.

The third picture was of an elderly lady. She was sitting in a wheelchair. The young Rosco was standing behind her. The woman had turned her face towards him and was smiling with great affection.

'That must be Grace Fanshaw,' Venn said. 'She does seem

very fond of him. You can believe, looking at this, that she might have left him her fortune.' He looked back at Ross. 'Let's bag them. I'm not sure if it would be technically possible, but it'd be great if we can improve the quality in some way. I'd like to know if that really is Greystone, and it would be good to ID the three kids round the fire. I'm pretty sure that one of them is Rosco and he might have kept in touch with the others.'

The concierge was waiting for them in the lobby as he'd promised. He was chatting to a frail older woman, who seemed likely to be a resident. He took her arm and helped her into the lift before turning back to them. Ross thought the owners would miss him when he finally retired. Perhaps he was the reason why some stayed so long.

'All done?' The voice was cheery. Rosco's death seemed not to have affected him personally.

'For now,' Venn said. 'Did Mr Rosco employ a cleaner?'

'Not exactly. It's a service the freeholder provides for an extra service fee. Lynn goes in once a month to air the place and keep it clean. She's here today if you'd like to speak to her.'

Ross waited for his boss to make a positive reply, but Venn shook his head. 'I'll take her contact details, though, in case we need them.'

Then they were back outside in the bright autumn sunshine.

Chapter Nineteen

MATTHEW STOOD FOR A MOMENT OUTSIDE the apartment block, looking out at the sea, thinking again about Rosco.

'We need to trace his movements in the weeks before he blew in to Greystone. He must have another home, possibly another family. It's as if he just appeared from nowhere.' He couldn't get any sort of grasp of Rosco the man, apart from the public persona: rugged, amiable, a little reckless.

'Vicki's working on it. And his solicitor might be able to help.'

'Maybe, but something specific brought him back to North Devon, and I want to know what it was.' Rationally, Venn understood that it wasn't Ross May's fault that they had so little information about Rosco, but he needed an outlet for the frustration, someone to blame. 'The train ticket would suggest he came from Liverpool. I know Vicki has been in touch with colleagues there, but we haven't heard anything back, have we? Let's push for a bit of speed. Can you prioritize tracking his recent movements? Have we got mobile records? Bank withdrawals?'

'As far as we've been able to find out, Rosco didn't own a mobile. Unless it was a pay as you go. It wasn't in the cottage.'

'Did he own a car? Just because he got the train doesn't mean he didn't have a vehicle. It's a killer of a drive and a driving licence or passport might give us a more recent address.'

'We've checked,' Ross said. 'He always gives the Morrisham apartment as his permanent home.'

'There must be a reason for him doing that.'

'What are you thinking?' Ross asked. 'Some kind of criminal activity?'

Matthew was about to discount the idea, but then he thought perhaps he could see the dead man being up to something piratical: smuggling booze or cigarettes, or even people. Rosco would love the risk and excitement of the venture and he wouldn't be the first charismatic individual to consider himself exempt from the rules other people had to follow. After all, politicians did it all the time.

'It's worth considering . . .'

'So, he might have another identity.'

'But there was no unopened mail in the apartment, and the concierge says he hasn't been there for months.' Matthew thought he'd been so seduced by the romance of the love story between Rosco and Eleanor that he hadn't focused sufficiently when they'd been looking at the flat. 'There'd surely be something. Council tax and utility bills. Junk mail. Even if the cleaner had picked it up, there'd have been a pile somewhere.'

'Perhaps it was forwarded somewhere by the concierge?'

'Wouldn't he have told us?' Matthew had already turned to go back into the building to find him. The frustration was building. Then, glancing into the cafe bar on the ground floor of the block, he saw Jonathan sitting at a high table in the window. He was talking to an older man, who did indeed have wrinkles and grey hair, pulled back into a ponytail. This must be the art teacher friend. Matthew looked at his watch. It was just past midday. The pair were in earnest conversation, and Jonathan was sitting side on to the window. He wasn't looking outside.

'Who's that guy with your bloke?' Ross had seen Jonathan too.

'Why?' Matthew felt his temper fraying. Ross had a tendency to gossip.

'He was in the sailing club when I went to see Bartholomew Lawson. Just a member, I guess.'

Matthew didn't answer. He knew it wasn't Jonathan's fault, but yet again he felt that his two worlds were colliding. Perhaps he should never have asked his husband to come to Greystone. Life was complicated enough. He said nothing and led May back into the building.

They found the concierge in his little office, the door open, so he could watch the residents coming and going. He'd miss nothing. If Rosco *had* been here, surely he'd know.

'Inspector, how can I help you now?' The man was smiling, but there was an edge of irritation in his voice.

'Mr Rosco's mail,' Venn said.

'Yes?' The same smile.

'What happens to it? I assume he receives some at this address. Do you forward it to him?'

'Ah, I don't. No.'

'But you must know what happens to it!' Venn could feel the tension in the muscles of his face and heard it in his voice.

He tried to breathe more slowly and to smile back. 'After all, you know everything that goes on here.'

The man's eyes flickered in acknowledgement of the compliment and the accuracy of the judgement. 'I think Mr Rosco came to some arrangement with his cleaner.'

'That's Lynn, who's working here today?'

'Yes.' A pause. 'I'm afraid I wasn't privy to the arrangement. Normally I carry out that sort of service for our residents.' He gave a little sniff.

'Where can I find Lynn?'

'Ah, I'm afraid you've just missed her. She left soon after you did.'

'I didn't see anyone leave the building with us.'

'She left,' the concierge said, enjoying the exchange now, 'through the back door. I believe I gave you her contact details. I'm sure you'll find her at home.'

Lynn Johnson lived on a housing association estate on the edge of the town. Even in the sunshine, the grey concrete was dispiriting. The place might have been built at the same time as the block where Rosco had his flat, but was a world away in terms of facilities and upkeep. Lynn's home was a semi on a long street, which curved through the length of the development. It was one of the smarter premises, with a window box hanging by the door and a neatly cut lawn. Next door had a window boarded up and a stained mattress in the garden. Lynn's car was parked on the street outside. An old Fiesta, which would probably not make it through another MOT.

She must just have come in, because when she opened the door to them, she was still wearing an anorak. That too had seen better days. She was in her fifties, thin and nervy, and she regarded them with an air of suspicion.

'Yes?'

'Mrs Johnson, we're detectives—'

She interrupted before Venn could finish the sentence. 'If you're after Dean, he's not here. He's back in rehab. Which is where he should have been from the start. Not locked up in a cell all day so he ended up nearly killing himself. I'm his mother, but I still couldn't look after him properly.' The words running over themselves.

'We're not looking for Dean. And I'm sorry he's not well.'

The suspicion remained. 'Addiction's an illness, and he's always had problems, even as a boy.'

'It's you we'd like to speak to, Mrs Johnson, not your son. Perhaps we could come in?'

She stepped aside, with a quick glance at the street to check the neighbours weren't watching.

'I don't have anything to do with drugs.' The thought obviously horrified her. 'You should go next door. Strangers turning up every hour of the day and night. If you're looking for a dealer on this estate—'

This time, it was Venn who interrupted. 'We're investigating Jeremy Rosco's murder, Mrs Johnson. This is nothing to do with drugs.'

'Oh!' At last, she fell silent. 'You'd best come into the lounge then. Poor Jeremy.' She shrugged herself out of the anorak.

The lounge was small but immaculately clean, dominated by a large television.

'You do clean Mr Rosco's flat?'

'Not a proper clean. He's never there, is he? So, no marks on the paintwork or spills on the kitchen tiles. I just dust and put the hoover over once a month. Open the windows while I'm there to let in some fresh air.'

'You were there this morning?'

'Yes, first thing. I start at the top of the block and work down. I do the communal areas every day.'

'And you collected Mr Rosco's mail as usual? Even though you knew he was dead?'

'Well, I'd seen the news, of course, and I didn't know what to do with the letters.' Lynn was sitting on the edge of a grey velour armchair. Matthew thought she'd seldom sit still. She was already twitchy, wanting to be up and moving. 'I didn't want to leave them there, making the place look untidy, and most of it was junk and could go in the bin anyway. Jem always said to use my judgement. No point sending on a pile of advertising. But if there was anything I wasn't sure about, I should send it on.'

'Have you already posted it?'

'I haven't had a chance, have I? Only just got in when you knocked. I was going to take it to the post office this afternoon, when I'd had a bit of dinner.'

'Even though you knew he was dead?'

'It doesn't get sent to him, does it? It's a different name with the address. So, *they* wouldn't have died. *They'd* know what to do with it.'

'What would you usually do, with the post you collect every month?' Venn kept the tone easy, conversational. She was already nervous, her bony fingers twisting the material of her trousers. 'Did you just forward each letter individually?'

'No! Jeremy said to send them all off in one go each month. It'd be less bother. He bought a pile of these last time I saw him. Enough to last a year, he said.' She opened a cupboard in the sideboard and showed him a pile of white padded envelopes. 'And he gave me money for the postage too, more than enough.' A pause. 'And he paid me for doing it. Thirty quid a month. Not bad just for packing them up and taking the envelope to the post office. Jem Rosco was always generous, though. I was paid by the company that owned the flats, but he always left a bit extra for me.'

Venn let that statement go for a while. It sounded as if Lynn had cleaned for the man while he was still in permanent residence in the apartment. 'Could we see the mail you picked up today, please?'

She fetched a large handbag from the hall, pulled out first an overall and then half a dozen envelopes. 'See, I'd ditch these.' She put obvious circulars on the arm of her chair. 'You can tell they're just junk. But I'd send those two on.'

'And where would you send them?' Venn asked. 'Of course, we'd like the address. And the name of the person who received them. I'll take care of those letters too. Have you got an evidence bag, Constable?'

Ross held open the bag and Lynn dropped them inside. Now she was wide-eyed and serious.

'If you could just let us have that forwarding address,' Venn said.

'It's here.' She picked up a card from the mantelpiece. 'You take it. I know it off by heart now. Years I've been forwarding Jeremy's mail.'

Venn slipped the card into an inside pocket without looking at it. He didn't want Lynn to know how important it might be and he'd wait until they were back at the Maiden's and he had time to consider it properly. Now he focused all his attention on the cleaner.

'You've known Mr Rosco for a long time? Perhaps since he first moved into the flats?'

'Oh, I knew him before that!' Lynn seemed a little more relaxed now. 'I was at school with him. Morrisham comp.'

'Really?' Matthew didn't have to feign interest.

'Well, there was only one high school in the town. Still is. And we were in the same year group.'

'You were friends?'

'Yeah. In the same set. Never part of the swotty gang. Then he joined the sailing club and mixed in different circles.'

Of course, Matthew thought. *Then he met Eleanor. And Bartholomew Lawson.*

'You came across him again when he came back from sailing round the world and bought the apartment on the seafront?'

'I needed a job that would keep me going all year round, not something seasonal that only paid out in the summer. I had a kid to support by then and the father ditched me as soon as our Dean was born. I like cleaning. It's useful and you can see the results. And then there he was in that flash apartment at the top of the block. Living like a film star! It was a real surprise when I saw him there. He recognized me, though. No airs and graces.'

'You didn't need to forward his mail at that point?'

'Nah, he was living in the apartment full time then, wasn't he? He'd get me in to clear up after his parties.'

Matthew, who was sensitive to any form of slight, wondered what this must have been like for Lynn. Once Rosco had been a friend, but she'd ended up skivvying for him.

Perhaps she guessed what he was thinking. 'He was being kind,' she said. 'He knew things were tough for me but I wouldn't want a handout. Not from the state and not from him. He paid well above the going rate, and I'd get to take home all the fancy leftovers. There were days when I ate better than a king.'

Matthew thought he'd rather go hungry, but pride had always been his greatest sin.

'You must have known his first wife.'

'Selena. Lovely girl. She wasn't at school with us but I'd seen her around. Her dad owned a fancy clothes shop in the high street. I couldn't understand why she left him. They seemed dead happy. That was when Jeremy started working away more.'

'And when he asked you to forward his letters?'

'That came later. Desmond, the concierge, dealt with any mail at first and Jeremy was still home more often then. It was before he was off on his travels for the telly. He asked me to look after the post a couple of years ago. He said he'd found a new base. Somewhere a bit more convenient for his work. And he could trust me not to be nosy.'

'Is Desmond nosy?' Ross broke in at this point. He was never much good at just listening.

Lynn considered the question. 'Well, yes, he's nosy, though I can't see him steaming open Jeremy's letters.' She gave a snort of derision. 'I don't think he'd stoop to that.'

'Did you ever meet Jeremy's friend Eleanor?' Matthew asked.

'I never met her. She didn't go to the same school as us. She went to the convent in Bideford. The place with the fancy uniform. But Jeremy talked about her.'

'Oh?'

'She lived in a big house out of town. She still does, I think. I remember him telling me he'd been invited to a party there. It happened not long after Jeremy got back from that first big trip, the one that made his name. I was in his flat cleaning the afternoon of the same day. He was all in a dither. So excited and full of it. I suppose it was a kind of acceptance, getting to go to a party in the big house. He'd be the celebrity, wouldn't he? All the people from the sailing club, who'd once looked down on him, would be there. He was nervous too. Worried about if he should take a present, what he should wear. I told him nobody would worry what he looked like. They'd just be proud of what he'd achieved. Putting Morrisham on the map. "You'll have a lovely time." That was what I said.'

'And did he?' Venn kept his voice bland. 'Did he have a lovely time?'

'Well, I didn't see him until a week later, did I? And by that time, he'd moved Selena into the place!'

Had the party at the big house been the occasion when Jeremy had realized that Eleanor was engaged to Bartholomew Lawson?

Matthew could picture it, the smart young things spilling out into the garden with their drinks as the sun went down. Jeremy Rosco being the centre of attention, telling the story of his great round-the-world adventure, glowing. At first, at least.

Then, perhaps Eleanor had taken him aside, stood with him under the trees in the dusk, and broken the news of her engagement to Barty. Though surely she wouldn't be so cruel as to tell him there, so publicly? Perhaps she hadn't even invited him. It could have been Bartholomew who'd added Jeremy to the guest list, just so that he could gloat. That would put the man in his place. Rosco might have sailed round the world but Barty had won the woman of his dreams. Matthew thought he would need to go back to talk to Eleanor.

His attention was pulled back into the room. Ross May was

as fidgety now as Lynn. He wouldn't see the point of this conversation. He'd want to open the letters that had arrived in Rosco's flat, and make contact with the person who received them still on Rosco's behalf.

Matthew stood up. 'You've been very helpful, Mrs Johnson. I'm sorry we've had to disturb you.'

Now, she seemed reluctant to see them go. 'If there's anything else . . .' She pulled a packet of cigarettes and a lighter from the cavernous bag, and, as they walked to the car, she was standing on her doorstep, smoking, watching them until they'd driven away.

Chapter Twenty

WHEN JEN RAFFERTY ARRIVED IN THE Maiden's Prayer, the place was empty, apart from Harry Carter pottering behind the bar. Matthew and Ross were in Morrisham and Jonathan had gone home.

'You got a key for the snug?' he called over to her. 'If not, I can let you in. I found a spare.'

So you can snoop when we're not here. Jen wondered what Matthew would make of that.

'I'm fine, thanks.' She'd had some keys cut when she was in Barnstaple, but that was no business of his.

'Feel free to light the fire.'

'I will.'

She was about to let herself in when she remembered what Davy Gregory had told Venn: that Harry had defrauded his father of all his savings and forced him to sell his land. She moved towards the bar and sat on a stool there. 'Any chance of a coffee while I wait for the team?'

'Sure.'

He came back a little later with a mug. There was no sign of Gwen. Her day off, perhaps.

'I'm surprised you don't make a bit more of this place,' Jen said. 'Now staycation is a thing. You could go upmarket, serve smart food. You'd get the tourists flocking. They're always complaining that the popular coastal villages are too crowded and they love a pub with character.'

'Well.' Carter set down his tea towel and leaned across the bar. 'I did have plans. We've already done a major refurb on the rooms. They're all en-suite now. I was thinking a gastropub kind of vibe. Maybe expand to the front with a restaurant extension. A lot of glass to make the most of the view. Specialize in local fish.' His voice was as enthusiastic as a child. Or Ross May talking rugby.

'Sounds fab,' Jen said. 'I'd come for a special meal out and then stay the night. What happened to your plans?'

Carter shook his head. 'We couldn't quite get the numbers to work.'

Jen was going to say she understood that some locals had invested, but Davy hadn't wanted Gwen to know that her father had sunk all his savings into the project and she might still be lurking somewhere behind the scenes. Besides, it was probably not a good idea to show her hand too soon.

'You could start with a new menu at least. That wouldn't be too expensive. A bit of local publicity and word would soon spread.'

The landlord shook his head. 'If I'm going to do it at all, I want to do it properly. I'm putting feelers out for some backers.' He looked across the bar at her.

'No good asking me!' She laughed. 'I've got two teenage

kids and an overdraft.' She slid from the stool and let herself into the snug.

Matthew and Ross turned up soon after. She had the fire lit. Despite the sunshine the air was chill. Ross was almost bouncing with impatience.

'Let's have a look then. See where the man was living.'

Matthew, almost teasing, took his time to hang up his coat.

'We don't know it's where he was living. Only where his post was sent.' He was still standing and took a piece of paper from his pocket, set it on the table.

'What is all this?' Jen hated the feeling of being excluded, of boys together playing their games.

'Jeremy Rosco hasn't stayed in his flat in Morrisham for months,' Venn said, 'and then it was only for a couple of weeks. His cleaner sends on all his post. This is who it was forwarded to.'

Jen looked at the name, which meant nothing, and at the address, which gave her a sudden jolt.

'The Wirral.' A pause. She never liked giving away too much information about her earlier life. It was private and the memories were too painful. 'That's where my ex's parents live. At least, only a couple of streets away.' She pictured the street. Large Victorian villas backing onto the green of a smart golf club and on to the Dee Estuary. 'It's very posh. Used to be part of Merseyside, but the locals didn't want to be linked with us scallies, so it's Cheshire these days.' She looked again at the name: I Holt. No title. 'Whoever Mr or Miss Holt is, they're not on the breadline.'

'That would tie in with the train ticket from Liverpool,'

Venn said. 'Holt could be a made-up name, I suppose. If Rosco was living there and not wanting anyone to know where he was. Or it could be a friend, someone agreeing to take in mail for him. Or a partner.'

'We'll be able to find out, won't we? Now we have an address, we should be able to check who lives there through the electoral roll.' Ross was already pulling his mobile out. 'I'll get Vicki onto it.'

'Yes.' Matthew spoke slowly. Again, it was impossible to tell what he was thinking. 'But tell Vicki no contact. Not yet. Jeremy Rosco's death has been all over the news, but Holt hasn't been in touch. If it's a friend or a partner, surely they would.'

'Not everyone wants to be involved with a murder investigation,' Ross said.

'Of course, that's true. But let's get all the details before we decide how we need to move forward.' An impassive stare fixed on the paper in front of him. 'We could be looking at a murder suspect here. The last thing we'd want is to scare them away.'

While they were waiting for official records to come through from Vicki, Ross was on his laptop googling, checking out social media. Matthew and Jen sat each side of him, looking at the screen. 'I think this must be her,' Ross said. 'Imogen Holt. No address but she's an actress. Small time. Had a part five years ago in a soap, and roles in a couple of ads.' He sat back so the others could look at the woman's photograph on the screen. 'Here she is.'

Jen looked at a woman with long blonde hair. It was a publicity shot, so of course she'd look glamorous, but she was certainly attractive. She had a sudden thought. 'This fits the description of the woman Alan Ford saw. Our mysterious woman who turned up in Greystone in the early hours of the day Rosco's body was found.'

'So it does, Jen.'

She could tell that Venn had already come to the same conclusion, but that he was letting her take the credit.

Almost immediately after, Vicki came through with the more official details. 'Imogen Holt. Age thirty-eight. Divorced. A graduate of Northumbria University, where she got a first in Performance. She teaches drama part time at an FE college in Liverpool, but still works for a small women's theatre group. No criminal record.'

'Does Jeremy feature in any of her social media posts?' Matthew directed the question to Ross.

'No, and that's a bit odd, isn't it, if they've been living together. If it was a long-term relationship, wouldn't he have his mail posted to him personally?'

'It could have been an arrangement that started years ago and just drifted on,' Jen said.

'Maybe.' Matthew seemed to come to a conclusion. 'Let's get some local officers round to that address, shall we? Discreetly, on the pretext of notifying her of the death. See what she has to say for herself. Let's find out if she has an alibi for the night of Jeremy Rosco's death.'

Chapter Twenty-One

WHILE HE WAS WAITING FOR NEWS from the Wirral about Imogen Holt, Matthew phoned the doctor's surgery. He thought that Smale might help him untangle some of the relationships within the village. It seemed that the Bartons and the Gregorys were Brethren members, and each was involved in some way with Rosco's death. But all he got was a recorded message saying that the surgery had closed for the day.

Venn couldn't stand the thought of another evening in the Maiden's Prayer and headed out for Willington, hoping to catch Ruth and Peter Smale at home. He still needed to confirm that Matilda Gregory had spent the night there when Rosco was being stabbed.

The wind was picking up again, a sign perhaps that another of the Atlantic fronts was rolling through. Venn had seen a weather forecast the night before: a hurricane was just about to hit the south-east states of the US and might be on its way soon. Perhaps by then, he thought, this would be over.

The curtains still hadn't been drawn but there was a light

in the downstairs window. Ruth must have seen his car on the drive because she opened the door before he knocked. She was small and slight and she looked too young to be living in this large house.

'Please be quiet.' She spoke in an urgent whisper. 'Emily's just gone off to bed. Come on through. The rest of us are in the kitchen.'

He had to squeeze past a large, old-fashioned pram to follow her. There was a brief moment of curiosity as he wondered what it would be like to have the responsibility of a parent. Jonathan had once spoken of their adopting a child. The thought had terrified Matthew. He was too selfish. Too self-absorbed. Too wrapped up in his work. But he knew that if Jonathan wanted it, really wanted it, he would agree. In the end, he would deny his husband nothing to make him happy.

Ruth led him into a room which looked as if little had been changed since the house was built. It was cramped. There was a solid fuel range, with a coal scuttle to one side, and hanging from the ceiling an airer on a pulley. On the airer hung baby clothes. The worktops were scratched and a cupboard door was slightly open, hanging on one hinge. He could see no space for a dishwasher. A modernized version of the space could be seen in the homes of the aspirational middle classes from the Cotswolds to the Lake District, but this, Matthew thought, would be hard work.

The family must just have eaten their evening meal. Peter was at the sink, sleeves rolled to the elbows, washing up. The woman looked tired. Venn felt a stab of sympathy. She had a young baby to care for, and a mother in hospital. And here he was to intrude on her peace. Of course, she would be under stress. Her faith might help, but it wouldn't shield her entirely from anxiety. Two girls were sitting at a scrubbed pine table, with exercise books, pencils and crayons.

'That's enough homework for now,' Ruth said. 'Let's have half an hour's television before bed.'

Mother and daughters left the room. Peter emptied water from the washing-up bowl, and offered tea. He must have seen Matthew's response to the kitchen. 'We loved the house when we first saw it. It's perfect for work, halfway between Greystone and Morrisham. We knew it would be a project, but things ran away with us. And then we found out Ruth was pregnant again. A joy, of course, but it threw our plans out a little. I'm not sure we'd have bought it if we knew quite how long the renovations would take.' He set mugs on the table. 'How's the investigation going? Or shouldn't I ask?'

There was a moment of silence, broken by the sound of children's television in an adjoining room. 'It's hard,' Matthew said at last. 'Coming from outside into a community as close as this.' He looked up at Peter. 'Some of the people closely linked to the dead man were Brethren members.' He expected a response – outrage perhaps – but none came and he continued. 'Rosco's body was found in Barton's boat, Davy Gregory went to school with him and someone looking very like Matilda Gregory was seen in the street close to his house in the early hours of the morning.'

'I'm not sure what you want from me,' Smale said.

'You know all these people. You worship with them every Sunday. Could one of them commit murder?'

'No!' Now the response did come immediately. 'No, of course not. They're good people. They look after each other.'

They, Venn noted, *not we.* He was about to ask more when

Ruth Smale came back into the room. She sat beside her husband, took the hand that was resting on the table.

'How is your mum?' Venn asked

'Better.' She smiled up at him. 'It's not as serious as they all thought when they took her in. We're still praying for her, but already it seems like a miracle.'

'I'm glad.'

'Tilly Gregory said you'd probably call in to check that she was here when that man was killed.'

'You've been friends for a long time?'

'Since she married Davy and we moved home. They've been brilliant neighbours. Davy's a lot more practical than Pete is, so he's the one we turn to in a domestic crisis. We had a nightmare with the septic tank, and really, you don't want to hear the details. I'm not sure how we'd have managed without them.'

'Can you tell me what happened on the night of the murder? Just for the record. You understand that we have to check?'

Ruth nodded. 'Tilly said that someone matching her description was seen at the bottom of Quarry Bank that night. So dreadful for her! But, of course, she was here all the time.'

'Just talk me through it.'

'I got the call about mum at about four o'clock. I'd just picked up my two older daughters from school in Greystone. It was my dad from the ambulance saying they were on their way into Barnstaple. He was distraught and he sounded so scared. Pete was in surgery in the village and Tilly was still at work, in a teachers' meeting, so she wasn't answering her phone. I got hold of Davy, who was actually brilliant, so reassuring. He texted Tilly, and she got the message at just after four thirty. She went home to pick up some overnight things and then she came here. By that time, Pete was already on his way back from Greystone. I'm still feeding Emily, so we took her into the hospital with us and Tilly stayed with the big ones.'

'What time did you get home from Barnstaple?'

Ruth turned to her husband. 'What do you think? Ten thirty? Ten forty-five?'

So, a little earlier than Matilda Gregory had said. Was that significant?

'But Mrs Gregory still decided to stay overnight with you?'

'Yes, she was already in her pyjamas when we got in. She heard our car outside and came down to see how we were, but it made far more sense for her to stay over.' She waved her hand to take in the space. 'We've got lots of room, after all. She made us a cup of tea and then we all went to bed.'

'You're sure she didn't go out later?'

'Well, we sleep at the front and her room was at the back, so I might not have heard her, but why would she?' When Venn didn't answer immediately, Ruth continued: 'Actually, I had to get up a couple of times with the baby, once at about two and once at five, and Ruth's car was still parked by the kitchen door then.'

'What does she drive?' As if it was a matter of idle curiosity.

'A little white Fiat.'

So, Venn thought, that wasn't the car Alan Ford had seen dropping a woman off at Quarry Bank. He supposed that Gregory could have picked up his wife in his taxi and taken her into Greystone, but none of it made sense. Matilda's parents might have known Rosco when he was young, but that wouldn't explain a secret visit in the middle of the night. A murder.

'What was she wearing when she came to look after your daughters?' Covering all bases. Just in case.

'Jeans and a sweater. And a down jacket. She knows how chilly this house can be. We've still not got the boiler working properly.'

So, not the skirt, the long coat and the scarf Alan Ford had seen.

'And what happened in the morning?'

'Tilly left early. The girls weren't even awake. I was up because the baby needed feeding. We had tea and toast together but Tilly had gone by seven thirty. She nipped home to change, but she would have been in school long before the kids. She's a dedicated teacher.'

Matthew supposed he'd got what he'd come for, but he still had other questions. More curiosity. Easy questions. They could have been friends, sitting around the table, catching up.

'Where did you do your medical training?' The question directed at Peter.

'Newcastle. About as far away from here as it's possible to be in England.'

Were you just a bright young man needing a new adventure? Or were you running away? From an oppressive family and the Brethren?

'You were already together then?'

Ruth laughed. 'Oh yes! We were childhood sweethearts. I'd already decided he'd be my husband before I left school. We both grew up in Greystone. Pete's a few years older than me, but he came back during the uni vacations.'

Matthew thought Ruth must have been there at the Greystone Brethren meetings, when he'd been brought along by his parents, but he couldn't remember her. She'd have been one of the gaggle of younger kids, timid, compliant, sitting with their parents.

'When did you marry?'

'I was nineteen. Pete was twenty-two. I moved north so he could finish his training.' She paused. 'It was difficult. He was working so hard. All hours in the hospital, and then doing his GP training. I didn't know anyone and money was very tight at first.'

'Did you work?'

'I don't have any formal qualifications – I always knew that university wasn't for me – but yes. I was a care assistant in an old people's home. It was very rewarding, but that was tough too. So many of the residents had dementia. And some weeks, it felt as if I was surrounded by the dying, and there was nothing I could do to save them.'

What would you want to save them from? Death? Or from damnation because they didn't share your beliefs? But of course, *that* question stayed in Matthew's head.

Ruth was still talking. There was something guileless about her. There was no protective skin between her and the world. No filter. She didn't seem to care what Venn made of her. She just wanted to tell the truth as she saw it.

'Things became easier, of course. Pete qualified and found a job in Gateshead. I got pregnant with Hannah and then Esther. We made friends there. But I could never really settle.' She turned to her husband again. 'You loved the north-east, didn't you? But I missed this place. My family. The community.'

'When did you move back to North Devon?'

Peter answered. 'Five years ago. There was a vacancy in the health centre in Morrisham, and they were keen to open a little surgery in the village here. It all seemed meant. We rented for a while in Morrisham, and then the old rectory came on the market. We've only been here for a year and, as you see, there's still a lot to do.'

Venn wondered what Peter Smale really made of it all. He'd
been used to the freedom of an anonymous city, challenging
work and new friends. Matthew had returned from the city to
North Devon to be with Jonathan, but he'd not returned to the
claustrophobic world of the Brethren. Their influence might
still lurk at the back of his mind, or as an awkward voice in his
head, but at home and at work, he could escape it. Smale didn't
come across as a happy man. It must seem that now, for *him*,
there was no escape at all.

Venn stood up. 'Thanks,' he said. 'That's all been very
helpful.' Outside, it was quite dark. He stood for a while,
looking in at the brightly lit home, still unsure what he made
of the family inside.

Chapter Twenty-Two

DESPITE THE TIME, JEN HUNG ON with Ross in the Maiden's Prayer for Venn to return from talking to the Smales. News had come through from the officers who'd been to visit Imogen Holt, and she wanted to be there to hear his response.

Ross shouted out the information as soon as Venn came in. 'There was no sign of the woman. They talked to neighbours and they haven't seen her for a couple of days.'

'She could have gone away to stay with friends,' Matthew said, 'to grieve perhaps, if she heard that Rosco was dead.'

'Nah!' Ross was triumphant. 'She left before he died. Her car disappeared the day before.'

'Did they confirm that she and Rosco were partners?'

'Yes. He's a bit of a hermit apparently, and hates publicity, so he's not seen out in the community much. But the neighbour said they were definitely a couple.'

There was a moment of silence, then Matthew turned to Jen. 'Any chance you could go up and see her? If she's turned up again. Track her down otherwise and see if she was anywhere near North Devon on the night Rosco died. Maybe sniff around and get a feel for the situation? Find out why Imogen hasn't admitted to any sort of relationship with the man on social media, and why she hasn't been in touch once the news of his death went public. I know it's awkward with the kids, but you're a Scouser. Your territory and you'll fit in.'

Jen's first response was a shock of excitement. Back working her patch. Though she hadn't often been called to the big houses in the smart Wirral villages, unless they'd been the targets of burglary. Then she started thinking through the practicalities. It might work. It wouldn't be the end of the world if the kids missed a bit of school. She could make up a story about a sick grandparent. Nobody would know. Robbie's parents would be delighted to have them for a couple of nights, and that would give her a cover story, a reason for being there. Robbie's mother was a gossip, and she might even know Imogen.

'Yeah,' she said. 'Why not?'

They'd moan, of course. Ella would have plans to see Zac and Ben would have to be prized away from his screen. But Ray and Joan had Wi-Fi, didn't they? And it would do them good to do something different.

'I'll make a few phone calls.' She walked out through the big bar and into the street. She didn't want to be overheard grovelling to her in-laws. She was feeling the pull of home. The smell of the Mersey. The Wirral wasn't quite the city she loved, but it was a lot closer to Liverpool than this place, with its cold cliffs and grey sea.

It was early the following evening by the time Jen and the kids arrived at her ex's parents' house in Hoylake, and by then she was frazzled. They'd stopped on the M5 to find something to eat and Ella had whinged because vegan options were limited, and Ben had left his phone in the cafeteria and they'd had to go back. Then there'd been an accident, closing the motorway, and a horrendous diversion through the Cheshire countryside.

Joan looked at her watch when she opened the door to them, making a point. *You said you'd be here soon after lunch.* Joan had always had a point to make, even when Jen had turned up on her doorstep with a black eye and broken ribs. Today, though, the woman seemed curious about the sudden decision to visit, and invited Jen in for tea.

Jen was shattered, and wanted to make a start looking for Imogen, but if she spoke to the couple now, she wouldn't have to come back until she picked up the kids.

They sat in the living room with its chintz and its polish, the curtains pulled tight around the bay window. The children had taken themselves off to the rooms where they always slept, to charge their phones and contact their mates at home. They seldom stayed with their father in his smart apartment on the Liverpool docks. This was their home in the north-west. Robbie might come to visit. Or he might not. It would depend if he had something more exciting on offer. The women drank tea. Ray poured himself a beer, but didn't offer one to her.

'Why the last-minute visit?' Usually, Joan was supremely confident in her own domain, but now, she seemed almost diffident.

'Work. I'm part of the Jeremy Rosco murder investigation. We think he might have had connections locally.' There was no need to explain who Jeremy Rosco was. For her parents-in-law's generation, he was still a hero, and they might not sail them-selves, but they'd certainly have friends who did. It was that sort of community. She looked across the glass coffee table to the woman opposite. 'You haven't come across him?'

Joan shook her head. 'There are lots of newcomers to the village. Things aren't the same as they were.' She sounded regretful and disapproving at the same time. Jen wondered if the new people were young families, people with noisy kids and arty, liberal views.

'You'd have heard, though, if he'd joined the sailing club?'

The woman's back straightened. 'Oh yes, we'd certainly have heard about that.'

There was a silence. Jen finished her tea and set her cup on the table. Now, it really was time to make a move. Ray and Joan exchanged a glance.

'We weren't sure if you knew,' Ray said. He drank the last of the beer.

'Knew what?'

'About Robert's young lady.'

'Is this a new one, or the one he had when the kids last visited?' Jen wasn't interested. Rob was attracted to pretty little things who liked his money and were prepared to meet his needs and desires to share it. Any with a mind of their own soon moved away, and he was more careful these days. No stalking. No physical violence. Nothing that could get him in trouble. Her close former colleagues had his card marked. He might be a hotshot lawyer, but they'd love to see him in court. In the dock, not addressing the bench.

'Her name's Amelia,' Joan said. 'Calls herself Millie.' A sniff. 'Sounds more like the name of a pet.'

Appropriate then. But Jen kept the words in her head. She was too tired to make a fuss.

'I'm sorry, I'll have to leave. I'm here for work.'

'She's pregnant.' Ray had been building up to the revelation since she'd arrived.

Jen felt a surge of broodiness, a physical longing more powerful than sex. In that moment she wanted another baby more than anything else in the world. The sensation had been bubbling in her sub-conscience for months, she realized now. The clock ticking. She needed a child with a man who cared for her. Someone who'd be a good father. She needed a chance to prove that after all the mistakes of the past, she could be a good mother. She wanted the swelling of the belly, the first kick, the labour, the suck of a greedy infant. Those sensations.

They were waiting for a reaction from her, but she'd never given them what they wanted. Her unwillingness to compromise with his parents had been the cause of Robbie's first assault.

'It was unplanned,' Joan said. 'By Robert at least. But it seems she's determined to go ahead.'

Jen stood up. 'I apologize, but I really must get on.'

'Why don't you come for lunch on Sunday?' Joan's voice was bright. 'It'll set you up for the long journey. All the way to Devon.'

It occurred to Jen that the couple must disapprove of Millie even more than they'd disliked her. They believed she'd trapped their only and beloved son into an unsuitable relationship. Her spirits lifted for a moment, but the broodiness, the jealousy was still there in the pit of her stomach. Besides, Sunday lunch! Overcooked beef in a floury gravy in the formal dining room. It had been a ritual in the early days of her marriage, and she'd only survived it by drinking too much. Several G&Ts before they got there, and too much thick red wine with the meal, topping up her glass when she thought they weren't looking. And Ella and Ben would hate it.

She smiled at them. 'Sorry, I'm not sure what time I'll be

done. It's a difficult case.' Lunch was always at one on the dot. They wouldn't compromise on that.

'Of course.' Joan was too proud to show her disappointment. 'We could do coffee afterwards, though. We'll make you coffee before you set off.'

'That would be lovely.' Because Jen saw now that they were old and lonely. Their world had changed and she could afford to be generous.

Chapter Twenty-Three

ROSS FOUND RODNEY BOTTLE IN A smart retirement flat in a little development on the edge of Morrisham. There was a gate with an intercom and, beyond that, manicured lawns.

Bottle himself was spry and jovial. When Ross phoned, it had been clear that the man would relish the company, and the chance to talk about his career. They met in the communal lounge, which was empty, apart from a woman in the far corner who was sitting with a newspaper, doing the crossword. There was a coffee bar at the end of the room, and the lawyer shouted across an order for drinks and scones. He walked with a stick and couldn't have managed the tray, so a young woman with pink hair carried it to their table.

'I saw the news about Jeremy Rosco's death. Of course, I've retired now and all the paperwork will be in the office, but I'll help if I can.'

'Rosco inherited a considerable fortune from Grace Fanshaw.'

'He did!' Rodney was spreading jam on his scone and looked up. 'It was all above board. The nephew tried to challenge it, but Grace Fanshaw was clearly of sound mind. I knew her, not as a client, but as a neighbour. She was frail at the end, but sharp as a tack.'

'How did she die?'

'Pancreatic cancer. Terrible disease. She went very quickly.' He looked at Ross again. 'And that was above board too, if you're thinking what I believe you are. She was in hospital for her last two weeks. There was no monkey business around her death.'

Ross smiled. He hadn't been thinking murder in relation to Grace Fanshaw; he was young and thought the elderly died all the time. The old man obviously had a colourful imagination.

'Were you surprised that Miss Fanshaw left everything to Rosco?'

'Not once I'd met the boy. He bounced into my office full of charm and confidence.' He nodded towards the teenager with the pink hair. 'Jasmine she's called. She brightens my life. Always full of chat and a joke. If I didn't have close dependents, I'd leave everything I had to her. Better that than the government have it all.' He gave a wink. 'I've left her a couple of thousand anyway. She doesn't know. It'll give her a nice holiday, or help her get her first car.'

'But Miss Fanshaw left him a fortune! Not quite the same.'

'Jeremy had been good to her, and was almost a permanent carer at one point. Not living in, but visiting to shop for her, and to keep her company. The nephew didn't even come to see her in the hospital when she was dying. It seemed harsh that she'd left the nephew out of her will, but I could see why it happened.'

'Do you think Rosco had expectations?'

'You think he was kind to her in the hope of inheriting? Probably! But there's nothing illegal in that.' Rodney dropped the last of the scone into his mouth, avoiding crumbs on his smart blazer. 'And it was years ago!'

'When was the last time you saw him?'

'It was just before I retired. Ten years ago. He turned up without an appointment, but he was a celebrity then, at the height of his fame, and my assistant squeezed him in.'

'What did he want?'

'This time it was *his* will he was thinking about.'

'Oh?' Ross thought this would be very helpful. It could tell them if Rosco had any kids, for example. He could get information about the sailor's private life here in North Devon, before Jen Rafferty got anywhere near to Merseyside.

'Yes, that was all very interesting.' The old man chuckled. '*That'll put the cat among the pigeons*, I thought. There was only one beneficiary.'

'It wasn't Eleanor Lawson?'

'It was!' Bottle was obviously disappointed that Ross had guessed. It was as if Rodney was a comedian, and a member of the audience had shouted out the tagline of his favourite joke. 'Respectable member of the community. Married to Barty, who is magistrate and commodore of the sailing club. It was almost as if Rosco wanted to disrupt the marriage.'

'Did Eleanor know?'

'Well, I didn't tell her! Not my place. I suppose Jeremy could have done.' A pause. 'I don't know how much he has to leave. I suppose he'd have made a bit from all those TV programmes. They seem to be repeated all the time.'

Ross was thinking of the visit to Rosco's home. 'He still owns an apartment in the block on the seafront. I bet the big ones there go for a fortune.'

'Oh, indeed. Yes, indeed. There was one for sale recently.

They wanted nearly half a million. Stupid prices. I don't know how young people can get on the housing ladder.'

Ross felt a little smug. He and Mel had bought before prices in the south-west went through the roof. They'd been sensible and got their priorities right.

'I wonder what Eleanor's husband will make of an old flame leaving her all that money.'

'I don't know.' That little chuckle again. 'I'm betting there'll be fireworks when he finds out. He's got a temper on him, Barty Lawson. He'll be glad of the money, though. His old man was a bit of a gambler and there wasn't much left for Barty to inherit. Eleanor has the big house and all that land, but word is that she'll never sell it.' He paused. 'You could build a good few homes for local people on that.'

Ross wondered how the former lawyer got all his information. He thought it was the gossip that kept the man so engaged and so lively. He must have visitors who enjoyed the chat as much as he did. But Ross was grateful. These were useful snippets to take back to Venn. He sat a little longer, listening to Bottle talking. He was a local history nut, full of stories of the old Morrisham, of pirates and wreckers and adventurers. Eventually boredom outweighed gratitude and Ross May got to his feet and left.

'So, Rosco left everything he had to Eleanor,' Venn said. 'I wonder what she'll make of that.' They were meeting in the cafe bar in the apartment block where Rosco had kept his flat.

'I thought he could have changed his will more recently, that this new woman on the Wirral might benefit now, but I phoned the solicitor's office, and apparently the one Rodney Bottle put together still stands.'

'You could do with a break and some time with Mel,' Venn

said. 'Have a couple of nights at home. Come back on Monday morning.'

Ross looked at Venn as if he was a bit mad. The boss wasn't given to those kinds of gesture, not to Ross at least. He was out of the door before Matthew could change his mind.

Chapter Twenty-Four

ON IMPULSE, MATTHEW DECIDED THAT HE would go home too. Suddenly, he longed to be in the calm house by the estuary. To spend a little time with Jonathan on home territory. The threatened wind still showed no real sign of arriving despite the isobars on the weather map.

He was going to phone or text, but in the end he didn't. He decided he'd show Jonathan that he could be spontaneous for once. He'd surprise him. Yet, when he drove along the toll road at the back of Braunton marsh and parked by the house, *he* was the person to be surprised. Jonathan's car was there, but there was another vehicle that Matthew didn't recognize. Something a bit old and battered. Some of Jonathan's arty friends, Matthew decided. He wondered how long it would take them to get rid of the visitors tactfully. This, he thought, was why spontaneity was rarely a good idea.

When Matthew let himself into the house, there was only one visitor. The teacher he'd seen having lunch with Jonathan in Morrisham. Jonathan beamed when Matthew walked in, and pulled him into a hug.

'Oh, that's great timing. I'm just making coffee.' The anxiety of the day before seemed to have disappeared. That was how Jonathan was. Bad moods passed like clouds blown across the moon. 'We've finished supper, but I can make you something if you're hungry?'

Matthew shook his head, and Jonathan continued: 'This is Guy. He teaches at Morrisham High. I thought I'd be on my own tonight, so I invited him round.'

'Of course.' Matthew held out his hand. His mother had considered manners important. 'You're a member of the yacht club.'

'Yeah . . .' The man looked at Jonathan, suddenly suspicious.

'I haven't been talking about you!' Jonathan laughed. 'He's a detective. He knows stuff.'

'My sergeant saw you there, the day he went to chat to the commodore.' Venn pulled mugs from the cupboard, and went to the fridge for milk. 'Did you know Jeremy Rosco?'

'I taught him. Introduced him to sailing. At least, I stuck some posters on the school noticeboard and he turned up. Ruffled a few feathers at the club, having a youngster like Jem trying to join us, but that was just what was needed. It was turning into a glorified gentlemen's club.'

'You must have been very proud when he set the round-the-world record.'

The man smiled. 'Well, I was glad to prove the old farts in the club wrong. They never thought Rosco would make anything of himself. I was young and radical back then. Now, I'm one of the old farts myself, just reliving the past.'

'When was the last time you saw him?'

'Oh, it was at least five years ago. He just turned up at the club. The poor commodore was almost apoplectic. He'd never

liked the man, and then in waltzed Jeremy, the centre of attention, all smiles and swagger. There was nothing Barty could
do. Rosco had been invited by one of the newer members,
who knew nothing of the bad feeling between the two men.
No rules broken so Barty had to grin and bear it.'

'Can you think why anyone would want to kill Rosco?' The
question came out almost without Venn thinking about it.

There was a silence in the room while the man considered
the question.

'Nobody specific,' Guy said at last. 'But he was an awkward
bugger. Nothing he liked better than winding people up to get
a reaction. Just the sort of kid you don't need in a class.'

Jonathan was up first again the next day. 'I'm going for my
swim. Want to join me?'

'Nah, I'll have coffee made when you get back.' Then, hit
by the fear that such happiness could never last: 'You will take
care? It's still rough out there.' Thinking that perhaps he should
go too, just in case there was an accident.

Jonathan only laughed.

At Jonathan's insistence, they had breakfast outside. 'This
could be the last day it's possible.' They sat in the lee of the
house, sheltered from the breeze, eating scrambled eggs.
Matthew was wearing a jersey but still felt cold. Jonathan was
in shorts and sandals, and was talking about his supper with
the teacher.

'As you'll have gathered last night, Guy found Rosco hard-
going, and that's not like him. He can find good things to say
about most of his students, but he was more honest when we
were on our own together. He said you couldn't trust Rosco.
He was the best liar he'd ever met. Perhaps because he believed

in his own lies. He was often on the edge of trouble, but there was always some other poor sod who got the blame.' Jonathan paused. 'There is something else.'

'Mmm?' Matthew was relaxed. He wasn't sure he wanted there to be anything else.

'You were wondering how the killer got from *Moon Crest*'s tender back to dry land.'

'Yes.' Now he was listening intently.

'I know I shouldn't interfere, but I've been looking at some large-scale maps and I think there's a place where you could get up the cliff to the coastal path.'

'Can you show me?'

'Sure! I'd be glad to.' A pause. 'I'd like to help and it'd be an adventure.'

Chapter Twenty-Five

JEN WOKE TO A MILD AND blustery day, and the sound of rain on her window. She'd done a brief recce of Imogen Holt's gaff the night before, but there'd been no lights on and she hadn't wanted to go creeping round the place in the dark. She'd persuaded herself that this was a fool's errand.

She helped herself to the buffet breakfast – hard fried eggs under warming lamps, and greasy tepid bacon – and drank several mugs of tea. She had the place almost to herself. Perhaps visitors to this part of the Wirral wanted more than a budget hotel. She decided to walk to Imogen Holt's place. The rain was showery, intermittent, it wasn't far and she'd brought her old waterproof jacket – which she wouldn't be seen dead in at home – and her boots. This way, she'd avoid the problem of residents' parking, and she needed the fresh air and exercise.

The road was quiet, tree-lined, not far from the estuary, with its smell of mud and salt. There were back gardens with trampolines and smart wooden climbing frames. These would be the newcomers Joan found so disturbing. A young father in running gear turned out of a wide drive and jogged along the pavement followed by two preschool boys on scooters. Jen would bet there was a super-mum inside, rustling up a breakfast for their return. Something healthy. Homemade granola and fresh fruit. Natural yoghurt. And the children would eat it without complaint. Jen could never aspire to that. It was probably as well that she'd never be a mother again.

Imogen Holt didn't live in a house, but a large ground-floor flat. There were two bells by the door. HOLT in neat printed writing next to one. SAVAGE next to the other. Not Rosco. Jen had wondered if Rosco might have been a close neighbour and that Imogen had been persuaded to accept the post for him because he travelled so much, but it seemed not.

There were wooden slatted blinds at the front windows and it was almost impossible to see inside without getting very close. This would be a neighbourhood of bored and vigilant old ladies, and Jen didn't want to raise suspicion.

An unbolted gate through a high wall led into the back garden, which was small, overgrown, with dripping shrubs and long grass. A fence at the end to keep out prying eyes, and a slimy crazy-paving path. More blinds at the back windows, except at the kitchen. On the draining board, there was a mug, half-filled with tea, a film on the top. A plate and a knife. Somebody had left quickly without clearing up. Jen had a moment of disquiet, her imagination running wild. She pictured another body. A beautiful woman with long blonde hair. A pool of blood. She saw again the blood in Rosco's bath. There was a door leading from the kitchen into the garden. Jen rattled it but it was firmly locked.

She moved on to the last set of windows. The blinds hadn't quite been closed and she could squint through to see something of the room beyond. It was a bedroom, cluttered and colourful, nothing like Rosco's spartan room in Quarry Bank. A double bed, the quilt thrown back, empty. Beyond the bed, something, which might just be a pile of clothes. The angle of the blinds made it impossible to see properly. The disquiet grew into something close to panic.

A small upper window was slightly open, held on a catch. No way would she be able to climb through – a small five-year-old would struggle – and she couldn't quite reach to open it properly. If she could do that, she'd be able to move the blinds to get a better view into the room. She'd seen an aluminium stepladder next to the back door. Only three steps but she'd be high enough.

The ground was a little uneven, and the steps were light. She rested against the frame to stop herself wobbling, and lifted the catch on the window, pushed it in, and the blinds to one side. At last, she had an uninterrupted view of the room. She was focused on what was inside, and she didn't hear the soft footsteps on wet grass. The steps were pulled suddenly away from her, and she fell. She hit her shoulder on the paving and the pain made her feel light-headed. As a kid, she'd always fainted when she hurt herself. She knew she had to stay awake, to face the person who'd attacked her, but the garden spun around her as if she was the worst kind of drunk, and in the end everything went black.

Chapter Twenty-Six

JONATHAN LED THE WAY OUT OF the village and onto the headland. They were walking with a blustery breeze behind them, the waves blowing back white foam. Soon, Matthew thought, there would be rain. The path led along the edge, with steep cliffs to one side and, inland, open ground of browning bracken and yellow gorse. The whole place was windswept and wild.

The headland was narrow, a finger of land jutting into the sea, and there was no way of getting down to the rocky beaches below. At the furthest point, they stopped to look at the view. From here, they could see back into Greystone with its jetty and cottages, and, in the other direction, on towards North Cornwall. Jonathan shook off his rucksack and pulled out a flask of coffee and two bars of chocolate. Now, Matthew almost took his husband's competence for granted.

Looking down to Scully Cove, he tried to work out where the *Moon Crest* tender had been anchored. He'd looked on maps and charts, but thought he should have come here sooner.

It made more sense to see the place in reality. Ground-truthing. Wasn't that what the experts called it?

He pointed to a spot in the water. 'I think that's where they found Rosco's body.'

'I thought it might be.' Jonathan was already on his feet, the flask stowed, eager to go on, bouncing on the balls of his feet. 'Look, I'll show you what I meant. There's a place where I think the killer might have come ashore. It's hard to tell on the map, but Guy mentioned it when we had lunch in Morrisham.'

'You wouldn't be able to get up from there.'

'Be patient! You'll see. Guy drew a little sketch for me.'

Despite his words, there was nothing patient about Jonathan. He set off at a pace that left Matthew breathless.

They'd travelled the length of the further edge of the headland when Matthew did begin to see. There was a gully, almost hidden by rocky outcrops, the end of a valley which led inland, a fold in the land. In the distance, at the top of the valley, stood a house, at once familiar but strange because of the different perspective.

'That's Ravenscroft Farm, where Davy and Matilda Gregory live.' Matthew tried to picture the map, to recreate in his head the view he'd seen from the farmhouse's garden.

And where the valley morphed into the gully to fall into the sea, there was a steep path down to a shingle beach, only visible now because they were almost at the top of it.

'Ready to give it a go?' Jonathan was like a puppy, straining at a lead, wanting to be let free. 'According to Guy, it's not too tricky.'

Matthew was about to be disapproving, to talk about contaminating crime scenes, to tell Jonathan that they should get the CSIs in before they did more damage. But there'd been a force-ten gale since any potential murderer had climbed up here, and anyway, what evidence did they have that this was the route that the killer had taken?

'Yeah,' he said. 'Why not?'

And so, Jonathan was away.

The path was, as Jonathan had said, less sheer than it had appeared from the top of the cliff. It snaked down the gully and there were shrubby trees to provide handholds.

'It wouldn't be possible to drag a boat up here,' Matthew said. They'd stopped for a moment. Every few yards, he was taking photos on his phone. 'I'm still not sure how it would have worked. Surely it's still more likely that there was another vessel, to tow out the dinghy, anchor it and then continue back to Greystone or even go on to Morrisham?'

'I reckon you'd be able to wade ashore if the tide was dead low.' Jonathan was convinced by his theory now, wanted it to be right, to have made an important contribution to the investigation.

'In that weather? Surely you'd be swept off your feet?'

'So, you think it's more likely that there were two people involved?'

'Honestly? I don't know what I think yet. The whole thing seems so overblown and melodramatic.' Matthew paused. 'A bit like the man himself.'

'We'll go to the bottom, though, shall we? No turning back?'

'Oh yes,' Matthew said. 'Definitely no turning back.'

On the shingle beach there was a little shelter from the wind, but further out, beyond the headland, the waves were bigger, and spindrift was blowing like a blizzard over the surface. Matthew thought there would be nothing to find here. There was a thin strip of sand where footwear prints might have formed, but any physical evidence would have scattered long ago. There was nothing to confirm or repudiate his husband's theory. Even after the climb down the path, Jonathan was restless, unable to keep still. He ranged across the beach, his boots clattering on the pebbles, jumping across the rockpools on each side of the narrow cove, occasionally picking up stray pieces of driftwood, as if they might provide insight into what had happened a little way out to sea.

Matthew called across to him. 'How close is the top of the path to any sort of track or road?' It seemed that the nearest house was the Gregorys' place. It might be possible to park a car in the track which led to it, but it would be a long walk across country to reach that, especially in the dark, and when tired and wet. He was still keeping an open mind about Jonathan's theory that the killer had waded ashore.

'I asked Guy about that. He said there's a lane less than a quarter of a mile away. It leads to a small parking place for people who want to walk the coastal path. Only room for two or three cars, so I doubt it's marked on any of the tourist maps, and I'm sure nobody would be using it at night. Not on a wild night like that.'

'Cool. We'll check when we've finished here.' Which wouldn't, Matthew thought, take very long. Something about the place creeped him out. It was the gloom, the black kelp and the grey water, the haunting call of the scavenging gulls. The fact that a short way offshore, Jeremy Rosco had been left naked in a small boat, posed for the lifeboat crew to find him.

Jonathan had been scrambling over boulders to the south of the cove. There was a spur of black rock, jutting into the bay, and he'd disappeared beyond it. Now he turned back and

Matthew thought they'd be able to start back up the cliff. His mind was on lunch somewhere a bit classier than the Maiden's – perhaps that cafe bar in Morrisham – and a large pot of coffee. And on the fact that he'd need to talk to the Gregorys again, now he had a clearer idea of the geography.

'Look at this!' Jonathan was standing where the shingle merged into rock, staring down into a pool. Something was caught there, half covered by water. Sodden fabric. Clothes, Matthew thought. His mind was racing. Could the killer have died trying to wade back from the dinghy where Rosco's body had been left? Could the case be over?

As he got closer, he saw that this was no body. It was a large bag, navy blue canvas, waxed to make it waterproof. Jeremy Rosco had been carrying all his belongings in this bag when he first blew into the Maiden's Prayer. And his killer had carried him in it, wrapped in a shower curtain from the little house at the top of Quarry Bank to Sammy Barton's tender. Then the murderer had dumped it, waded ashore and climbed up the steep path to the lane. The bag had been washed up here.

'There should be a plastic shower curtain.' He spoke under his breath, but Jonathan was off, climbing further round the rocks until he was out of sight, a hunting dog wanting to please its master.

Matthew was taking photos. The bag was on the tideline but could be washed away by the next high water. Sodden and unwieldy, it would be too awkward to carry back up the path. It would be best to pull it further up the beach and get one of Brian's team to look at it there, before arranging for it to be brought back to the lab.

Jonathan appeared round the curve of the cliff and started making his way towards Matthew. He was waving.

So, Matthew thought, *he's found the curtain. More evidence that it happened as I thought. The right scenario to move us forward.* Jonathan seemed to open his mouth to shout, but no sound came out. He didn't speak until he was close enough to reach out and touch his husband's arm.

'You have to see this.' Then he turned away, ran over the shingle towards the shallows and retched into the water. 'I'm sorry.'

Matthew had never seen him so shaken. Jonathan was never ill. Still the man seemed unable to speak. Perhaps there was still blood on the curtain. So much blood that its use was obvious. Jonathan took Matthew's hand and pulled him across the beach to the rockpools. Here the cliff was sheer above them, with only narrow ledges pocked by white muck, evidence of the birds that had nested in the spring. At high tide, the water would almost reach where they were standing and it would be a struggle to escape back to the beach and the path to the top.

At last Jonathan stopped. At his feet a body. Twisted. Limbs broken and out of shape. A face nibbled in places. There must be rats here. Or perhaps it was the work of gulls. Matthew could understand why Jonathan had been sick. Now, though, his husband could speak. It seemed the reality wasn't as shocking when Matthew was with him. Or that his imagination had conjured up a sight that was even worse on his scramble back to the beach. 'He must have fallen from the top. Slipped, I suppose. A dog-walker, do you think, out in the gale?' He turned to Matthew. 'Or is it related to Rosco's death? A bit of a coincidence that he's here, so close to where they found his body. Could this be your killer, drowned on his way back from the *Moon Crest* tender?'

'This didn't happen in the gale.'

Matthew thought this had happened more recently than the night of Rosco's murder. There was too little animal damage, and the clothing was bone dry, even, as far as Matthew could tell, beneath the body. Besides, he'd seen this man since Rosco's body had been found. Only a glimpse then, but he recognized him now from the photograph Ross had shown the team at their last meeting in the Maiden's Prayer snug. One of many he'd downloaded to his laptop. The equivalent to the office Murder Wall.

'His name's Bartholomew Lawson,' Matthew said. 'His wife is Eleanor Lawson. Nelly Wren. Jeremy Rosco's first love.'

Chapter Twenty-Seven

MATTHEW STOOD FOR A MOMENT STARING out to sea, the wind blowing into his face, but he couldn't shift the image of Bartholomew Lawson from his head. He breathed in the salt and the stink of rotting seaweed and at last his brain started to work again, to consider the practicalities. This was a logistical nightmare. Just getting the body back up the cliff would take a specialist team. He looked at his phone. Of course, there was no signal, here in the shadow of the cliff.

He looked at Jonathan. 'Could you go back up the path? You'll be quicker than me. As soon as you get a signal, call it in. Jen will still be on Merseyside, but you'll get Ross on his mobile and then let the team know in Barnstaple. If you can direct them to the parking space you mentioned and lead them down the path.'

Oh God. This is a health and safety disaster. A whole search team scrambling down that path! He should probably do a risk assessment. But they needed Lawson's body shifted before high tide made it even more dangerous.

'Can you see if anything's already parked in the space? Make a note of the registration and call that in too?'

'Sure.'

'When's high water?' Because Jonathan would surely know. That competence again.

'About three this afternoon.' The man had taken in the instructions, nodded, and was already moving away to start the climb up the path.

So, they had just under four hours, Matthew thought. It could be a lot worse. Jonathan was out of sight now. Matthew could hear his boots rattling the shingle, the noise sending gulls into the air. He was running.

Soon, everything was quiet again, except for the sound of the waves on the shore. Matthew sat on a dry rock, still with his back to Lawson's body, and tried to make sense of the man's death. Lawson was on the periphery of the case. He'd known Rosco when they'd been boys, but the pair had never been close. If anything, there'd been hostility, barely concealed. And he was the husband of Eleanor, Rosco's childhood sweetheart, haunted by her, it seemed, until his death. It would just make sense if Lawson had murdered Rosco, though the elaborate staging of the body seemed completely out of character, but why would anyone want to kill both men? Matthew rejected the idea immediately that this was an accident; that Lawson had slipped and fallen to his death. From Ross's description he wasn't the sort of person for bracing country walks. And he'd never quite believed in coincidence. Not when it came to murder.

His thoughts then turned to Eleanor. If her husband had died late the night before, or early this morning, she might not even know that he was missing. He could even have been in the habit of disappearing when he was drunk, ending up on a friend's sofa or in a strange woman's bed. Matthew hoped the team would arrive soon, so he could be the person to notify Eleanor of his death.

The woman connected both victims. It can't have been easy living with Bartholomew and of all the people involved in the case, she was the closest to him, the person with a motive. She could have stood next to him at the top of the cliff and pushed him. If he'd been drinking, it wouldn't have taken any strength. Matthew could believe that of Eleanor: an impulse when she was stretched beyond endurance by his selfishness, wanting at last some peace, but not the pantomime with Rosco. He'd believed her when she'd said she'd loved *him*.

He started to feel cold. The breeze was stronger and the clouds had darkened. Perhaps the forecast storm was on its way. Matthew got to his feet and started to move, frustrated now to be here waiting. Powerless. There was no doubt that Bartholomew had fallen from the top of the cliff; nothing else would explain the extensive injuries. It was possible, of course, that the man had already been dead before he was tipped over. Would a pathologist be able to tell the difference between trauma to the head caused by a weapon, and from injuries sustained as a body fell from height, bouncing into sharp rock as it fell?

Matthew looked at his watch. Time seemed to be crawling, but only half an hour had passed. Then, above the natural sounds of wind and waves, he thought he heard another. A siren at the top of the cliff above him. A little while longer, and there was the scuffle of boots on the steep path. He left his post and climbed over the rocks to the beach. He saw two uniformed officers, panting, because they'd been moving as quickly as they could and they weren't built for the job: Jimmy Rainston again, and his friend; the officers he'd met in

Greystone that first morning, who had been part of the search team in the village.

'This way.'

The three of them stood, looking down at the body.

'It won't be easy getting him up the cliff,' Rainston said. 'He's a big bloke. A fall then, was it? Your mate wasn't clear.'

Matthew ignored the question. 'His name's Bartholomew Lawson. Have you come across him?'

'Big cheese in the yacht club.' A pause. 'Boozer. Lucky not to have lost his licence.' He looked up at Matthew. 'Not the sort, I'd say, to be walking the coastal path. I only ever see him in a car or propping up the bar in the club. Unless he's changed his ways and suddenly gone in for healthy living.'

'I can leave you to it then?' Matthew didn't want to speculate about what might have happened. 'And we treat it as unexplained until we know any different. I don't imagine you get many people down here, but there might be some rubberneckers when we take him up.'

It struck him that if it hadn't been for Jonathan's restlessness, Lawson's body would probably never have been found. There was a gale forecast and a high tide, and anything left by the rats and the gulls would soon be swept out to sea. Even if the tide hadn't taken it, time would reduce it to bone. The killer, if the man *had* been killed, had chosen the perfect spot. Surely this was the work of a local, someone who understood the coast.

Jonathan was waiting for him at the top of the cliff.

'Do you want to see the layby, the nearest spot to the road?'

'Sure. Then we'll need to get back to Greystone to our cars. I want to inform his wife.' Because it was the kind thing to do, before she heard through the media, but also because he wanted to see Eleanor's response to the news.

They could see the road after a couple of hundred yards. It was running parallel to the coast and would have been invisible, bounded by a hedge, apart from the top of a lorry, moving along it. After ten minutes the lane swerved and almost hit the path. There was a thin spinney of windblown trees separating the two, and a pull-off where the police car was parked.

'I should have told them to park elsewhere. We need to check for tyre marks. I'll let the team know to keep it clear.' There was no other vehicle parked there.

'So, Lawson definitely didn't drive here.' Matthew was still talking to himself as much as to Jonathan. 'Surely not an accident then? Even if he fancied a midnight stroll, he wouldn't have walked here all the way from Morrisham.'

Matthew made his way through the trees to the marked coastal path, close to the cliff edge. He didn't go too close. He could feel the tug of the wind.

'This must be where he went over, don't you think? If he was already dead, the killer wouldn't want to drag him any further than they needed. And if you look at the layout of the bay, this is where you found him.'

'Definitely.' Jonathan was nearly at the edge, looking over. Matthew was tempted to call him back. But Jonathan was a risk-taker and hated him fussing. At last, he turned and walked away.

Ross May was approaching, just as they arrived back at the parking spot. Matthew motioned for him to keep the spot clear and park on the lane. 'We need an officer to keep any vehicles away. There are two below. They've got radios. Can you get one of them back up?'

'So, what's going on?' Ross was already out of the car, looking very smart and sleek after his night at home.

'Just wait until we have someone to secure this place. Then you can give us a lift back to Greystone and I'll tell you.'

'You just stumbled over his body?' They were almost at the village and Matthew had explained what had happened. Ross sounded suspicious, as if Matthew had some secret form of intelligence that he wasn't passing on. 'By chance?'

'Purely by chance,' Matthew said, 'and if Jonathan hadn't found out about the path down to the beach, it could have laid there, rotting, and we'd never have known the man was dead.'

'What do you want me to do now?'

'Go back and supervise the removal of the body. We need it up before high tide. And we're treating this as a crime scene. Even if a coroner comes up with an open verdict, this is a murder.'

Chapter Twenty-Eight

JEN OPENED HER EYES SLOWLY. THE garden had stopped spinning.

'What the fuck do you think you were doing?'

It was a woman's voice, clear, theatrical. There was no sympathy. Jen could see brown bare feet, slightly muddy. She pushed herself up to a sitting position, rubbed her arm and looked at Imogen Holt, who was wrapped in a dressing gown. She was staring down at her victim with the unfocused look of somebody who has just woken up. But she was lovely all the same, even without the make-up of her publicity photo.

'I thought you were a yob, breaking into my house. The neighbour over the road said some shifty bloke had gone round the back.'

That would be the waterproof and the boots. The hood up with the hair tucked inside to keep it dry.

'Were you trying to break into my house?'

'No,' Jen said. She thought she could only have been out for seconds. 'I'm a cop. I need to talk to you.'

'Why didn't you just ring the bell?'

'Your car's not here. We thought you were away.' She got unsteadily to her feet. 'Look, can't we go inside? I could murder a brew.'

'I don't know . . .' She peered at Jen. She'd not had time to get her specs or put in her contacts. 'My car's not here because it got bloody clamped near the airport. I've left it there before, with no bother . . .' She broke off and looked at Jen again. 'I'm not sure what you want.'

Jen fished in her pocket for her warrant card. 'Let me come in and I'll explain.'

Imogen must have come out through the front door and round the side of the house, because that was the way she led Jen.

'I've been away for a few days,' she said. 'Work. I didn't get in until late and my neighbour's phone call woke me.'

As if to prove it, there was a suitcase standing in the hall, airline label still attached, coat flung on top of it.

Imogen stood just inside the door. 'What is going on?'

'I believe you know Jeremy Rosco.'

'Yeah, why? I thought he'd be back from his adventures by now.'

'He lived with you?'

'Still does unless he's wandered off for good this time.' Only then did Imogen seem to properly wake up. 'What's happened to him? Bloody travel always turns my brain to mush, even if I don't have the excuse of jet lag. I don't know what you're telling me.'

'Could we sit down somewhere?' Jen didn't want to do this in the hall, with the woman half-dressed and blinking like an owl.

'Let me get some clothes on. Go on through.' She nodded to the living room.

Jen made her way into a comfortable living room. Bookshelves had been built on either side of the fireplace, and they were crammed tight, and piled with extra copies. There were two sofas, well-made. Jen thought of the little house in Greystone, where Rosco had spent his last weeks. The minimalist order was very different from this. This was very definitely Imogen's flat.

Imogen came into the room. She was wearing running gear – Lycra leggings and a baggy top. Her feet were still bare but her hair had been tied back. She'd put on her glasses. Large, with designer frames.

'Where have you been?' Jen thought it was best to get in a few early questions in case the woman lost it when she heard that Rosco was dead.

'Morocco. Two days. Work. A drinks ad.'

So, it was just possible that she'd been the woman Alan Ford had seen at the bottom of Quarry Terrace. She could have gone straight to the airport afterwards.

'Jeremy left home some time before that?'

'Yeah, he went a few weeks ago. Some mysterious project.' She was starting to get suspicious, but was still relaxed, curled on one of the sofas, her feet beneath her. Jen thought she probably did yoga. Pilates. She was fit and flexible. And, of course, she would run. These days, everyone ran.

'He didn't tell you where he was going?'

'Not in any detail. He's always disappearing on some exped- ition or other, or a recce for a show. We don't have the sort of relationship where we have to account for our movements.'

'But you *were* in a relationship?'

Now, Imogen stared at her. 'What is this? What's going on?'

'Jeremy Rosco is dead. He was murdered in a village called Greystone on the North Devon coast. You hadn't heard?'

'No! Jem's dead?' She seemed shocked, horrified. But then she was an actress. It seemed as if her world had fallen apart.

'It was all over the news.'

'We were filming in the mountains. Ten-hour-a-day shoots. No phone signal. And when I got in last night I just went to bed. No, I hadn't heard.'

Jen thought about that. The first thing she did when she arrived into the country off a flight was to check her phone. Someone would have sent a message to Imogen surely. A text of condolence. Or curiosity. And if she hadn't picked them up in Morocco, she would certainly have seen them once she got off the plane.

'None of your friends got in touch to let you know? The film crew would surely have had access to news of the outside world.'

'Jeremy and I didn't have that sort of relationship.'

'What *was* the nature of your relationship, Miss Holt?'

A moment of silence.

'It wasn't exactly public knowledge that Jem and I were together.'

'Why would you keep it secret?'

Imogen shrugged. 'It wasn't my decision. Jeremy always said he didn't want his private life plastered all over the media.' She looked across at Jen. 'I could see why he wanted a bit of privacy. He was always being pestered to stick his name to good causes, donate to charities, be the public face of some business. I have a bit of that hassle and I'm not half as famous as he was.'

'How long have you been together?'

'Years,' she said. 'Bloody years.'

Then the tears started. Jen thought they weren't just about loss and grief, but for the wasted time spent with a man who hadn't even acknowledged their relationship. Time when she could have found a real partner, someone who would celebrate her, someone with whom she might have children. *Children again.* Jen thought *she* was becoming obsessed with them. She waited. Imogen pulled a tissue from a pocket, blew her nose and dried her eyes.

'How did you meet?' Jen asked.

'At a Royal Television Society bash. I was still a minor character in a minor soap, and Jeremy was up for some award for a documentary he'd made. We were sitting at the same table. He charmed me.' A pause. 'He charmed me almost until he died. I thought I was supporting a great man, a hero. Deep down, I suppose I knew it was a relationship of convenience, that he was using me. I gave him stability, a home. Sex on tap. And he had no responsibility. I did all the adult stuff. I even booked his tickets when he went off travelling and did his tax return. I was a cross between a mother and a PA.' Imogen looked up at her. 'But I loved him. I really loved him.'

'Did you book his tickets for the most recent trip?'

'No.' The woman wiped her eyes again. 'He said the company would do it for him.' A pause. 'I was suspicious. He was so mysterious about it all. I wondered if he'd met someone else and he couldn't face telling me.'

'Did he tell you where he was going?'

She shook her head. 'I didn't want to push him. Besides, I was distracted. I had an audition and it was a job I *really* wanted.'

'Did you get the part?'

Her face brightened briefly. 'Yeah, I did! We start rehearsals at the beginning of next month.'

'Did you ever go to his flat in Morrisham on the North Devon coast?'

'Once,' she said. 'Soon after we met. For a romantic long weekend.'

'He had all his mail from there redirected to you.'

'He did. An envelope would turn up every month.'

'Why the secrecy? Why use your name instead of his own?'

She shrugged. 'Because he enjoyed making a drama out of everything? I always thought he was like a pirate in a kids' adventure story, swashbuckling, larger than life.'

'Did you see what was in the letters?'

'Of course not! I wouldn't pry into personal correspondence.'

'Really?' Jen said. 'I'd have been tempted.'

Imogen caught her eye and gave a little laugh. 'Well, of course I was *tempted*. But I didn't. The letters came in a sealed jiffy bag. Impossible to do without being found out!'

'Does the name Eleanor Lawson mean anything to you? Nell Lawson? Nelly Wren?'

At the last name, Imogen looked up. 'Wasn't that the name of his first proper boat? The one he completed the round-the-world in?'

Jen nodded. 'It was named after a real woman.'

'Ah,' Imogen said. 'His first girlfriend. The love of his life.'

'So, he did mention her to you?'

'At the beginning of the relationship, when we spent hours talking, baring our souls. You know how it is.'

No, not really. I've never had a relationship that intense. That honest.

'Did he seem anxious recently? Any threats? Any disagree-ments that might have led to his murder?'

'No! Jeremy didn't provoke people. He wanted them to like him.' Imogen paused. 'If anything, he seemed quite excited in the last few weeks before he disappeared. He'd get like that before a fresh project. That itch for a new expedition. A new adventure.' She looked up at Jen. 'Or a new woman. It would be like him just to slide away. I wasn't entirely surprised that he wasn't here when I got back.'

'Did he keep any of the letters? I'd like to see them.'

'I never saw them once the big envelope arrived. He always took it away to open. He didn't discuss them. I asked once what had come in the mail. "Nothing interesting," he said. And that was it. But you're welcome to look for them. He used one of the bedrooms as a kind of office. If he kept them, they'd be in there.'

It was a box room at the back, dark and shady, just big enough to make a child's bedroom. There was a desk under the window, a map of the world on the wall. With pins, presumably marking all the places that he'd travelled to. There were a lot of pins. A filing cabinet, not locked, and shelves containing travel guides, books. A few of them written by Rosco himself. The place was ordered, tidy. Much more like the spartan house in Greystone. The only thing on the desk was a PC with monitor and keyboard. Jen thought she'd bag that and take it away for the digital team to poke into. No point her looking at it now.

The top desk drawer held pens and notebooks. She opened a couple. They all seemed to be journals of his travels. She couldn't imagine what that must be like. The restlessness. Always moving. Never able to settle. Would it have been different if he'd managed to persuade Eleanor to marry him? Probably not, she thought. That was just a dream and eventually he would have felt the need to be on the move again. As Imogen had said, no home meant no real responsibility. No growing up.

At first, she found nothing significant in the filing cabinet. Old contracts with production companies. Invoices and statements. Nothing recent. Was that because most business was being done online or because he wasn't so much in demand as he was getting older? Then she came across a fat envelope which looked as if it was full of fan mail. Some of it seemed to go back years, but she took it with her. There could be some weird, obsessed stalker, who'd been rejected and felt the need for revenge. They could have followed Rosco to Devon and killed him.

She unplugged the computer and went back into the living room. 'I'm afraid I'll have to take this.'

Imogen was still sitting on the sofa. 'No worries. I use my laptop.'

'Did Jeremy have any overenthusiastic admirers? Stalkers who hassled him?'

Imogen shook her head. 'Maybe in the early days. I think that was one reason why he wanted to protect his privacy. But not recently. These days, he wasn't even recognized when we were out together. He pretended to be pleased, but I rather think he missed the attention.'

'Are you okay? Have you got friends to keep you company?'

'Sure.' She looked up. 'I'll be fine. It was a shock, you know, and I'll miss him.'

Jen nodded and left the building.

Chapter Twenty-Nine

By the time Ross got back from Greystone to the parking spot close to the coastal path, the lane was so full of vehicles that it was tight to squeeze past. Ross recognized Sally Pengelly's VW and there was a coastguard's Land Rover. He had to pull right onto the verge, and when he climbed out of his car, he stepped into mud, covering his new trainers and splashing his jeans. Jimmy Rainston was managing the traffic and waved at Ross.

'They asked me to point you to the way down to the cove.'

'Is it safe?'

From here, the cliffs seemed sheer all the way along to Greystone in the distance. May felt dizzy just looking.

'Depends what you call safe.' Rainston directed Ross along the coastal path. 'We've marked where you turn in with tape. It might be a bit slippery now, all the buggers that have been up and down. Best take care. Don't want no more accidents.' The constable saw a tractor approaching and walked back to the road to see it through.

There was a bit of blue and white tape wrapped around a

prickly bush, and from here Ross could see a path twisting down a gully to the beach. Below him a group of men dressed in navy jackets stood, apparently waiting to be called to action. Perhaps they'd been drafted in to lift the body to the top. Ross considered himself fit, and he started down the path at speed. The tide was on its way in and he wanted to be there before everything was over. This was what he'd joined the job for: drama and adventure. He and Mel had planned a lazy morning, but she'd understood when he was called in again. Zigzagging down the stony path, he thought how lucky he was. He tried not to take her for granted these days. He couldn't imagine life without her.

When he hit the beach, it started to rain. A gusty squall from the north-west. From the sea. The tide was inching in, the wind behind it. There'd been some shelter in the gully but now the weather hit him with full force. He recognized one of the men in the navy jackets. He played rugby for a Bideford team and they'd had a few wild nights out together after the local derby. So wild that Ross struggled now to remember his name. It didn't much matter because the noise of the wind and the sea was so fierce that they could hardly hear each other. The man pointed to the rocks to the south of the bay, then bent down and yelled into Ross's ear.

'Tell them they'd best get a wiggle on or they'll all be stranded.'

Ross stuck up a thumb to show he understood, and wished he'd brought gloves.

He scrambled across the rocks, slipped on some seaweed and his foot went into a pool. It took a moment for the cold water to seep through the leather of his trainer and his sock. Sally Pengelly straightened when she heard him swear. 'Want a quick look? I understand you met him. We're just about to move him.'

The man looked more twisted than May would have thought possible. Lawson had been an arrogant, drunken sod, but he hadn't deserved this. 'Yeah,' he was bellowing and his voice seemed to bounce back from the cliff. 'It's definitely him. Bartholomew Lawson.'

'Let's get the volunteers in then. You okay to give them a shout?'

Ross didn't stop to answer. He couldn't imagine anything worse than being stuck here, in the cold and the wet, stranded beyond the rocky spur and waiting for the tide to go out. When he returned with them, Lawson was already in a body bag. The team strapped him onto a stretcher and carried him away.

Ross was the last person back on the beach, and the water was lapping at his feet as he crossed the rocks. It was still an hour from high water, and safe now on higher ground at the top of the cove, he stood for a moment, alone, buffeted by the storm. It occurred to him suddenly that there must be something significant to the killer about this place. That was why there'd been the elaborate ritual of towing Rosco out in the *Moon Crest*'s tender. That was why Bartholomew Lawson's body had been thrown over the cliff at this particular point. He decided that he needed to discuss his theory with Venn as soon as possible. Jen Rafferty wouldn't be back in North Devon until the following day. There was even a chance that they'd have this all wrapped up by then. Without her.

He phoned Venn when he reached the top of the cliff, but there was no answer. He headed back towards Greystone. He knew the boss had planned to talk to Eleanor Lawson, but he might be back by now. In the village, instead of stopping at the Maiden's he drove on and pulled up a little way from the jetty, and ran through the rain and the spray to Sammy Barton's cottage. He banged on the door. It was opened by Barton's wife, Jane.

'Come in, come in.' She stood aside to let him past. 'What strange weather we're having. All over the place. Let me take your jacket.'

'Is Sammy in?'

'He's not, my love. He's out at a meeting.'

'At the lifeboat station?' Ross imagined it would take some organization, running a show like that.

She didn't answer immediately and he wondered if he'd been tactless in some way for asking. Perhaps Barton was a recovering alcoholic, or in some other kind of therapy.

'No,' she said. 'He's an elder of our church. It's one of their days for a get-together.'

'You're Barum Brethren?' Ross had never heard of the group until the body of a lonely man had been found on Crow Point. Now, it seemed, they haunted every case he worked on.

She nodded briefly, surprised that he'd heard of them, but not wanting to discuss the matter further. 'Perhaps I can help you?'

'That bay beyond the headland where the *Moon Crest* tender was anchored . . .'

'Scully Bay.'

'Is that what it's called?'

'These days. The story goes that it used to be Skull Bay. After the bodies found there when ships came aground, lured in by wreckers.' She laughed, more relaxed now. 'But I love my local history and I've seen old maps and charts. It was always Scully headland and Scully Bay. The rest is just made up.'

'I wondered if anything more recent had happened there? I don't know. A suicide? An accident?'

'Why are you asking?' Her voice was sharper. Suspicious.

Ross shook his head. 'Just a theory. Just trying to work out why anyone would tow your bloke's dinghy all that way. It's as if someone's making a point.'

'No,' she said. 'I can't think why anyone would want to make a point like that.'

'I'll come back later,' Ross said easily. 'See if your husband can help me. It was his boat that was stolen after all. Perhaps that was making a point too.'

'Sammy won't be able to help any more than me.' She was impatient now. 'You're just making a story. Like the people who believe in the wreckers and smugglers and skulls rolling up on the shore. Stick to the truth, boy. Stick to the truth.'

She opened the door and stood watching as he ran back to his car, as if she wanted to make sure that he'd gone.

Chapter Thirty

THIS TIME, INSTEAD OF WALKING UP the drive, Venn drove the car through the stone pillars and parked right outside the big house. He wanted to tell Eleanor Lawson that her husband was dead before she found out from another source. Besides, the weather had changed, and this wasn't a good day for a walk. The place looked different. Everything was damp and grey. When he got out of the car, he could hear the wind in the trees, and howling around the tall chimneys. It was so dark that there was a light on in the kitchen on the side of the house, and that was where he went. He knocked on the door and Eleanor opened it almost immediately. There was a smell of bread baking, and she had a smudge of flour on one cheek.

'Inspector, what a dreadful day to be out, come along in.' She seemed untroubled. Had she even noticed that her husband was missing?

'I have some bad news,' Venn said.

Perhaps something in his voice made her realize that this was serious. 'Just a moment, Inspector.' She took a tea towel, and bent and lifted a loaf from the oven and slid it onto a wire

cooling tray. She turned to him, and gave him her full attention. 'What is it?'

'When did you last see your husband?'

'Yesterday evening before he set off for the sailing club.' A
pause. 'Oh, he didn't insist on driving, did he?' A pause, then
a confession. 'He's an alcoholic, you know, and he has no
judgement after a few drinks. The staff at the club usually
manage to get his keys off him, but not always.' She looked
up. 'Did he have an accident? Hurt someone? Are you telling
me he's under arrest?'

'Had you noticed that he hadn't come home last night?'

She nodded. 'Not until this morning. We have separate
rooms. A house this size, there's no reason to live on top of
each other. But when he didn't emerge for coffee at eleven
. . . That's our ritual. It's when we catch up and make our
plans for the day. Then, I went up and saw that his bed hadn't
been slept in.'

'You weren't anxious?'

She shook her head. 'It's not so unusual. A sailing chum
invites him back for a nightcap and he falls asleep on the sofa.
Wakes the next day with an even worse headache than usual.
He turns up later, full of apologies, clutching a bunch of
supermarket flowers.' Another pause and a little smile to take
the edge off any criticism. The loyal wife, even now. 'What's
happened, Inspector? Where is he?'

'He's dead,' Venn said. 'I'm so sorry. His body was found
earlier this morning.'

She didn't move. Then he saw that she was crying. She lifted
the edge of her apron to dry her eyes.

'Stupid man,' she said, her voice affectionate. 'I knew it
might happen one day. But that it should happen now, so

soon after Jem. I've lost both my men within a week.' She dropped the hem of her apron. 'It does seem a very odd coincidence, Inspector.'

There was the trace of a question in the last sentence. Her brown, bird-like eyes were sharp.

'Your husband's death is unexplained so far,' Venn said. 'It doesn't seem as if it were a vehicle-related incident.'

'So, nobody else was hurt?'

'No, there are no other victims.'

'Victims? That's a very odd word to use.'

Venn took a breath. Outside, it was raining in earnest now, drops battering the old sash windows like pebbles. 'Your husband's body was found at the bottom of cliffs near Scully Cove.'

Again, she was quite still. Waiting.

'It could, of course, have been an accident, but his car wasn't anywhere close by. Our officers are searching for it.' Venn had a sudden thought. 'It isn't here?'

Eleanor shook her head. 'I looked when I realized he wasn't in his room.'

'It could perhaps have been suicide.' Venn had been thinking of this since seeing the body, had wondered perhaps if Bartholomew Lawson had killed Rosco, and then himself. 'But again, we would have expected to find his car somewhere near the top of the cliff.'

'I don't think Barty would have killed himself. His father took his own life and Barty always said it was a very selfish act. He'd been close to his father and rather despised him for taking an easy way out. One never knows, of course, quite what is in another person's head, but really, I think Bartholomew was quite comfortable with the ritual of his life. The evenings at the sailing club, coffee here with me. Then he was a JP and many of his afternoons were spent in court. That seemed more like a social club than a position of responsibility. Many of the magistrates were people he knew well, and they seemed rather a clubbable bunch. The older ones at least. The more recently appointed were more earnest. He was disappointed that things hadn't worked out as he'd imagined when he was a young man, but we led quite a civilized life together. No, I don't think he'd be so desperate that suicide would seem a sensible option.'

'How has he been recently? Anxious? Under any kind of threat?'

'You think that he was murdered too? Is that what you've been trying to tell me, Inspector?'

'I think,' he said, 'that's it's a possibility we need to consider.'

'If anything, perhaps Jeremy's death caused him some satisfaction. Barty had always disliked Jem. That was almost tribal. It was about the difference in their backgrounds. It upset his sensibilities that a feral, ill-educated boy, son of a poor single mother, should become almost a national hero.'

'So, your husband wasn't worried in the last few days, scared even?'

Eleanor thought about that. 'Honestly, no. There was nothing different about him.'

They sat for a moment without speaking, the rain whipping at the window.

'I can't understand why anyone would kill him,' Eleanor said at last. 'Robbery perhaps? He would have had cash on his person. Credit cards, a mobile phone. Morrisham might seem very genteel, but there are areas of deprivation. I understand that drugs are a problem.' She paused for a moment. 'Or could it have been revenge? Someone he met in court perhaps and sentenced a little harshly. He wouldn't have been the most lenient of magistrates. He had no sympathy for law-breakers, despite his blindness about drink driving.'

'We come back to the coincidence.' Venn leaned back in his chair. 'Your husband's body was found near Scully Head. Just across the cove from where the boat holding Jeremy Rosco's body was anchored. As you said, your two men.'

'You think I might have killed them both?' Now the bird eyes sparkled. Anger? Amusement? Matthew found it hard to tell.

Venn shook his head. 'I'm not saying that, but you were the connection. You might have useful information.' He paused for a moment. 'Did you know that you're the only beneficiary in Mr Rosco's will?'

'No!' She appeared genuinely shocked. 'The stupid boy!' She gave a little smile and was, it seemed, lost in thought. Venn thought the romantic gesture had moved and pleased her.

'Let's go back to Scully Cove,' he said after a while. 'Is there anything about that place that has any special significance for you?'

She pulled her attention back to the present. 'Only in the way that it has significance for everyone living on this coast. We all grew up with stories of smuggling and shipwrecks. Kipling has a lot to answer for.'

'Locals would have known about the path down to the beach then?'

'Of course. I think every generation of teenager claimed it as their own.' She got to her feet and knelt on the floor, stroking the head of the dog that lay sleeping in front of the range. 'I'm sorry, Inspector, I would help you if I could. Might I see my husband?'

Venn thought of the body, twisted, the face already pocked with bites. 'You don't need to do that. My sergeant was able to identify him. You might prefer to remember him as he was.'

She seemed to understand and nodded. 'I see. You're very kind. Can I think about it and let you know?'

'Of course,' he said. 'I wonder if I could look in your husband's room? And if there was somewhere he used as an office?'

She got to her feet. 'I'll show you, Inspector.' She led him up a grand wooden staircase, along a corridor and opened the door to a bedroom. In the hall downstairs a phone started ringing. 'If you'll excuse me.' She left the door open and he heard her feet on the stairs and then her voice, even, controlled. 'Thank you. Yes, it is rather terrible. No, we don't know yet exactly what happened. The police are still here. That's really very kind, but at the moment I think I need to be alone.' Then the click of the receiver being replaced.

The news was out then, Matthew thought. There'd be more pressure from the top – from his boss Joe Oldham – but little support. The adrenaline which had kept him going since Jonathan found Lawson's body drained away, and he felt flat and very tired.

Eleanor stayed downstairs and he was left to explore Lawson's room alone. Lawson's rooms. Because the door led into a suite of rooms, almost a small apartment. Everything was very brown and large; the furniture must surely have been in the place since Eleanor's parents had been in charge here. Probably before that. The wind was as strong as ever, and rattled the windows. Matthew had to switch on the light.

He came to the bedroom first. It was big and square and at the front of the house. This was where Bartholomew had been standing when Venn had first seen him, staring out of the window at the frosty garden. The bed was made and seemed not to have been slept in. Blankets and faded linen sheets and pillowcases. A shiny quilt patterned in cream and beige. They'd need to check if Lawson had made it to the sailing club the night before. Ross was a familiar face. He could do that once the place opened.

There were two cavernous wardrobes and a matching chest of drawers. In the wardrobes, there was a lot of tweed, every-thing muted. Green and brown. A couple of work suits which presumably the man had worn to court. Checked shirts for casual wear and white and pale blue ones to go with the suits. Nothing was new. Matthew pulled open the drawers hoping for letters, documents, something to give him a handle on the man. A smell of lavender and mothballs floated out. The drawers contained underwear, knitted jerseys. Navy, not green. A couple of pairs of navy shorts. These would be his sailing clothes. Not quite a uniform, but somehow defining him.

A door on the furthest side of the room led to a short, dark corridor and two more doors. One opened into a bathroom, which must have been renovated in the seventies or eighties. An avocado-green bath, sink and lavatory. No natural light and with a background smell of mould. No shower and no visible form of heating. A bentwood towel rail looked incon-gruous against the green plastic. It held a large, threadbare towel, which had once been white.

The other door led to a more attractive space, again at the front of the house. A living room and office rolled into one. There was a large desk under the window, and against the opposite wall a leather chesterfield. Bare floorboards and a faded rug in reds and golds. Bookshelves on either side of

When he joined her in the kitchen, she'd already made the coffee. The pot stood on the edge of the range, keeping warm. There was milk in a jug and brown sugar in a matching bowl. She'd taken off her apron. It was almost as if she felt the need to impress.

'I've taken all the paperwork in Mr Lawson's drawers. There's nothing you're likely to need immediately?'

She shook her head. 'Both our wills are held by our solicitor.' A pause. 'I don't think there'll be life insurance. Nothing like that.' She was staring out into the garden but there was nothing to see except the rain.

'I'll miss him,' she said at last. 'As you'll have realized, we led very separate lives, but we did meet every day for coffee and lunch. He was a presence in the house. We could be quite companiable in our own way.'

now. Free and available. Come and comfort me. How ironic that I'm free and he's dead.'

'Did you know,' Matthew said, very gently, 'that Mr Rosco had been living with a woman on the Wirral for a number of years? An actress younger than him.'

'No. I didn't know that. I could have guessed he'd be living with someone. He was never very good on his own. He'd have left her and come to me, though, if I'd asked him. Even after all this time, I can be certain of that.'

There was a moment of silence.

'I'll send an officer to be with you. They can pass on any information as we find it, and stop you being pestered by the press. You won't mind the company?'

She shook her head again. 'No, I won't mind. But you call in too, Inspector, whenever you think I can help. Barty wasn't

a good husband, but I wasn't a very good wife, and he didn't deserve to die in that way.'

'If you think of anything that might help, here's my card.'

Eleanor took it and propped it on a shelf over the range.

Matthew let himself out. The rain had stopped for a moment, but a gust of wind blew a shower off the nearby trees and into his face as he ran for the car.

Chapter Thirty-One

Jen spent the afternoon in a police station in Birkenhead, bringing colleagues up to speed. They gave her a desk in the open-plan office and she felt strangely at home. It was the accents and the humour. She even recognized some of the names they were discussing. Men she'd arrested as lads now had kids of their own but were still thieving. Or dealing drugs. She'd been to school with a couple of lasses who'd just been done for large-scale shoplifting. Poor cows, she thought. She'd admired them then. They'd been super cool.

'Has Jeremy Rosco come onto your radar at all?' There was no record, but these officers knew the patch. Nobody had come across him, though. The younger ones hadn't even heard of him.

She waited for and received confirmation that Imogen Holt had been working in Morocco and that she'd been on the same flight home as the rest of the crew, then she spoke to the producer who'd organized the audition that the actress had attended. It had taken place the week before Rosco's

death. Imogen could still have driven to Devon. There was a possibility that she was Alan Ford's mysterious woman. It seemed she had no alibi for the relevant date.

Jen called in a favour from an old mate and dropped off Rosco's computer with the digital team. She could have gone back to the hotel then, arranged to meet up with friends in Liverpool, but instead she stayed in the police station and started to read the envelope of fan mail. She loved the buzz here. The noise of policing. The view of the river and *her* city on the other bank.

She almost missed it because the letter was one of the less graphic efforts. There was a declaration of admiration, of love, but no promise of sexual favours. Then Jen came across others signed by the same name. They seemed to have arrived over two time periods, with a gap of several years in between. The first few appeared to have been written by a gushing teenager, decorated with painted hearts. In the later bunch, the writer bared her soul: *I'm going through a tough time. Please can we meet? I think you might understand and be able to help.* A description of an unhappy relationship. They were beautifully handwritten. There was nothing recent and no indication that any had been answered. No threats of violence. Perhaps the writing itself had been cathartic. Each letter was signed by both a first and a family name. Mary Ford.

Jen was on her feet, just about to head to the hotel, where it would be quieter, to catch up with the team when Ross phoned.

'There's been another body.'

'Who?'

'Bartholomew Lawson. Nelly Wren's husband. Commodore of the yacht club. The boss found him on a beach close to where that boat with Rosco's body was anchored.'

'I'll get a couple of hours' kip and then I'll be on my way.' Mary Ford's love letters went out of her head then, until the call was over.

Chapter Thirty-Two

MATTHEW AND ROSS WERE BACK AGAIN in the snug in the Maiden's Prayer. The waves in the bay were blown into small white peaks like meringue. Matthew supposed that if you lived in a place like this, you'd always notice the weather. In Greystone, the sea was the first thing he looked at when he woke up. At the house by the estuary, the bedroom only had a view of the river.

Jonathan had driven home the night before, saying that he had a Woodyard Trust meeting to prepare for, but probably not wanting to get in the way. Or perhaps he still needed time to sort out the personal matter that had been haunting him. He'd seemed distracted. Gwen Gregory was bustling in and out with coffee and toast.

'Lawson's death is all over the news,' she said. 'You'll be looking into that too, I dare say.'

'You knew him?'

'Nah, we didn't move in the same circles. He was sent away to boarding school, and when he was back, he didn't mix with the likes of us.'

'You must have known *of* him, though. Your brother gave him a lift home from the sailing club most nights.'

'Well, yes. I knew *of* him. He was a magistrate, wasn't he? Always on the local radio, spouting about law and order.'

'Davy must have known him better?'

She sniffed. 'I suppose, though from what I hear, the man was so pissed most nights, there was hardly much of a conversation. I can't see how someone like that had the nerve to pass judgement on other people.'

She walked away. Matthew looked through the hatch to the bar. Carter was chatting to an elderly couple who'd come in for coffee.

'I've just heard a forecast. The wind's getting up again and there are already trees down further up the coast.' Matthew thought of all the trees surrounding Eleanor's home and wondered how many of them would still be standing the following day.

Carter disappeared back into his personal domain. At last, he and May could talk with no danger of being overheard.

'They've found Lawson's car,' May said. 'It was outside the sailing club. I'll go later and speak to the members.'

'I think I should talk to Davy Gregory.' Matthew believed Davy would have been closer to Lawson than Gwen had implied. He'd acted as a kind of nursemaid to the man, and would surely know his secrets. Besides, if Lawson had been at the sailing club the night before, wouldn't Davy have expected to pick him up later?

'What do you want from me?'

'By the time I get back from Gregory's place, Jen should be here. She's going to drop the kids at home and then come on to Greystone. She reckons she'll be able to stay over. The kids can look after themselves because it's the weekend and she doesn't have to see them off to school. Can you do a bit more digging on Imogen Holt? She couldn't have killed *Lawson*, but Jen says she meets the description of the woman Alan Ford saw in the street. And she suspected he'd run away to meet another woman.'

'Bit of a stretch, isn't it? No way she'd be able to get him in a boat and out to Scully Bay if she wasn't local.'

'She could be a witness, though. If she'd come for a quick visit before going away to work in Morocco. To surprise him perhaps. Or to check up on him. She might have seen something.'

'Nah!' Ross was dismissive. 'That's surely too much of a coincidence. And why wouldn't she have told Jen if that was how it happened?'

'Because she didn't want to be involved in a murder investigation? She's just about to start a new acting role. You could see that the last thing she'd need would be adverse publicity. Very few people seem to have known that she and Rosco were an item.'

May shook his head. 'I just don't see it.'

Matthew drove along the wet roads towards the Gregory house. There was a brief startling flash of sunlight, so the tarmac shone gold, and then the clouds blew in again. When he got to the farmhouse, he saw that each of the couple's cars were there. Matilda opened the door to him. She was dressed in jeans and a long black sweater, her blonde hair loose about her shoulders.

'Inspector.' Her voice was neutral. Not hostile, but hardly welcoming.

ANN CLEEVES

'There's been another killing,' Venn said. 'I expect you've heard.'

'No,' she said. He couldn't tell if she were shocked or not. 'We were out all morning and I've been adding up the cash we raised for Artie's fund at the fayre, so I can announce it at school on Monday. I haven't been listening to the news.'

'And Davy?'

'I think he's been watching an old film.' A little smile. 'And probably snoozing. He works late with the taxis. He quite often has a daytime nap.'

'Was he late home yesterday evening?'

'He was. I'm not sure what time he got in, though. I was fast asleep when he came back.' She stood aside to let Matthew in. 'When we were first married, I would wait up for him, but I'm an early morning person. I soon realized I'd have to give up on the late-night vigils.' Now she asked the question that he'd have thought she would have put to him earlier. 'Who has died?'

'Bartholomew Lawson,' Matthew said. 'One of Davy's regular customers.'

'Oh!' At last, she seemed almost dismayed. 'Davy will be upset. Barty had his problems, of course, but Davy did rather like him.'

She walked through into the living room, with its view down the valley towards Scully Bay. Gregory was stretched out on the sofa. In the corner daytime television burbled. Gregory was gently snoring. Matilda touched him on the shoulder. 'We've got a visitor, love.'

He woke and smiled at her, stretched and sat upright, then saw Venn. 'What are you doing here at the weekend?' Trying to keep his voice pleasant, but not quite managing it.

'The inspector's come with some bad news.' She moved away towards the door. 'He wanted to tell you himself. I'll leave you both to it and get back to my marking.'

'I'd rather speak to you both,' Matthew said. 'If you could give me a few moments.'

'Of course.' She sounded reluctant, though. She took a seat next to her husband on the sofa.

'What's all this about?'

'It's about one of your regular customers. Bartholomew Lawson.'

'Ah,' Gregory said. 'Poor chap. His liver finally packed up, has it? It was only a matter of time.'

'No.' Again, Matthew looked down the valley. He wondered how long it would take to walk to the coastal path. Perhaps he'd walk it when he'd finished here. Perhaps. Or he might send one of the local officers to give it a go. 'Mr Lawson's death is unexplained. Suspicious even. His body was found at the bottom of the cliffs on the edge of Scully Bay.'

There was a moment of complete silence, before Matthew continued speaking.

'I understand that Mr Lawson was a regular customer. You'd pick him up most nights from the sailing club in Morrisham and take him home.'

'Not every night,' Davy said. 'Sometimes I had another job, something that paid better.'

'How did Mr Lawson get home if you couldn't collect him?'

Davy shrugged. 'I suppose one of his friends gave him a lift. Or one of the staff took him. I know they took his keys off him as soon as he got there. He was a magistrate. It wouldn't look good for him or the club if he was done for drunk driving.'

'And the night before last? Did you pick him up then?'

Davy shook his head. He was wide awake now and quite sharp. 'I probably would have been able to. I had another job later, but he was usually ready to go before eleven. Or the staff wanted him gone before he started making a scene. But nobody phoned me. That was the deal. Someone would book me if Barty was there. But he wasn't there every night and I wasn't going to save the slot unless I knew for definite that he'd need taking back.'

'I understand.' Matthew thought the man was probably telling the truth, about this at least. He was intelligent enough to know that they'd check with the sailing club staff. But that didn't mean he hadn't been waiting for Bartholomew when he'd arrived at the club. Lawson's car had been there after all, and somebody with a vehicle had brought him to Scully Bay and pushed or thrown him over the cliff. 'When was the last time you did see him?'

'Wednesday night, the night after the big storm. Barty was in the club on Wednesday night and I picked him up as I usually did and I took him home.'

'How did he seem?'

'Good,' Gregory said. 'Not quite as drunk as he usually was. Quite chatty. He even gave me a tip when he dropped me off. The rides were usually on the club account, and that didn't happen very often.'

Venn thought for a moment and then he turned his attention to Matilda. 'You told me that your father worked for Mr Lawson's father. Did you know the family?'

She shook her head. 'My father was an accountant. He worked in the office. The Lawsons had a portfolio of properties and Dad made sure the rents were paid and accounts were in order. He left, though, while I was still a young child, and set up in business on his own. I don't remember meeting the Lawsons at all.'

'Not even at the sailing club?'

'No.' She gave a little laugh. 'I'm terrified of the water. I can't even swim. My parents were into it, and had their own boat, but no, it wasn't for me and I never joined the club.'

'You told me that your parents knew Jeremy Rosco when he was a teenager.'

'Yes, but that was before I was old enough to remember.' She paused. 'They had great faith and they believed they were doing the Lord's work in their care for Jeremy. I don't think he responded as they might have hoped.' She frowned. 'Later, when I asked about him, they told me that he'd let them down. They were never specific about what he'd done. I suspect that he stole from them. They hoped he might come back to them when he was ready, but he never did.'

'I wonder if I might speak to your parents.'

She seemed reluctant but at last she answered. 'I suppose so. They're retired now and living in Barnstaple.' She jotted down their contact details on a scrap of paper and handed it to him.

'Is there a footpath from here down to the coastal path?'

'What are you thinking?' Davy was defensive. 'I told you, I didn't see Barty that night, and even if I had, I wouldn't bring him back here and set him walking out towards the shore.'

Matilda put a warning hand on her husband's knee.

'I'm just exploring possibilities,' Venn said. 'Trying to get my head round the geography of the place. Don't worry. I've got an OS map in the car. I can check with that.'

'There's a footpath leading from the lane at the end of our drive to the coast. It was a real nuisance in the summer when we were farming the place, because there's no parking, and tourists would block the gate into the field there. They still do, but it's not my problem these days.'

'Thanks,' Matthew said. 'That's very helpful.'

'If you see Barty's wife,' Matilda said, 'please pass on our condolences.'

'Do you know her?' Matthew was surprised. He didn't think they'd move in the same circles. Besides anything else, there was the religious divide. Eleanor had told him that hers was a Catholic family.

'Not really.' It was Davy who answered. 'I'd meet her sometimes when the man was too drunk to let himself into the house. She always seemed a nice woman.'

Matthew realized that there might well have been a connection between Eleanor and this family. Perhaps not with Matilda, but with Davy at least. He'd claimed to be big mates with Rosco when they were at school and Eleanor had been Jem's girlfriend then for a while at least.

'You never met her when she was going out with Jeremy Rosco? When you were all kids?'

Davy shook his head. 'Jeremy was always talking about her. He claimed she was the love of his life. But he never really introduced us. He thought we were a bit rough and ready for his lovely Nell, that we'd frighten her off.'

'Wasn't he a bit rough and ready himself?' *That was the myth at least. Rosco was the scally falling for the princess in the big house.*

'He could always put on a show, though, could Jem.' Davy paused for a moment and seemed lost in thought. 'I did see her with him once or twice, at a party, I think, and when they were in the marina at Morrisham about to go sailing, but I never really knew her.' There was another silence. 'And really, when they were together, they only had eyes for each other. I might as well not have been there.'

Outside, Matthew looked again down the valley. He took his car to the end of the Gregorys' drive and pulled onto the verge. There was a wooden signpost pointing to the footpath. Everything seemed very sharp and very close to him, an indication perhaps that the weather was about to break again. He thought he'd come to regret this, but he climbed the stile and set off. He set the stopwatch on his phone. The footpath crossed two fields of sheep, separated by a fence and another stile, the grass wet, the path ill-defined, not well used. The light was already starting to fade, but there was no sign that a body had been dragged here. No trail of flattened grass. But then his footprints disappeared almost as soon as he'd made them, the sheep-cropped sward too short to leave a mark. Only a small kissing gate in the opposite corner showed where the path should end. Through that, there was a foot-bridge over a stream, very fast flowing after the earlier down-pour. Beyond the bridge, the path led sharply downhill and through a patch of woodland. And then he'd already arrived at the lane. He could see cars still parked on the verge, Jimmy Rainston back on duty, looking bored, keeping drivers out of the layby.

Venn stood and watched. Rainston was talking into his phone and didn't notice him. Anyone could have crossed the lane here and made their way down by the steep and hidden path to the beach. He checked his watch. The walk had taken fifteen minutes and Venn hadn't been moving quickly. He turned and made his way back to his car, his mind playing out various scenarios. None of them quite fitted this particular landscape, these particular facts.

In the car, he checked his phone. Jen Rafferty had left a message. She was home, and was heading out to Greystone now.

Chapter Thirty-Three

Ross May had found nothing more useful on Imogen Holt. There was a local news report in the *Liverpool Echo* about her being axed from the soap. A review of a play she'd starred in. He moved on to check the CCTV footage sent through by Vicki from Barnstaple, looking for Lawson's car and Gregory's taxi on the night of the commodore's disappearance. He still hadn't got any results. Now he was bored of staring at a screen and was ready to do some proper policing. He felt an itch of resentment: he could have been doing this routine stuff in Barnstaple, and gone home at the end of it for a night with Mel. And why did they have to wait for Rafferty anyway?

Venn arrived back from his visit to the Gregory house. He stuck his head round the door of the snug.

'See if you can rustle up some coffee, can you, Ross? Thanks. I won't be long.'

Then he went again, apparently going up to his room, perhaps for a quick shower or to call his husband on the phone. Ross's resentment grew. He wasn't some sort of tea boy. When

Venn returned Jen was already coming through the door, so Ross didn't have the chance to talk to him alone, to share his theories and perhaps influence the progress of the investigation without her interference. He'd been getting on better with Jen and the boss lately, but there were still times when he felt like the new boy.

'So, tell us about Rosco's new partner.' Venn directed the question at his sergeant. 'Let's catch up with that before we move on to Lawson's death.'

'Imogen Holt.' Jen looked tired. She grabbed the coffee mug with both hands, like an addict desperate for the caffeine. *No stamina*, Ross thought.

She drank deeply, then continued.

'As you know, Imogen's an actress. Not a major celebrity, but doing okay. Usually in work. A bit of telly but mostly live theatre. She owns a nice flat in a smart part of the Wirral. Rosco moved in with her a few years ago. Nobody locally seems to have been aware that he was living there, and that's a bit odd considering his celebrity. I checked with the local sailing club and he wasn't a member. She fell for his charm and I think she's still besotted even if the gloss is wearing a bit thin. When he disappeared this time, without giving her any real explanation, she suspected he was having an affair.'

'Did she strike you as the jealous type?'

'She's certainly impulsive,' Jen said. 'She thought I was breaking into her house and took me on. But really? I can't imagine her stabbing Rosco, planning the whole thing with the boat.'

'But she could have tracked him down?' Ross said. 'She still could be the mysterious woman at the bottom of Quarry Bank?'

'Maybe. But it's a long way to come to check up on her bloke.'

'Did she give any reason for Rosco keeping such a low profile?' Venn asked.

Jen shrugged. 'He told Imogen he just didn't need the hassle. People bothering him to be patrons of their charities, open school fetes, be mentors for sporty youngsters from deprived backgrounds. That was why he kept the flat in Morrisham as his official address and had his mail forwarded to Imogen.'

'I had the impression of someone who quite liked being in the public eye, though.' Venn leaned back in his chair and yawned. Ross thought he had as little stamina as the sergeant. 'I wonder if there was some other reason why he might want to avoid the public's gaze. Can we have another dig into his past, Jen? He might not have a record, but let's see if there were any complaints made against him. Official or unofficial. It's almost as if he were trying to hide.'

She nodded. 'I did come across something interesting. Rosco had an office in Imogen's flat. I found these there.'

She set an envelope on the table in front of them. 'He kept all his fan mail. He obviously needed an ego boost from time to time. Check these out.'

She spread out a fan of handwritten letters. Ross looked at the name at the bottom before reading them. 'Mary Ford. I wouldn't have had her down as a fan girl.'

Venn read them carefully. Time passed slowly.

Ross found himself losing focus, distracted. It had been like that at school. He'd keep his attention on what was being said for a short time, but then it would slide away, despite his best efforts. When Venn looked up, Ross couldn't help jumping in, sharing the ideas that had been rattling round his head, even though they had nothing to do with Mary Ford or Imogen Holt.

'I was wondering if there was anything significant about Scully Bay. I mean, there must have been easier places to dispose of a body. All that pantomime with getting the tender there. I know we thought it was about Rosco having been a sailor, but then when Lawson ended up there too . . . It can't just be random, can it?'

'What sort of significance were you thinking of?' Venn leaned forward across the varnished table. 'I asked Eleanor about the bay. She said they'd all grown up with myths about the place, stories about smuggling and wrecking. She implied it was romantic nonsense dreamed up for the tourists. You're thinking there might have been something more recent?'

'Yes,' Ross said. 'These killings feel almost like revenge. Someone sending a message maybe. I wonder if there was a case of negligence that was put down as an accident. Some other tragedy.'

He could tell now that Venn was listening intently. *The boss's* attention never wandered, even when he was tired. 'I went to see Sammy Barton, to ask if any lives had been lost near the headland. The *Moon Crest* tender was used after all, and he'd know about any fatalities as he manages the lifeboat crew. He wasn't there – he was at a Brethren meeting apparently – and I spoke to his wife.'

'What did she say?'

'The same as Eleanor. That it was all childish adventure stories. But I'm not sure. I had the feeling she might have been hiding something.'

'It might be worth asking Mary Ford,' Venn said. 'She's an incomer and might not feel the same need to protect local reputations. Why don't we talk to her in the morning? And at the same time, we can ask about these letters.'

Ross was left with the sense, not exactly that he'd been vindicated, but at least that the boss had taken him seriously.

The sea was still wild from the wind of the night before. It was dark by the time Ross reached the sailing club, but the tide was high and he could hear the breakers on the shore. He parked at the back and rang the bell. A woman's voice answered and he was let in. The bar was much as it had been on his last visit. There was the same woman serving drinks; the person who'd taken Barty's keys from him to stop him driving home.

'You'll be here about the commodore. We're all in shock.' And there *was* a quietness about the place. It was less raucous than it had been before. The woman, though, seemed more curious than upset. 'What happened exactly then? Nobody seems to know.'

'Mr Lawson's body was found at the bottom of cliffs close to Scully Bay. We're treating it as an unexplained death.' Which, Ross thought, was what she knew already, and he wasn't about to pass on any other gruesome details. 'Was he here the night before his body was found?'

'No.' She started polishing glasses. 'We were expecting him. Usually, he's regular as clockwork.'

'His car was parked outside.'

'Well, I was on duty all night and he didn't show up.'

'You didn't check with anyone? To find out why he wasn't here?'

She shook her head. 'Why would I? He was an adult! Only needed looking after when he'd had a few too many whiskies.

Besides, he didn't like anyone interfering in his personal affairs.'

'Oh?' Ross managed to appear interested, but not *too* interested.

The woman lowered her voice into a stage whisper. 'Only last week he got into a row with one of the newer members. It all got a bit unpleasant. I'm not sure how it all started, but it ended with Mr Lawson standing up and yelling that "the whole bloody lot of you should mind your own business."'

'Who was Mr Lawson arguing with?' Ross asked. 'Is he here today?'

Now the barmaid looked as if she was already regretting the gossip. Her voice dropped even lower. 'It's Brian Moore,' she said. 'Over there by the window with Helen, his wife. He used to own that car showroom on the edge of the town, and a couple more in the county. He sold them about three years ago. Everyone says he's minted. He's got a fancy yacht in the marina.'

Ross didn't look across the room, but continued talking. 'I'll need a list of all your members. I can talk to the people who are here now, but, as I said, Mr Lawson left his car outside this building and somebody must have noticed him. That was probably the last time he was seen alive.'

He took his time making his way to Brian Moore and his wife, stopping on his way at all the tables, taking names and contact addresses, asking who had been in the club the night of Lawson's disappearance. Nobody said that they'd seen Lawson or his car.

'Sorry, I didn't notice.'

'It gets dark so early these days, doesn't it? Really, we should get some better lighting.

'The commodore? No, we were all saying how strange it was that he wasn't here that night.'

Ross moved slowly across the room, glancing up occasionally to check that the Moores were making no move to leave. They had the best view in the house, and could look down at the marina and the shore beyond. Again, Ross was distracted for a moment, his attention pulled to the white hulls below, moored along the pontoons, caught in bright security lights. While the car park at the back of the clubhouse might not be lit, from here it was possible to see every detail.

'You're asking about Lawson?' Moore had a Midlands accent. 'I'm sure one of them has told you we had a row last week. Almost came to blows. But that was two guys, old enough to know better, behaving like teenage kids. It soon blew over.' He was drinking beer and paused long enough to take a sip. 'The commodore had a temper, though. He completely lost it, turned in a moment. And that night he hadn't even had much to drink.'

'What triggered the argument?'

'It was the night after Jem Rosco died. I went over to the commodore and suggested we should have some sort of memorial here in the club. I'd fund it if cash was short. He'd been here as a junior, hadn't he? It was where he started his sailing career. I couldn't understand why we hadn't made him an honorary member, invited him to speak at one of the dinners. A celebrity like him and we'd draw a crowd.'

'Mr Lawson hadn't liked the suggestion?'

'That's putting it mildly, isn't it, bab?'

Helen Moore nodded. She was middle-aged, comfortable, still good-looking, and she wore a lot of gold – bangles, earrings and a chunky necklace. She could carry off the look. 'You'd think a bloke of that age would have a bit more self-control. The language! And he was frothing at the mouth. Literally.'

'What exactly did Mr Lawson say?'

'That Jeremy Rosco had been a disgrace to the town and the county. That he had behaved despicably throughout his life. And if he'd ever been made a member of the club, it would have been over Lawson's dead body.' Helen looked over the table at Ross. Her face was plump, almost without lines. 'He picked up Bri's empty beer glass. I thought he was going to smash it on the table and stick him one. But one of the other members came over and took it off him.'

'It was a shame,' Brian said. 'Embarrassing when a famous man had just died. It did Lawson no favours. There was already talk in the club that someone should stand against him as commodore.'

'Would you have put yourself forward?'

'No way! Too much like hard work. That's why I sold up and retired early: so that I wouldn't have any stress in my life. Doctor's orders after a heart attack. I came to sailing later than most. Never thought it would be for someone like me, to be honest. I've still got that working-class chip on my shoulder. But I love it! Just the sailing, mind you. Not all the bollocks that goes with it.'

'Did you see Mr Lawson the night before last? His car was parked here, but nobody seems to have noticed him arriving.'

He shook his head. 'We weren't here. It was our wedding anniversary. Thirty years. We had a night away in our favourite hotel in Cornwall. I can give you the name. You can check.'

Ross wrote down the details, but he thought the couple would have been there. They were too relaxed, too confident and easy in each other's company, to have made up a story like that. He'd check, of course, and he'd make a note of the hotel's name. Maybe he'd take Mel there on a special occasion. Their next anniversary.

Chapter Thirty-Four

WHEN MARY FORD GOT BACK FROM the school run, the two male detectives were waiting on the doorstep. She'd been hoping to lose herself in her work and swore under her breath.

'How can I help you?' A pause. 'If you want to talk to my father again, he's gone home. His neighbour's really understanding about feeding his animals, but he wanted to get back to them. He was quite certain that he'd seen that woman on the night Jem Rosco died.'

The older detective introduced himself, though she knew exactly who he was. In a place like Greystone, everyone was known.

'We will want to talk to Mr Ford. We'd like him to look at a photo of a woman who might possibly be the person he saw that night. But this morning, we'd like to talk to you. If you can spare the time.'

'Sure.' She stepped aside. 'My head's not really in the right place for work today anyway. Artie was disturbed in the night. I thought he might be building up to a seizure. He hasn't suffered like that yet, but it's one of the symptoms that could happen as the disease progresses.' She felt her voice tighten. Keeping the panic and the grief at bay. But aware, at the same time, that the sick child card was always worth playing.

'I'm sorry.' The words were pathetic, inadequate, but she thought that he meant them. She'd heard the rumours in the village, that he'd grown up in the Brethren but he'd lost his faith.

'No, come on in. I'll be glad of the distraction. You'll have to excuse the mess, though.'

There *was* a mess. This wasn't the false modesty of a house-proud mother. In her life there was more to deal with than a mucky home. There were toys scattered on the floor, and in the kitchen at the back of the room, a table with cereal bowls, a carton of milk, spills and crumbs. Mary piled the toys into a big wicker basket and gathered up stray children's clothes from the chairs, so there was somewhere for them to sit.

'We've found out where Jeremy Rosco was staying in the last few years.'

'Oh?' Once she would have pretended to be uninterested. Now, it wasn't an act.

'He was living with a woman on the Wirral. Of course, we had to search their flat. Routine. I'm sure you understand.'

She felt a flush spread from her neck and to her cheeks. She hadn't thought that she could do embarrassment any more. It was such a petty emotion in comparison to her other feelings. But now she wanted to shrink away from the men, who were sitting on her sofa, smiling at the photo of her son on the mantelpiece.

'We found some letters.' There was no judgement in Venn's voice.

'I used to write to him.' She looked up to them. 'It began

when I was a kid, then I started again when I was older. Lonely. He never replied. I thought perhaps he never received them. I sent them to his Morrisham address and he wasn't often there.'

'But you carried on writing anyway?'

'I needed to tell someone what I was going through. My husband and I were having a crap time, and my mother was ill. My father had enough on his mind looking after her. Jem was, I suppose, the equivalent of a child's imaginary friend.'

'More than a friend surely. More like a lover?'

Mary could feel the flush deepening. Venn was right, of course. Her dreams had been erotic, exciting. 'I met him a couple of times when I was still at school. He came to the sailing club. I was young, a bit wild. He said I reminded him of himself at that age. I was flattered. And I fancied him rotten. Became a bit obsessed by him when my marriage started falling apart. But I knew, deep down, that nothing would come of it. I wasn't sure how I'd feel if he finally agreed to meet up with me.'

'And then he turned up in Greystone.'

She nodded. 'My fantasy made real.'

'Did you go to the house he was renting?'

'No!'

'Really? After writing to him all that time? Asking him to meet you? And all you had to do was wander up the hill and knock at the door.'

'I went to the Maiden's,' she said. 'A few nights after he arrived. Dad came to babysit. The village was full of it. Jem Rosco blowing in, almost taking up residence at the bar.'

I dressed up for him. Not a frock, nothing like that. But nice underwear and my tightest jeans. My black boots. I used straighteners on my hair.

'What happened?' This time the young detective asked the

question. Not quite smirking, but ready to mock. She thought her story would be all around the police station. The mother with two kids who lost her head over an old sailor.

'Nothing happened.' She was determined not to cry. 'I went up to him, reminded him who I was. He was charming. But I could tell he couldn't remember reading my letters. I suppose he got so many. "Oh yes," he said at last. "You're Alan Ford's maid. I remember. A bit of a sailor." That was all I was to him: a bit of a sailor.'

I slunk out of the pub and ran home, pretended to my father that I'd got the flu, wept into my pillow so he and the kids wouldn't hear. But the next morning I was cured of my obsession with my imaginary lover.

'You didn't try to see him on his own?'

'No. I came to my senses. Life isn't a fairy story, is it? It's about just getting through.'

'Sometimes,' Venn said. 'But there's nothing wrong with wanting more.'

That last sentence surprised her. He didn't seem like a man who would demand very much.

'Will you get rid of the letters?' she said. 'Burn them.'

'Once the case is over,' Venn said, 'they're yours to do what you like with.'

She thought she'd put them in a cotton shopping bag weighed down by a very large rock and drop them into the sea when the lifeboat was next out on exercise.

'Had you heard there's been another unexplained death?'

'Yes. Bartholomew Lawson, wasn't it?' It had been all over the news the night before.

'You knew him?'

'I'd met him a few times. He was commodore of the yacht

263

club. They did occasional fundraisers for the lifeboat. We had to bail out his members a couple of times.'

'When they got into difficulty?'

'They aren't all the great sailors they think themselves to be. They like the idea of the sea, but don't always show it the respect it deserves.'

'Have there been more incidents at Scully Bay?' Venn asked. 'It seems an odd coincidence. Two men's bodies found dead there. Two sailors of the same generation.'

'I'm not sure what you mean.'

'Honestly? Nor do I. We wondered if there'd been some sort of tragedy there. Other lives lost. If these men's bodies had been placed there as a kind of homage to the past.'

Mary thought about that, and remembered the crew mumbling behind her as she took them into the cove. 'There are lots of superstitions about the place. Some of the older crew don't like going there on exercise. When we enter the bay, they mutter to themselves.'

'Mutter?'

She didn't explain directly. 'All sorts of things are considered bad luck at sea. Having a woman on board. Not wearing the same boots every time you're out. Whistling. Honestly, it's not unusual, especially in the fishing community, and most of our men have been fishermen.'

'But they put up with you as helm?'

'They haven't got a choice! It's hard to get regular volunteers. And most of them are used to it now.' For the first time since the men had arrived, she smiled. 'I think they see me as an honorary man.'

'So, the mutter is a kind of incantation to ward off evil spirits?'

'I know it's ridiculous, but it's not only sailors, is it? Sportsmen and women have the same need for ritual. Sometimes going out on a shout is literally a matter of life and death. I don't believe any of it, and I'm not sure the crew do either, but I can understand why it happens. It's a kind of insurance policy.' She wondered if that was why people in the Brethren, like Matilda Gregory, could believe in their God, in the rapture, and that only they would be saved. Just in case it turned out to be true.

'What do the crew say to ward off ill luck?'

'Skulls and bones and the white, white light.' She grinned. 'It's supposed to be a reference to the wreckers who lured sailors to the beach with torches, mimicking the harbour light at Greystone, which guided boats into the jetty. The sailors would drown and the locals would loot the ships, of course.' Another grin. 'Personally, I think the words were made up in the Maiden's Prayer by some old guys having a laugh a generation ago.'

'So, local people would know about the path down to the cove from the coastal path?'

'Sure. When I was growing up round here, it was a secret hangout for young teenagers wanting to drink, or have the occasional spliff. A way of avoiding our parents and the tourists, even in high summer. We didn't care at all about the skulls and the bones, and the white, white light.'

'But you can't think of anything more recent that would have triggered that old fear about the place?' Venn thought about the events of the previous summer, when a boy had fallen to his death from a cliff nearer to the home that he shared with Jonathan. 'A suicide perhaps? Accidental drowning if someone got caught in the tide?'

'There might have been a suicide,' Mary said. 'I think I remember hearing about it, when I was a young kid. Some chap from Morrisham whose business went tits up threw himself over the cliff. But Dad would be able to tell you more about that.'

Venn thought they'd be able to check the details, but it seemed unlikely that a tragedy that had happened decades before would link together the Rosco and Lawson murders.

Ross May had been quiet throughout the discussion, but just as Venn was about to leave, he asked a question of his own.

'What did people make of Barty Lawson? Other Greystone locals, I mean. The lifeboat crew? People like Sammy Barton?'

'They despised him, I think. He was a bit of a laughing stock, all bluster and fine words. A couple of the youngsters had been before him in the court. A brawl outside a bar in Morrisham that got out of hand. Local feeling was that Lawson had been heavy-handed with the sentence. Sammy couldn't stand him, but that was down to Barty's wife's family, and the quarry closing. Sammy must have seen it coming but he'd been foreman there. Important. Good wages and a reputation within the village.'

'The quarry closure wasn't Eleanor Lawson's fault, though,' Ross said. 'Hadn't the family sold out years before to a bigger business?'

'Yeah, but that didn't stop Sammy being resentful. You don't allow the truth to get in the way when you need someone to blame!'

Chapter Thirty-Five

THE KIDS HAD MOANED ALL THE way back from Hoylake, and Jen had struggled to sleep in the coffin-like room at the back of the pub. She was sure Ross had been given something slightly more luxurious and resentment had simmered until she'd finally dropped off.

Apparently, Robbie had told Ella and Ben about the baby after he'd taken them out for brunch. Some burger joint that had made Ella moan again because there was nothing veggie for her to eat. *I haven't eaten meat since I was, like, twelve. You'd think he'd remember. Make a bit of an effort.* And then he'd walked them along the seafront and told them that his girlfriend was pregnant.

That had understandably grossed them out a bit, because after all he was *so* old. Though, Jen thought, only three years older than she was. Ella had shown a bit of interest on the drive home.

'I suppose it might be quite cute to have a baby sister, but then we hardly see Dad, do we? It's never going to be a close relationship. And I've not even met the mother. It's not even

267

the same woman as when we were last staying with Gran and Grandad.'

'The baby is a girl then?' Jen had tried not to sound too eager for information, not wishing to give the impression that it particularly mattered to her.

'So he said.'

Ben had just stuck in his Airpods to listen to his music. He wasn't bothered, it seemed, one way or the other.

After Venn and Ross left to interview Mary Ford, Jen walked out to the quay to clear her head, an attempt to make sense of the deaths. Two middle-aged men. Apart from a love of sailing they seemed as different as it was possible to be. Connected only by a woman. Eleanor. Nell. Both men had been infatuated by her.

Then she thought that perhaps Rosco and Lawson had had more in common than she'd first believed. Both full of themselves, entitled in their own way. Both unable to form proper relationships. They'd been lonely men, hadn't they? Despite Lawson's apparent bonhomie at the yacht club, Ross had described him as sitting, and drinking, alone. And Rosco had hooked up with Imogen to provide him with company, but it seemed there was little warmth towards her. He'd kept all his fan mail, but never replied to the women who wrote to him. Adoration, it seemed, was enough for him.

She remembered the photograph Venn had shown her: Rosco with two other teenagers on a shingle beach, which might have been Greystone. The man seemed to have had friends then. And he'd had Eleanor, which had been a fantasy; the sort of infatuation which surely wouldn't have lasted if they'd married. The sort of infatuation that Mary had felt for *him*.

Jen had believed herself in love with Robbie when they'd first got together; had even imagined her wedding as the happiest day of her life. Such self-delusion! She'd dreamed about him at night, and he'd been at the back of her mind every minute of the day. It had been a kind of madness. She'd put up with too much hurt because the dream had lingered. Because she'd invested so much of herself in the make-believe.

'What do you want me to do, boss?' she'd asked, over breakfast.

He hadn't answered immediately. That wasn't Venn's way. Everything was considered.

'I'd like to know more about Lawson. Let's have a dig into his finances. He lives in that big house, but that came to him through Eleanor's family, and there's no sense of any wealth there. It's all a bit run-down and shabby. The land alone would be worth a fortune, and if you converted the house into apartments, you'd make an eye-watering sum. But I can't ever see Eleanor selling out to a developer. It means too much to her.' Then he'd passed on the contact details for Matilda Gregory's parents. 'Give them a ring. They probably won't be able to help much but they knew Rosco when he was a troubled boy. There might be something . . .'

She'd nodded. She understood Venn's need for background detail.

'Can you chat to your friend Cynthia, see what she knows about him? He was a magistrate. She might have some gossip.'

Oh yes! Cynth always has the gossip. And it'd be a chance to catch up over lunch or a coffee.

Venn had continued talking. 'Lawson's grandfather must have had money – he was the leading light behind the yacht club. Bartholomew was sent away to school, so his family can't have been on the breadline when he was growing up. Perhaps Cynthia will know what happened to all the cash.'

'Shall I go and see Eleanor?' Jen thought it had taken some nerve to ask the question. 'Might be good to get a fresh perspective on her? You're the only one of the team to have met her.'

There'd been a moment of silence before Venn had nodded. 'Yes. Go and see her first. Ask about Lawson and his finances. It'll help you to know where to start digging. Her family owned the quarry here in Greystone. Another link with the place, I suppose. Another connection.'

Now, with her back to the wind and the sea, she phoned Roxy, the officer who was acting as family liaison for Eleanor.

'The boss has asked me to come and chat to her. How's she holding up?'

'Well,' the woman said. 'She doesn't say much. She's very self-contained. There've been calls from friends who wanted to visit, but she wouldn't talk to them, and asked me to tell them she wasn't ready yet for company. I have the impression that she and Barty led very separate lives.' There was silence on the end of the phone. 'But really? She's one of those stoic women. Very British stiff upper lip. She could be weeping inside and I'd never know.'

As Jen approached the house, she thought it looked from the outside like something from an old-fashioned horror movie: all soot-stained stone, chimneys and turrets. She rang the front doorbell and heard it echoing inside. Then there were footsteps on a hard floor, and the door opened. It was Roxy, the police officer: cropped hair, leggings and a big jumper. Tattoos where they wouldn't show at work. Jen had seen her off-duty at parties.

'I hope you're wearing your thermals. It's a bit parky in here,' Roxy whispered. She then added in a louder voice: 'Eleanor's in the kitchen. She's expecting you. We were just about to make coffee.'

Jen followed her through the house, and had glimpses of large wood-panelled rooms, with dark paintings and leather furniture. As Venn had said, it was all rather shabby, and gloomy. He'd obviously been very taken by the building, but she couldn't see the attraction. Not for one person. Not even for a couple. You'd be rattling round in the place. Why not sell up, buy somewhere a bit more manageable, spoil yourself, travel? The kitchen was more comfortable, warmer. And sitting at the table, with a dog at her feet, was Eleanor. Nell. Rosco's Nelly Wren.

The woman was small, round, dressed in a brown cord skirt and a brown jumper, which was pilling and fraying a little at the cuffs. And yet, Jen thought, you wouldn't overlook her. In a crowd, she would be the person you'd notice. Cynthia would say she had an energy, an aura. But it was also her eyes, round and expressive. She got to her feet, held out a hand, and that was brown too. Jen imagined a summer of pottering in the garden.

'You must work with Inspector Venn,' Eleanor said. 'Lucky you! What a very nice man he is!'

'Yes. He is. Very nice.'

'Roxy here said you had more questions. She's been brilliant at fending off the press and my more inquisitive and pushy acquaintances. But we'll make some coffee first, shall we?' She moved a kettle onto the hob. It must have recently boiled because it whistled almost immediately. The noise was horrible but the dog scarcely stirred.

'Frankie's deaf,' Eleanor said. 'I think that may be a blessing, don't you?' She looked at Jen as if she really wanted to hear the answer.

'Perhaps for a dog. I'd miss the chat, the gossip.'

Eleanor laughed. 'I'd probably have said the same when I was your age. Now, I value silence.'

'I have to ask you more questions, I'm afraid. Silence isn't really possible in my work.'

'Of course, you must ask. I do understand.'

'Do you have any idea why anyone would want to kill your husband? Because we're sure now that he was murdered.'

'He was an alcoholic,' Eleanor said. 'Functioning, but unpredictable when he'd been drinking heavily. I did try to persuade him to get help, you know, but in the end, he had to want to be sober, and he enjoyed drinking too much. Or perhaps he needed to drink.'

Jen said nothing. There were times when she too knew the value of silence and she could tell that Eleanor had more to say.

'He had a temper. Usually he could control it, but sometimes it flared. Wild like fire. Triggered by a word or a look.'

'Was he violent towards you?'

Eleanor shook her head. 'No. Never.' A pause. 'But I can see how it might happen. Someone saying something to which Barty took exception. He'd lash out. Unsteady on his feet and no danger really to anyone. But if the person were provoked to retaliate . . .' Her voice tailed off.

'So random, you think? Not in any sense premeditated.' Jen gave that time to sink in. 'Doesn't that seem rather a coincidence? After Mr Rosco's murder?'

'You believe the same person killed them both?' Eleanor

looked up sharply. The sudden movement made the dog stir in his sleep.

'It would seem a reasonable assumption.'

'Oh no!' Eleanor said. 'Not at all. The men barely knew each other. Even when we were all young, they mixed in quite different circles.'

Jen let that ride. 'What did Mr Lawson do for a living?'

It took Eleanor a little time to answer. 'His family had property all over the county. Barty managed the portfolio, collected the rents.' A pause. 'His father was a gambler. Another form of addiction, so I assume there was probably some inherited trait. One by one the properties were sold. In the end there was no rent. Nothing to manage.'

'Your husband couldn't find work?' Jen's dad had been a docker. When the docks had closed, he'd laboured on the buildings. When he'd got too old for that, he'd driven a van.

'Nothing that suited,' Eleanor said. 'We managed here very well. I have a little savings. My parents were more prudent with their investments than Barty's.'

'You didn't consider selling this house? All this land?'

'Barty might have considered it, but it's in my name and he knew I'd never agree.' She looked, and answered the question Jen hadn't felt able to ask. 'He would have inherited it, of course, if he'd survived me, and then, I suppose, he could have done what he liked with it. At that point, I'd be beyond caring.'

'And now that he's died first?'

'I have no heirs and no close relatives. I'll leave it to charity. I've still to decide which one. Perhaps one caring for deaf dogs like this one.' She caught Jen's eye, saw how shocked the detective was and laughed again.

'There's no possibility that Mr Rosco and your husband met up while he was staying in Greystone?'

Eleanor shook her head. 'They weren't friends. There was always bad feeling between them. A strange kind of jealousy. I'm not even sure that they would have recognized each other after all these years.'

Chapter Thirty-Six

Jen had texted her friend Cynthia Prior before heading for Eleanor Lawson's place. **You free for lunch?** There'd been an immediate and enthusiastic reply saying that she was. Before setting out to meet her, Jen phoned the number Venn had given her for Matilda's parents. There was no reply. He'd have to contact them later.

She and Cynthia met in the cafe in the Woodyard, the arts centre managed by Matthew's husband, Jonathan. The tide was out and, through the big windows facing the river, there was a view of mud and stranded, rotting boats. Jen got there first and had time to chat with Lucy Braddick, the woman with Down's Syndrome who worked there and who'd become a friend.

'How's your dad, love?' Maurice Braddick missed Lucy now she'd moved into independent living. Jen thought he needed looking after more than his daughter these days.

'He's okay.' Lucy paused. 'I go and see him every weekend I'm not working here, stay the Saturday night. Just to keep him company. We go to the Fleece for our tea.'

'Ah,' Jen said. 'That's kind.'

Lucy smiled. 'Nah, they do great steak pie. Dad and me both love steak pie.' She moved away to clear another table.

Cynthia flew in late, wearing a new pink coat, trailing scarves, carrying a smart bag. She was newly single and revelling in the freedom, giddy with possibilities. She'd already decided that she'd stay in Barnstaple, in the pleasant house she'd shared with her husband. She must have done well from the divorce, Jen thought. Jen's ex, Robbie, was a lawyer and he'd screwed her over big style financially. When they'd separated, money had been the last thing on *her* mind; she'd just been relieved to have the kids safe and to be away from him. Jen wondered where Roger, Cynthia's former husband, was now.

Cynthia must have read her mind. 'I think the bastard's slunk back to the city and conned himself into another flash job. We still had cash left over from the sale of the London property and I've bought him out of the Barnstaple house with my share of that.'

'I'm working on the Bartholomew Lawson case.' They'd ordered food and coffee from Bob in the kitchen. This weather and this time of the year, there weren't many visitors, and they had the place almost to themselves. The windows were still streaked with salt and muck from an earlier gale, so the people who walked past seemed blurred and shadowy. 'You must have known him.'

Cynthia was a magistrate too and took the role seriously. She leaned forward across the table, suddenly earnest. 'Bartholomew Lawson was a horrible man. Honestly, he'd have brought back hanging and flogging given half a chance, and he was lazy as well as bigoted. He'd already made up his mind about the disposal of the offenders before reading the pre-sentence reports; he just skipped through them and took no notice of any recommendations. There was no sympathy, no understanding.' A pause. 'If it weren't for our lovely clerk to the court, he'd have exceeded sentencing guidelines on more than one occasion. He was a bully and some other members of the panel wouldn't stand up to him. He was lucky still to be on the bench. I should have reported him for incompetence really.' She paused for breath. 'And he was a patronizing git.'

'So, you tried to avoid being in court with him?'

'No! It was a pain, but if there was nobody else with a mind of their own on the panel, I tried to make sure I was there. Just to be certain that justice was tempered with a bit of mercy. Otherwise, every single mother who'd shoplifted would be sent down, leaving social services to be responsible for their children. He had a real downer on women with kids.' Cynthia finished her sandwich and looked up. 'What happened to him? Really, there were times when I felt like killing him myself.'

Jen didn't answer directly. Her mind was elsewhere. 'He and his wife were never able to have children. Apparently, it affected him deeply.'

'God, I can't imagine him as a father. He'd be the sort to pack them off to boarding school as soon as he could. He'd like the idea of them, carrying on the bloodline and the family name as if they were race horses, but not the reality.'

Is that me too? Is this longing for another child about the fantasy, not the real thing?

'Is there anyone who hated Lawson enough to kill him?' Jen tried to focus on the present. 'We're treating the death as unexplained, but really we can't see it as anything other than murder. Was there an offender who threatened him? Someone who might actually have carried out the threat?'

'His body was found under the cliffs at Scully according to the news. Really, I can't see any of our chaps getting out there. A stabbing outside a bar in the middle of town if Lawson was walking past I could understand, but not something out in the wild.'

'You can't think of any offender based in Morrisham?'

Cynthia shook her head. 'Not at the moment. I'll have a think and ask around, though.'

Later, they stood outside in the car park for a moment, enjoying each other's presence, not wanting to go their separate ways. Jen wanted to tell Cynthia about Robbie and the baby, her irrational longing, but Cynthia had never shown any interest in having children and she probably wouldn't understand.

'Let's have a girls' night in when your case is over,' Cynthia said. 'A film, and some of the very good wine Roger left behind. Lots of his very good wine.' She started to walk towards her car, but turned back for a moment. 'You can tell me what's troubling you then. Because I can tell that something is . . .' Then there was a flash of pink coat and she was gone.

Chapter Thirty-Seven

MATTHEW AND ROSS WERE WALKING AWAY from Mary Ford's house.

'What do you think?' Ross said. 'Seems a bit odd. A grown woman sending love letters to some bloke she scarcely knew.'

Venn said nothing. His romantic dreaming had begun when he was an adult too. He'd first met Jonathan at a training session in a smart hotel in Barnstaple and suddenly his world had expanded and seemed full of possibilities.

He thought he'd send Ross and Jen back to Barnstaple at the end of the day. There was no point all of them camping out any longer in the Maiden's Prayer, and they'd be more useful with the rest of the team in the police station. Matthew decided that he would stay in Greystone, though. He still believed that the answer to both murders lay there.

Alan Ford's house was on the edge of a grand country estate; they'd glimpsed a stately home with parkland as they'd approached. Once, perhaps, the cottage had been the home of an employee of the big house, of a gamekeeper or gardener.

It was semi-detached and the adjoining house mirrored its neighbour, and must have been a tied cottage too. Mary Ford would have grown up here, surrounded by woodland and birdsong. Venn wondered when the sea had first worked its magic and pulled her to Greystone. There was a small garden to the front, still bright with autumn colour. Venn moved along the lane so he could see into the land at the back. Here the garden was thin, but long, stretching all the way to the wood. Close to the house there was a pond, with muddy edges; further away, vegetable patches and a coop with hens. Matthew was reminded of his first meeting with Eleanor Lawson, as she appeared out of the mist with a basket of eggs on her arm. Right at the end of the strip, there was an orchard, so it was hard to tell where Ford's land ended and the woodland belonging to the estate began.

A car was pulled into a space by the side of the house. Matthew was thinking that Ford must be at home, or at least not very far away, when suddenly the man appeared, walking round the house and past the car towards them, a dog at his heels, a pair of binoculars round his neck.

'Come in!' His voice was welcoming. 'Mary said you might come along.'

He led them, not to the front door, but the way that he'd come. Close to the house there was a flagged area, with varnished wooden furniture tipped up so any rain would run off. Matthew could see the garden more clearly now. There were bird feeders hanging from posts along the border fence, and in one of the more substantial trees in the orchard, a wooden tree house had been built. Perhaps that had once been Mary's, used now by the man's grandchildren.

Ford opened the back door and pulled off his boots. 'Tea?'

he said. 'If my wife were still alive, there'd be homemade cake in the tin, but at least I can run to supermarket biscuits.'

'Did Mary tell you why we wanted to speak to you?' They were sitting in the kitchen with its window facing out into the garden. Occasionally Ford would lift the binoculars to check a bird on the feeder, but Venn thought they had his full attention. 'We have a photograph of a woman. She might have been the person you saw at the bottom of Quarry Bank the night Rosco was killed. Could you take a look?'

'Sure.' A pause. 'I don't think I can be certain, though. I only saw her briefly in the street light. I wouldn't want you to convict someone just on what I might have seen.'

Venn shook his head. 'Really, there's no danger of that. We're much more wary of identification evidence these days. We know how people's memories can play tricks. But you're good at holding details in your head and it might just help us to look in the right direction.'

Ross put his tablet on the table and the image of Imogen Holt came onto the screen.

'Could that have been her?'

Ford stared at the photograph. It was sharp and close up, a publicity shot of the face. He took a while to respond.

'Honestly, I can't say. I was upstairs looking down and I didn't see her face at all clearly. It was more of a silhouette. Do you have something taken from further away? Sometimes the way someone stands and moves helps us to recognize them, don't you think?'

Ross pressed some buttons on his device and there was Imogen on the screen again. The picture had been taken outdoors on set when Imogen had been acting in a soap opera. It was full-length and she was dressed in a long coat, much as the one Ford had described the mysterious woman as wearing.

'You know,' Ford said, 'that could be her. I certainly couldn't go into court and swear to it, but there's something about the stance . . . She's very upright, the spine very straight, the neck long, as if she's a dancer.'

'Thank you.' Venn wasn't sure that this got them much further. The team was already checking with other taxi drivers, who could have met trains in Tiverton or Exeter on the night of Rosco's death. Nobody reported having collected the woman, but that didn't eliminate Imogen altogether. 'There was something else we wanted to ask. I don't know if Mary mentioned it.'

'Something about Scully Head?'

'Two bodies were found there within a week. It would have taken some effort to get them there. Rosco's death seemed especially elaborate. Why bother with all the show? We know about the superstitions – the skulls and the bones and the white, white light – but we wondered if there was something more tangible about the place that might link the two men. Mary thought you might have some idea.'

'Did she?' Ford frowned. 'I can't think why.'

'Because you've lived locally for most of your career. I'm guessing you'd have been doing a seabird census along those cliffs over the years. You might remember some incident, another death or a suicide perhaps.' As he spoke, Matthew thought how tenuous this sounded. Two experienced detectives were here, drinking tea and fishing for stories, when there were so many more important things to do. It seemed faintly ridiculous.

'You think Scully might have some significance to the killer?'

'It's one theory we're exploring. Mary thought there might once have been a suicide there.'

'I think there was something. A Morrisham businessman who went bust, and jumped to his death, but that was years ago.'

That triggered a memory for Venn. Someone else had mentioned the incident in connection with the case, but he hadn't heard the precise location of the suicide and he hadn't made the link.

'Can you remember his name?'

There was a silence. Ford seemed to be scrolling through his memory. He was a naturalist, used to recalling and identifying birds and insects. He would, as Venn had already said, have a good memory. He looked across the table at them, with a new awareness. 'His name was Lawson. Henry Lawson. He was Bartholomew Lawson's father.'

Just as Venn had expected.

They left soon after to drive back to Greystone. Venn asked Ross to take the wheel; he knew he would struggle to concentrate. His mind was racing, running once more through various scenarios, questioning his judgement, everything he'd previously treated as a certainty. Could Bartholomew's death be suicide, after all? It would be almost impossible for a post-mortem to tell how the man had begun the long fall to the bottom of the cliff. Then, the thought came more insistently: why hadn't Eleanor given Venn or his sergeant the details of her father-in-law's suicide? Matthew only had her word for the fact that Barty's mood had been stable, and that he wasn't the sort of man to kill himself. She was of a generation to be reticent about matters of mental health. Would she have confided in Venn if her husband *had* been severely depressed? If he had decided to take the same way out as his father? Would she consider suicide cowardice? A scar on her husband's reputation. As a Catholic, would she consider it a sin?

Matthew pushed the theory on, and let another possibility scroll out in his mind. Could Eleanor have assisted in her husband's suicide? Could she have picked him up from the sailing club car park and driven him to the coastal path? Venn imagined her, standing there beside him at the top of the cliff, looking down into the darkness, quiet, resolute on her husband's behalf, waiting for him to jump. But why would she do that?

The answer came to Matthew immediately and with clarity. Because she knew that Bartholomew was a killer. Perhaps the man had confided in Eleanor when he was drunk. Matthew could picture him, maudlin and sentimental, not strong enough to keep the details of his guilt to himself, wanting to offload them onto his wife. And Eleanor *would* be strong. She would hate the publicity of a trial, but she would want retribution for the death of her former lover. Could she have persuaded Bartholomew to take the same way out as his father? Matthew thought it was possible.

They were approaching Greystone now, but Venn hardly noticed. He was juggling ideas. Could Bartholomew, the drunken boor, have planned the murder of Rosco? They'd thought it unlikely, but perhaps it was possible. According to Jen's feedback after her chat with Cynthia Prior, Lawson had managed to maintain his role as magistrate, despite his drinking, his bullying and his arrogance. And he'd been sailing for as long as the victim had. He knew the coast, the tide and the weather. He might be unfit but he was a big man. It wouldn't be hard for him to overpower Rosco, especially if he'd taken him by surprise. And he would have taken him by surprise. There'd been no lock on the bathroom door in the house in Quarry Bank.

Again, Venn let the possible scenario roll out in his head. Ross had stopped asking questions about Ford and the ID of Imogen, once he'd realized Matthew was preoccupied with thoughts of his own, and now Matthew could see the little house by the quarry more clearly in his mind than the approach to the village outside the car windows.

Had Lawson got wind of Rosco's arrival in Greystone? News would have spread in the area. Harry Carter would have seen it as an opportunity to pull in the punters to the Maiden's Prayer. *Guess who comes in for a pint with us every night, boys.* The Morrisham darts team had played there, so word would have got out that way, even if Carter had been more discreet about his celebrity drinker. Had Lawson been scared that Eleanor would leave him for her childhood sweetheart and come to Greystone to challenge him?

Again, Venn believed he could see how that might have played out. Rosco would have mocked Bartholomew, challenged him, provoked him. That was the sort of man Rosco had been. Perhaps the champagne and the glasses had been set out to taunt Lawson. *Guess who I'm expecting later! Of course. My own sweet little Nelly Wren.* So, when Rosco had gone to the bathroom to use the lavatory or wash his hands, Lawson had followed him. Stabbed him. Either with a knife he'd brought from home, a knife he'd use on his boat, or with one of Rosco's. And he'd killed him, driven at last to a sort of frenzy.

Venn ran the theory on, trying to find holes, something that wouldn't hang together. Bartholomew would know Sammy Barton and know the *Moon Crest.* As commodore of the sailing club, he'd surely have had dealings with the lifeboat operations manager. Matthew thought there might well have been bad feeling between them. Two powerful men fighting over their own territory, separated by class and religion. A toxic mix. Venn couldn't imagine that they'd get on.

It would please Bartholomew to implicate Barton, by taking the *Moon Crest* tender. He was a large man, strong if he still sailed. He could have bundled Rosco's body into the enormous canvas bag, wrapping it first in the shower curtain, and then he would have carried it down to the quay. The village would have been empty at that time and in such a gale. Except for the strange woman seen by Alan Ford. Venn wished they could know for certain who she was. She could be a vital witness.

Then, if Venn was right, Lawson had loaded Rosco into the tender and, using its outboard motor, taken it out to Scully where his father had died. Afterwards, it wouldn't, as Jonathan had said, have been too hard to wade ashore at low water. And to call the coastguard with a fake emergency shout. Involving Sammy Barton again. But how would Bartholomew have got home from there? The storm would have been blowing again. The weather that morning had been foul. Venn couldn't picture Lawson scrambling up the steep path and walking miles back to the gloomy house and his wife. It would just have been getting light by then, and he'd have been drenched. Someone would have noticed him, even that early in the morning.

Of course, that wasn't how it happened, Matthew thought. Bartholomew would have phoned Eleanor. Already shocked at what he'd done, panicking, unravelling, he'd have needed her.

And she would have come to fetch him. Which would make her complicit, not just in Lawson's suicide, but in the murder of Jeremy Rosco.

They'd arrived outside the Maiden's Prayer. Venn had already told Ross he could go back to Barnstaple, but now he hesitated. He needed to share these thoughts. He wanted to hear what the others made of his ideas. He hoped that they'd pull them apart.

'There's something I'd like to discuss. With you *and* with Jen. We'll have supper together. Then, I promise, you can both go home.'

He didn't see Ross roll his eyes, but he could sense it.

Chapter Thirty-Eight

WHEN THEY WENT INSIDE, HARRY CARTER was alone behind the bar. He seemed to have been waiting for them.

'My regulars don't like you poking around at Scully,' he said as soon as they got through the door. 'They're a superstitious lot, some of them. You're scaring them away. It's bad for business.'

'Even the Brethren?' Venn was genuinely curious. 'Don't they see superstition as the devil's work? Close to witchcraft.'

Carter kept silent, and Venn continued talking.

'Two men died there. Better to poke around on the beach, don't you think, than to leave the bodies to be eaten by rats, and the bones washed away into the sea.'

Carter turned away towards the kitchen, but Venn called after him. 'The more information we get from the people who drink in the Maiden's, the sooner we'll leave Scully alone. Perhaps you could tell your regulars that.'

In the end, they had an early dinner in the stylish cafe bar in Morrisham, in the building where Rosco had still owned an apartment. The apartment, which now, Venn thought, must be owned by Eleanor. Although he'd never had her down as a woman motivated by money, financially she must be doing very nicely after the two men's deaths.

The bar was full of the wealthy elderly, smart couples who had probably been coming since the place first opened. In the background, there was relaxed jazz that swum into his head and relieved some of his tension. It was very different from the Maiden's, and Venn was glad he'd brought the team here, and not just because he'd felt the need to spite Carter. They were anonymous, three colleagues out for a meal, straight from work. It might, he thought, provide a new perspective, and at least lighten the mood.

'So, Ford reckoned the woman he saw could have been Imogen Holt?' Jen seemed tired. Perhaps that was because of the long drive from Merseyside, and the visit bringing back unsettling memories.

'Could have been her,' Venn said, 'but that's not really good enough, is it? We still don't have a record of her travelling to the south-west on the day Rosco died, and we can't find anyone who gave her a lift.' He paused. 'If I'm right, the woman could just be coincidental, someone visiting in the area. I know we've put the word out, asking for information about her, but Greystone hasn't exactly rushed to support us, especially since Lawson died.'

'According to Cynthia, Lawson was a drunken bully. Nobody liked him. I can see why people aren't prepared to put themselves out to find his killer.' Jen paused. 'I got through to Matilda Gregory's parents in the end too, but they didn't give anything away. I don't think they liked speaking on the phone.'

Ross turned to Venn. 'What's your theory?' He was fidgety,

impatient. Matthew understood that he wanted to be home, with his wife.

'I think we should consider Lawson as Rosco's killer again. And I believe that Eleanor was complicit.'

Carefully, Venn took them through his reasoning.

'I don't know,' Ross said. 'I just don't believe the man could hold it together . . .'

'He wouldn't have needed to, would he?' Jen leaned forward so she could talk to them both. 'From what Cynthia told me, I can see the man reacting with an irrational flash of anger, like the boss described. He's the sort to lash out at someone he resented and envied. Then he'd have to cover it up as best he could. It would surely sober you up, being landed with a dead body and a bath full of blood.'

'One of the sailing club members said Lawson had a foul temper,' Ross conceded. He thought for a moment. 'The woman Ford saw, it couldn't have been Lawson's wife? Summoned to Greystone to help once Rosco was dead and Lawson was panicking?'

Venn shook his head. 'The description's nothing like.' A pause. 'Eleanor might still have planned it, though, once Lawson had done the killing. Leaving Rosco in the boat at Scully might have been her idea of a fitting end for the man. A kind of respect.'

'What do we do next?' Ross was done with talking, with theories.

'You and I will go to see Eleanor tomorrow. I'd like someone with me while we talk to her.' Venn hesitated, before coming out with an admission. 'I've been rather blinkered where she's concerned. She never struck me as someone who could be a liar.'

'And me?' Jen asked.

'If Eleanor lied about the circumstances surrounding Rosco's death, she might have lied about other things. The man's relationship with the elderly woman who left him all her money.' Venn thought Eleanor could have been complicit in that too. It could have been a kind of fraud. A scam. 'Apparently, there was a living relative who questioned Miss Fanshaw's will. Could you see if he's still alive and talk to him?'

'Sure,' Jen said. Then: 'If there's nothing more, boss, I think I'll go back home to the kids.'

'And okay if I go straight back too?' Ross was already on his feet, keys in his hand. 'What time do you want to meet at the Lawson place?'

'Not too early. There's a couple I want to talk to first. Matilda Gregory's parents. They live in Barnstaple. Go into the station and I'll see you there.'

Matthew stayed where he was, finishing the last of his coffee, enjoying the moment of peace and the music.

He was about to leave when he heard voices that he recognized and saw Matilda and Davy Gregory come into the bar. Matthew was sitting in a shadowy corner and they didn't notice him. Gregory had his arm around his wife, helped her out of her coat and they sat down together.

'So, my love,' Davy said, 'we have a night out together at last.'

Matilda must have said something, but her voice was soft and Venn couldn't make it out.

'I'm not celebrating a man's death. Not exactly.' Gregory reached across the table and took her hand. 'But I can't pretend to be sorry that Bartholomew Lawson is dead.'

Venn got to his feet. He made for the door, avoiding a route that would take him past the couple's table. Turning back before leaving, it occurred to him that Matilda Gregory and Imogen Holt did look very much alike with their long blonde hair and dancer's bearing. A coincidence, he told himself. Nothing more than that.

Standing on the pavement, and looking across the road to the promenade and the water, he realized he couldn't face going back to the pub in Greystone, the scowling locals and the gloom. He phoned Jonathan.

'Listen, I'm coming home tonight. I need to be in Barnstaple tomorrow morning. And I want to see you.'

Chapter Thirty-Nine

WHEN JEN GOT HOME, THE KIDS were holed up in their rooms again. They answered when she shouted up at them, but they didn't come down. There was evidence that they'd scavenged for food. She thought that prison wouldn't be any sort of deterrent for this generation, as long as they were allowed phones and internet access in their cells.

If she were starting out as a parent again, she'd do things differently. She wouldn't be so focused on her work. There'd be more outside play, more time having adventures. North Devon would be a fabulous place to bring up a child. Jen pictured a toddler, nut brown, running across a beach towards her, arm stretched out for a swing or a cuddle, laughing into the sun.

She told herself she was only dreaming about a baby because her former husband was about to get something she couldn't have. She was behaving like a three-year-old. It had never occurred to her that she might want another child until she'd heard of his girlfriend's pregnancy. A word from her Catholic upbringing came into her head. She was *coveting* this child, and it was a sin.

ANN CLEEVES

Soon, she told herself, the longing would be gone. In another few years, her kids would both be independent, they'd have flown the nest for work or university. She'd be unencumbered, free to pursue her ambition, her career, and to enjoy whatever life she wanted. Why give up that freedom? Besides, a child needed a father, Jen had no regular man in her life, and any other route to motherhood would surely be complicated, a little embarrassing.

There was a third of a bottle of white left in the fridge and she poured it into a large tumbler. The meal in the Morrisham bar had been stylish but not very filling. She discovered that she was still hungry. She found a few remnants of cheese and some grapes that the kids must have dismissed as being too old and wrinkled, put them on a plate with a handful of crackers and went back to the living room. She finished the wine before starting on the food.

She fired up her laptop, googled Grace Fanshaw, and saw that there were a surprising number of references to the name. She had an entry in Wikipedia. It seemed that she'd been a writer, a poet, but was most famous for a series of children's fantasy novels written in the 1970s towards the end of her career. One had been turned into a feature film. Jen had a flash of memory. It had turned up most Christmases on television when she was a child. Presumably, the money left to Jeremy Rosco had come from the proceeds of the books and the adaptation, as well as the sale of her home.

Wikipedia had Grace Fanshaw as unmarried. There was no mention of a fiancé who'd died soon after the war, but there was of a brother, the father perhaps of the nephew who had disputed her will. The brother – Roderick – warranted an entry in his own right, and Jen clicked on the link and turned her attention to him. Roderick had been an adventurer too, though not a sailor like Rosco. He'd set up businesses in South America and the Middle East and, it seemed, fortunes had come and gone. No wonder Grace had taken to the young Jeremy, with his confidence and his recklessness. Perhaps he'd reminded her of her brother. Perhaps he'd become the child she'd never had.

Roderick had been married and, according to the entry, there was one son, David, who would have been Grace's only nephew. He must have been the person to contest the will. There were a number of David Fanshaws of the right age to wade through, but Jen drew up a shortlist. According to Eleanor, the man had lived in London. One was the headmaster of a prep school in Putney, one was an employment lawyer, partner in a big firm based in the city, and the third managed a betting shop in Kentish Town. He seemed unlikely, but Jen knew better than to make judgements on such limited information.

At least now she had somewhere to start the following day. She took her plate into the kitchen and made her way to bed.

The next morning, Jen started first with the firm of city lawyers. She'd decided someone with legal training and the right contacts might have had the confidence to challenge Grace's will. She spoke to a woman with a high-pitched voice and a cockney accent, who seemed surprised that anyone would expect one of the partners to be in so early in the working day.

'It is rather important.' Jen explained that she was a detective. 'We think that Mr Fanshaw might be able to help us. Could you let me have a mobile number for him?'

There was a pause on the other end of the line. Fear of her

employers overcame curiosity and her anxiety to help the police. 'Oh, I'd like to help, honest, but I'm afraid I can't. We've been told never to give out personal numbers. Not for anyone!'

'Perhaps you can help then but in another way. I don't suppose you know the first name of Mr Fanshaw's father?'

'Of course! He was David too. He was a partner of the firm until he retired ten years ago. Shall I get Mr Fanshaw to call you when he gets in?'

Jen thanked her and said that she would get back to him if she needed to but she didn't think that would be necessary. Not Roderick then. Not Grace's brother.

The number for the betting shop in Kentish Town was no longer operational, so Jen took a deep breath and phoned the private day school in Putney. She'd always been scared of teachers. Many of the nuns in the convent she'd attended had terrified her, and even the kind ones had left her unsettled and tense. When her kids were at school, before she'd moved south with them, she'd felt inadequate. She didn't live in the perfect family home you saw on the ads. Her children were growing up in a battlefield, and even though they'd never seen any actual physical violence – Robbie had been too clever for that – they must have sensed her humiliation and her fear. The teachers would judge her for her appalling parenting, and they had every right to do that. Even when she'd moved to North Devon, she'd sensed the school's disapproval when the kids forgot games kit or she turned up late for parents' evening. It was the Scouse accent and the lack of a husband. It was being different.

'Could I speak to David Fanshaw, please?' She told herself that she was an officer of the law. There was no need at all to be nervous.

Chapter Forty

MATILDA'S PARENTS WERE NAMED SUSAN AND Philip Vickery. They lived just outside the town, very close to Matthew's mother. Venn didn't recognize them. They would have been living in Bideford when he'd been growing up, and had still been a member of the Brethren. His mother would know them now, though, if they still went regularly to meetings.

He'd phoned them the evening before. There'd still been no reply but Venn had left a message and Philip had phoned back. There'd been no explanation for not responding to Jen Rafferty's calls. Perhaps he'd recognized Venn's name. He'd agreed that Matthew could come early: 'Oh yes, we're not ones for lying in bed all day.' His voice disapproving, as if staying in bed was a sin.

Matthew was feeling more relaxed than he'd been for a while. Jonathan had been waiting for him when he'd got home the night before and they'd sat together, watching an old film, not needing to speak. Matthew had the sense that whatever had been troubling him had been decided. He didn't ask about that. He was too selfish to spoil the evening. He thought that Jonathan would tell him when he was ready.

Matilda's parents' house was solid, a detached red-brick in an anonymous street on the edge of the town. Nothing to set it apart. Philip opened the door to Matthew. He was tall, wiry. In his seventies, perhaps, but wearing well. Susan was tall, rather elegant.

'Come in,' the man said. 'We know your mother. She's spoken of you.' Like the house, his tone gave nothing away.

They sat in the living room. There was a well-kept garden to look out at. Photos of Matilda on the wall. Otherwise, it was bland, featureless.

'You only have one child?'

'Yes,' Susan said. 'She's been a great blessing.' *Not*, she seemed to imply, *like you. We know how you behaved: you made such a scene when you lost your faith that you were unfellowshipped in the middle of a meeting.*

Or perhaps, Matthew thought, he was reading too much into one sentence.

'Matilda has a lovely home at Ravenscroft.'

'We were able to help them both out when her grandparents died. And she's always been artistic.'

Venn sat on a grey velour armchair. The couple were opposite on a matching sofa.

'You'll have heard that Bartholomew Lawson has died?'

'Yes,' Philip said.

Nothing more. He would be accustomed to silence and wouldn't find it intimidating, so Venn pressed on. 'I understand that you used to work for his father.'

'Briefly,' Philip said, before reluctantly adding, 'I didn't know what was going on in the business. As soon as I realized what

I was letting myself in for, I left to set up on my own. It felt like a big step, but the right one.'

'What *was* going on?'

'Lawson senior had a problem. He gambled, then tried to fiddle the books to hide his losses.' Vickery stared for a moment out of the window. 'He wanted me to put them down as business expenses. Of course, I couldn't do that, even when he came up with receipts for building work that had never been done.'

'You didn't tell the police or the revenue what was going on?'

'No.' Philip didn't quite look at Venn. 'I suppose I should have done, as soon as I realized what Mr Lawson was doing, but I knew that it would all fall apart soon enough.'

'Did you know Bartholomew, the son?'

'He came into the office during his school holidays to learn the business, but I didn't know him well.'

'What did you make of him?' Venn thought this was worse than pulling teeth.

There was a moment of silence before Vickery shrugged. 'A chip off the old block. I couldn't take to him.'

'In what way?'

'He was bright enough, but arrogant. He thought he knew it all. He was spoiled rotten by his family. Not his fault really.' The man paused. 'They all lived in this kind of fantasy world. They'd grown up with money and privilege, and thought it would be theirs for ever, even when the business was collapsing around them.'

'You knew them socially too? Through the sailing club?'

'Yes.' Again, Vickery seemed to think an explanation was needed and took his time to pull his thoughts together. His wife had remained silent throughout the conversation and still she didn't speak. 'I've always loved being out on the water. My father built a boat and handed it on to me. I didn't think the club was for me – we don't drink – but Lawson joined me up when I started working for him. One of the perks of the job, he said. It was handy to have a mooring there and to use the facilities.'

'Did you meet Bartholomew's girlfriend, Eleanor?'

'He brought her into the club some evenings. I knew of her family, of course. They'd owned the quarry at Greystone and lived in that big house out of town.'

'What did you make of her?'

Philip looked at Venn as if he couldn't see the point of these questions, but was prepared to humour him. Just about. 'She was a sparky little thing. Polite, though, to all the staff. I liked that. I thought she deserved better than Barty.'

'And the sailing club was where you met Jeremy Rosco? Matilda said you took him under your wing.'

At last, Susan Vickery did speak. 'We could tell that he was choosing the wrong path. We invited him to spend some time with us. He used to come for his tea sometimes. I'm not sure his mother ever cooked for him. He seemed to live off white bread and chips.'

'In what way was he taking the wrong path?' Venn thought that could be anything, from swearing to attempted murder. To eating too many chips. All would be sins in the eyes of the Brethren.

'He was living a rackety kind of life,' Philip said. 'I don't think he knew the difference between lies and the truth. He'd tell you anything to get what he wanted. We tried to show him a different way. We had Matilda by then and we invited him into our home and tried to make him part of the family. There was something appealing about him. You couldn't help liking the boy and he seemed grateful for what we did for him. But in the end, we couldn't trust him.'

'Why?'

'Some money went missing from my purse,' Susan said. 'Twenty pounds. I'd left the purse on the table when he was alone in the room. Twenty pounds was a lot in those days.'

'You didn't tell anyone?'

'No. I had no proof and I could have been mistaken. You wouldn't want to blacken a man's name without being certain.'

'We were already having doubts about him by then,' Vickery broke in. 'His behaviour hadn't changed. He was pleasant enough when he was in our home, eating our food, but he hadn't really changed his ways.'

'Yet, it must have been around that time that he started helping Grace Fanshaw, an elderly woman. You must have been pleased about that.'

'She left him all that money in her will!' The words flew out, but immediately Susan shut her mouth tight, as if to prevent another uncharitable outburst.

'You think that was why he befriended her? In the hope of becoming her beneficiary?'

'In the hope of getting something out of her, at least,' Susan said. 'That boy did nothing good without expectation of getting something out of it.'

They sat for a moment, quite still in the room.

'Did you ever see Jeremy with Eleanor? It seems they were close friends too.'

'He brought her here once.' There was a pause. Venn waited for her to continue and at last Susan filled the silence. 'I'm not sure what was going on between them. They didn't seem particularly close to me. I had the impression that Jeremy was showing her off to us. What she got out of the relationship, I'm not sure. But she was the one in control, I'd say.'

'Both Rosco's and Lawson's bodies were found in Scully Cove,' Venn said. 'Is there any significance in that, do you think?'

Susan and Philip shot a glance at each other. 'Barty's father Henry killed himself there.' It was Philip who spoke.

'He took the easy way out.' Susan's voice was at once disapproving and self-righteous.

Philip said nothing, and Venn sensed an unease. He waited.

This time, Vickery seemed to find the silence uncomfortable, and at last he spoke. 'I wanted to give him a chance to put things right. I'd left the business by then. It was nothing to do with saving my own skin. I just thought it must be terrible, living with the mess of it. I thought it'd be eating away at him.'

'What happened, Mr Vickery?'

'He was at the marina one evening. He was a fine sailor, intuitive, you know. Like he could smell the wind and knew the tide. It was just the two of us, late one summer's evening. I wasn't doing much on the boat – just a tidy at the end of the season – but I was enjoying being there, close to the water. He was moored next to me, sitting on deck. We started talking. I said he should tell the revenue what was going on. They wouldn't prosecute, not if he came clean and offered to pay the money back.'

Venn could imagine the scene. Vickery, not content with saving his own soul, would feel the need to save Lawson's. 'Did you threaten to go to the authorities, if Lawson didn't go himself?'

Another silence, which stretched until Venn himself felt unnerved by the tension in the room.

'I told him my conscience wouldn't allow me to let it go any longer. He wasn't just stealing from the revenue, but from local contractors and some of his tenants. It was going to unravel. I said I'd give him until the end of the month to sort it out.'

'But instead, he jumped from the cliff at Scully and ended it all.'

'We don't know that Phil's words had anything to do with that!' Susan reached out and took her husband's hand.

'Why did he choose Scully as the place to end it all?' Venn wasn't sure how this was helping his investigation, but he wanted to know.

Another silence.

'Mr Vickery?' Venn was becoming impatient now. This pious self-justification touched too many nerves.

'It was just a place that he loved,' Vickery said at last. 'He'd sail round there with the family and they'd anchor and take the tender ashore for a picnic. He said it was always peaceful. A lot of the locals didn't like it because of the old superstitions. You might get a few kids there, but only in the evenings. It was as if it was his own private domain.' He looked directly at Venn. 'I think he could believe that he owned it. Just as everything else he owned was slipping away from him.'

'I suppose he would have taken Bartholomew there.' Matthew wondered if that made the suicide theory even stronger. Scully wasn't just the place where Lawson's father had died. It was a place where the man had been happy and at peace.

'Oh yes! Bartholomew and his young woman. They always included her in family outings.'

Which took Venn back to Eleanor.

Out in the street, Matthew sat in the car for a moment, wondering if he should go and see his mother, as he was so close to her home. Jonathan would approve. He believed they should build bridges with Dorothy, even though he had little contact with his own family. *She's a lonely old woman. And you need some sort of resolution as much as she does.* Venn's mother was still making him feel guilty, indirectly, after all this time.

He left the car where it was and walked the short distance to her house. Dorothy took a little time to answer, and he'd thought for a moment that she might not be in.

'Matthew, come in!' Her voice was warm, almost welcoming. She'd mellowed since he'd first come back to North Devon. He was thrown by the change in her, a little unsettled.

'I haven't got long, but I was just down the road and I've called in to see how you are.'

'I'd have thought you'd be out at Greystone. That murder has been all over the news.' A pause. 'I suppose he was a famous man. There's bound to be a fuss.'

'I've been staying there for a while.' He looked directly at her. 'It brought back lots of memories.'

'Oh yes! Do you remember that picnic in the grand garden? The children played rounders. Such a lovely day! I've got a picture of you somewhere . . .' She disappeared from the room and came back with a shoebox.

'I should go,' he said gently. 'It's a busy time.'

'Just a few moments. It won't take long.'

She rifled through the pile of prints and pulled out a

photograph. It was the image of his memory. A small boy wearing shorts and sandals on a swing, his head tipped to the sky. A wide smile on his face.

He'd been gone for ten minutes, but when he returned to his car, Philip and Susan Vickery were still standing at the window of their living room, watching, anxious because he was still in the neighbourhood.

In the police station, Ross was waiting for him. They were just about to set off to speak to Eleanor Lawson when the phone on Ross's desk rang. The man listened for a moment, making uncharacteristically sympathetic responses, before replacing the receiver.

'That was Roxy, the family liaison officer. She arrived at the Lawson place this morning to pass on the latest news, and to tell Eleanor to expect us, but nobody was home. The doors were unlocked, but there was no sign of the woman.' A pause. 'She says there's blood. In the bath. Like with Rosco.'

Chapter Forty-One

JEN NAVIGATED HER WAY THROUGH THE Tube system from Paddington and arrived at the school where David Fanshaw taught just after noon. It wasn't particularly grand from the outside, and she might have walked past if it weren't for the discreet sign on the door. Fanshaw's name was as big as that of the school. She wondered if he was a small man, in need of validation.

It looked as if a number of terraced Victorian houses had been knocked through to form one establishment. The entrance was set back from the street a little, and the district was pleasant enough, but it could have been an office or a boutique city hotel. A bell rang, and then she did hear children's voices. There must be outside space at the back of the building.

She had to press a buzzer to be let in, the door opened and a hatch, with a sliding glass door, led into an office. She signed a large book and was given a lanyard and a pass. Nothing unusual. It would have been the same at her kids' school. Except here the small room where she was asked to wait was wood-panelled, with a bowl of real flowers on a side table, and she was invited to help herself to coffee from a filter machine in one corner.

Fanshaw came in ten minutes later, just as she was thinking she'd go back to the office and start to throw her weight about, tell them that she'd come all the way from Devon so she wouldn't have to inconvenience the man. He was apologetic, which mollified her a little, and he *wasn't* a small man. He was tall, fatherly, wearing a crumpled suit. She found herself liking him. He seemed as if he'd care about the kids he was in charge of. Perhaps the safeguarding issue wasn't his responsibility after all. At her last appraisal, Venn had told her that she jumped too quickly to conclusions:

'You've got a good instinct, but that's not enough. You need a clear head. And maybe allow for that chip you're carrying on your shoulder. Be aware of it, at least.'

In person, there was nothing intimidating about David Fanshaw. Or perhaps, Jen thought, he just talked a good game.

He led her into his office, talking as he went, offering her sandwiches, more coffee. 'If you've come straight from the train, you'll be starving.'

The office was at the back of the building and looked out over a garden with playing fields beyond. Children were chasing each other. A few were skipping with long ropes. There were boys and girls, the boys in shorts and long grey socks, green jerseys, the girls in pinafores. It looked idyllic. Very different from the city Catholic school she'd attended. The chip was making itself felt again. At least, Jen thought, she was aware of it.

There were two chairs facing each other, away from the desk. The head teacher took one of them and nodded for her to sit in the other. 'You wanted to know about my aunt and Jeremy Rosco. It was such a long time ago.'

'It must still rankle, though, that she left everything she had to a lad she scarcely knew. You challenged the will.'

'There was a small bequest to me.' He smiled. 'She didn't leave me out altogether. But yes, I was young, just out of university. My parents had died in a dreadful car accident. They weren't wealthy people, and I suppose I was relying on my aunt's money to set me up. I was complacent. Selfish even. I'd rather taken the legacy for granted. I seldom went to see her and, when I did, it felt like a chore. I know now that she was an intelligent woman. I'm sure she picked up on the fact that I was there under sufferance.'

'So, you don't resent the fact that she left all her money to Rosco?'

'At the time I did, certainly, but not after all these years! I'm sure it was good for me in the end. I had to earn my own way. I went into teaching because of the holidays, the security and the regular pay cheque, but I found that I love it.'

'Why this sort of school?'

'You disapprove of private education?' That smile again, very warm, very understanding. 'I worked in the state system for twenty years. I wanted to spend the end of my career doing what I've always enjoyed: educating young children, broadening their experience, opening their minds to the world. Not fighting for funds and teaching an ever narrower curriculum.' A pause. 'We've established a very generous bursary scheme for city kids whose parents can't pay.'

'Did you ever meet Rosco?'

There was a moment of silence, not, Jen thought, because Fanshaw was uncertain how to answer, but because he was trying to remember the occasions in detail.

'Twice,' Fanshaw said. 'Once was one of my irregular visits

to see my aunt. I had expected her to be on her own and it
threw me when a young man opened the door. A scruffy young
man with long hair, in cut-off jeans and flip-flops. I thought
he must be some kind of tradesman. I was rather pompous in
those days and I was probably horribly rude to him. I know
that he laughed at me. He called into the house, "Hey, Gracie,
there's someone to see you." And my aunt just shouted back,
"Send them through then, Jem, love." My aunt Grace, whom
I'd always considered so prim and unapproachable, calling this
man *love*. I couldn't get my head round it. I thought she must
have been scammed by him. Or that she'd lost her marbles.
I didn't handle the situation well. I was very prickly, rather
juvenile and arrogant. I suspect that was when she changed
her will.'

'Do you think Rosco *had* scammed her?'

'I think he charmed her for his own ends, but that's not
quite the same, is it? It's not illegal.'

'Was Rosco on his own with your aunt? There wasn't
anyone else with him?'

'No, it was just the two of them. They'd been having lunch
together. Mackerel that Rosco had caught, salad and white
wine. How odd that I can remember the details so precisely!
My aunt was obviously enjoying the meal. She pulled a piece
of bread from a loaf and wiped up the juice from the mackerel
with it. They offered me a glass of wine and I turned it down.
What a priggish, obnoxious man I was!'

'And the second time you met Rosco?' Jen thought there
was nothing obnoxious about Fanshaw now. He had become
charming too.

'Before I started legal proceedings to challenge the will, I
went to Morrisham to appeal, I suppose, to his better nature.

I thought we might split the inheritance between us, or that he might at least leave me something. Either the house or her savings. I couldn't understand that a man like that would need both. All he seemed to want was to be on the water. I was Aunt Grace's only relative. It seemed so unfair that I should have to beg for a share of her estate.'

'Where did you meet?'

'In her house. He was preparing it for sale, packing up her things.' Fanshaw looked across at Jen. 'He asked me if there was anything I'd like to remember her by. It seemed a terrible insult. Humiliating.'

Jen said nothing.

'I tried to control myself, not to lose my temper. I do think I was quite reasonable on that occasion. I explained that I intended to challenge the will, that he'd have to go to court, which would be expensive. Better, I said, that we should sort things out between ourselves.'

'How did he respond?' Jen knew what the outcome had been, but she was fascinated by this insight into Rosco's early life.

'He laughed at me. Not exactly in a cruel way, but making me feel ridiculous all the same. "See, boy, I've got nothing to lose. I want to make my name and be out on the sea. I want to sail round the world. My life's made for adventure. Gracie understood that. She left me everything so my dreams could come true. You can take me to court, but she was in sound mind. Everyone will tell you. I brought a bit of fun into her life at the end and she was grateful. The way I see it, it'd be wrong not to respect her wishes. And I think that's the way the court would see it too. I might lose it all, but I'm willing to take the risk."'

'But you still challenged the will?'

He nodded. 'Partly it was pride. I'd gone that far and I didn't want to back down. There was a strange sort of snobbishness too. But it wasn't just that. Something about his attitude really made me believe he'd tricked her. I don't mean that he'd forced her to write the will, but that he hadn't been honest with her.'

Jen wondered if that had been wishful thinking, a privileged young man not quite believing that his aunt could choose a feral working-class lad over him. 'According to people we've spoken to, it was the fact that he returned the locket, which was all she had left of her sweetheart, that endeared her to him. That was just chance.'

'I suppose so.' David looked up at her. 'I'm probably being foolish, but when we met that time, Rosco was triumphant. It was as if he wanted me to realize how clever he was. He was almost on the point of telling me how he'd pulled it off. There are children like that, who can't resist bragging about how naughty they've been.'

'Was he on his own that second time?'

'No,' Fanshaw said. 'There was a girl in the house with him. She wasn't there when we discussed the will, but she let me in.'

'Can you remember anything about her? Did you have a name?'

He shook his head. 'She was small, pretty, with a lovely smile. She made us both coffee before she disappeared. Rosco was almost dismissive, a bit patronizing. "Leave us to it, there's a good maid." I suppose things were different then. I've got daughters. They wouldn't put up with that sort of treatment.' A pause. 'But there was something about the way she looked at him as she left the room that again made me think they

313

were playing some sort of game. The role of dutiful girlfriend didn't really suit her.'

Fanshaw looked at the clock on his office wall and at the same time a bell rang again. The children were pulled back towards the building like iron filings to a magnet.

'I'm sorry,' he said. 'There's nothing more that I can tell you and I have a meeting.'

She nodded. She had no more questions. He stayed with her while she signed out and left her pass at reception.

'I've had a good life,' he said, as he held open the main door for her to leave. 'A brilliant wife and kids, work that I love. Even if Rosco did cheat me out of my inheritance, I don't bear him any ill will. In the end, he did me a favour.'

She walked out into the peaceful city street. She switched on her phone and saw that there were missed calls from both Venn and May. She called back as she was walking towards the Tube station and had the news that Eleanor Lawson was missing. At Paddington, she just had time to grab a sandwich before catching her train. David Fanshaw had been right. She was starving.

Chapter Forty-Two

ROXY MET THEM AT THE BACK door to the big house. She was white, drawn.

'I'm so sorry. I should have stayed last night.' She looked up at Venn. 'Frankie's gone too.'

It took Venn a moment to remember that Frankie was the dog.

Venn thought she'd been crying. She seemed more upset by the dog's disappearance than Eleanor's. He recalled seeing her at a works Christmas bash in a sleeveless top, her arm covered in tattoos. The largest had been of an Alsatian's face. Then he remembered that she was vegan and volunteered in her time off at the animal rescue shelter.

'You said there was blood.'

'In her bathroom.'

As in the Rosco murder.

'Let's get the CSIs in. Notify Brian, will you, Ross?'

Ross nodded and left the room.

'Show me.' Venn pulled on a scene suit and mask, and threw one to Roxy. She led him upstairs. Eleanor's rooms matched

Bartholomew's. The bathroom door was open as she'd left it. The fittings were equally outdated. They didn't need to go inside.

'Eleanor wasn't in the kitchen when I arrived. I thought she must have taken Frankie for a walk. He's old, though, and he can't go very far. I waited for them. I waited too long. I thought perhaps she'd slept in, and I came upstairs. Her bed had been slept in but there was no sign of her. Then I came in here.'

The bath was old, enamel, stained where a tap had dripped. And now it was stained with splashes of red. Red like the hips and haws scattered over the North Devon hedgerows.

'We don't know that it's hers.' Venn was speaking almost to himself. If it *was* Eleanor's, he'd been very wrong. He'd have to reassess the whole case. 'We need to get a test as soon as we can. In the meantime, of course, we treat this as a crime scene. Let's go and talk somewhere more comfortable.'

She led him downstairs and into a room he'd not been in before. A little living room, with a faded chintz sofa and matching armchair, an old-fashioned, bulky television in one corner. Everything comfortable but a little dusty.

'You'll have checked if Eleanor's car is still here?' He sat on the sofa.

Roxy nodded. 'It is.'

'And the house was unlocked when you got here?'

'Yes. That didn't surprise me. She's an early riser and she'd go to let out the hens. Besides, even after the men's deaths she didn't seem very fussed about security.'

Venn wondered if that was a class thing. Had landowners always had that supreme confidence that set them apart, believing that they were untouchable, that nobody would dare to breach the castle walls?

Ross must have heard them talking because he came back into the room. He nodded to show that the CSIs were on their way.

'Can you organize a search of the house and grounds?' Venn said. 'We'll need a team, but perhaps you can make a start?' Roxy was about to interrupt when he added, turning to her, 'I know you'll have looked for her, but it's a big place. It would be easy to miss a small woman, even inside.' *Especially if she were motionless, or dead. Besides, we should be doing something.* 'I'd start at the top of the house and work down.'

Ross nodded and left the room. They heard his footsteps on the bare wooden floorboards of the corridor, and then on the stairs.

'When did you last see Eleanor?'

'Yesterday evening at about six thirty. I offered to stay the night, as I have since I was first involved. Her husband had died. They might not have been close, but she wasn't used to being on her own, and rattling around in this place . . .' Roxy looked up. 'She's always refused. In the politest way possible, but she was adamant. She was alone now and it would be better to get used to the situation as soon as she could. Besides, she said, she had Frankie to keep her company.' There was a moment of silence. 'I should have insisted.'

Venn didn't say anything to that. Rationally, Roxy knew that Eleanor's disappearance wasn't her responsibility, but that didn't ease the guilt, and nothing he could add would help. 'How did she seem?'

'Quiet, but then she's been like that since Bartholomew died.'

'Any visitors? Phone calls?'

'There were phone calls,' Roxy said, 'but I took most of them. Mostly press. Some friends checking to see if she was

317

okay, wanting to visit. There could have been others later that evening, of course.'

'Of course.' They would check. 'What about her mobile?'

'I don't think she had one! I never saw one, at least.'

'Surely everyone these days has a mobile!' Even as he spoke, Venn's brain was flooded with questions, muddling his response, preventing clear thinking. Suddenly, this felt like madness, some crazy revenge killing. Like the death of Rosco, and the streams of blood, the stuff of a horror movie, not real life. What had these three middle-aged people done to provoke such a response? And if he was right, and there was a history to this story, why wait until now to take revenge?

He'd put together a list of difficult questions for Eleanor, thinking that she might be complicit in the killings. Now, his view of the case pivoted, swung on its axis. He had to start again from the beginning.

He turned back to Roxy. 'Have you checked her room?'

'Just a quick look to make sure she wasn't there.'

'Let's see what's gone. Outdoor clothes. That sort of thing.'

'I checked the corridor by the kitchen. That was where she kept her boots and her big waterproof. They're still there. I didn't go through the things in her room.'

'Was she on any medication?'

'Yes,' Roxy said. 'Eleanor told me she'd had breast cancer five years ago. They caught it early and she only had minimal surgery. But she takes tamoxifen.' She looked up at him. 'My mother was diagnosed a couple of weeks ago. Eleanor was lovely. Reassuring. She offered to go with Mum for the first session of chemo, if she needed it.'

So, if the blood isn't hers, if Eleanor had left the house of her own free will, she'd have taken the pills with her.

Roxy led the way up the grand staircase, and down a corridor opposite to the one leading to Bartholomew's room. It was a pretty room. Matching curtains and quilt cover with a little floral print. Something yellow and delicate. Jasmine? Jonathan would know. This could have been Eleanor's room when she was a child. There was a dressing table, which now seemed to operate as a desk. It had a laptop on it, and some letters, which caught his attention immediately. They looked old, the handwriting a little faded. Then, another thought intruded.

If she had a laptop, surely she'd use a mobile phone. Still, he found it hard to consider Eleanor, indomitable and very alive, as a victim.

Venn pulled open a wardrobe door. It was large, Victorian. Inside, there were outdoor clothes, but there could well have been others.

'Do you know where she kept her medication?'

'In the drawer in the little cupboard by her bed. I came up here with her the day Bartholomew died. She said she needed to rest.' Roxy opened the drawer. The pills were still there.

'Not taking them wouldn't be immediately life-threatening.' Roxy turned so Venn could see how serious she thought this was. 'But Eleanor always did. Religiously. "The NHS saved my life," she once said. "Now it's my turn to do what I can to prevent the horrible illness returning."'

Unlikely, then, that Eleanor had taken herself away, to escape the pity of her friends or to avoid awkward questions from the police. Besides, there was the blood.

Venn looked more closely at the letters. They were from Rosco. Real passionate love letters, which could only have been written by an adolescent. Venn thought of the letters that Mary Ford had written to Rosco. In comparison, those were measured, almost distant. Mary had talked about having a teenage crush, an imaginary lover, but her letters had been written by an adult, needing an outlet for her unhappiness. These were outpourings of emotion.

Eleanor must have kept them all these years. Had Bartholomew known? How would that make him feel? Had they been hidden and only brought out after Jeremy Rosco's death? Two sentences caught Venn's attention: *I'm sailing the world for you. I'll make my fortune and I'll be back to claim you.* In a different letter, another piece jumped out: *Remember the night of the skulls and the bones and the white, white light. Remember it for ever!*

Venn bagged the letters and carried them downstairs, his brain still tumbling with ideas and images. *If I found a stack of letters like that in Jonathan's things, and the lover had come back to claim him, how would I feel? I'd be jealous,* Venn thought. Not jealous enough to kill, but deeply wounded, and he could imagine that Bartholomew was a man who would nurture a grudge. A grudge which could fester for years. All this pointed to his theory that Lawson had killed Rosco. But Eleanor's disappearance, and the blood in the bath, didn't fit in to the scenario at all.

The day passed in a muddle of activity. Brian Branscombe appeared to work in the bathroom.

'I've taken the toothbrush to compare DNA. I've asked them to fast-track it, but don't expect miracles.'

A team came in to search the grounds. Venn didn't expect them to find anything. No small woman dressed in brown, and stabbed to death. If this had been staged like Rosco's murder, Eleanor's body would be found elsewhere. He'd be better sending his officers to Scully Cove.

Ross arrived back in the kitchen to say he'd covered the house. 'I even got into the attic. It's full of junk, but there's no sign of the woman.'

'There is a cellar,' Roxy said. 'Eleanor took me there to get a bottle of wine. Barty had a collection and she wanted to choose something special. I had a glass with her. I've never tasted anything like it.'

Venn wondered if that was the action of a woman mourning her husband, or of celebrating his death. The words of Rosco's love letters were still rattling around in his head.

The door to the cellar was hidden in a cupboard in the kitchen. There were steep stone steps and the room below was lit by a single, dusty light bulb. A rack of wine stood in one corner and the rest of the space was filled with the junk of everyday life: a lawnmower which looked as if it hadn't been used for years, suitcases, a box with Christmas decorations spilling from the top, empty bottles waiting to be recycled. A lot of bottles. Against one wall, shelves contained jars of jam and preserves.

Roxy was the first to reach the bottom. 'What's that?'

Venn could see nothing out of the ordinary.

'Listen!'

A low moan seemed to come from behind a pile of cardboard boxes. Roxy scrambled over them. Venn followed, heart racing, then felt a moment of anticlimax. It was Frankie. There was a lead round his neck, tied to one of the pipes that ran around the walls. He was straining to get free. Roxy, openly weeping, released him and put her arms around him.

Upstairs, back in the small sitting room, which they'd taken over as the hub of the operation, he saw that he'd had two missed calls. One was from Jen, who'd left a voicemail. She was on her way back from London. '*It was interesting, boss. I'll fill you in when I get back. Shall I come straight to you?*'

The other was from Jonathan. No voicemail but a text: **Give me a ring when you get a chance.**

Matthew asked Ross to contact Jen. 'Let her know what's happened. Get her to come here. She talked to Eleanor too and there's an outside chance she might have some idea where she could be.'

He phoned Jonathan back. The man answered, but kept his voice low. In the background, it seemed that some reading group was taking place, a discussion about unreliable narration. Jonathan must have moved out of the room because the background noise faded away.

'I know you must be busy, but Guy was asking if you still wanted him to look at that photo.'

It took Matthew a moment to remember what Jonathan was talking about. He'd asked if the teacher might identify the teenagers in the photo they'd found in Rosco's flat.

'Sure, but there's a been a development.' He explained about Eleanor's disappearance. 'Sorry, I can't get away.' A pause. 'If I email you the photo, could you show Guy? See if he can ID the people involved. We're stretched here.'

There was a moment's silence. Matthew thought there'd be some crack about allowing Jonathan to meddle in his work. But there was nothing. 'Sure. No problem, I can do that. I'll give you a shout if he can place the kids.' Another pause. 'I'll be keeping my fingers crossed that Eleanor's safe.'

Matthew thought it would take more than crossed fingers, or even an incantation about skulls and bones and white, white light to save Eleanor. In this situation, his mother would pray, of course. At this moment Matthew wished he had her faith, and then thought that a prayer of his own would do no harm. He closed his eyes briefly, but the right words wouldn't come.

It was late afternoon when Jen arrived. The search had widened and in Barnstaple they were checking CCTV and the registered vehicles of everyone on the edge of the Greystone investigation. Venn was still in Eleanor's house. He still half hoped that the woman would come in, pushing open the back door, with a story to explain her absence:

I've been in the farmer's market in Morrisham selling my eggs. Or: *I had to go to Exeter to see Barty's solicitor and I thought I'd make a day of it.*

But none of that would make sense because of the dog tied in the cellar and the blood in the bath.

They were sitting in the small living room. It was colder than the kitchen and there was little light but the crime scene investigators had taken over there, looking for fingerprints on the cellar door. Jen was full of the conversation she'd had with David Fanshaw. 'He says he doesn't bear any grudge against Rosco, and I think that's true. He's got his life pretty sorted. He's certain the man scammed his aunt, though. He says Rosco was almost boasting about getting away with it.'

Venn was struggling to focus on what Jen was saying. If willpower alone could have brought Eleanor back to the house, she'd have arrived already. Venn was just about to ask his sergeant to repeat herself when one of the local constables burst into the room.

'I've just heard from Sammy Barton, the RNLI guy at

Greystone. They've got some news.' He stopped for a moment, looking at them, and enjoying the limelight. 'They had a shout. A boat adrift. In Scully Cove.'

Venn thought this was what he'd been expecting, without quite realizing, since they'd had the news of Eleanor's disappearance.

Chapter Forty-Three

MARY FORD HADN'T EXPECTED TO SEE her father that day. She thought he had his own life to lead and she didn't want to make too many demands. Besides, she was embarrassed. Should she tell him about her letters to Rosco and let him know that they'd been found by the police? What would he make of her foolishness?

When he turned up at her house just before lunch, she felt ridiculously awkward. He didn't knock – he had his own key and never wanted her to leave work in the studio to let him in – but he shouted as soon as he got into the house, always respecting her privacy, not wanting to surprise her. Always hoping, she suspected, that there might be a man in the house. A suitable man. His marriage had been very happy, even at the end when his wife was slipping away from him, and he wanted the same for her.

She came down from the attic to make coffee for them.

'Don't stop!' he said, when he saw her appearing at the top of the narrow stairs. 'I was going to bring one up for you.'

She shook her head. 'I'm finding it hard to concentrate.'

She'd found it difficult to focus for months, since Arthur's diagnosis, even on days like this when he was well enough to be in school. Recently work had become more of an escape than a struggle, but now, the discovery of Rosco's body had thrown her again, the image of the dead man worming its way into her mind so she could see little else.

'I thought I'd stay over.' He was carrying his overnight bag. 'You could have a night in the pub with your friends. A bit of a break.'

She shook her head. The last thing she needed was to be surrounded by the gossip and speculation about two deaths in Scully Cove. Gossip about Jeremy Rosco. 'I might put myself down as available for the lifeboat, though. If that's okay with you?'

'You sure? You don't want a break? A few drinks with your mates?'

'Nah!' She gave his arm a squeeze. 'But a bit of adult company tonight is just what I need, so thanks for coming along.'

They went for a walk after lunch, out onto the headland, a strong breeze in their faces. Alan pointed out seabirds, and she pretended to recognize them, as she had throughout her childhood. She loved his enthusiasm, but couldn't share his passion. She loved the glory of the scenery, not the minute details of the natural history of the place.

'So that's where they found Rosco?' He was looking down into the bay.

'Yeah.' A pause. 'I had a bit of a crush on him when I was younger.'

'I know you did! Posters of the *Nelly Wren* on your bedroom wall.'

'I wrote to him a few times.'

But the wind seemed to blow her words away, and she didn't try to talk to him about it again.

On the way back, they picked up the children from school. Alan had offered to go for them alone: 'Go home, put your feet up and enjoy a few minutes' peace.' But in the end, Mary had decided she'd like to be there too. Alan waited in the playground with Isla, while Mary went in to get Arthur from Tilly Gregory. The teacher seemed drained, exhausted, unusually quiet.

'Are you okay?' Mary had never been close to Matilda, though they were of an age. The whole religion thing got in the way. The certainty and the way the Brethren stuck together. Sammy Barton's mistrust of Mary as lifeboat helm wasn't only that she was a woman and an outsider. It was because she was a non-believer. Matilda had been brilliant with Arthur, though, patient and kind even before his illness had been diagnosed and he'd just been considered awkward by other adults. Mary would always be grateful for that.

The teacher gave a wry smile. 'It's stress, I think. Living in a community now where bad things have happened. Not quite knowing who to trust.'

Mary wondered if Matilda had anyone specific in mind. Had a close friend triggered suspicion? One of the Brethren? Surely not Davy! Despite the difference in age, Matilda and Davy were as close as any couple Mary knew. Sometimes other people's relationships made her jealous. She wanted what they had. She'd always seen the Gregorys as one of those envied couples. They lit up when they saw each other. She was trying to form a response to Matilda's comment when the teacher walked away back into the school.

Back at home, Alan found snacks for the kids and she made an early supper for them all. The call from Sammy Barton came on her pager just as she was taking her first mouthful. A lifeboat call-out. Could she helm? She was straight on her feet, experiencing the usual surge of adrenaline, of excitement. The high. Almost immediately afterwards, her mood shifted, dropped. There was the irrational feeling that had haunted her since the last time she was out in the lifeboat, that Rosco's death was her fault and that she could have done something to prevent it. She hesitated for a moment before responding.

Sod it! Of course, I'll go.

After all, it might be good to have another call so quickly. To be forced to take responsibility for another incident. It might erase the memory of finding Rosco's body. It would be like getting on a horse after a fall or driving a car after a crash.

She turned to her father. 'This *is* okay?'

There was a moment's pause when she thought he might object and ask her to stay at home, but he just smiled. 'Sure.' Another hesitation. 'But take care, yeah?'

By the time he'd finished speaking, she'd picked up her gear and was at the door.

This was different from the last time, of course. There was daylight and the weather wasn't quite so wild. The shout seemed to have come from a reputable source: a member of the public walking along the coastal path had called it in to the coastguard. But the location was the same. The vessel had been seen at the mouth of Scully Cove, just off the headland.

If we'd stayed a little longer on our walk, Mary thought, *we'd have seen the boat in trouble. We could have called it in ourselves.*

But then, I wouldn't have been home in time to get the shout. Someone else would have been helm.

The monster tractor had them pushed into the water in seconds, the huge wheels crunching the shingle, the sound deafening. This time, Mary took the wheel. She knew exactly where she was going and she wanted control, to be at the front of the RIB with the spray on her face. They bounced over the waves breaking on the beach, the lifeboat bucking and twisting as if it were alive, and headed out for open sea.

Even before they rounded the headland, she became aware of the murmurs behind her. They were low and unsettling. More a vibration than a sound, felt through her body, not heard with her ears. They were muttered under the breath, barely audible over the noise of the engine, but Mary knew what the men were saying: *Skulls and bones and the white, white light.* The words running into each other, so they sounded like a hummed familiar tune. Reassuring, but somehow menacing at the same time. She didn't turn round.

Like her, the men were thinking of the last time they were here, and even the most rational young crew member was turning to the old superstition. Just in case. She wondered if they considered her part of the problem, part of the place's curse. She found herself repeating the line in her head too, a feeble attempt to appease them or the power they were calling to. To make herself part of the team.

The boat was there just where they'd been told. It was small enough for an experienced person to manage single-handed. The message had said that they were to expect only one casualty.

Mary tried shouting, but there was no response. In this weather it shouldn't be too hard to get alongside, and she slowed the RIB until it was sliding towards the smaller boat, until the hulls were touching. There was no sign of the sailor. The sails had been lowered but not furled. Then Mary realized that like the tender where they'd found Rosco, this boat too had been anchored. The silence and the lack of life made her jumpy. She reached for a line and tied it to the lifeboat to steady it. There was an outboard motor, but presumably that had failed too. Otherwise, there would have been no reason for the mayday. But where was the sailor? The sea was choppy, but not rough enough to send a person overboard.

Behind her, she sensed the crew becoming restless. Tense. They didn't want to be here. She needed to act quickly if she were to hold on to any authority.

'Go in.' The words were directed to the man behind her. 'There might be someone sick below.'

Or a body, white as wax, drained of blood.

Daniel was young, just out of his teens, fit and he'd climbed across in seconds.

There was a small cabin, below the level of the deck, and for a moment he disappeared from sight. His head emerged. Mary held her breath.

'Nothing here.' He looked across at her, raising his voice above the sound of the lifeboat's engine. She thought that he'd been expecting the worst too and could hardly believe it. 'No sign of an accident. I've checked everywhere. It's empty.'

Again, she heard a murmur behind her. A release of tension, but also perhaps a sense of disappointment. The empty boat was an anticlimax. Scully Cove had promised more drama.

'We'll tow it back with us.' Mary turned to the rest of the crew. 'Anyone recognize her?'

'I do.' Daniel again. He was a member of Morrisham Yacht

Club, had been since he'd been a child. 'She's the *Scully Maid.*' A pause. 'She belonged to the commodore, Mr Lawson. I don't know how she got out here. I was at the club last night – working a shift in the bar – and I noticed that she was still in the marina then.'

Chapter Forty-Four

VENN WAITED FOR NEWS FROM THE Greystone lifeboat in Eleanor Lawson's grand house, restless and distracted. His team thought him unnaturally patient, but he hated waiting. He'd once told Jonathan that hours of boredom in Brethren meetings was perfect preparation for being a cop. *I can be as impatient as any of my colleagues, but I've learned to hide it.*

He'd sent Roxy home, and she'd taken the dog with her. 'Just until Eleanor comes back and can look after her again.'

He didn't like to say that Eleanor could be dead in the boat, or at the bottom of the sea.

The call came in the evening, just as the light was starting to fade. Sammy Barton again phoned with the news.

'There was nobody there. No sign of a struggle. They towed the boat into Greystone and I checked it myself. It was anchored, just like the *Moon Crest* tender.' The operations manager paused. 'It belonged to Bartholomew Lawson.'

Then Venn demanded information from Rainston. 'One of the lifeboat crew recognized Bartholomew's boat. He's a student but he works part-time in the sailing club bar. He reckons it was definitely still in the marina last night. Can you check? I need to know if it was there this morning, if anyone saw it leave.'

'Sure. Want me to head over to Morrisham now?'

'Yes.' Venn paused briefly and tried to order his thoughts. 'Make a start on canvassing there. And ask if Eleanor Lawson was seen at all. Her car's still here, so we know she didn't drive there to take the boat out herself.'

It was too much of a coincidence, Venn thought, to believe that the discovery of Barty's boat and the disappearance of his wife were unconnected. He was still talking, putting his thoughts into words, sharing them with the team:

'But she could have a got a lift there if she wanted to go for a sail in her husband's boat. A taxi.' A thought occurred to him. 'Do we know that her car's working? It hasn't just run out of petrol or failed to start?' Because that could have been the logical explanation for her disappearance that he'd been seeking all day.

'Roxy tried it first thing,' Ross said. 'She found the keys on a hook in the kitchen. It started fine.'

Venn nodded. He sent Jen back to Greystone. 'Talk to Mary Ford. There might be something about the state of the boat which could give us an idea what happened there.'

'Sure.'

Rainston was making his way out of the room, had the door half open, when Venn shouted across to him. 'What's the name of Lawson's boat? Do you know?'

'*Scully Maid*,' Rainston said. 'That's what Sammy Barton, the lifeboat operations manager called her.'

Everything takes us back to Scully.

But now it was dark. Venn was tempted to get everyone out

to the cove with torches and headlamps, but that wouldn't have been safe and a search would have to wait until the following day.

He sent Ross home. He thought of Jonathan, troubled, it seemed, by some dilemma that he wasn't ready to share. Matthew knew he should go back to him, should offer his support. It wasn't late and Jonathan would still be up, a glass of red wine in his hand, the fire lit. It was tempting, and certainly, Matthew had no desire to go back to Greystone and the Maiden's Prayer.

Instead, he stayed where he was, dozing in front of the kitchen range, just in case Eleanor should return, just in case there was news of her.

Chapter Forty-Five

MARY WAS FEELING FLAT. AFTER THE drama of yesterday's lifeboat call-out, there was a sense of anticlimax, and the everyday anxieties were crowding back. Her father had gone home, and she missed him. She missed the adult company and the optimism he carried with him. He still thought that Artie would be saved by a miracle cure, and she'd always been too realistic to put her faith in that. Even if the Illinois doctor peddling a new life wasn't some sort of quack, the sale of knitted toy animals and traybakes would hardly raise the cash needed to get him treatment. Her father had offered to sell his house to fund the trip to the US, but he'd remortgaged it already when he'd given up work to care for her mother, and even if he could get a buyer, the resulting profit wouldn't scratch the surface.

It was time to be practical. Perhaps she should sell this house in Greystone and move in with her father. His place was bigger and there'd be space to extend. They could perhaps provide a ground floor adapted for her son's needs and there'd be the garden. But no view of the sea. And she needed the sea at times of darkness. She needed the ebb and flow of it to feel alive.

She was thinking of this as she took the children to school. She was a little early for the bell and the parents were in small groups chatting. If she'd attached herself and joined in one of the conversations, they'd have tried to make her a part of it, but it would have been an effort. She always felt awkward butting in, as if she were intruding. Rarely did anyone else make the first move.

Today, though, Ruth Smale, the doctor's wife, did notice her and waved her over. Mary was moving through the yard to be close to the door when the kids were let in. As always, she skirted past the groups of gossiping parents as if magnetically repelled by them, not wanting to be pulled in by their pity. It was as if she were some sort of alien planet in the playground universe. Ruth was chatting to one other woman, but now she pushed her pram in Mary's direction.

'I heard you were out in the lifeboat again yesterday.'

Mary was surprised by the approach. Ruth Smale was always polite enough, but usually in the playground she stayed with the other Brethren mums.

'Yes,' she said. 'It was a busy day. No drama, though, this time. Just an empty boat.'

'Oh.'

The word was almost a question, but Mary didn't respond.

'How's Arthur?' Ruth put on the sympathetic face of a parent with perfectly healthy children. Not understanding in the slightest how hard it was, and not really wanting to hear. Just wanting to show that she cared.

Mary replied as she always did on these occasions, with a smile and a brisk no-nonsense voice. 'Oh, you know. There are good days and bad days.'

'We're all praying for you.'

Mary might have let loose then and said that she didn't need their prayers. She needed a scientist who wasn't a fraud to discover a cure. Backed by immediate proper peer-reviewed research. After all, if they could come up with cures for other diseases, shouldn't it be possible? But Arthur was one small boy, with no power or influence. Mary had even opened her mouth to speak, but the words were covered by the noise of the bell, and the school door opened and the kids streamed in.

Mary waited for Matilda Gregory to arrive to collect Arthur. That was what happened every morning. The yard had cleared except for a few last-minute stragglers, like Isla, who were still playing. Ruth Smale shouted that she had to get the baby home and it would be great to catch up another time. That complacent expression still on her face. As if Mary had done something to cause Arthur's illness and if she'd been happily married and devout like Ruth, he'd still be well and strong.

Not if I see you first, lady.

But Mary waved and smiled, before turning back to her son.

When Matilda appeared, Mary thought the teacher seemed distracted this morning. Usually there was time for proper feedback about Arthur's condition, how he'd been overnight and any problems he might have during the day. But the handover was perfunctory, and added to Mary's frustration, her sense that she was the only person to care about him. Isla still hadn't gone into the building and was swinging on the climbing frame with one of her friends. Mary shouted to her to get in, that class was about to start, that Mrs Gregory was taking Arthur in now. Taking out her fury on her daughter.

It seemed, though, that Matilda did want to speak, just not about Arthur.

'I heard there was another incident at Scully.'

'Yes,' Mary said. 'There was.' She looked straight at Matilda, challenging her to ask more questions, but the teacher's eyes slid away, and when she spoke again, it was almost as if she was talking to the boy in the chair.

'It seems that Eleanor Lawson's gone missing.'

'Oh?'

'When the police turned up at her house yesterday, apparently there was no sign of her.'

Mary wondered how Matilda could have got that information. 'Her husband's just died. I suppose she wants a bit of time on her own.'

'Of course,' the teacher said. 'I expect that's it.'

'I should get back.' Mary wanted to be in her studio, working. The exchange was making her uncomfortable.

'Of course,' Matilda said, her face flushed. 'I'm sorry.' Mary couldn't really see what there was to be sorry for. She didn't understand what the conversation had been about at all. 'I'll have to get in too.'

'Sure.' Mary released the brake on the wheelchair, and turned it so Matilda could take Arthur inside. She had to shout to tell Isla again to go into school, because whose kids ever responded on the first time of asking?

Ruth Smale's. I bet her girls do just what they're told. First time.

Mary had read somewhere that well-behaved little girls often turned into teenage monsters. Wouldn't that be great, if it were true? All the way home she fantasized about Ruth's darlings falling prey to teenage pregnancy and heroin addiction, and then she felt guilty for wishing that on any mother.

She was just unlocking her door when she saw Jen Rafferty walking towards her. It seemed that today there would be no peace, no chance to become engrossed in making her art. 'Are you looking for me?'

'Please. I was hoping for more advice.'

'I suppose you'd better come in.' After the encounter with Ruth and Matilda, Mary didn't care if she sounded churlish. Instead of taking Jen into her living space, she led her upstairs to the loft, the room she used as a studio.

I work too. My time is as precious as yours.

'What did you make of the incident yesterday?' Jen asked. 'A bit odd, wasn't it?'

'Really odd.' Despite herself, Mary was curious to know what the police had made of the empty boat. 'There was no real sign of damage and the weather wasn't that bad. And coming so soon after finding Mr Rosco's body in the same place . . .' Her voice tailed off.

'We're checking to see if anyone saw who took it out from the marina. Someone must have seen it leave.'

'I guess so. But in the middle of the day, and midweek, there wouldn't be so many people down there.' Mary paused. 'It's unlikely that it was taken very early in the morning, not if it was sailed straight to the cove. Dad and I were on the headland at lunchtime and we didn't see it then.'

'One person could have sailed it?'

'Sure, if they knew what they were doing. But if you knew what you were doing, you wouldn't get into trouble on an afternoon like yesterday.'

'What's the most likely scenario?'

There was a moment of silence. Mary considered the possibilities.

'I think it was done deliberately. Posed.' A pause. 'Honestly, I can't think of any other explanation.'

'Like Jeremy Rosco in the *Moon Crest* dinghy?' Jen asked.

'Yeah, but why would anyone want to do that?'

A silence. The room was lit by a skylight and Mary could see a gull, very white against grey clouds. Its beak was open, and she knew it would be screaming but she could hear nothing.

'Bartholomew's wife has gone missing,' Jen said at last.

'I heard.'

'Who told you?' The detective seemed surprised that the news had got out, disturbed even.

'Matilda Gregory, when I dropped Artie off at school.'

There was another silence before Jen spoke again. 'We were wondering if Eleanor could have taken out the boat.'

'You think she had some sort of accident? Went overboard?'

'That might be one explanation. There'll be a team searching the beach at Scully today.'

'They won't see much there until mid-afternoon,' Mary said. 'It's the spring tide, and with this wind behind it . . .'

'Spring tide?'

'The biggest tide of the year. At the equinox.' Mary loved the magic of the tides, the suck and flow of them, pulled somehow by the tug of the moon. 'It'll cover the beach over the middle of the day. Right up to where the path ends. Even if they've already started searching, they won't get far before they have to go back up the cliff.'

'There's nothing else you can tell me?'

Now Mary was losing patience. She wanted this woman out of her house. 'Why don't you talk to Sammy Barton? He's a bit old school – he's never really believed that a woman should be lifeboat crew – but he knows this coast better than anyone else for miles. And he grew up here, understands the people and taught most of them to sail. He might have an idea who'd pull that sort of stunt.'

Chapter Forty-Six

VENN WOKE, UNCOMFORTABLE IN HIS CHAIR by the range, just as it was getting light. He threw more logs into the stove and moved the kettle onto the hotplate to make coffee. If he'd hoped for inspiration about where Eleanor might be by staying in this strange old house, he was disappointed. All he'd achieved was aching joints and a sense of failure. And an obsession with Scully Cove. The place and the old stories surrounding it had drifted in and out of his dreams throughout the night.

He'd kept his overnight bag in his car and he'd washed and changed by the time Ross arrived with bacon sandwiches from the cafe in Morrisham.

'So, what's the plan, boss?' He was speaking with his mouth full, too eager, it seemed, to wait until he'd swallowed. He made Venn feel middle-aged and stale.

'I want to go back to Scully. Let's see what's been washed ashore now that it's light.'

'I thought the coastguard team were on that.'

They were, until they were pushed back by the tide, but Venn still wanted to be there, to check for himself. In the end there was a compromise. He waited until the coastguards had finished their search. He stayed in Eleanor's house, the spider in the middle of a web, soaking up the information coming from outside, from Jen, and Ross, and from the team canvassing in Morrisham, becoming more frustrated as only fragments of news filtered through. Then in the late afternoon, he decided to move and he and Ross made their way back to the cove.

He made Ross drive – he was anxious about his ability to concentrate – down the narrow lanes through the overgrown hedges and past trees bent by the wind. Ross wouldn't stop talking:

'Are we looking for a body?'

It seemed to Venn that the last question was almost gleeful. Excited at least. He bit back a sharp response, partly because he had no idea why he felt they *should* go there. Why they might find something that the coastguard had missed.

'Or a cold and tired woman,' he said. Though after a night and a day, and the blood in the bath, he knew that was unlikely.

Venn wondered why he was so keen to go. Perhaps because he hoped to see himself as Eleanor's saviour, the white knight galloping to the rescue. Perhaps she'd become his own means to redemption.

When they arrived at the top of the cliff path at Scully, there was building cloud and a chill breeze. They parked in the layby and walked through the scrubby thicket of hawthorn and elder until they reached the path down the cliff towards the cove. Ross wasn't dressed for the weather and started moaning before they were halfway down.

Venn thought that if Eleanor had been in the boat and somehow found her way ashore, she'd already have had a night in the open air. She'd be freezing and miserable. If he'd been thinking more rationally, they'd have come prepared with blankets and a flask of coffee. He'd have allowed Ross to get a coat and boots before setting out. Besides, this was a fool's errand. A fantasy, stirred by the superstition surrounding the place. If Eleanor had found her way ashore, the coastguard would have found her. Still, he was pulled back to the place. In his gut, he knew that it was important.

There were signs of the search party on the beach: boot marks on the wet sand below the tideline. Ross wanted to turn back immediately. 'You can see that it's already been searched. We've no phone signal down here. The team's got no way of getting in touch if she *does* turn up.' He made a show of shivering. He too thought this was a waste of time.

'Now we're here, let's do the thing properly. We didn't see Lawson's body at first, when I was here with Jonathan. It was around the cliff on that narrow beach at the edge of the bay. If the tide was still up when the coastguard came, they wouldn't be able to make their way there.' It was low water now. Rocks were exposed that would only be seen at a spring tide. But the tide was already on the turn, and soon the sea would slide up the cove again. They had to take their opportunity.

Venn started to clamber across, following the path that Jonathan had taken. He heard Ross, splashing and cursing behind him, and allowed himself a smile, before thinking that he should be more charitable.

All trace of Lawson's body, and the investigators' work, had disappeared, swept away by the high autumn tide. There was no space between the tideline, marked by seaweed, the white bones of driftwood and the glints of sea glass, and the bottom of the cliff. They walked along it. Venn poked at the kelp with his boot, more he realized to slow their progress and to annoy

Ross than in the hope of finding anything. From here, there was no view of the path, and Venn was aware that the tide was already turning. In a couple of hours, they would have to retreat to the shingle beach and begin their climb back. He might as well admit to Ross and to himself now that this had been a wild goose chase.

There was a sound above them. They were so close to the cliff bottom and the grey granite was so steep that it was impossible to get a glimpse of what might be happening there. If anyone was at the top, the angle prevented them from being seen. Venn stepped further away towards the water, and looked up in the hope of a better view. He became aware of a movement and thought he could see a figure, shadowy in the fading light. Then he told himself that he was being melodramatic, was seeing ghosts, affected by the superstition surrounding the place, by his almost sleepless night in Eleanor's house.

The boulder, though, was no figment of his imagination. While Venn had been focused on the person above, a rock, so big that it could have been quarried from the Greystone works, must have bounced down the grassy, sloping, upper reaches of the cliff and now was in freefall from an overhang. Venn started to shout a warning, but it was already too late. As he watched in horror, too far now from Ross to throw him to safety, the boulder hit the man on his shoulder and felled him. Ross crumpled, and collapsed onto the shore, his head hitting the seaweed-covered rocks. For a brief moment, there was no noise and no movement.

Venn started to clamber towards his colleague, but had only moved a few steps when more rocks followed. A trickle became an avalanche. It was as if the cliff was collapsing in on itself and falling towards the shore. Venn stepped further back from the onslaught and found the water almost covering his boots. The tide would be sweeping in very quickly soon. He looked up at the clifftop but the shower of rocks blurred his view.

Suddenly everything was still. The avalanche, if that was what it had been, stopped as suddenly as it had started. Ross was lying motionless. Venn climbed towards him, panicking, thinking he must be dead and knowing that he was responsible. He didn't see the final boulder until the last moment, and then his boot was caught in a cleft in the rock. He couldn't shift out of the way in time. It hit him in the chest, and he lost balance and fell.

He was woken by the water lapping his cheek. The approaching tide, icy cold. He must have lost consciousness for a while, but despite the headache and the nausea, he found that he was already thinking clearly. The stone that hit him had been hurled out from the clifftop. Aimed. It hadn't rolled and bounced like the others. The person throwing must have been a good shot. Or been lucky. Venn thought that he'd been lucky too – if the stone had hit his head, he would surely be dead. Because he'd been standing away from the cliff, the earlier tumbling rocks had missed him. He sat up, and the world swam for a moment and then settled. Ross was further away from the water, safe from drowning but lying still. Venn scrambled to the man's side, felt for a pulse, and began to breathe again when he realized that his sergeant was alive.

One of Ross's legs was pinned down by a mound of boulders. Venn started to move them and saw that the bone was broken and twisted. Ross stirred, groaned. Opened his eyes. They were hazy, unfocused and he closed them again almost immediately. Venn had fallen with his face towards the sea, and his clothes were still mostly dry. He took off his jacket and put it over Ross.

All the time he was thinking. Here, in the growing dusk, his mind was startlingly clear. This was meant to look like an accident. A rockfall. It must happen all the time. Fissures in the cliff weakened by frost or storm would cause a mini-avalanche. But this was no accident. Venn could picture the boulder thrown towards him. No rockfall would send a boulder flying out like that.

Fuelled by superstition, the locals would believe the theory, though. Two detectives, drowned while they were investigating the suicide of a man who'd killed himself in the same spot. An unlucky place. They'd put it down to supernatural influences, to the skulls and the bones and the white, white light. But Venn had stopped quite believing in the supernatural when he'd renounced his faith at eighteen.

He and Ross were still alive, however, and whoever had let loose the rockfall couldn't be sure that they were dead. Surely the killer would check. Venn couldn't do anything now, while the tide was coming in and getting higher by the minute. He was stranded. Even if he waded, it wouldn't be safe to make his way to the cliff path to get help for Ross. He thought the killer would be waiting too, and they'd know the tides better than he did. They'd make their way down the cliff as soon as the water started to ebb again. They'd want to make sure that neither of the detectives were living to tell the story.

Chapter Forty-Seven

JEN SPENT THE AFTERNOON IN MORRISHAM with a team of uniformed officers, checking for witnesses who might have seen the *Scully Maid* leave the day before. While they moved along the promenade, talking to the dog-walkers and runners, she stood at the entrance to the marina. It would be other sailors who would have noticed the boat go out, not passers-by who knew nothing of the sea.

An older, grey-haired man unlocked the gate onto the pontoon, and started making his way along to his mooring. He was wearing baggy jeans and a threadbare jersey, heavy boots and carrying what looked like a bag of tools. She called him back, and introduced herself.

'One of these boats belong to you?'

'Ha! As if I could afford one of these. I'm just doing a bit of work on this beauty. Tarting it up for the owner, like.' He nodded fondly towards a gleaming hull.

'One was found anchored off Scully Cove yesterday. Empty. Were you working here then?'

He nodded. 'I came around lunchtime.'

'Did you see anything go out?'

'One or two. Making the most of it while the wind had dropped.'

'I'm interested in the *Scully Maid*.'

He looked up sharply. 'Belonged to the commodore? He's dead, you know. It wouldn't have been him.' His accent was so thick that she struggled to understand him, and he looked at *her* as if she was from another planet.

'I know he's dead. But his boat ended up in the cove so somebody took it out. Any idea who that might have been?'

'Could have been the bloke in the hat.' A pause. 'Must have been him, because nobody else came this side of the marina. And that's where the *Scully Maid* was moored.'

'Which bloke?' She was almost wishing she had Ross with her. He was good with the locals.

'Came along in the afternoon. I started chatting, but he just walked on. Rude really. Odd because most of the owners don't mind a natter.'

'What did he look like?'

'Like I said, he was wearing a hat. Woollen. Dark blue. I didn't really see his face. He walked so quickly he had his back to me before I had a chance to look.'

'It definitely was a man? It couldn't have been a woman?'

'Nah. Wrong build. And the way he was walking. Heavy.' He paused. 'And he was wearing boots. Rubber sea boots. His feet were too big. Couldn't have been a lady.'

So, Eleanor hadn't taken the boat out herself.

The man started to walk on. She called after him again. 'One last question!'

'What now? I've got work to do.'

'Was he carrying anything? Your man in the hat?'

ANN CLEEVES

He stopped in his tracks, thinking for a moment. 'He had a bag. One of those black plastic bin bags. Heavy duty you'd use for rubble or garden waste. Might have been planning to dump it overboard. Save paying for the tip. But I don't know what he had inside. Could have been anything.'

Excited, Jen phoned Matthew and Ross, but she received no answer. They must be somewhere with poor reception. They'd talked about going down to Scully Cove, but they should be back by now.

She headed back to Greystone. It seemed even more sensible now to follow up Mary Ford's suggestion to talk to Sammy Barton – he might recognize the description of the man with the hat – and Venn and May might be there. She parked outside the Maiden's. It was darker than it should have been. Only early evening, but there was a mountain of low cloud and the first spots of rain. The wind making a noise around the chimney pots. There'd been the forecast of another deep low coming in from the Atlantic. She drove slowly through the village, but there was no sign of Venn's car. Perhaps he'd given up and gone back to Jonathan, and she'd had a wasted trip. She could have gone straight home, enjoyed the peace of an evening with a bottle of wine and crap telly; she could have invited Cynthia to join her. She phoned the mobile again. The same message. She tried Matthew's landline. Jonathan answered.

'Nah, he's not here. He stayed in Eleanor Lawson's house last night and I've not heard from him since lunchtime. Everything okay?'

'Yeah,' she said. 'All fine.' Because what was the point of ruining Jonathan's evening by making him anxious too?

Out of the vehicle, she hesitated, wondering if she should

be worried about Matthew, if she should alert the team to look for him. But he was with Ross, and they were adults. What could have happened? The wind was increasing and she pulled up the hood of her coat, hiding her red hair, making herself as anonymous as she could. She couldn't face questions from the locals about the progress of the investigation. Walking past the Maiden's Prayer, she glimpsed in. The door was a little ajar, and she could see a couple of elderly men in the bar, with Harry Carter behind it. No sign of Ross or the boss.

There was a light on in the doctor's surgery, and, as she walked past, Jen saw Matilda Gregory and Ruth Smale inside, so deep in conversation that they wouldn't have noticed her, even if her face hadn't been half hidden by the hood. Matilda was crying, and Ruth had her arm around her friend. There was no sign of the doctor. Surgery must be over, because the reception desk was unmanned. There was no sign of Ruth's kids either, so presumably Peter Smale was at home babysitting. Rows of strange knitted animals stared down at the scene, a weird audience to the theatre playing out below.

Jen walked on past to allow herself time to decide what to do next. While there seemed to be some drama happening between the women, she thought there was no certainty that it concerned the murders. Jen had spent enough time at the school gate to know that some women enjoyed a little excitement, and could create it out of nothing. She paused on the corner of the street, with its view of the quay and the lifeboat station, the tide breaking over the shingle, and tried to work out whether she should talk to these women, who were on the edge of the investigation, or whether the conversation would be a distraction.

Before she could make up her mind, the light in the surgery was switched off and both Ruth and Matilda appeared on the pavement. Just in the way that they made their way up the street, Jen had the sense that they'd come to a decision, and were determined on some course of action.

Curious, she was tempted to follow them, but she continued walking down the quay towards Sammy Barton's house. Her phone rang. There was a moment of relief. It must be Venn. They might meet up for dinner and she could pass on the news from Morrisham marina.

It was Jonathan on the end of the line. 'I've tried to call Matthew but he's still not answering. Busy, I guess. I've been with Guy, the teacher at Morrisham High. He was able to identify those kids in the photo he found in Rosco's flat. I thought it might be important. Can you pass on the message?'

'Sure,' she said. 'No probs.' But a worm of unease had squirmed its way into her head and it wouldn't come out.

Chapter Forty-Eight

ROSS WAS CONSCIOUS ALMOST ALL THE time now, but obviously in such pain that he drifted off occasionally, scaring Venn until he came back to life, groaning and swearing. Venn sat with him, trying to shelter him from the weather with his body, but wary and frustrated. He needed to get Ross treatment, but with no phone signal and trapped by the tide that had already reached the spur of cliff separating them from the main cove, there was nothing he could do. It was dark now, but as soon as the water was low enough, he'd get up the cliff and phone for an ambulance, even taking the risk of bumping into the killer. Because Venn still thought that the killer would need to know that the detectives were dead. At some point they'd be here to check.

We must be close to an answer, Venn thought, *for them to risk killing us. Or they must be mad.* He shivered, and thought the cold must be stopping him thinking this through properly. His mind slid over possible outcomes, not coming to grips with anything substantial or real.

When the light appeared, it came not from the land as he'd been expecting, but from the sea.

Of course, Venn thought, the killer wouldn't wait for the tide to go out before coming to find us. This part of the world, the sea is the natural way to travel. It came to him that their only chance was to play dead, to hope the attacker wouldn't come too close, that seeing the bodies would be enough. Ross seemed to be sleeping. Venn took his jacket from his constable and put it back on, then lay where he'd fallen after the boulder had hit him. The tide was ebbing now, but his head and shoulders were still in the shallows. He tried not to move, even when the cold seeped through his clothes, and he prayed to a God in whom he no longer believed that Ross too would keep still and quiet.

There was the hum of an engine. They weren't creeping in. He supposed they'd see no point in silence if their victims were already dead, and if they were alive, there was no place yet for them to escape. Then the engine stopped and all he could hear was the lapping of waves on the shore. If it weren't for the light, he'd believe he was imagining it all. As the light came closer, he heard the splash of oars in the water. And then voices. He strained to listen but couldn't make out what was being said. There was more than one person then, and neither was making any effort to be quiet. Quite the reverse. He became aware of another sound: the keel scraping against the shingle and then a woman's voice shouted his name.

'Matthew! Are you there?'

It was Jen Rafferty, Scouse and miraculous. He sat up awkwardly, raised his hand and was blinded by the white light of her torch. 'Yes! We're here!'

Jen was carrying dry clothes, blankets and flasks of coffee. She started to take his wet jacket off, and then his jersey. Her hands were on his skin. He was still disorientated and thought he'd never been so intimate with a woman close to his own age.

'No!' He could hear the panic in his voice. 'We need to help Ross. He's badly hurt.'

'Sammy's done the first responder training.' Jen's voice was gentle. 'He's checking him out.'

There were a few moments when the only sound came from the waves on the shore.

'There are a few bones broken,' Sammy said. 'But we need to move him. Quickly. He's cold already and hypothermia could kill him.'

Venn finished putting on the dry shirt and jumper. They must have belonged to Barton because they were too big. The jumper was hand-knitted, the wool a little scratchy on his skin. He turned down the tracksuit bottoms. He'd rather be wet and cold than be seen in those.

Gently they lifted Ross into the boat. Again, he seemed to slide in and out of consciousness.

'What made you come to look for us?'

'You've always said this place was important and we knew where you were heading for. It's not like you to be out of touch for so long; you trained us to maintain contact. Mary suggested I talk to Sammy about the *Scully Maid*. She thought he might know who could have sailed her and how she came to be abandoned. I tried phoning again while I was chatting to him, but you still weren't picking up, so I asked if there was some way to try and find you.' Jen made it all sound very simple. Very normal. 'We didn't want the whole of Greystone knowing what was happening so we decided against the lifeboat.' After the drama and anxiety of the previous hours, her calm explanation was just what Venn needed.

Barton was standing in the shallow water, holding on to the boat, the water lapping around his long rubber boots. 'We need to get this chap back to Greystone. The doctor will be waiting for us.'

'Smale?'

'Yeah. We work with him all the time. He's on standby. He doesn't know all the details, of course, but he'll have realized it's not a usual lifeboat shout.' Barton looked across to Venn. 'That *is* okay?'

Venn thought for a moment, but then he nodded. Getting Ross treated was the most urgent priority. 'Sure.'

He stood at the water's edge while Barton settled Ross as well as he could in the dinghy. His headtorch moved, throwing weird shadows, picking up odd details, but it seemed to Venn that, warmer and drier, the sergeant must already be more comfortable. Matthew turned to Jen. 'Any news on Eleanor?'

'Nothing. Jonathan phoned, though, with some news for you.' She passed on the message about the photo of the teenagers. 'That's the real reason why we came. It seemed very odd that you hadn't been in touch with him.'

'You coming then? I want to get this chap back,' Barton interrupted, impatient.

'Someone tried to kill us.' Venn was still talking to Jen. 'The rockfall wasn't an accident and we were deliberately targeted. I think they'll come back to check that we're dead. I want to be here to see.'

'We could have people staked out at the top of the cliff.' She was horrified. 'No need to have you here as a kind of decoy.'

But Venn had already thought through the options. He shouted to Barton. 'How long until the tide goes out far enough so someone could get round the cliff to where we were lying?'

'An hour if you didn't mind getting your feet wet.'

Venn turned back to Jen. 'How many people could you round up to be here in an hour? You won't have any phone signal until you're almost in Greystone. One officer? Two if you're lucky? And even if they caught our killer at the top of the cliff, there'd be no proof of what they were up to.'

'But then at least we'd know,' she said, 'who we were looking for.'

'Oh, I believe I already know.' Because the thoughts that had been sliding away from him, slippery as the kelp on the shore, had made sense at last, and Jonathan's message had confirmed it. 'Not the details, not yet. But why. At least I know why.'

'You're injured,' she said. 'You can't sit here for the rest of the night. You need to see a doctor.'

'I had a bit of concussion. It's Ross that we need to worry about, and if we don't get him treated, Oldham will kill me.' A pause. 'Get me sacked at least.'

Oldham was their superintendent, idle and incompetent, and Ross was his favourite. Venn had meant it as a joke, but it wasn't far from the truth.

'I'll stay too.' Her voice was strong and resolute and he could have kissed her. He was a coward and he didn't want to be here on his own. 'They'll be looking for two bodies,' she went on. 'And while we're waiting you can tell me what this is all about.'

Venn knew that if he was any sort of boss, he'd send her back in the boat with Barton. He was the senior investigating officer and she had two kids. But he was grateful. He only nodded and shouted across to the man. 'You can manage Ross on your own?'

'Of course I can. Peter will be waiting at the other end.'

Barton might have had more to say, but they couldn't hear, because he'd already tugged the cord to start the outboard, and the boat disappeared into the darkness.

'Where did he get the dinghy?' The thought only occurred to Venn once they were back under the cliff. 'The *Moon Crest* tender is still in Appledore with the forensics team.'

She hesitated for a moment. 'He nicked it. From one of his neighbours. He said he could get it back before anyone noticed.' Another pause. 'Not his fault. I told him to do it.'

There was the first grey light of dawn when Venn heard the sound of pebbles rattling down the cliff path. The breeze was blowing back the waves and the first light caught the foam, forming white lines against the grey water. He'd been dozing and his first response was panic. Was this the beginning of another manufactured rockfall? Another attack? The fear of the previous day returned, a sharp jolt of adrenaline, a kind of muscle memory, but almost immediately he realized that this was the sound of someone scrambling down the cliff path. Jen was sitting beside him. Quiet. Waiting too. They'd decided not to play dead. Now it was light that would fool nobody.

From where they were sitting, beyond the spur in the cliff, they couldn't see where the path hit the shingle. The first they heard of the approaching person was whistling. Joyful. Some song Venn had heard as a child. A traditional tune that they'd learned at school. Something about morning and dew. Appropriate. They must be walking on the pebbles now because they could hear footsteps. Then there was the splashing of boots in rockpools. Wading birds disturbed from their roost and calling. Only then did he realize that there were two sets of footsteps, and he saw very clearly that this plan to entrap the killer had been folly.

'Inspector, you shouldn't be here. It's a dangerous place, Scully Cove. Us locals know that.' Davy Gregory sounded genuinely sorry. 'You should have taken notice and stayed away.'

'I'm sure you'd have found another way to scare us off.' Venn paused. 'Or to stop the inquiry altogether. You tried to kill us last night.'

The other man, in the blue knitted hat, stood a little apart and said nothing.

'You can't hope to get away with this.' Venn knew he sounded desperate.

Now the man in the hat did speak. 'We don't need to get away with it. We just need time. A bit more time.' The voice was high-pitched, a little manic. He started to move, to circle behind Jen, who was sitting, apparently calm and quiet on a rock, a little distance away. He was carrying a scarf, each end twisted round a hand. A weapon. Venn watched him, waiting. He knew Jen would be aware of him too and wondered why she didn't stand to confront him.

'My team know that we're here,' Venn said. 'They're on their way.'

'We'll be gone before they get here,' Davy said. 'And they'll have more than enough to keep them busy with two officers injured. They're terribly fragile, the rocks on these cliffs. Anything can happen.'

The other man was edging closer to Jen with every step. She was looking at Davy, seeming not to realize the danger she was in. Venn was about to shout a warning, but she looked at her boss and gave a slow, imperceptible wink. She knew exactly what was happening and was prepared to take the risk.

She knew there was no proof to convict the man in the blue hat. Who would believe that a pillar of the community could be guilty of two murders? She wanted to force him to show his hand. Jen turned her attention to Gregory.

'What would your wife make of all this?'

Davy Gregory stared at her. 'This has nothing to do with my Tilly.'

'I think she's guessed, though. I saw her yesterday afternoon, talking to Ruth Smale. In tears. It must be hard to believe that the man you love is involved in a murder. Did you see her last night?'

'I was working until late.' He too sounded as if he was almost in tears. 'I wouldn't hurt her for the world.'

Venn got to his feet slowly. He'd only have one chance and the rocks were slick with weed. He'd have to wait until the man was behind Jen, slipping the scarf around her neck. He thought that Davy would remain a bystander, not a killer, but he'd have to take that risk too.

Now Jen did attempt to confront the danger, to challenge her attacker. She tried to stand up, to step away, but the shingle shifted under her feet and threw her off balance. The man had thrown the scarf around her neck and was pulling it tight. Venn moved towards him, a large boulder, heavy and smooth in his hand. The man saw him coming but not the weapon he carried. He continued to twist the scarf around Jen's neck and shouted to Davy. 'Do something, man! Stop him.' Imperious.

Still, Davy made no move.

Venn was behind the strangler. Everything seemed to be happening very slowly. Venn lifted the boulder and brought it down very hard on the man's head. He watched his victim crumple and fall onto the shingle. Jen pulled the scarf from her throat, coughing and spluttering. Venn looked at the blood on the rock he was still holding, and then down at Alan Ford, sprawled at his feet. In his head, there came a plea, a prayer, that he hadn't killed the man.

From the top of the cliff came the sound of sirens.

Before Rainston and the others arrived, Venn turned to Gregory. His voice was as imperious as Ford's had been. 'Where's Eleanor Lawson?' A pause. 'Where will we find her?'

Chapter Forty-Nine

JEN WALKED WITH RAINSTON AND GREGORY up the cliff path. Venn stayed below with Ford and the paramedics. Jen had seen the relief on Venn's face when they'd said the man would survive without long-term ill effects.

They'd just reached the top when Matilda Gregory appeared, frantic, some avenging angel, her hair shining in the early morning light. She'd run from the layby where the cars were parked and past the officer who tried to block the way.

She stood in front of her husband, ignoring everyone else, her question directed at him. The others might not have been there. 'Is it true? Did you help kill those two men? Rosco and Lawson.'

Davy Gregory answered before Jen could intervene.

'To save a child!' It came out as a cry and a plea for understanding.

'That was not your judgement to make.' Now the teacher sounded horrified. Perhaps she'd been hoping for denial and explanation. Proof that her suspicion was unfounded. Instead, it had been confirmed.

'Alan said it was the only way to get Arthur the treatment he needed. To get the cure in America.'

'And this!' She was almost spitting. 'Attacking police officers. How can that ever be right?'

'That was to buy Alan time. He's got the tickets. He and the boy could have been on a plane tonight to Illinois. He said he'd take the blame then. Once they were there. Nobody would ever know I had anything to do with it.'

'I would know!' Matilda's voice was so loud and harsh that Jen could hear how the effort was scratching the woman's throat. 'God would know.' She stood aside so Rainston could lead her husband into the police car and custody.

Jen wanted to go home, to be warm and dry, but Venn was on a mission to find Eleanor Lawson, and she couldn't let him do that alone. They drove to Morrisham and walked a little way along the promenade, then up a quiet street of Georgian houses.

'Detectives! What a surprise to see you here!'

'Really? I'd thought you'd be expecting us.'

Eleanor Lawson was sitting in the courtyard garden of a small boutique hotel. She was on a white wooden bench, surrounded by pots of late-flowering plants, and she looked as round and small as a wren. As harmless.

She smiled at the inspector. 'I'd have thought you'd have more important things to do than look for me. I needed some time on my own to grieve for the two most important men in my life. I'm sure you can understand.'

'The two men that you killed?'

'I think, Inspector, that the intricacies of this case must have disturbed your mind. How would I have the strength to kill two grown men?'

Venn shook his head. 'It's all over,' he said.

Jen could tell he was thinking how he'd been duped by the woman, and how clever she'd been.

She smiled. 'I don't think so. Oh no, not at all, Inspector.'

'I didn't want to believe it.' Venn's voice was sad. 'You were a part of my childhood. I visited your house with my parents.'

There was a moment of silence. 'How's Frankie?'

'He's fine. At home with Roxy.'

'How lucky,' Eleanor said, 'that you sent a dog-lover to look after me! I knew she wouldn't rest until she'd found him.'

'You'll have to come with us to the station.'

'A new experience, Inspector. How exciting!' Her voice was flinty now. 'But I assure you that I'll not be there for very long. You have no proof, you see, that I was involved in anything criminal at all.'

Venn gave a tight, angry smile. 'Oh, we'll be charging you immediately, Mrs Lawson. Davy Gregory has a conscience. Unlike you. He's already started to talk.'

Chapter Fifty

THEY WERE ALL BACK IN BARNSTAPLE. After Eleanor had been delivered to the station, Matthew went home for a shower and a change of clothes. He thought she might be less sure of herself after a couple of hours in the cells. He drank coffee and discovered that he was starving. Jonathan made him a sausage sandwich and nothing had ever tasted so good. He played down the events of the previous night – all there was to show for his ordeal was a small lump on his head, hardly noticeable because his hair was so thick – and he wasn't ready yet to relive his fear as the rocks had showered down on them. Fear for Ross and terror for himself.

Instead, Matthew focused on the investigation. He asked Jonathan about the blurred photo recovered from Rosco's apartment and the teacher's response. It would provide confirmation.

'Thanks for meeting Guy and asking him about the boys in the picture. I could identify Rosco but I didn't have a clue about the others. It helped put everything into perspective.'

'No problem. He said Ford and Gregory were very close at

one time. Thick as thieves. But Ford was always in charge. The leader of the pack.' Jonathan seemed settled, relaxed.

'Is everything okay?'

'Yeah. There are things we need to talk about. I'll tell you when this case is completely over. There's no rush now.'

Ross was in the North Devon Infirmary. He had a broken collarbone, cracked ribs, a broken leg and the after-effects of hypothermia. No damage to the skull. They'd keep him in for the night, but then he'd be home. Mel was with him. Venn had spoken to her on the phone. 'You saved his life,' she'd said. He could tell that she was crying. 'I don't know how to thank you.'

I put him in danger in the first place.

They met for coffee the next day in Ross's house. Mel had taken a week's leave from the care home she managed so she could look after her husband. It seemed to Venn that Ross was loving every minute of the convalescence. He was lying on the sofa with a duvet tucked round him, a small table within easy reach, and Mel on hand, devoted to fulfilling his every need. Venn had wondered if the incident on the beach would have shocked him into introspection or maturity. But it seemed to have left him untouched emotionally, and despite the plaster cast on his leg, he'd weathered the physical injuries well. He was young and fit, and it probably helped that he was a man with little imagination. He couldn't contemplate the reality of serious injury or death.

'So, what is this all about?' Jen directed the question to Venn. 'I want all the details.'

'Yeah, talk us through it, boss, right from the start.' Ross pushed himself more upright with his good arm. Matthew saw that the plaster cast was covered in signatures. How could anyone acquire all those friends? It was a skill *he'd* never acquired.

Venn knew that meant going a long way back. The actors in this tawdry piece of theatre had been twisted together for years.

'Ford, Gregory and Rosco knew each other from school. Jonathan showed the photo we found in Rosco's flat to a chap who taught them, and he recognized all three. According to the teacher, Ford was the ringleader and the brightest of the bunch. I think it was Eleanor who took the picture, and that it was taken on Scully Cove. Apparently, it was their special place.' It seemed to Venn that every generation had claimed it as their own.

'I thought Eleanor went to some private school.' Jen didn't quite sneer at the idea.

'She did, but she knew Rosco through the sailing club, and Ford was a member too in those early days, though his interests changed when he went on to university. Perhaps Mary inherited her love of the sea from him.' Matthew paused. 'They tolerated Rosco, but he was considered a bit of a clown. They despised him.'

'When I was interviewing Eleanor yesterday, she said Rosco had never really been *one of them.*' Jen was sitting on the floor, legs curled under her body and had to look up at him.

'Ford was the intellectual, very bright, rather intense. Gregory's parents were farmers and quite wealthy before his father squandered his money on Carter's scheme at the pub. Bartholomew was on the scene in school holidays too. He came from the landed gentry, even if his father was gambling away most of the cash. Rosco's mum was a single mother, surviving on seasonal work. So no, he didn't quite fit into their social circle.'

There was a moment of silence. Venn had never quite fitted in at school either. He hadn't fitted in anywhere, until he'd joined the police, and found his own role, his own tribe.

'I think Rosco amused Eleanor,' Venn went on. 'She'd never met anyone quite like him. And she certainly loved the adoration. She kept all his love letters. That came in useful later on, of course, when she needed to persuade us that she'd reciprocated the sentiment, that he was her first true love and she couldn't contemplate killing him.'

'She talked about Grace Fanshaw's locket too yesterday,' Jen said. 'Once she realized that Gregory was confessing everything to us, she couldn't stop talking, boasting that the murders were her idea. That she was some sort of mastermind.'

'Where did the locket fit in?' Ross might be restricted to the sofa, but he was still impatient.

'Apparently,' Venn said, 'Rosco wanted to sell the necklace as soon as they found it on the beach at Morrisham. All he could see was an immediate profit. Later, he put out the story that *he'd* thought it might have sentimental value for the owner and that he'd made the effort to track her down. Eleanor claims that she was the one who persuaded him to do that, and that she'd actually found Grace Fanshaw.'

'He was the person who befriended the old lady, though,' Ross said. 'Doing her shopping, keeping her company.'

'I think he enjoyed her company too. He never had much of a family. Matilda Gregory's parents recognized that when they took him in.'

Venn shifted his position so he was facing Ross. 'Eleanor

claimed that Rosco would never have had the money to buy the *Nellie Wren*, would never have become famous, if it weren't for her. Yet, when Alan and Davy asked Jeremy to contribute to the fund to send Arthur Ford to the States for treatment, he refused. The refusal was her excuse for getting involved.'

'A lame kind of excuse for murder!'

'I don't think murder was suggested at first. The men hoped Eleanor might persuade Rosco to make a donation, or use his celebrity to raise awareness of the campaign. Instead, she came up with the more elaborate plan of luring him to meet her. She chose Greystone as a place where she was relatively unknown, and pointed him to the cottage in Quarry Bank, owned by Gregory's father. Davy still had a key. The men got caught up with the excitement and adventure of it. The scheme was very elaborate, and pandered to Rosco's romantic nature.' Venn paused. 'She kept him waiting there for two weeks before arranging the rendezvous. She'd have enjoyed that too.'

'Imogen, Rosco's girlfriend, said he used a forwarding address to save being tapped for cash by good causes.' Jen looked up at Venn. 'Selfish bastard. None of them were very pleasant individuals, were they? They were all as bad as each other.'

Nobody spoke for a moment. Outside in the street, two young mothers were chatting. Venn couldn't make out the words, but they seemed animated, happy. The women walked on and he turned back to the room.

'Did they go there intending to kill him?' Jen still couldn't quite believe it. 'Was it premeditated?

'By Eleanor, though I don't think any of the group would have committed murder as individuals. They fed off each other's resentments and fears and Rosco was a convenient scapegoat. Ford's only thought was for his grandson. He'd have done anything to save Arthur. He knew that Jeremy had left Eleanor money in his will, and she promised it would be used to send the child to the US. I think Davy was swept along, desperate to be a member of the gang again.'

'How did they set it up?'

'Eleanor got in touch with Rosco, implying she wanted to rekindle the relationship. His attraction to Imogen was already starting to fade and he responded. The plan fed into Eleanor's desire to be the object of the man's passion. After being married for all those years to Bartholomew, she wanted that thrill again. She guessed he'd still be obsessed, interested enough, at least, to do as she said, and to come to Greystone to wait for her to seek him out.' A pause. Venn tried to find the words to explain. 'For her it was all about power. Regaining the power of her youth, pulling strings. The thrill of getting the men to do what she asked of them. Even if that was murder.'

'Of course, she was the mysterious woman Rosco told the village he was waiting for.'

Venn nodded. 'It was all very, very carefully planned. Eleanor's doing. She was bored in that house with nothing to do but walk the ancient dog and feed the hens. Bartholomew was drinking himself to death. I think she was slowly going mad there. The plot to kill Jeremy was a weird distraction, a fantasy.' He paused, thinking again that wasn't enough to explain Eleanor's impulse to murder or the sway she'd held over her co-conspirators. And that she'd held for a while over *him*. 'She's a charming narcissist, completely self-centred. As I said, she loved the power. I don't think anything that has happened to her since lived up to that sense of being adored by Rosco.'

'In interview, Gregory said he had no idea that Eleanor was planning to kill Rosco,' Jen said. 'He thought she was going to seduce him, to persuade him then to make the donation. He claims he was shocked when he knew what violence had taken place in his dad's little house.'

'He helped the others cover it up, though.' Ross stretched again.

'Grace Fanshaw's nephew said he had the impression that she was using Rosco when he met them all those years ago,' Jen said. 'She certainly had a way of manipulating people, of getting what she wanted.'

Venn shot her a look. He wondered if Jen was including him in the people who'd been manipulated by the woman. If so, she was right.

'Which of them actually killed Rosco?' Ross was getting impatient with all the talk of a time before he'd been born.

'I think Eleanor and Ford did it together. Gregory gave them the key and they surprised Rosco in the bathroom. She couldn't have carried Rosco down to the quay on her own. Ford's still a competent sailor. Perhaps he stole Barton's dinghy because the man had been giving Mary a bad time. He took the boat round to Scully and anchored it there, before wading ashore. That was when Gregory became involved. We've checked Ford's phone records. He called Davy from Greystone and the taxi was waiting at the top of the cliff to give him a lift back to his daughter's house. They waited for Ford to get in before they called in the fake lifeboat emergency. Mary said her father was awake when she was called out. It was all about the story, the unreliable narration.'

'What do you mean?'

'They kept feeding us stories. And we fell for them. Ford claimed to have seen a mysterious woman get out of a car in the early hours of the morning, but Rosco would have been killed well before that, I think. No wonder Brennan didn't see anyone. And Ford described Matilda Gregory, knowing absolutely that she had a perfect alibi. It was just to confuse us and to lead us astray.' Venn paused. 'We couldn't make it work when we thought there was just one killer. Once I considered the idea of a group working together it all made more sense.'

'What made you so sure that a group was behind it?' Ross held out his cup for Mel to refill.

'In the end, it was too complicated for one person to have been the culprit.' He paused. 'It was a construct of Eleanor's strange imagination and it was bound to unravel.'

'Why did Bartholomew have to die?'

'Because he guessed that Eleanor might be involved. He'd known that she'd never actually fallen for Rosco, that the man had been obsessed by her, but that she was too self-centred actually to fall in love with *anyone*. And perhaps he'd known she'd been out the night Rosco was killed and he challenged her about it. They might have slept in separate rooms, but he could have been aware of her coming and going.' *And she was bored by him. When she killed Rosco, she was given a sense of new possibilities, new adventures.*

'She pushed Bartholomew over the cliff?'

'Oh yes,' Venn said. 'I don't think anyone else could have done that. Gregory probably gave them a lift, picked them both up from the sailing club after they'd left their car there. Eleanor would have come up with a reason for an evening walk along the path at Scully with her husband. She might have said it was to mourn his father or for old time's sake. Barty was still susceptible to her charms and, as we know, Scully was a special place for them all.' He paused. 'She couldn't face killing the dog – instead she left him in the cellar for Roxy to find – but she seems to have had no qualms about Rosco or her husband.'

'And then she tried to finish us off,' Ross said, his voice ridiculously cheerful.

'Well, I don't think she started the rockfall. That would have been the men. But yes, it would have been her idea. She persuaded herself, and them, that we were getting too close, perhaps. Or she'd just got caught up in the violence, the stories and the recklessness.' Venn gave a little smile. 'The skulls and the bones and the white, white light.'

There was a silence. Mel offered to make more coffee and disappeared into the kitchen.

'Matilda Gregory can't have had anything to do with it,' Jen said. 'She was distraught when she suspected her husband was involved.'

'I think Davy had been behaving strangely. Of all of them, he was the least committed. He was the first person to confess to the whole thing last night.'

Mel came in with a tray, more biscuits, but Jen got to her feet. 'I'm going to see Mary Ford. I want to get it over with. She knows we've arrested her father, but I wanted to talk to her. To explain, though I suppose no explanation is going to help. She's on her own now, with a daughter and a very sick son.'

'I don't envy you that.' Venn wondered if he should offer again to speak to Mary, but he and Jen had discussed it. She'd said she thought that the conversation would be better coming from her.

She looked up at him and smiled. 'I'm not exactly looking forward to it, myself.'

Chapter Fifty-One

IT WAS LUNCHTIME WHEN JEN ARRIVED in Greystone, but she didn't feel much like eating. Certainly, she wasn't tempted to go into the Maiden's Prayer for a half of bitter and a pasty. She thought that after today she never wanted to go back to the village again. A weak sun shone on rain-soaked pavements, but it didn't make the place seem any more attractive.

In the end, Jen didn't find Mary Ford alone. Matilda Gregory was there when Jen arrived. She saw them both through the living room window before knocking at the door. They had mugs in hand, but any conversation appeared desultory. Mary let her in. Matilda looked up as they came back into the room, then got to her feet.

'I should go. Lunch break is nearly over. The kids will be back in class in five minutes.'

'You're working today?' Jen wasn't sure how the teacher could be doing that. Her world must have collapsed. Her husband had been charged with killing two people. He might get away in the end with facing the charge of being an accomplice to murder, but he'd still spend years in prison. Perhaps the woman's faith was getting her through it. But then, Jen thought, *she'd* always fallen back on work when things were tough too.

Matilda nodded. 'It helps. And I didn't want to be on my own. Brooding. That's why I'm here. I didn't want Mary brooding alone either.' She gave Mary a quick hug and left.

After the door had shut, Jen turned to Mary. 'You up for that? The sympathy?'

'Tilly's in the same boat, isn't she? Her bloke's been charged too. And she really is alone. At least I have the kids.'

'I'm so sorry,' Jen said, 'that Arthur won't make it to the States any more. Not yet anyway.' She'd been thinking they could do some fundraising at work. No way was she knitting, but some of the lads were into running. She was thinking sponsored marathons, a bucket in the tea room to collect spare change.

'He wouldn't have gone anyway.' Mary was crying. Great fat tears were running down her cheeks. 'I looked into the bloke who was supposed to have the miracle cure. It was a con. I tried to tell all the fundraisers in the village that they were wasting their time, but that just seemed ungrateful. I'd told Dad. But he'd got sucked into this social media site about the cure, with all the stories from supporters.' She looked straight at Jen. 'Dad's a scientist. I don't know how he could believe all that crap. The posts were undermining the real medical research. According to them, all Arthur needed was a change in his diet and an operation that only the professor could provide. It was like the doctor was some sort of God. Or witch doctor.'

'You're sure that was why your father got involved in the plot to kill Rosco?' Jen thought there might be more to it. A background resentment. Jealousy because Rosco, the boy they'd all despised, had done so well. And because Eleanor, who had even conned the boss, had sucked him in and stoked his obsession.

'Of course! Dad really believed he was doing it for us. Eleanor just fed into his certainties and convinced him that with Rosco gone, there'd be a happy ending.' A pause. 'There were times when I wanted to believe too, to think that we could sit on a plane and fly into the sunset and suddenly Arthur would be well again. But I couldn't.'

'What will you do now?'

'The same as every parent with a child with a life-limiting illness. I'll wait and hope, and make sure that what life Arthur has left is as good as it can possibly be.' She wiped her tears with a grubby sleeve, and looked like a child herself. 'Peter Smale has put him forward for a trial in Oxford. We won't know if he's had the drug or the placebo, but it's something to hang on to.' A pause. 'When your colleagues first phoned me about Dad, I was going to run away. I couldn't face the village. All the gossip. The judgement. I thought I'd have to move, even if it was only to his house.'

'But now?'

Mary shrugged. 'Matilda was here to offer to babysit a few nights a month. So I can go out. Or put my name on the lifeboat rota. A kindness. Maybe there are worse things than gossip.'

'Did you have any idea what your dad was up to?'

Mary didn't reply immediately. 'He'd been weird for a while, disappearing down this rabbit hole of the internet, following the stories of wonder cures, believing the lies. I thought it was depression – Mum dying and Artie being ill. He had no energy, no plans for new adventures. He'd taken early retirement to lead tours all over the world before Mum was ill. Then more recently, he'd been his old self again. I thought the depression was lifting. He was off to meet people, getting texts and phone calls.' She gave a wry little laugh. 'I thought he'd got back into the natural history group, was spending time with his old colleagues. But when he talked about planning meetings, I guess there was something completely different on the agenda.'

The word was unspoken between them.

Murder.

Jen got to her feet. 'I should go. You will be okay?'

Mary stood up too and looked out at the sea. 'Yeah,' she said. Then: 'I'll have to be, won't I? That's what parents do.'

Chapter Fifty-Two

ON HIS WAY BACK FROM ROSS and Mel's house, Matthew stopped at the police station. Ford and Gregory had given their formal statements the evening before, but Eleanor had wanted a lawyer, and nobody had been immediately available. Now, they sat in the grey room and went through the formalities. Venn had Vicki Robb with him, but the conversation was between him and Eleanor, and the others remained silent.

He'd thought she might try to bluff her way out of the charges. She had, after all, deceived him from the beginning. She had the charisma of a brilliant general leading his troops into an unwinnable battle, or a guru convincing his followers to sell all their worldly goods and believe in him. She could tell a good story and she'd had time to make one up.

In the end, though, she admitted that she was behind the plan to kill Jeremy Rosco. She almost seemed proud of the fact.

'He was such a mean and greedy little man. Petty. He'd have done anything for Alan when they were boys. That summer he joined the sailing club, he so wanted to belong to our group.

Then when Alan asked him for a donation to Arthur's fund, he didn't even reply. Alan wrote again, and Rosco just sent a two-line response: he was sorry but there were so many demands on him that he couldn't help. He supported his own charities.' A pause. 'He still owned that flat in Morrisham, which he never used. If he'd sold that, the cost of Arthur's treatment would have been covered. After all, he had no dependents. Nobody to leave it to.'

'That was hardly a motive for murder,' Venn said. 'You have no dependents, and your house is far too big for you. You could have sold that.'

She answered immediately. 'Impossible! The house has been in our family for more than a hundred years. Besides, Barty had a position in the county. We couldn't have lived in some box on an estate.' Her mouth snapped shut, and Venn realized now that the monstrous events of the past weeks had nothing to do with charity, or a sick little boy. It was about an older woman feeling alive and powerful again, and pushing to the limits the men who followed her. A strange game of chicken or dare.

'Why did Bartholomew have to die?'

'He was still awake when I got in the night that Rosco died. A little less drunk than usual. Everyone thinks he was very stupid, but I could never have married a stupid man. I could see him wondering . . . I hadn't thought he'd mind my killing Rosco. He never had any time for him, called him feral. But he was a magistrate and had this pompous notion about the law. And when he'd been drinking, he was unreliable. He might have shared his suspicions.'

'Did Davy Gregory drive you from the sailing club to the coast path that night?'

She paused. 'No, Davy was becoming unreliable too by then. No spine. I picked Barty up before he could get into the building and I drove us there. He thought we were going on a romantic walk. He was standing with his back to the edge. I had my arms around him and he thought I was leaning in to kiss him. It didn't take much of a push.' She looked up at Venn and gave a wicked grin, mischievous, almost appealing, so he could understand again why Rosco had been so obsessed by her. 'He might have had his suspicions, but he died happy, believing that I cared for him.'

'And then you just drove home.' Venn paused. 'Were you able to sleep that night?'

'Oh yes! I've never had any problem sleeping.' She looked directly into his eyes. 'I really thought everybody would believe he'd killed Rosco and had thrown himself over the cliff in remorse.'

'I almost believed that,' Venn said.

'I wasn't sure, you see. I thought you suspected me.'

'How did you manage the blood in the bath? It *was* yours?'

She gave a little smile. 'Oh yes! I've suffered from nose-bleeds since I was a child. I needed to throw you off the scent.'

'Hence the charade with your disappearance, and the *Scully Maid* found floundering in the cove. I suppose Alan Ford took that out.' *Wearing a hat knitted by one of the fundraisers.*

'You think that was a little over the top?' There was the same smile, which now made her seem a little unbalanced. 'By then, I admit, I was rather getting caught up in the adventure.'

'Causing a rockfall, which almost killed my sergeant, was certainly over the top.'

The smile again. 'Come now, Inspector, I think I've

confessed to enough, don't you? I'm sure confession's good for the soul, but you have enough here to send me to prison for the rest of my life.'

So that wasn't you? And in the end, do the details matter? Venn felt exhausted by the business now. Eleanor might enjoy drama but he was very much happier without it.

When he got home, Jonathan was there. It was raining again and the wind was singing through the bare trees in the garden. Usually, at this time of the evening, they went for a walk together, but today Jonathan lit a fire and they sat there together on the rug, their backs to the sofa, somehow wanting the comfort, even though it wasn't a cold day. Jonathan had suggested opening champagne to celebrate the successful end to the case, but Matthew said it was too early. An excuse of sorts.

'Tea,' he said. 'If that's okay with you. It doesn't feel as if there's much to celebrate. I was duped by Eleanor Lawson. I imagined what it might be like to be part of all that, that house, that family. She was an exciting and appealing woman.' *And I was very happy there, when I was a boy, on the swing under the tree. That memory coloured my sense of the place and of her.*

'Ah, boring Dorothy suits you much better.'

'You're saying I'm boring?' He leaned his head on his husband's shoulder. 'Well, you're probably right.'

'Not at all!' Jonathan threw another log onto the fire. 'I've been thinking about mothers too.' He took a breath. 'You're not the only one with a screwed-up parental relationship. I've decided to see if I can find my natural mum, to find out if she'd like to meet me.'

Matthew's first response was dismay. He knew that Jonathan

had never felt at ease with his adoptive parents, but he'd hoped that they were enough for each other, that neither of them needed more family around them. Then he saw how eager Jonathan was, and how anxious, and he was flooded with guilt that he could be so selfish.

'Of course she'd want to meet you! And once she does, she'll adore you.' He got to his feet. 'I'll get that tea.'

In the kitchen, he looked out over the dark garden, waiting for the kettle to boil. A red light-buoy marked the entrance to the estuary. It was all very ordinary, rather mundane, but he had the sense that nothing would quite be the same again.

Chapter One

IT'S NOVEMBER TODAY. I HATE NOVEMBER. *Two years ago, in November, my dad ran off. A year ago, Mam stopped eating and started slipping away. She got the sack from the travel agency in town, and I caught her talking to the TV when it wasn't even switched on. She had the idea that it was talking back. There was just her and me, and I felt I was drowning. I'm only fourteen, so what could I do to help?*

I tried to tell Miss at school. I'd always thought she was okay, but in the end, she was only interested that I wasn't wearing the uniform socks and that I hadn't got my homework in on time. When I told her about Mam, she frowned and said I was making excuses. I needed to stick to the rules, whatever was happening at home. If I had real problems, I should talk to pupil welfare.

But pupil welfare is run by Mrs Saltburn, and she hates me, because she takes RE and I told her that I couldn't believe in a God that allows war and famine and anyway, what about the climate emergency?

'Salvation is an academy with a Christian ethos, Chloe. That was made clear before your parents chose it as your place of education.'

I wanted to tell her that I was getting into Wicca, which made far more sense to me, but then I'd have been in detention for the rest of the week. Also, that my parents put Salvation at the top of the list because the only other school in the catchment is Birks Comp, and a year nine kid got stabbed there, and the GCSE results are shite. But then she would have said I was being cheeky and that would have got me detention too.

Now it's November again. Mam's back in hospital, and I'm having to live here: Rosebank Home for the teenage kids nobody wants. I don't blame Mam. She's ill. And Dad's not even in the country. Apparently, he's in Dubai, making a fortune selling fancy apartments to rich people. He's not answering my calls or texts and I'm not even sure I've got the right number for him. Maybe he has a new woman in his life. A new family. Maybe he doesn't need me anymore. So I have tried talking to Miss and to Dad, and I'm not going to bother with Nana and Grandpa. They've always hated Mam and taken Dad's side and when I talk, they don't seem to hear. Nana's like Miss – only bothered about what I'm wearing and what I look like.

BUT NOBODY LISTENS.

That's not fair. Josh listens. But he's only agency staff and he's not here all the time. He listens when I tell him about the pervy guy waiting in his car outside the home – though maybe I was wrong about that – and that Brad Russell is like some sort of gangster in a crap movie, wearing that stupid parka even indoors, and dealing crack, and that I'm scared because there's no lock on my door. I'm not sure if Josh passes on the information though, or if anyone listens to him.

Josh told me to keep this diary to let out my thoughts and feelings, and we go through it when he's working and when he has time. Mostly he works in the evenings and at weekends. Today's Sunday, so he should be here, covering for *Jan* who's got the weekend off, but with agency staff you never know. Agency staff cost money, so sometimes Dave has to manage and it's just him and Tracey sleeping in. I don't think Dave minds when it's just the two of them.

Josh was supposed to have a shift tonight, and I thought I saw his car draw up. I was looking out of the window, watching out for him. Usually, I can see the light at the end of the quay where the coal ships used to tie up, and the big container ships heading for the docks, and the ghost ships with no crew lurking on the horizon, but it's misty, with that drizzle that feels like a heavy fog. I can't see anything. It's as if this house is on its own in the world, as if I'm on my own in the world and nobody would care if I died. Sometimes I dream about killing myself, then I think about *Josh*. It seems to me that he might care.

This place is worse than the bin where Mam's locked up. It's worse than prison.

Miss said I could be someone special when I started at Salvation, and my SATs were good. That was when Dad was still at home, and he came with Mam to parents' evening. She said I could be a poet or a songwriter. Then everything went wrong at home, and I couldn't concentrate, and I couldn't sleep. Miss didn't care about me anymore. Salvation only cares about the swotty kids who can make the school look good. When I got taken into care, I could tell they hoped I'd have to move to a new school, but the home's still in the catchment, and social services said I'd had enough disruption already, so they have to put up with me.

I might go down and meet *Josh*. We could go through the diary in the kitchen, and then he'll play cards with me if he's not too busy. The others are watching a film in the lounge. Tracey made them pizza and popcorn. But I'd rather play cards with *Josh*.

I think I could be in love with him.

Chapter Two

DETECTIVE INSPECTOR VERA STANHOPE LOOKED UP from the teenager's scrawl.

'It's got today's date. Chloe must have written it this evening.'

The manager of the children's home was faded, dusty. He had grey hair tied back in a ponytail. He seemed well out of his depth. Vera had seen the same ashamed look in some of her older colleagues' eyes: the people who were desperate to retire, but who couldn't quite make the jump. Because what would be the point of getting up in the morning if there were no work, nothing to get out of bed for? These were the lonely people, the bored ones, the introverts. Vera knew how they felt. She had no desire to retire, not even now when she felt like a failure. Especially now. Work was a kind of penance. They'd have to push her out.

She and David Limbrick, the manager, were standing outside in the corridor looking in at the room. The diary had been on the floor, close to the door. She'd reached in to pick it up with a blue-gloved hand, breaking every rule, but curious, because time was important now and it would take the CSIs a while to get here.

Vera was first on the scene because she'd still been in her office when the 999 call came through. Working late because she couldn't quite face driving into the hills to her empty house, so she'd sat at her desk, even though it was Sunday and the rest of the team had better things to do. Brooding about a dead young woman who'd once been a colleague, and thinking about how pointless her own life had become. Holly might have called it an existential crisis. Vera had heard the term, without understanding what it meant. Now, she had an inkling.

It was midnight and the CSIs were on their way. The pathologist would be there as soon as he could make it. He'd asked if it could wait until the morning, but she'd explained where she was, and the nature of the victim they'd found outside. And that a lass was missing. Now, it was just her and the manager. It seemed that David Limbrick slept in one of the staff rooms if he was on duty overnight, but he'd still been up when this tragedy had happened. When the body had been found, at least. Vera knew they'd be unlikely to get an accurate time of death. Paul Keating, the pathologist, made that clear every time they met. Dave told her he'd been working too. Catching up with things in the office. 'The bosses want up-to-date occupancy figures. It's all they seem to care about.' Moaning. Vera had guessed on first sight that he'd be a moaner.

Now they were both hovering outside the room, the door still open.

'I'll head outside again.' There was a uniformed officer with the body, but Vera wanted to take another look at the scene, despite the damp and the autumn chill. 'I just wanted to see Chloe's room.'

But she didn't move immediately and turned back to Limbrick.

'Anyone else here this evening?'

'Tracey,' he said. 'She was here until ten. She was in the lounge with the kids watching the movie, but she's not sleeping in tonight. It would just have been Josh and me on duty.'

'Tracey's one of the social workers?'

'Aye.'

'What time was Josh supposed to get here?'

'Eight-ish. I heard his car. He was always early.'

'But you didn't see him?'

'Nah, he was just sleeping in. Filling in for another staff member. I assumed he'd gone up to his room, and then that he was in the lounge with the others.'

'And Chloe? When did you last see her?'

He shrugged.

'You didn't notice her leave?'

'She's a wanderer that one. We never know where she is.'

The corridor ahead of them was empty, but Vera was aware of a couple of slightly open doors, young eyes peering through, muttered conversations. Muted excitement. Murder could generate excitement. She could understand that. But not here. Not this.

'Can we do anything with the other kids? Is there somewhere they can go?'

For the first time since the man had opened the main door to her, he seemed to come to life. 'No! They're only here because there's nowhere else for them. They're troubled. Disturbed.'

'I don't mean parents, families. Another home to take them in on a temporary basis. So my chaps can have a clear run.'

He looked at her as if she were mad. 'You don't understand. There is nowhere else. The whole system is falling apart.'

She thought he was being melodramatic. She'd contact social services in the morning. There must be some sort of emergency placement. She'd have to cope as best she could until then. But Limbrick was still talking. 'Most of them have been through foster care. But they're older, often aggressive. Hard to manage.'

Vera nodded down at the pages of the diary. 'Even Chloe?'

He shrugged. 'Yeah. Even her.' But he looked away and Vera could tell he didn't mean it, that he thought this hadn't been the right place for her. At least now that he'd read the girl's diary.

'You can leave me to it for now,' she said. 'Maybe you could talk to the kids. Tell them I'll be speaking to them in the morning, but that they should get some sleep.' A pause. 'Did Chloe have a special friend here?'

He shook his head. 'She was a bit of a loner.'

'Except for Josh.' Vera looked at the diary she was still holding in her hand. 'It seems that she got on with *him*.'

Limbrick didn't answer. He wandered back down the corridor. One of the kids shouted out to him through a half-open door. He gave them a few words, but told them nothing. Vera shot a quick look back into Chloe Spence's room and made her way outside.

Josh Woodburn was young. He lay on the edge of a rough path through a piece of scrub, close enough to the road for the street lamp outside Rosebank to cast a little light on his body. The PC had his back to Josh, looking out towards the sea and the lights of the town. Vera took out her torch to get a better look. Josh hardly looked old enough to be in a position of responsibility in a place like Rosebank, even if he was only on a temporary contract. He had floppy hair the colour of wheat and long, loose limbs. He was wearing jeans, a university sweatshirt and trainers. His face was turned towards Vera, but she could see the back of his head, the large round hole in the skull where he'd been hit, the blood that clotted and matted in the pale hay-coloured hair.

Oh Chloe, Vera thought. *What have you done? And where are you now? And if this wasn't you – and really there's nothing in your diary to suggest that it was – are you still alive?*

Because Chloe Spence had disappeared.

Vera stood next to the body and stared back towards Rosebank. She'd spent a bit of time volunteering in a children's home when she was a cadet. In those days, young trainee cops were sent out into the community to get to know their patch. It wouldn't hurt, Vera thought, if police training still included more good works and less sitting at a desk in the uni being talked at. The kids' home had been a big house on the corner of a leafy street. There'd been a garden with bikes and a tyre swing tied on a big tree. She'd been there in November, and they'd built a bonfire, and the house parents had let off fireworks. The children had swung sparklers around their heads, eyes wide and bright. There were potatoes baked in foil and sausages and toffee the kids had made that afternoon. It had been nothing like this place.

To be fair, the kids in that home had been nothing like the Rosebank kids. They were younger. Distressed and traumatized maybe, but easier to handle. You could cuddle a seven-year-old, couldn't you? Distract them with lights and sweets and stories. It would be hard to cuddle a fifteen-year-old lad, who'd punched his grandmother and stolen her pension to buy smack. Who'd just avoided the Young Offenders' Institution because of the tales of abuse he'd suffered. Who was handed over to social services to be cared for instead.

All the same, Vera couldn't see how being in that place was helping them. Inside, it was shabby and grey. It was as if all the light and the life had been sucked from it. Once, it had been a guest house for the workers who'd put up the new battery factory just up the coast. Before that, maybe for families who wanted a cheap holiday on the coast, though the beach here was still black with sea coal. Then it had become a bail hostel. Then a hostel for asylum seekers. And now this. A bleak house on the edge of a former pit village, with threadbare carpets and everywhere small signs of violence: a door almost pulled off its hinges, a sofa with a scorch mark, not quite hidden by a cushion. How could a child feel safe or loved here? Vera knew what it felt like to be unloved, but she'd grown up in the hills, with space and clean air, and couldn't remember ever feeling unsafe.

She said a few words to the officer, reassuring him that someone would be along to relieve him soon, and then reluctantly made her way back inside.

THE TWO RIVERS SERIES

Discover Ann's latest lead character
Detective Matthew Venn

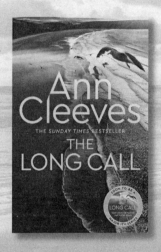

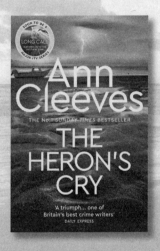